PRAISE FOR *GEEK TO GU*

"Alex Skolnick's journey from introverted
metal/jazz/any style guitar virtuoso is singularly awesome. _
metal scene comes alive in these pages, from teenage Skolnick's guitar
lessons with the legendary Joe Satriani to all manner of war stories with
Testament. Written entirely by Skolnick, the man's humble yet confident,
sensitive and opinionated observance of life shines through like a well-placed
note on the high E string. "
  – Anthony Bozza, author of four New York Times bestsellers
including *Whatever you say I am: The Life and Times of Eminem* and
Slash, co-written with Slash; writer and editor for *Rolling Stone*

"A surprisingly personal book about his evolution from pained adolescent to
one of the most remarkable guitarists in hard rock history. Alex Skolnick
holds nothing back in this excellent memoir that describes the passions,
pleasures and pains of being a professional musician."
  – Brad Tolinski, Editor-In-Chief, *Guitar World Magazine*

"If you come to Alex Skolnick's memoirs simply expecting the thrash-metal
version of Mötley Crüe's *The Dirt*, you're going to be challenged – Skolnick
is a searching, opinionated and fearless thinker. He opens up the Bay Area
'80s' metal scene, shedding light on Metallica and Megadeth and
crystallizing the strange moment when major labels were willing to risk
money on burnouts pushing the boundaries of speed. Besides, no one in Crüe
to my knowledge ever made love to a woman on a bowling-ball return
machine."
  – Ned Vizzini, author of *It's Kind of a Funny Story* & *The Other Normals*

"If every child of sixties Berkeley Jewish intellectuals quit playing piano
after a brief period of frustrating lessons and, deflated by family failures, was
deemed never to be a musician, but then turned fate on its ear to end up not
just a prodigy metal guitarist but one of the world's most agile rock/jazz
virtuosos, Alex Skolnick's memoir wouldn't be the inspiring read that it is.
Here is an honest, raw, articulate story of a life whose problems were forged
in the crucible of music into something triumphant."
  – Bradford Morrow, author of *The Diviner's Tale* and *The Uninnocent*

(contd.)

"...Alex Skolnick became the lead guitarist of thrash metal band Testament at age 16. He was the band's youngest member, and by the time he was 18, they had their first record deal. By age 19, he was touring the world. Today, naturally, he fronts a titular jazz trio. He tells the wild tales of his transition to jazz in his new biography, *Geek to Guitar Hero*, which he wrote without a co-author. About the book's title: Onstage, Skolnick shreds with confidence. Offstage, he has struggled his whole life with feeling out of place and socially awkward. Alex Skolnick, revered the world over as one of the greatest living guitar players, is painfully shy.....Skolnick's choice not to work with a co-writer is similar both to his independent pursuit of guitar and to his entry into the jazz world.... There might be writers who look at a guitarist who writes his own book with a jaundiced eye. However, Skolnick's words are eloquent and insightful—and frequently entertaining. *Geek* is an engaging read, and, in the context of the author's dutiful, DIY personality, it makes a whole hell of a lot of sense that he chose not to use a co-writer. The story is his, after all. And for someone who has battled insecurities for as long as he can remember, it's fearless."

— *The Village Voice*, December 2012

"Born of brilliant left-leaning academics into a family fraught with parental inhibition and sibling rivalry, and coming of age amidst the "social experiment gone amuck" that was '70s-era Berkeley, California, the precocious Master Skolnick negotiated a perilous trajectory culminating in redemption by guitar and a revelatory induction into the Kiss Army. That experience, his subsequent ascension to teen maestro in Testament, and related adventures are detailed in this engaging memoir—including milestones such as the guitarist's discovery of Miles and Coltrane, and his disillusionment with the music business. Personal photos, pithy pronouncements, and behind-the-scenes disclosures provide context, fun, and occasional titillation."

— Barry Cleveland, Associate Editor *Guitar Player Magazine*

ALEX SKOLNICK

Geek

to

Guitar Hero

LOUDER
EDUCATION
PRESS
Brooklyn, New York

Book Design by Maddy Samaddar © nomad9design.com
Cover photos by Tom Couture © Tom Couture Photography

For more information, go to:
www.geektoguitarhero.com

This book can also be ordered at these independent book stores:
McNally Jackson Books
52 Prince Street
New York, NY 10012
&
Harvard Book Store
1256 Massachusetts Ave,
Cambridge, MA 02138

First Paperback Edition

ISBN 978-0-9885419-0-0

www.geektoguitarhero.com
www.alexskolnick.com

GEEK TO GUITAR HERO

CONTENTS

ACKNOWLEDGEMENTS

This book would be unimaginable without the assistance of literary guru Nettie Reynolds, who pre-read, advised and motivated. Some great writer friends—Bradford Morrow, Anthony Bozza and Ned Vizzini—helped shed light on the writing process and inspired with their tremendous body of work. Huge thanks to the people at Nomad 9 Design and Louder Education Press for their incredible hard work and rising to the occasion in the face of various challenges. I'd also like to thank my early pre-readers Mike Fine, Katie Jacoby, Laura Whitmore and Brad Tolinski.

Though some difficult periods are described, these words are in no way a reflection of relations today, especially when it comes to the Skolnick family and my brothers from Testament. To all friends, family and others who are mentioned: thanks for putting up with the brutal honesty and I apologize if any of this is hard to read. Thanks especially to my mother Arlene, who I know did the best she could and whose beautiful photography, long deserving of wider recognition, is displayed throughout.

Finally, my deepest thanks to Maddy, whose immense dedication, intellect and input have been invaluable, whose elegant design work adorns this book and whose loving presence in my life has helped heal many of the scars left by wounds described within these pages.

FOREWORD

I've accomplished some goals that I've been told were impossible: going from a shy, socially awkward kid with an inability to look another person in the eye to becoming a fearless performer on stage; carving out a career in the strangest and toughest of all industries (the music business) and having a professional impact with the most played instrument in the Western world (the guitar). Yet looking back it feels—at least at this very moment—that the writing of my first book, *Geek to Guitar Hero*, has been the toughest project of all.

The main period of this book's creation was late 2008 to early 2011. The majority was written on tour—in the bunks and lounges of various tour buses as well as cafes and bars all over the world. The rest of the time, it was written in the coffeehouses of Brooklyn, NY, which I'm proud to call my home.

The book's germination goes back a couple of decades. Over the years, many false starts have been attempted and aborted. Being a longtime fan of novelists with autobiographical elements such as Kurt Vonnegut, Phillip Roth, Erica Jong and Thomas Wolfe, I couldn't bear to write anything that didn't at least partially reflect the standards I had as a reader. While the goal was to write a novel, this story—with so many real life events and figures—became increasingly difficult to convey through fiction.

All through the 1990s and beyond, I read books on writing, took creative writing classes and struggled, often uninspired. At the same time, I was working hard to reinvent myself as a guitarist and musician, so writing often had to take a back seat.

Then, in the early 2000s, I discovered contemporary writers such as Nick Hornby, David Sedaris, Dave Eggers and Chuck Klosterman, all who peppered their work with musical and cultural references I could relate to. Their non-fiction read like the novels I enjoyed and helped point me towards the right literary vehicle with which to finally tell my own story: the autobiographical memoir.

Little did I know that by the time I would finally accomplish this goal of writing a book, it would be 2012— the age of the "rock bio," where having a book (usually co-written) is about as common among artists as having a signature guitar. At least I can say I have written this entire work myself. And I must confess that throughout this process, I've often felt more like a writer that plays music than a musician who writes.

As if by fate, I soon found myself back in the band I'd left after nearly a dozen years, surrounded by many of the same characters—band members, road crew and old friends. Although the social environment was much improved from the time I'd left, many old memories and feelings came flooding back. Suddenly I was re-living all the classic stories, many of these recounted over beers and laughs. Lying awake at night, or first thing in the morning, I'd take it all in with a little MacBook-Pro to capture my thoughts.

By this time, we had entered the age of blogging. Being a blogger has been a huge stepping-stone in cultivating this content. Some sections originally appeared on my own blog, SkolNotes (alexskolnick.com) and on GuitarPlayer.com. "On Being Metal" originally appeared on MTV's "Headbangers Blog."

While this book is based on facts, actual events and real characters, some names are changed, as well as a few specific details, in the interest of privacy. It is not my intention to cause discomfort and embarrassment to anyone. I only wish to recount events as I experienced them through my own admittedly subjective point of view. There are many more great stories that have been left out in the interest of time constraints and/or further embarrassment (to myself and others). Those may show up in some form—fiction or otherwise—in the future.

To anyone who has ever felt confused, alienated and isolated while growing up: let this story show that if you stay true to your goals and make the right choices, no matter how difficult, then things have a way of working out.

~Alex Skolnick
Brooklyn, New York,
September, 2012

PRELUDE

Many believe that things fell into place quite naturally for me—they assume I was born with recognizable talent, that it was nurtured and developed by those around me and I achieved a distinguished musical career with relative ease.

I'm here to tell you that nothing could be further from the truth. I wasn't good at anything, not even music. My family and friends acted like the guitar was the equivalent of sucking my thumb—an immature and annoying habit they were forced to begrudgingly tolerate until I came to my senses. My early career couldn't have been more disillusioning and disheartening.

Only by going against the expectations of everyone around me, doing the opposite of what I was told, have I been able to find a place of my own in life and in music. Even today, as I write this, there are difficult choices to make, risks to take and a feeling of uncertainty, as if the life I've created for myself could fade out like one of BB King's Blues bends.

Don't get me wrong: I've fared better than most who attempt playing the guitar as a career choice. I wouldn't change my life as a guitarist for anything. Life these days is very good. It just hasn't been what I once imagined: sprawling homes on both coasts and in Europe, a Ferrari sports car and unlimited resources. But I do okay, especially in a profession that is very hard to make a good living in. I'm not complaining.

Most importantly, I get to wake up every day and do what I love, fill the world with creativity and (hopefully) inspire others in the process. I've achieved something that many others, including some with much bigger bank accounts have not achieved: fulfillment, integrity and individuality. That's worth more than any house, car or portfolio in the world.

When asked exactly how I managed to carve out a name for myself as a guitarist—something that is aspired to by many yet so few attain—there are many answers. I suppose there is truth to the "10,000 hour theory."[1] But more important than the amount of time one puts into practice is the effective use of that practice time, as well as learning to apply one's practice to real life situations. I would also say that from the beginning, I've had a feeling of

---

[1] The 10,000 Hour Theory, originally based on a study by Swedish psychologist K. Anders Ericsson, has been adapted universally. *"Ten thousand hours of practice is required to achieve the level of mastery associated with being a world-class expert — in anything. In study after study, of composers, basketball players, fiction writers, ice skaters, concert pianists, chess players, master criminals, and what have you, this number comes up again and again."* Daniel J. Levitin *"This Is Your Brain On Music"*

faith, not in a religious context, but one in which I felt destined and determined to go against all the resistance surrounding me at all costs. Playing the guitar was just, as they say in Eastern cultures, "in my nature." But to get to the root of the question, it helps to ask a couple of other questions:

What would compel me to devote 10,000 hours locked away with a slab of wood and a set of strings?

Once amuck in the treacherous jungles of the music world, what set me apart from the herd?

Those answers can be found within the story I'm about to tell you.

Part I

LOBBY CALL 4:00 PM

"Birth is probably a major musical experience."

-Keith Jarrett

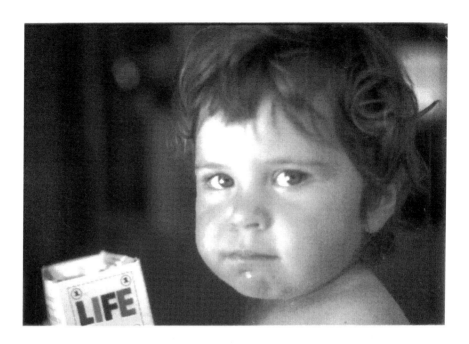

1. LEAST LIKELY TO SUCCEED

Personality. It seemed like everyone else was born with it except me. From pre-school to high school, all the other kids seemed to know who they were, where they stood, what to say and how to react to the daily situations life threw at them. Me? I was afraid of everyone and everything. I didn't know how to talk to people. Everything I said or did felt stupid, and life consisted of daily mocking and humiliation. I was left out of some exclusive club.

I never got the memo.

When I speak of this now, people are shocked. "You?" they say. I can understand this. After all, so many dream about doing what I do today: commanding a stage with a guitar in my hands; traveling the world like it's my own backyard, being warmly greeted by fans across the globe, appearing in music magazines, newspapers, on cable and network television and being acknowledged as one of the best guitarists from the Bay Area, alongside guitarists much more famous than me (Carlos Santana, for example).

Meanwhile, the 21st century launched a whole new industry, fueled by video games enabling millions to step into a fantasy world that lets them pretend, for a few moments, that they're like me: a "guitar hero," if you will. But as a child, if you had told me that anyone would try to emulate me in any way, I never would have believed you.

Though not exactly a "tabloid celebrity," it occasionally feels as if I am. When out and about, I sometimes get asked to pose for pictures. These incidents create small scenes in which bystanders glance, stare or approach, wondering if I'm someone that they've heard of. At concerts, music stores and anywhere guitar fans congregate, people yell out my name from a distance or approach me with trepidation. Here are a few things I've been told by fans I've run into:

"You're Alex Skolnick right? Wow. Can I have your autograph?"

"I started playing guitar because of you"

"You're like this rock star but also a serious jazz musician who's highly respected. That's cool."

(Couple with baby boy): *"This is our son. His name's Alex. We named him after you."*

All this has been augmented by the fact that I've received compliments from female fans of all ages who see me as a sort of sex symbol—the tall, lean, blue-eyed man with the guitar in his hands and the white streak in his hair. In recent years, I've dated some women that are as gorgeous as any actress, pop singer or model.

I bring all this up not to brag about it, but because I remember being obsessed and terrified by women and feeling unworthy of them. From an early age, I felt a painfully strong physical attraction to girls, but my lack of social skills prevented me from getting to know them, let alone having a romance with any of them. This continued through my teens, when I was ignored, snickered at, taken advantage of and rejected by more girls than I care to remember. I was one of those hopeless, desperate, stereotypical losers, the kind depicted in '80s' teen films, such as *Pretty In Pink, Weird Science,* or *Bedazzled.* But in more recent years, beautiful women have told me things like:

"You're one of the hottest guys I know. All my girlfriends think so too."

"You? A shy kid?! You're not shy at all!"

"If I wasn't married, I'd ask you to leave a white streak in MY hair."

*

When I hear things like that, I'm caught off guard and surprised. As a pre-teen and teenager, I was the least likely candidate to ever be considered "hot," "cool," or an "alpha male." I felt like a poor wretched young soul with no place in the world, an unwanted insect.

I will never forget what that feels like, even today, as I find myself "cool" enough to be courted by guitar companies, placed in advertisements and sent to millions of homes adorning the cover of the monthly catalog of the nation's largest music retail chain, *Guitar Center*. I've gone from feeling ugly, awkward and useless, to someone whose "hotness" is used to help sell guitars and other musical products. I even did some modeling for a rock clothing line—one picture features me with two gorgeous female models laying on my lap, the three of us looking at the camera with a collective expression that seems to say: *"You're not even cool enough to be looking at us."*

Despite all this, I don't feel "cool" most of the time. Having been on the other side, I see it where others don't and hang out with many guys and girls who are cool in my book but don't fit the textbook definition of "cool." Being honest with yourself and recognizing your successes and failures is what creates genuine coolness. It's also part of what makes a good musician.

So while a snapshot of my life in recent years, with concerts, guitars, beautiful girls, exotic locales and appearances in the media might make me seem very "cool" by some standards, it's been a long, hard road getting here with many humbling lessons learned along the way. And none of this would have been possible without many lonely hours locked away with a guitar.

2. PEOPLE ARE STRANGE

*S*emptember 29, 1968, Alta Bates Hospital, Berkeley, CA. A television *drones in a hospital waiting room. The music of The Doors, The Byrds, Jimi Hendrix and The Beatles is heard as if in a film soundtrack to all that is going on: in Vietnam, an ugly war in the jungle has led to innumerable local civilian casualties and Americans taken prisoner, tortured and dying by the thousands. Bloody revolutions are taking place in Latin America, China and Africa. In April, the great black civil rights leader Rev. Martin Luther King was shot dead while standing on the balcony of a Memphis motel. The likely next President, Senator Robert F. Kennedy, went on live television and made a plea for calm, only to be assassinated himself in June. Meanwhile the Democratic National Convention in Chicago has turned into a battleground, with Chicago Police gassing, beating and killing protestors.*

I've absorbed all these events and the music, as my mother listened to the radio, watched the news, read the paper. She's subconsciously taken on the weight of the world while waiting for me to be born. Soon it will be time to leave the darkness of the womb and move forward into the bright void.

*

Music was the first thing that had actually made sense to me, adding meaning and logic to an otherwise very strange existence. What, you might

5

ask, was so strange about it?

Let's take a look:

Berkeley, 1974. Cars and vans drive by spray painted with peace signs, clouds and other psychedelic decor. Panhandlers stand left and right, and streets are full of vendors selling drug paraphernalia, homemade jewelry, signs, banners, incense, bumper stickers and tie-die. Everyone wants a buck, everyone has a cause:

"Save the whales! No more nukes! Spare change for a beer!"

A couple of the kooks out here are particularly memorable. There's the "Ashby Bum," covered in soot, with a long scraggily beard and a tattered suit. He wanders up and down Ashby Avenue in a haze—like a cartoon character that just walked out of an explosion. Then there is the "Orange Man." He has wild red hair, a red beard and is seen all over Berkeley, a clear plastic bag in his hand with four oranges, the other hand out for spare change. "Drink four glasses of orange juice a day, okay?" he says to everyone within earshot. Then there is this short fat clown with curly rainbow-colored hair. He is always on campus passing out leaflets for some cause or another. A key figure at such seminal '60s events such as the Merry Prankster movement and Woodstock, he will one day be immortalized by a couple of hippie entrepreneurs named Ben and Jerry in the form of an ice cream flavor bearing his name: Wavy Gravy.

As my father would carry me through the streets of Berkeley in one of those baby-backpacks, I'd experience a case of sensory overload and promptly throw up all over his neck. Somehow, I was supposed to accept that all this was normal.

What kind of people would choose to raise a family in an environment like this—where the streets were a veritable carnival of the bizarre? Where the public school they'd send me to was named after the leader of a controversial black power organization with a Jew hating fringe[1]? And where the babysitter they'd hired to watch me would wind up dead in a police raid, the result of her affiliation with radical left wing revolutionists[2]?

Reading this so far, you might get the impression that I was raised by hippies. Although my parents shared some overlapping political beliefs with the hippies, all similarities ended there. Would you believe it if I told you they were Ivy League scholars?

---

[1] Malcolm X Elementary School. Malcolm X once led the Nation of Islam.

[2] The Symbionese Liberation Army—the same group responsible for the crime of the decade: the kidnapping of heiress Patty Hearst.

My father is widely regarded as one of the brightest and most respected in the academic world of criminal sociology. Besides UC Berkeley, he has taught at Yale University, New York University, UC San Diego, the University of Chicago, spent a year at Harvard on a fellowship, and has been a visiting professor at Oxford. His awards include Carnegie, Guggenheim and National Science Foundation fellowships as well as prizes for distinguished scholarship from the American Society of Criminology, the Academy of Criminal Justice Sciences and the Western Society of Criminology. Those who studied with him were always among the top of their class. His early students included a future celebrity lawyer, Alan Dershowitz, as well as a future legal analyst and CNN television host (and *Dancing with the Stars* contestant) Nancy Grace. They and pretty much everyone else who had him as a professor used the same word to describe him: brilliant.

As a child in Berkeley, I never saw anyone on TV or in real life who resembled my father. However, there is someone I could point to today, and that would be actor/commentator Ben Stein. Politically, my left wing liberal father couldn't be more removed from the conservative Stein, a former attorney for Presidents Nixon and Ford. But physically, the resemblance between the two men in both appearance and expression is uncanny. The similarities don't end there. Both have held positions as law professors and both are graduates of Yale University. If you took Ben Stein's famous character, the economics professor in *"Ferris Bueller's Day Off,"* made him awkward among strangers, confident in front of his students and controlling at home—that would be my dad.

Although humorless much of the time, my father would speak in jest about his brief experience in the US Army during the peacetime draft of the 1950s, particularly the time he was placed in charge of creating the official bulletin boards for the squadron. He picked a few other Jewish privates to assist, and the group promptly spent all their designated time playing poker. Realizing they only had one day left to complete the assignment, they put all their poker money together and hired a local design service to complete the assignment for them, winning accolades from their unsuspecting commander.

Despite his self-deprecating view of his military experience and disagreement with the US foreign policy being implemented (the roots of the Vietnam War), I couldn't help but think the US Army had a tremendous affect on his demeanor. He ran our household with a drill-sergeant-like intensity, oddly combined with a sense of flagrant incompetence when it came to matters outside his studies, particularly domestic activity. When attaching a bike rack to the back of our Audi sedan, he'd put it on the wrong way, causing severe paint scratches to the rear of the car. When peeling an orange for me, he'd hand me a horrible looking squashed, wet pile of pulp. He was often bumping into things, yelling out a name I only heard when he was angry: "Jesus Christ!"

When I heard the term "absent-minded professor," I knew exactly what it meant.

My mother, meanwhile, had a respectable, though less decorated career in social psychology. Over the years, I've encountered numerous psychology students who've come across her textbooks, a few of which have pictures of me at different stages of development. At one point, she was even brought on the Oprah Winfrey Show expecting to discuss her book, but reluctantly placed in the awkward position of mediator for dysfunctional families who fought during the holiday season. Like my brother and me, she was cast in the shadow of our father and his brilliant academic career.

If I had to pick a public figure who resembles her, it would be someone who has had an influence on her own field of study—feminist and political activist Gloria Steinem. The two attractive women were born the same year and never seemed to age. The resemblance is so uncanny, in fact, that I've seen pictures of Steinem over the years and sworn that was my mother.

In 1968, the University of California at Berkeley offered a tenured professorship to my father and a position in the psychology department for my mother. This brought in a salary that, despite their borderline socialist ideals, provided a comfortable living, enabling them to purchase a house where they moved in with my seven-year-old brother. I was born in September of that year.

Berkeley provided the perfect backdrop to their political ideology. With everything in place, it was assumed that their eggs would hatch into tiny left-leaning academics who looked, dressed and behaved just as they wanted—monotone discussions of the news, breakfasts in silence pouring over the New York Times and the bland styles of people who only wear clothing out of necessity of having to cover themselves.

The thought of their newborn baby one day wearing black jeans, leather vests, long hair and playing electric guitars for an audience of wild-haired, screaming, tattooed headbangers never crossed their minds.

3. THE LONG AND WINDING ROAD

I f I could go back in time and speak to the much younger me, I might say something like this:

"Alright, kid. Basically, it's like this—your mom and dad are raising you in the weirdest place on Earth, among hippies, homeless, hippies-turned-yuppies, Hare-Krishnas, Moonies and other people they don't relate to. You'll grow up with the offspring of these people your parents have nothing in common with, many of whom are viewed somewhat as freaks. Yet, compared to everyone else around, your family is so odd that YOU'RE the freaks.

"Your parents are a relic of another time and place. Their mannerisms and expressions are antiquated, they don't understand any of your expressions or ways of communicating. The way they interact with you and your brother, even each other—people just don't communicate that way anymore.

"This is going to cause you serious problems in school and camp. You're not going to be able to communicate with other kids. They're going to single you out as an oddball and make your life miserable. You won't be able to talk about this with your parents. It'll make no sense to them, and they're not comfortable discussing about their own feelings, let alone yours.

"At home, you're going to get a lot of puzzled expressions from your folks, as well as yelling and confrontation. Of course, no-one can do well at school under these social conditions, but they won't get that. They'll only see you not doing well in school and be convinced it has to be YOUR fault. Something's wrong with YOU.

"One day you'll understand more about the differences between them and you, which are drastic. There's the '30s and '40s when they grew up versus the '70s and '80s for you. There's the fact that they grew up before the social changes of the '60s and '70s; although they study and support the ideals of those movements, they cannot fathom you being affected by them. They'll expect you to be the quiet nerd—perhaps someone who studies sex, drugs and rock 'n' roll in terms of sociological statistics and their effects on society as a whole, but never the person who is involved in those activities firsthand.

"Are they brilliant scholars? Yes. But by choosing to raise you here in Berkeley and expecting you to magically turn out the way they envision (like miniature versions of themselves), they are behaving as though mentally disabled.

"They're going to do a series of negligent, inconsiderate things, repeatedly. For example, your mom will continually forget that she's promised to take you to fairs and other fun events, disappearing or making conflicting plans. Other times, she'll pack your lunch with sandwiches made with butter, despite you telling her again and again that you hate butter in your sandwiches. For your day camp hiking trip, she'll pack your canteen with only ice so by the time you've hiked up the mountains, it's evaporated into a few tiny drops of water, leaving you embarrassed, suffering from thirst and reduced to begging for sips from all the other kids. The next time, she'll do the same thing again (despite her title of "social scientist," she'll demonstrate little understanding of actual science). Inexcusably and inexplicably, she'll get angry at YOU for being upset. As a result, listening skills will be the most important quality you seek in others one day, as a musician and as a person. Something is off— she should know better. But you'll try to forgive her one day.

"Your dad, meanwhile, will at times exhibit what is known as cerebral narcissism—ruthless dominance and dismissal, powered by academic achievement and intelligence. He'll embarrass you all through your childhood and teens, screaming at you in public and in front of your friends. He'll cause you to miss or be late to social gatherings, with complete and utter disregard for your own feelings. He'll force you to cut your hair, resulting in the worst look of your whole life, at your most vulnerable time—

your early teens. This will cause you to vow to never cut your hair. As your hair grows, so will his yelling.

"Meanwhile, your brother is only going to make things worse. He's going to come out of all this seriously damaged and you're actually going to get through it. So as tough as it is, try not to hate him.

"None of this will be helped by the fact that, being born late in the year, you'll be the youngest in your class, causing everyone else to have social advantages over you. The resulting experiences will chip away at your self-esteem like a jackhammer. In a few decades, there will be much greater awareness of this predicament, with parents scrambling to do everything they can so their own kids don't have to go through what you'll be going through. This is thanks in large part to a study by a popular book that shines light on your situation.[3] Adding to that is the fact that, despite your mother holding a doctorate in psychology, she has zero interest or awareness of the fact that, according to a widely referred to psychological test, yours is a personality-type represented by only the smallest fraction of the population.[4]

"I know this is all really hard for you to accept right now, but as far as your family is concerned, they're really not bad people. They love you. They just don't know any better. If they had any idea how much damage they were causing you they would think beforehand and perhaps do things differently.

"One day you'll understand all this. For now, just hang in there bud. It's going to suck for a while. But you're going to be alright."

*

"Jewish" was this label attached to us, but I had no idea or understanding of what exactly that meant. My father griped and grumbled about how my brother and I should be more "Jewish." Yet he completely disregarded the fact that, as our father, it was ultimately his responsibility. Ironically, it was our father's one lone feeble attempt at enlightening us to our heritage and ethnicity that led to my brother wishing to play guitar. This would eventually lead to me picking up a guitar.

---

[3] *"Outliers: The Story of Success,"* Malcolm Gladwell (Little Brown, 2008) chapter 1 "The Matthew Effect", mostly based on the original research study on Relative Age Effect: Barnsley, R. H., Thompson, A. H., & Barnsley, P. E. (1985) *Hockey Success and Birthdate: The Relative Age effect, Journal of the Canadian Association of Health, Physical Education & Recreation, 51, 23–28.* The term "Matthew Effect" was coined by sociologist Robert Merton.

[4] Test: MBTI (Meyers-Briggs Type Indicator) Type: INTJ (Introverted, Intuitive, Thinking, Judging) considered to be the rarest (1-2% of the population) and most independent of all sixteen MBTI personality types.

Berkeley, 1978. Dad takes my brother and me to a fundraiser for Jewish causes at the Zellerbach Hall on the Cal campus. It is hoped that this event will somehow raise our awareness of our heritage.

This evening, there is a young Jewish rock band performing. They're pretty good. Although mom and dad have been to one or two rock concerts in their lives, it is rare and, for the most part, our father doesn't seem to understand rock music. Even the fifties rock star Elvis Presley, who has recently passed away and been all over the news, represents "loud, crazy music."

But as we walk out of the concert, my brother announces that he has enjoyed the concert and would like to play the electric guitar too. It is a rare moment of vulnerability for our father who just then sees a connection between rock music, the University and Jewish causes. It presents the perfect opening for my brother, who within a week is presented with a brand new, shiny red electric guitar.

*

My brother's role in my life so far had only been that of a wicked, taunting face. His glaring, menacing presence would point and laugh silently anytime I hurt myself, always just out of sight and sound of our parents. Then he'd complain that I was the bane of his existence.

The seeds of my brother's hostility may have been planted on the day I was born. For it was on that very day when, in honor of the arrival of his new baby brother, our father took him out for a celebratory dinner at a recently opened exotic food establishment. The evening ended with a frantic trip to the emergency room, where my brother spent the night uncontrollably vomiting, violently defecating and being hovered around by doctors, who'd never seen a worse case of food poisoning. The restaurant was promptly shut down by the health department.

Our parents reluctantly agreed to let me try an instrument too, but discouraged me from choosing guitar. They said that at eight years old, I wasn't old enough. They may have feared, rightfully so, that it would add to my brother's burgeoning sibling rivalry.

I chose piano lessons. A piano was a huge "pain in the ass," according to my father. Reluctantly, he agreed to allow an upright piano to be brought to my bedroom, courtesy of several large employees of the Sherman Clay Piano store in Oakland. It was a rental, with the understanding that if I became "serious" about it, we could possibly talk about extending the rental. Buying a piano for the living room was never considered, which I couldn't understand—other families had pianos in their living rooms, and there was a sense of fun and joy surrounding the instrument. I immediately thought of my rented piano as something as unwelcome in our house as fun and joy itself. Both parents made it clear they didn't want to hear any "goddamn noise" while they were trying to get work done.

I had a teacher, Claudia, a mediocre player who didn't inspire me. Things went okay for a few months, until one week when she was out of town and couldn't be there for the lesson. Admittedly, I hadn't practiced enough. At that time, I had zero discipline. I didn't know how to go about practicing on my own. But instead of encouraging me to try harder, Claudia tore into me at the next lesson two weeks later.

"Alex! You've had two weeks to practice and it sounds like shit!"

It was my last piano lesson. A few days later, I relived that day in a dream:

"Alex! You've had two weeks to practice and it sounds like shit." As soon as she says that, a man walks into the room. He has longish hair, black clothes and looks like some kind of action hero from a futuristic movie. He starts glaring at my piano teacher, his eyes looking as though they are going to kill her.

"How dare you."

"Who the hell are you?"

"I'm him."

"Who's him?" He points at me. She looks over and says "Him?!"

"That's right. It's thirty years in the future, and I have a career as a well-known and respected guitarist."

"But he, uh you, sound terrible."

"I'm seven fucking years old! I'm too distracted by etch-a-sketch, Lucky Charms, my dirt bike and Saturday morning cartoons"

"You don't look like a little boy to me. Quite the opposite." She smiles.

"Shut up and listen! Because of you, I quit piano. All I needed was a little encouragement. You could've played me some great piano music. Have you ever heard of Herbie Hancock? Bill Evans? Keith Jarrett? You could've taught me to find joy in the process of learning. You could've been my mentor."

"I don't want to be anyone's mentor. I was hired by your...uh, his mother to give piano lessons. I just need the money. She should be encouraging him, not me."

"Yeah, his mother. Former art school student, decided she wasn't good enough, quit to study psychology, which she says is more "sensible." A lot of good she's going to do."

"Give her some credit. She's the one who hired me. And rented this

13

piano."

"That's because she feels guilty. The psychologist in her knows it's unhealthy to repress a child's creative urges. But the damaged artist in her wants to let him try this music thing in a manner almost guaranteed to make it go away. That piano is rented right? Translation—temporary. Did she look for the best teacher available? No. She found you."

"You sound really ungrateful. I mean, an instrument and lessons, what else does he, I mean you, need?"

"A lot more. I'm only seven and don't realize this yet, but by not having the piano in the living room and only renting one for the bedroom, there are negative messages being sent, as if to say, "This is something not approved of by Mom and Dad." At this age, all any child wants more than anything is parental approval. It's looked down upon because of the noise it makes and the space it takes up. But guess what? That noise is the healthiest thing in the world."

"So you're a guitarist now?"

"I am. Two years from now, I'm going to take up guitar. My parents will give in again, out of Jewish guilt, but this time the teacher will be a lot more encouraging and patient than you, even going so far as to say I have a natural talent. But I'll never lose my love for the piano. I'll buy one and keep it in my living room to make up for what you did to me. And to have another outlet in which to compose music."

"Okay, so I screwed up your piano thing, I'm sorry. But at least your folks are going to get behind your guitar playing. At least it sounds like that's what's going to happen."

"You couldn't be more wrong. Oh, they'll try to make this a temporary thing again. We'll go on this three-month trip to Oxford and they'll put off letting me have a guitar for weeks despite my pleas. Only when I stop eating and sob all day everyday will they relent. Then a few years later, they'll try every trick in the book to get me to quit—bribing me with college trips to Europe, screaming at me, all but disowning me. It won't matter. I'll disown them first and choose the guitar. Then I'll become a heavy metal guitar hero."

"But it sounds like despite all that, everything turned out fine. Why are you still so angry? You're world famous."

"That's me now! I always wonder how my piano playing would've been if you hadn't said those words to me.

"I guess I'm like your mom. I was once a devoted artist. But I started listening to "reason," and trying to be more "sensible," so I pushed my artistic side away. I'll never have a career in music other than teaching

beginners, which I hate. I'm taking this all out on you, it's true."

"It's so obvious you hate it. And it's one thing for you to hurt yourself, but it's another thing entirely to inflict your pain on innocent young minds and hearts such as mine."

"You're right." She starts to cry. "I don't know what I'm doing anymore."

"You're listening to a voice inside—the wrong voice! It's been inflicted on you by your own teachers, relatives and other sources of negativity. Listen, there're some great books written for artists, which help you work out these issues."

"Really?"

"Yes, I swear and...oh fuck."

"What?"

"The books that have helped me the most haven't been written yet. Listen, there's nothing we can do about this now. I'm just here to try to repair damage from the past. I've been able to accomplish what I have partly because of checking out inspirational books and blogs on the internet. "

"WHAT on the inter-WHAT?"

"Um, never mind. You'll find out one day. Please keep in mind what I've said. I've got to go now." He vanishes in a puff of smoke.

I wake up and don't remember any of this.

*

I told my mother that I don't want to play anymore, piano playing is stupid, it's just pressing on keys. Her only argument was that sound comes out of those keys. I said, "I don't care." Then she answered, "Ok, if you're sure. You know dinner is almost ready. You should go wash up."

There was no inquiry into what might have caused me quit. There was no questioning of my lessons or my teacher, no inspirational talk and no incentive to keep going. Anything would have helped, perhaps words from songs she grew up with, *"Every time I find myself flat on my face, I pick myself up and get back in the race"*[5] or *"Pick yourself up, dust yourself off, start all over again."*[6]

It was Failure—something we were very comfortable with. Although my brother and I each had a sharp knife at our throats in the form of expectations to become "successes," the truth was that we were psychologically steered towards failure. My mother would guide us to failure by setting bad examples for us and being helpless against our father's

---

[5] "That's Life," Frank Sinatra
[6] "Pick Yourself Up," Nat King Cole. Also Fred Astaire/Ginger Rogers

dismissive behavior towards us, allowing him to trample over our confidence and ambitions in a stampede of disrespect. My piano and the intense negativity surrounding it *("It's a pain in the ass, I don't want that thing nearby, I'd better not hear the goddamn noise")* was just the tip of the proverbial iceberg that sank each Titanic of inspiration.

The most glaring example of failure had been commenced in the form of an unfinished "darkroom." During my mother's short-lived decision to become serious about photography, workers had been hired for the first phase of the installation—doors, cabinets, sinks, lights—only to be never called back in.

Now the former vision of inspiration lay dormant in the shed behind the house. Given up on for eternity. The never-completed "darkroom" sent a signal to me and my brother that failure was not only encouraged but actually *expected.* It was simply given up on, like my piano playing. There was a similar process with my brother's model rockets that he'd worked on for weeks, only to never be able to get one off the ground. I'd been embarrassed for him as our father and a crowd of strangers watched him in the park counting "3-2-1 Ignition," only to have nothing happen.

Then there were the interminable grant proposals, studies and other deadlines that my father was constantly haranguing my mother about—often not finished on time or abandoned. Outside of my father's towering success in his own academic field, and the fact that my mother had completed a PhD amidst less than ideal circumstances (Yale had many courses off limits to women at the time), our family seemed to secretly embrace failure. Patience, encouragement and moral support existed as invisible stars in distant galaxies.

It would take a lot of courage and self-help to break this awful cycle. I'd become determined not to let my own musical aspirations suffer from this fatal illness.

Within a week, the piano went back to the store and with it, all hopes of my becoming a musician. Or so I thought...

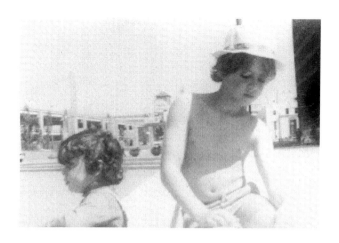

4. DO YOU FEEL LIKE WE DO?

It was the late seventies. *Frampton Comes Alive* was all the rage. Peter Frampton became my brother's hero. I think he somehow thought he could be like him. There was a slight physical resemblance; this further propelled my brother's musical delusions.

He'd claim he wanted to be a musician, but in truth, he only wanted to be a "rock star." There was little interest in music as an art form—he never approached learning his instrument as a "craft." Practicing was a chore, one he stopped doing as soon as his playing was mediocre enough to perform in local clubs. He lacked the passion for music found not just in devoted musicians but even in record collectors and concert goers. If there's any reason I would become what some might call a rock star, it's because my heart was in the right place—having a passion for the craft.

Despite having a long career before and after *FCA*, Frampton would have one of the shortest-lived periods as a superstar in the history of rock 'n' roll. Even as a child, I couldn't help notice that he'd disappeared. Where did he go?

For reasons not entirely his fault, Frampton became a music industry scapegoat. He'd been talked into putting out a live album with all his greatest songs, completely overshadowing any studio recording he had done. While the smash success of the live album had been wonderful, the aftermath was not. He was subsequently rushed into the studio by his label to do a follow up to *Frampton Comes Alive* with all-new material. It flopped, causing him to disappear as fast as he'd burst upon the scene.

There was no way Frampton could compete with his own live album, which ended up being responsible for the live album phenomenon of the seventies. The first live albums I'd own would be *Kiss Alive I and II*. Later, there'd be Iron Maiden's *Maiden Japan* and Judas Priest's *Unleashed in the East*. All of these are albums with live crowds but much or all of the recordings are "doctored" in the studio, in some cases re-recorded entirely.

It would be a rock producer, one that had worked with Aerosmith and other hard rock giants of the 1970s, who would one day explain this to me, shattering the illusion of all my favorite live albums. "Alex, you know that in rock 'n' roll, there's no such thing as a 'live' record right?" he'd say. I'd ask him what he meant. "Usually what they do is record everything on multi track, but they only keep the drums. In fact, it may claim to be one concert, but often, it's the best tracks compiled over several concerts. Then the guitars are fixed or redone entirely. And the vocals are almost always redone unless you have the rare singer that can pull it off live, but that's unheard of in hard rock. The crowd noise is usually real, but it's sometimes taken from other sources. When all is said and done, it sounds like a perfectly recorded concert, but it's more like a studio album than a live one."

"Isn't that lying?" I'd ask.

"Well, Alex, it's like this," he'd say, "In rock 'n' roll, there is 'the truth' and there is 'the legend.' If the legend is more exciting than the truth, go with the legend."

*

One day, my brother, at the urging of our grandma Rose, who was visiting from Florida and in the kitchen nearby, begrudgingly let me play his guitar. He watched over me as though I was a suspicious street vagrant that might run off with it.

The strings were very difficult to press down on, but I managed to squeak out a sound. Soon, I was able to find another note, followed by another. Suddenly, I was drawn into another world, one where I was creating my own reality. It was a world that felt new, different and exciting, a world of color in my black and white.

"Hey, what are you doin'?!" my brother screamed. I was back in reality. Apparently in my dreamlike state, a small drop of drool had descended from my mouth unknowingly. He snatched the guitar out of my hands. "You spit on my guitar!!"

"Did not!" I said.

"Shut up!" He turned his head and yelled. "Grandma! He spit on my guitar."

Grandma rushed over. "I'm sure he didn't mean to, dear."

"Yeah, well that's the last time he ever plays this guitar. And when I get my Les Paul, he'd better stay the hell away from it!"

*

Another time, my brother put *Frampton Comes Alive* on the living room stereo. Using a small cassette recorder, he recorded himself playing along to it. My friend Josh from up the street was there. He and I were listening as our Grandma wandered in. She noticed my plastic bunny guitar lying dormant nearby.

"Alex, why don't you play too, doll?"

My brother looked disgusted. "No!" he said. "I'm playing now."

"He doesn't want me to," I said. "And that's not even a real guitar!"

"Boys, boys!" said my Grandmother. "You're my grandchildren and I love you both. I want to hear you both play. Please Michael?"

"Fine!" he muttered under his breath, his eyes shooting poisonous daggers in my direction.

I decided to make one last attempt to diffuse the situation: "I don't want to. You can't hear this stupid thing anyway." I pointed to the plastic bunny guitar. But Grandma and Josh argued with me; they weren't going to let it go.

I picked up the toy guitar and started noodling along. I didn't even know what I was doing. With my toy bunny guitar and he with his brand new Les Paul (which I wasn't allowed to touch), it was as though we were enemies in the battlefield—he had a US Army issued M-16, while I had a pellet gun. A modern day David and Goliath.

Nonetheless, I managed to find some rhythms or something that somehow fit. "I think Alex is starting to catch up," I overheard Josh say to our grandmother. She agreed. I hoped my brother didn't hear them.

Afterwards, we listened to the tape. It was a jumble of mush: tape hiss, Peter Frampton in the background, my brother's fumbling on his proper guitar and far in the distance, occasionally peaking around the corners, me tinkering on a little plastic toy. But there was no denying a hint of musicality, desperately struggling to break through.

"That's very good, boys," said Grandma as she and my friend clapped their hands for the impromptu living room performance.

"That's all me!" my brother said with a cat-like grin, flashing me another dismissive look.

He was fifteen years old. I was eight. By the time I was his age, I'd be practicing for my first gig in a nightclub. He, on the other hand, was competing with an eight year old with a toy guitar who hadn't learned how to play yet. My brother turned out to be the first jealous, insecure guitar player I'd have to share the stage with. He wouldn't be the last.

5. ESCAPE FROM BERKELEY

So what exactly would draw me to heavy metal? I would say there are a few main factors. Whether you liked it or not, if you played music in Berkeley, you couldn't avoid metal. For another, it was music that put the guitar and guitar solos in the front seat, much more so than ska, punk, new wave and other popular music of the early '80s.

But I'd say that what would most draw me to metal was something that, for my own unique reasons, I, despite being an Ivy League professor's son, would have in common with the kids of Hell's Angels, construction workers, mechanics and other tough working class backgrounds: I felt confused, out of place and pissed off.

Perhaps if someone would have explained things to me, I might have had a gleam of understanding about the cards I'd been dealt. Instead, I didn't know what was going on. I only knew that my life up to this point was mostly terrible: castigated by an overbearing father, undefended by a mother in denial, taunted by a jealous, reckless older brother and mocked, sneered and sniveled at by peers in school.

Some musicians apply their angst to the form of music named after an emotional state known as "the blues." I certainly felt the blues. As I got older, I would listen to the blues heartily—BB King, John Lee Hooker, Freddy King, Johnny Winter, Albert Collins…I'd connect with the feelings expressed. It would make me feel a bit better, as though I wasn't alone. Naturally, this affected how I'd approached guitar (to this day, there is a connection to the blues in the way I play certain notes and phrases). But I wasn't growing up in Chicago, Texas or some other blues town. I was growing up in the Bay Area.

I would take my "blues" and put it into heavy metal lead guitar.

*

If you only know me from my adult incarnation, with an infinite amount of great friends, legions of fans (many of them female) and listed among the world's most respected guitarists, it might be hard to imagine me as an awkward loner with zero confidence and even less social skills.

But ask anyone who knew me in my youth. They'll remember someone unable to speak his mind, stand up for himself or even look another person in the eye. Back then, my life was a bastion of loneliness, embarrassment, shame and confusion.

I wished I had some simple explanation. Something like:

"My dad's in jail."
"My mother is an alcoholic."
"I was adopted."
"My parents are divorced."
"I was abused."
"I grew up in a tough neighborhood."
"I'm black."

It's not that I wanted to experience any of these things firsthand. But at least then, I'd have something to pinpoint as a source of my challenges. But I wasn't being raised by criminals, alcoholics or single parents. I wasn't abused, lived in a well-off neighborhood and was white. So what the fuck was wrong with me?

I attribute a good part of my troubles to Berkeley. This tiny Bay Area city with the big reputation has legions of fans who love the steady climate, where every day feels the same. They embrace the progressive, hippie-influenced culture and left of left political views, which are not to be questioned for risk of being labeled a Republican.

I, on the other hand, was part of a lost generation, born and raised there. We were like the proverbial handicapped children locked in the attic, lost souls with little direction in our lives, laboratory rats in a social experiment gone amuck.

Berkeley was the embodiment of so-called "solutions" which created more problems than they set out to solve. It was a mashing together of creeds, ethnicities and socio-economic backgrounds in an attempt to pretend that everyone is exactly the same and receptive to the same educational and parental needs. This well-meaning conspiracy kept many of us kids in the dark about who we were, where we'd come from and what our potential was. As a result, most of us never felt the glow and charm of Berkeley as experienced by those who arrive there at later points in their lives.

I should have had all the tools at my disposal in order to get by in the world and be happy, but I didn't. The Berkeley Public School System, its teachings, and its social environment were supposed to provide any additional answers and experiences I needed. They didn't. Any problems that came up, and there were many, should have been easily solved. They weren't.

I couldn't explain what my problems were—I only knew that there were many and I felt stupid for asking questions. Making matters worse, I didn't know how to communicate effectively, especially about personal and emotional issues.

It wasn't until I'd grow up, travel the world, interact with many different personality types and do a lot of soul searching that I'd finally begin to put the pieces of this puzzle together. Each time I'd unlock a key to the mystery of my painful past, the research would yield the same conclusion, which was summed up with the following assessment: *"No wonder I was so fucked up."*

*

A big part of my woes stemmed from the fact that my family fit into Berkeley the way Berkeley fits in to the rest of the United States: awkwardly. From the outside, a postcard-worthy picture: a seemingly "normal" family living on a quiet, tree-lined street at the foot of the quaint green Berkeley Hills. But on the inside: an island of dysfunction in a sea of confusion.

In many ways, we were like a reflection of Alcatraz, which you could see from our neighborhood. From afar: a pretty little rock drifting in the San Francisco Bay. From up close: a ruthless Federal Penitentiary. Alcatraz, back when it was in operation, had an added, traumatizing effect that was exclusive to its location. Being so close to the wharfs of San Francisco, the sounds of civilization, traffic and voices would carry over, sending a message to the inmates that while they were trapped in their cells, the rest of the world was going forward with their lives. This was what it felt like for me in our house.

On a comfort level, everything was fine. We had a roof over our heads, two cars, clothes, plenty to eat, a family doctor, a family dentist and occasional ski trips. There was never any doubt that while not wealthy, we were financially secure. But emotionally, creatively and communicatively, we were impoverished.

Like those inmates from a different era who'd been locked inside Alcatraz, I would witness others enjoying their freedom from the confines of my psychological cell. In real life and in the media, I saw kids my own age who seemed free to express themselves as they pleased. Not me.

Like Alcatraz we had rules and regulations. Ours were mostly unwritten. Here were a few:

A. Shut up and keep quiet.

B. Speak only when spoken to.

C. If you must speak, do so in a manner that is compliant, quiet and careful.

D. If any questions—revert to rule "A."

It was a dictatorship enforced by my father, unchallenged by a meek and subservient mother and made worse by an older brother who was unable to handle the pressures of our parents' behavior and our strange surroundings. He'd grow into a lost soul with no sense of purpose, no self-identity in terms of culture or socio-economic class and a work ethic that consisted of avoiding work at all costs.

My brother's problems would become worse as a result of the complexities of life outside our home, his infantile sibling rivalry and years of hallucinogenic narcotics abuse. A source of bewilderment and concern for our parents and me, my brother would retain the insecurity, mannerisms and immaturity of a pre-teen well into adulthood. I would feel a lot of passive resentment towards him for, at seven years my senior, never being the older brother-figure I needed. But as I grew up, I became the "older brother," and tried not to blame him for how he turned out. I recognized him as a helpless, incompetent private in the platoon of our father, an heir to my mother's lack of confidence and a product of all that was wrong with Berkeley.

*

24

Every day, my brother and I were sent out into a world in which people's speech, mannerisms, and general behavior were very different than that within our walls. Our parents had subconsciously decided that we would fit their image of perfect children: compliant, obedient and with no strong opinions of our own. Any signs of confidence had been quickly dismissed or shot down, as were attempts to communicate like our own peers and others outside our walls. Our attempts at adopting humor and expressiveness like those we'd witnessed on the outside were received with blank stares and hostility.

In order to win parental approval, I'd inadvertently molded myself into the son they'd be comfortable with: a spineless blob with no communication skills and no sense of self-worth, the result of an unspoken message being sent, announcing that only one personality type—that of someone meek, submissive, soft spoken and easily taken advantage of—would be accepted in this household. My resulting social weaknesses would be further perpetuated as I was thrown to the wolves of Berkeley's schools and camps to be feasted upon in the form of jokes at my expense.

I would have to find a way to change things or go through life forever scarred and trapped in this shell, in which case there'd be no point in living at all. I'd have to fight against the underlying twisted logic perpetuating the idea that life under our roof, from which my brother and I would both suffer severe emotional damage, was normal. *"Our way is the normal way, the right way,"* both parents seemed to be saying, *"Out there, people are meshuggah."*[7]

But I knew the truth: this was anything but normal. It was unhealthy.

Berkeley was not the right place for us. If there was any place where life was worth living, it was someplace beyond the walls of our house, and most likely, beyond the Berkeley City Limits. "Out there" could only be better than what was going on "in here." That's why my brother would escape to the safe, rent-free solitude of ashrams, yoga centers and other counter-cultural living situations. That's why I'd escape into the subculture of metal, rubbing elbows with drop-outs, addicts and ex-convicts.

Yet metal would soon turn from my savior to my oppressor. I'd one day realize that the very scene in which I'd sought my freedom and self-identity would be fraught with its own perilous limitations, while the intellect and higher education that I'd so fiercely resisted being forced upon me could be invaluable when sought on one's own terms.

---

[7] Yiddish word for "crazy." Adopted by a 21st century Swedish Metal band.

But before all that, metal would become my sole form of honest communication. I'd use that electric guitar to escape from the parental expectations and repudiations. To escape from the schoolyard bullying and humiliation. To escape the blind hypocrisy of a region that was as repressive as it was progressive. To...ESCAPE FROM BERKELEY!

Part II

LOAD IN 5:00 PM

"The most important thing we learn at school is the fact that the most important things can't be learned at school."

-Haruki Murakami

6. ENTER THE GUITAR

My mother had forgotten to turn on the coffee, quickly drawing the wrath of my father. A dramatic screaming match ensued. I started crying. Just then there was a knock at the door. It was our neighbor, letting us know that my carpool to school had arrived.

"Time for school, kid!" my father said, as if nothing had happened. Noticing a tiny Oakland A's baseball cap lying nearby, he took it and gruffly stuck it on my head. With the sensitivity of a grizzly bear, he patted me on the back, saying I looked like a champ. Then, he shoved me out the door and into a trap he'd unwittingly placed me in.

I remember nothing else about that day except the constant ridicule. From the grown-ups: *"What the hell's the matter with you, kid?"* From the other kids: *"Are you a goddamn moron or something?"* I didn't know what to say. I had no idea why everyone, complete strangers, had a beef with me.

It turns out that the night before, the Oakland A's had lost the American League Championship to the Boston Red Sox in their most embarrassing performance of all time—losing every game in the series. Before that moment, they'd been defending champions, having won three straight World Series (1972, 1973, 1974). In other words—*this was the worst possible day in the history of baseball to wear an Oakland A's hat.*

Being so young and naïve, I was unprepared to be an instant target for negative attention from complete strangers. It never occurred to me to take it off—my father had put it on me. I was only six. Such was my introduction to sports in America and the culture surrounding it.

My father should have known better. The social implications of putting the hat on me caused me to immediately develop a fear of strangers and other kids at school. It also caused a negative association with sports in general, giving me less in common with those around me than I already had. As a direct result of this incident, I would avoid activities such as the collecting of baseball cards. But there was one day, when I was called over to look at some baseball cards, or so I thought. It turned into a day I'll always remember.

*

1978 Malcolm X Elementary School: I'm in the fifth grade. It's recess. I'm out on the playground where a giant bed of tanbark lies opposite the basketball courts, forming a red island in a sea of concrete. I sit alone, playing with a piece of tanbark, watching a small crowd from class gathering over by the monkey bars.

One of the boys is showing off his new baseball cards. Big deal. Everyone at school is obsessed with baseball cards and sports in general. I don't get it.

Just then I see Tom, the kid from up the street. I don't know him well, but he's nice enough. He sees me sitting alone and waves me over. Oh great. *I think to myself, reluctantly walking there to join the gawkers. As soon as I get over there, the realization hits me like a fiery explosion: these are not baseball players on the cards.*

What I see instead are pictures of glittery masked creatures with musical instruments. There are four of them. They are all wearing slick, shiny costumes, have black and white faces and giant shoes. One looks like some kind of demon clown, sticking out a tongue that is so long, he can't be human, and wearing boots that look like gargoyles. He is breathing fire. Another one has a star on his eye, a hairy chest, the wildest hair I've ever seen and a cool looking guitar that appears to be made of cracked mirrors. The third is playing a Les Paul guitar like my brother's, only this one has smoke pouring out of the middle. He's wearing an outfit that looks like he just flew in on a UFO. And the fourth is playing drums on what looks like the biggest drum set in the world. He has a face like a cat and there is a giant green cloud of smoke next to him.

Their names are Gene, Paul, Ace and Peter. There is a picture of all four together on a concert stage with lights, fire, smoke and guitars. Behind them is a giant neon sign that announces to us just who this is we are looking at:

KISS

My life has just changed forever.

*

A short time later, a family meal at a local Chinese restaurant was followed by a visit to a neighboring record store for my brother, who'd just cut his hair short and become convinced that new wave music was his ticket to making it. He picked up an album by British synth/pop singer Gary Numan.

For the first time, our parents allowed me to have a record too—I chose Kiss's *Double Platinum.* I just liked the way it looked, the chrome mirror-like cover. Besides, it was two records, two had to be better than one, right?

As I acquired more Kiss albums, I'd be surprised to find they had some of the same songs as *Double Platinum,* not realizing that it had been what is known as a compilation or "greatest hits" album. Nonetheless, I listened to it religiously, and it was a perfect introduction to Kiss's music.

My repeated requests for an electric guitar were met with less success. I was, however, allowed to have a cheap nylon-strung classical guitar from a garage sale in the neighborhood. The neck was too wide for my hands and the strings felt a mile away from the neck.

In retrospect, I suppose I really couldn't complain; at least I had an instrument. But in context, I felt a bit cheated—my brother continued to have the red carpet rolled out for him in terms of music equipment. I wasn't expecting the Les Pauls and Marshalls he'd been given (later to be replaced by Fender P-Basses and Ampeg SVT amps). But I at least wanted an instrument that wasn't painful to play.

It seemed as though my parents were once again subconsciously trying to make things difficult for me, in hopes that I would just give up. How they expected that the culture of failure they were instilling would somehow parlay into success in life was perplexing. But at least it was a step up from the plastic guitar with rubber bands and a cartoon bunny.

Still feeling the pain of failure with the piano, I became determined to give my guitar playing everything I could, even with this awkward, cheap instrument. Discovering Kiss gave me new motivation and incentive. Within weeks, I was sitting in my room having my first guitar lesson.

*

A warm, easy-going Brooklyn native who'd moved to Berkeley, Gary Lapow would one day go on to become a very successful children's artist. Sitting with him in my bedroom on a summer afternoon in 1980, I couldn't have been more excited to get started on Kiss songs. Since that day on the playground, nothing had mattered except Kiss. Gary promised to teach me Kiss music when I was ready, but he started by asking if there was any other music I liked.

"The Beatles!" I said.

"Okay," he laughed. "That's a good start. Anything else?"

"American Hot Wax!"[8] I exclaimed.

"That's the '50s movie right?" he asked.

"Yeah," I said. "It's really cool." I showed him the album.

"What songs do you like from this?" he asked.

"All of them!" I said.

"What are your favorites?"

"I like the ones by Chuck Berry," I said.

"Great, we're going to have no problem. It's going to go a little slow at first, as your fingers get used to making the shapes. You're going to get calluses."

I froze in horror. "Am I going to have to have surgery?"

"What do you mean?"

"Is that something like tonsillitis?"

"A callus is just something that happens on your fingertip," he explained, chuckling. "The skin gets tough, and it helps you play better. Nothing to worry about at all!"

Gary Lapow was the first adult to communicate with me in a language I could understand. He was the first one who seemed to have my own interests at heart, not just his. It was such a revelation that I was very sorry he had to be out of town the following week.

Gravely, I thought of my ill-fated piano lessons. The voice of Claudia the piano teacher ringing in my head like the Wicked Witch of the West in the *Wizard of Oz* movie. Instead of *"I'll get you my pretty and your little dog, too,"* I heard, *"You've had two weeks to practice, and it sounds like shit."*

Would this be the end? Would he come back transformed into a

---

[8] *American Hot Wax*: 1978 film about the influential Fifties disc jockey Alan Freed, credited with coining the term "rock'n'roll." The largely unknown cast included future TV stars Jay Leno and Fran Drescher and featured performances by music legends Chuck Berry, Jerry Lee Lewis and Screamin' Jay Hawkins playing themselves. A box office flop never released on video, this film is an essential crash course in early rock history.

monster as she had? Not if I could help it.

Diligently, I went to work, first memorizing the names of the strings. Elegant Animals Don't Go Bathroom Ever. E.A.D.G.B.E. To this day, the silliest music moniker I've heard, but it made sense.

Next: the tuning. Gary had loaned me a 'pitch pipe' until I could get my own.[9] It sounded like a harmonica but only had one note, which matched the A or fifth string. Once you tuned that string, you just went to the fifth fret on the lower string and matched that pitch to the open A. Then the fifth fret on the open A matched the open D. And so on. The only trick was to remember that on the third string, you had to go down one fret, to the fourth, and then tune the 2nd string, B, from there. Once that was done, back up to the 5th fret for the open first string, which should be the same pitch as the low 6th string, only higher. I could handle this.

Then: the chords. Since then, I've met several other guitarists who have started on G and C chords. I guess this is okay, but I'm really glad to have started with E and A. Moving on to bar chords a short time later, it would be that much simpler since we were moving the E and A shapes up and down the neck, ones I was already comfortable with.

Conceptually, it made more sense to learn E and A first—E was based on the lowest string of the guitar, and I played all six strings. A was only five strings—you had to skip the lowest string. Technically, you could play it, but most of the time, it sounded better without it. Finally, there was the D chord. The root was on the open fourth string and like the A chord, you could play the string below the root, but it was best to just play the root. And with the D chord, you had to skip the low E entirely.

Every time I could get one of the strings to make a pitch, I was happy. But it seemed like forever before I was able to press down hard enough with one string and keep that sound—when I got sound out of two strings, it felt like a miracle. I became determined that in a day or so, I'd be fingering three notes of this chord. I kept it up every single day, for more than an hour.

Within a week, I was able to play each chord, and make it sound like it had color. I'd never worked so hard on anything in my life, yet strangely, it was satisfying. And once I'd achieved a chord, playing it was actually fun.

When Gary came over two weeks later for the lesson, I played for him, ready for disaster. He was silent. "Alex, I don't know what to say." he

---

[9] Electronic tuners existed but were very expensive and had not yet become affordable—today we have headstock tuners that are cheap, easy and precise. But it's still important to be able to tune by ear, as well.

finally muttered. I'd just demonstrated going back and forth between A and E chords. It was our second lesson.

Was he going to yell at me? Echoes of the evil piano teacher ringing like the chime of the bells at the gallows pole.

"Alex, it sounds terrific!" he said with a grin.

Huh? I thought. *I did something right? For the first time in my life?* "Do you know how rare that is? You're playing the chords!"

"I've been practicing," I said.

"I can tell!" he exclaimed, just before providing the corrective words I needed to hear: *"Alex, you've had two weeks to practice and it sounds like you've been playing for a year!"*

*

For the first time in my life, thanks to my own hard work and Gary's support and encouragement, I had something that I felt confident about. I certainly wasn't a boy genius or prodigy like Mozart or Paganini. But I had found something that was natural for me and which I enjoyed. This gave me the necessary tools and inner motivation to spend many hours working at my craft. It didn't hurt that I was emotionally tormented either. That would prove to be an asset, later on.

I think in a way Gary was a genius of a teacher. He was able to hone in on the music I was passionate about and apply that to my learning process.

The following week I had the chords and the strum and we applied that to my very first song, "Act Naturally" by the Beatles (sung by Ringo Starr). Even though "Act Naturally" wasn't one of the songs that grabbed my attention like "Day Tripper" and "A Day in the Life" (those would have to wait), I was still playing a song by The Beatles, and that was cool.

From there we moved to bar chords, blues vamps and other basic tools of rhythm guitar.

Gary was easily making a connection between these tools and actual pieces of music. And what a great excuse to show me chord after chord. Not in the context of some song I was being forced to learn, but in parts of songs I could relate to. This concept was very different than how I was being taught grammar, math, history and other subjects of elementary school, where I was forced to adapt to this predetermined curriculum that made no accounting of individual needs.

Within a few months, I was learning my favorite '50s song from the *American Hot Wax* soundtrack, from which Gary was able to make what for me was the ultimate connection: you take a vamp, like in Chuck Berry's "Roll Over Beethoven" and apply it to a Kiss song. As it turned out, one of my favorite Kiss songs, "Let Me Go, Rock 'n' Roll" was like an amped up version of Chuck Berry. This would be the first Kiss song I'd ever learn; and thinking about it now, it seems like their tribute to the '50s classics—along the lines of Led Zeppelin's "Rock 'n' Roll."

Was Kiss as good as Led Zeppelin? Knowing what I know now, I don't think so, at least in terms of musicianship. But early Kiss is not to be discounted—the songs were great and so were Ace's solos—both still stand up to this day. As a ten year old, I thought they were the best band in the world—better than Zeppelin, better than anyone! And it was only a matter of time before I'd build up a whole vocabulary of songs by Kiss, The Beatles, The Rolling Stones, Chuck Berry and other rock 'n' roll legends.

7. FAILURE IS NOT AN OPTION

The lessons with Gary provided a shining light to an otherwise dark and painful existence at school and increasingly, at home. I quickly got the message my guitar playing was being accepted begrudgingly, and I was not to express passion or enthusiasm for it.

There is probably nothing more disheartening for an eleven year old than wishing to share with his mother and father something he is passionate about, as I was about the guitar, only to be interrupted mid-sentence, the conversation suddenly shifted to one between his parents about a subject that doesn't concern him—an upcoming faculty meeting, a grant proposal, or a random item seen in the op-ed section of the New York Times. It was as though they'd sold their souls to intellectual academia, unable to discuss anything outside their comfort circle, especially personal matters or interests of my brother and me. These dismissals took place nightly at the dinner table, usually by my father and rarely ever challenged by my mother (although it was clear that she recognized what was happening, choosing to look away rather than confront reality).

It became increasingly clear that in our house, expression and emotion were not to be tolerated—arts and artistry were to be kept at a distance and unthinkable as career choices. A few mysterious pieces of art adorned the house but they seemed to have no meaning and were never explained or shared with us. Years later I would read that failed or unfulfilled artists were the most detrimental to developing artists like me. And I didn't realize it at the time, but I was being raised by two of them.

My mother had attended the High School of the Arts in New York, the same school that the movie and TV series *Fame* is based on. She'd had diverse artistic interests including painting, photography and, yes, guitar. Inexplicably, she had given up the pursuit of art and music and, possibly to hide the pain of this loss, gave up being a serious appreciator of the arts, as well. She had decided that in light of her own failures, a career in the arts and anything more than a distant, passing interest, was unacceptable.

In addition to my mother's decision that she would never become good enough for the arts, my father had wanted to play the drums. Being a fan of the great big bands, like Artie Shaw, Benny Goodman and Buddy Rich, my father had asked his parents for a drum set, but growing up in the Great Depression, was denied one—a fact he sadly reminisces of to this day. He had no friends or relatives who were musicians and no other link to following his dream of playing drums. Again, he decided that a career in the arts was impossible.

So as it turned out, both parents had poured their passions into their academic pursuits which, while very respectable, carried the baggage of their unfulfilled artistry. It was up to me to make up for their lack of success in the arts.

While extremely smart on a scholastic level, both parents showed an inability to engage in a meaningful discussion about anything outside their limited comfort zone of scholastic journals, op-ed pieces and the news. Uncomfortable subjects included anything I wanted to discuss—music, arts, pop culture and more importantly, difficulties I was going through in my personal life. They showed no passion except during family arguments, of which there were many, usually senseless in nature—household issues, false assumptions and unrealistic expectations.

*

Our father had, at an early age, found something at which he'd shown a natural aptitude: Social Sciences and Criminology. He had always seemed like one of the best from day one—as if everything since had fallen into place for him. It was a process my brother and I hadn't witnessed, for it had taken place in a different era. I wouldn't realize the full implications of his expertise until years later, when I'd encounter former students who'd enlighten me that our father was a towering figure in his field.

As brilliant as he was, I sometimes questioned whether he'd have the same success if placed in the shoes of my brother and me. Granted he'd had his own challenges—his own parents made the turbocharged neurotic parents of George Costanza on *Seinfeld*[10] look like the Dalai Lama. Having to walk through Catholic neighborhoods and receive anti-Semitic taunts was no picnic, but at least he'd grown up with others around him with similar challenges: Jewish kids who looked similar and were the offspring of immigrant parents. For some reason, his area of Brooklyn seems to have spawned a wave of ultra-successful Jewish men from his generation— scholars, doctors, lawyers, playwrights etc.

In my family, there was no one else around remotely like us. We were all under the shadow of my father, someone who was considered by many to be *the best*. It was made all the more intimidating by the fact that his field, criminal sociology, was a world so distant it felt unapproachable, like Vatican City to working class Italians or the Forbidden City in Beijing to the surrounding Chinese peasants...

Everyone else in our family was doomed to fail.

*

Part of the reason my family had been so confusing was this very backwards, unspoken way of looking at careers and goals. It was never stated but implied: unless you show potential of being the very best at something early (as our father had been), you shouldn't even try. If someone better comes along, you should just quit. This form of irrational thinking is destructive, psychologically damaging and career killing.

My mother had given up on art school because when she got there, there were others *better than her*. My brother had shown tremendous potential in downhill ski racing—he gave up after attending ski camp and finding there were people *better than him*.

If I decided to give up every time I encountered a guitarist who seemed *better than me*, I never would have gotten anywhere. Many times I have encountered those who come across as better, but it's had no effect on the ultimate outcome. I've often channeled these experiences into questions such as this: *Is this person really better than me or is it just the situation?*

For example, take a guitarist who picks an instrument at Guitar Center or some other music store, starts wailing and causes a small crowd to gather around whispering that this person is great. Put that same person in a real-life professional situation where he or she has to create actual *music*, not just guitar pyrotechnics—a studio or live gig where he or she has to interact with other musicians on a professional level—and very often this person doesn't have what it takes.

---

[10] Played by Jerry Stiller and Ann Mearr

As this is being written, there is an internet phenomenon known as "bed shredders," or people—some of them very young—who demonstrate high level guitar skill in their bedrooms. Take them out and put them on a real stage, with a real crowd and real life situations and they'll likely sound very different.

Some players get a shallow stamp of approval from the crowd just because they're doing whatever the flavor of the month is, playing like the guitarist who is most popular at the moment. On the flipside, there are players who might not be very good at showing off when picking up a guitar at a music store, but when placed in the context of their own professional situations, are downright captivating.

And what if you come across someone who is truly at a higher level than you are at that moment? *Quit now! Right?* Wrong! Instead, ask yourself—what can I learn from this person? How can I apply what they are doing to what I am doing? And most of all, what can I do to get more focused and try harder?

I always remembered a line that Frank Sinatra sang: *"Every time I find myself flat on my face, I pick myself up and get back in the race."* Of course, it takes a lot of humility to be able to achieve this headspace that enables you to recover from stumbles, accept the level you're at and still find joy in the endeavor, whatever it is, writing, painting, skiing, guitar playing, etc... But it's like exercising: the more you do it, the stronger you get.

It is tragic to let your endeavors be brought down by something as silly as someone being *"better than you."* If you approach it with the attitude that you will learn more by being around people who are at a higher level, you will go much farther than creating an illusion of comfort that you are the best in your immediate surroundings.

In fact, it's one of my favorite musicians of all time, guitarist Pat Metheny, who stresses the importance of being around better musicians. Here's something he often says, usually with a laugh:

"Whenever young guys ask me what they should do to get better, I always say, 'Try to be the worst guy in whatever band you're in.' That's the secret."

8. SHOUT IT OUT LOUD

For the next year or so, I struggled on that nylon string acoustic guitar, dreaming of one day owning an electric.

One time, my brother allowed me to accompany him to Leo's Music.[11] He'd said he was bringing in his Les Paul to see about a possible repair or adjustment. While he talked with someone behind the counter I wandered around and looked at the sleek, shiny works of art.

Most of these instruments were hanging, but there was one on a stand that was easily accessible. I didn't dare play it for fear of getting in trouble with my brother, as well as the store personnel. But when no one was looking, I carefully felt it up and down, without removing the guitar from the

---

[11]The original Leo's Music was on College Avenue in Oakland. It later moved to Telegraph Avenue, becoming a pro-audio specialty store.

stand.

The neck felt so thin and the strings felt so tiny. I could only imagine what I'd be able to achieve with a guitar like that, as opposed to my cheap classical clunker; it was like comparing a speedboat to a rowboat.

I walked around some more and looked at the electric guitars hanging on the wall—there were many colors and shapes. Red, orange, strange swirly mixtures (which I found out was called sunburst), black, white, chrome, even one where you could look through and see all the electronics. Pointy bodies, smooth bodies, curvy bodies, funny V-shaped bodies...

Suddenly my eyes glanced at the corner of the wall to an instrument that caused me to question whether I was seeing correctly. It was one of the strangest things I'd ever seen—was it two guitars? No, it was one guitar. It had a single body but two necks. It looked like those people I'd heard about that were joined together, Siamese Twins.

"She's a beauty, ain't she?" a voice startled me. It was a salesman, a really nice one. In the future, I would learn that not all music store salesmen were this nice.[12] He said, "That's a Gibson Doubleneck SG. Just like Jimmy Page from Led Zeppelin. Maybe you'll have one someday."

About twenty-five years later, in the winter of 2004, I'd be rehearsing at SIR studios in New York City to tour with the holiday-themed rock show, Trans-Siberian Orchestra. During a run-through, the show's creator, Paul O'Neil would walk in with a giant hard-shell guitar case, plop it at my feet, pat me on the shoulder and just nod. This guitar would be for a special song in the show where the entire band and string section would stop and I'd be the only one playing for the entire arena, green lasers shooting through me. At the end of the tour, Paul would point to the guitar and tell me, "Take it home, it's yours."

It's hanging on my wall now—a white Gibson Double Neck SG, exactly like the one I saw hanging on the wall at Leo's music that day.

*

On the way out of the store, I noticed my brother's guitar case looked different. "Did you get a different case?" I asked.

"Yep."

"Is that the same guitar?"

"Nope."

"Where's your Les Paul?"

---

[12] In 2010, I would write a blog for Guitar Player magazine, entitled "Music Store Horror Stories."

"I traded it."

"For what?"

"A bass."

"A bass?"

"Yep," he said.

"How come?" I asked.

"The guitar's harder, it's got six strings. The bass only has four!"

*

My brother switching from guitar to electric bass because it had less strings was metaphoric of his entire outlook on music and life. His thought process could be summed up with the following: What's the simplest way to "make it?" How can I "get signed?"

Of course, he had no clear idea of what making it or getting signed actually entailed. He seemed to believe that becoming a rock star like Peter Frampton happened overnight. In fact, Frampton himself had been hanging in there for many years—he'd already recorded five albums with the band Humble Pie and released four solo albums with disappointing results before *Frampton Comes Alive.* That's nine albums!

If you've ever done an album, you know—it's not easy. Success in music wasn't impossible by any means, but required the developing of an iron-clad strength, focus and determination.

Yet, to my brother, music represented a one-way ticket to easy street: a way to avoid work and school. He would play bass in a few surprisingly good local bands, only to be kicked out of each one. Watching this, I'd become more determined than ever to one day join a band and become the biggest strength, not the weakest link. I would listen mortified as he would explain his plans to my parents—it always involved some delusional idea about how he was going to make it. One time, he had a concept that he just knew would be a hit—a band called Fleet of Flounders with fish song titles like "Tuna Head" (tune ahead) and "Just for the Halibut."

By this time, my brother had become a habitual user of LSD, which only further fueled his delusions. While LSD had arguably enhanced the creative process of great psychedelic music like the Beatles and Jimi Hendrix, who had tried it only *after* they had already reached great heights as musicians, my brother, like many other Berkeley teens, believed that taking acid was the answer to their dreams. It resulted in no higher creativity, no productivity and ended up resulting in nothing but wasted time and energy. After all, it was Hendrix himself who sang, *"Castles made of sand fall in the sea eventually."*

My brother would use music as an excuse to drop out of college, avoid working and receive a monthly check of support from our parents who, quite understandably, would grow tired of rolling out the red carpet for him. The example he set for our parents was this: *Musician = Flake*. Attempts to differentiate myself and my musical pursuits from my brother would be in vain—he'd try telling our parents I was going to be *exactly like him!*

This would strengthen our parents' resolve that I was to be kept from becoming like Michael or the deadbeats he hung around. Unsure of how to handle their unraveling family vision, our parents' attitude towards me and my guitar would become increasingly negative.

There were, however, two incidents for which I would be grateful to my brother.

The first was giving me my first electric guitar. It didn't matter that it was a nameless, paper-thin piece of plywood that he somehow obtained and passed on to me, and an "amp" made from a transistor radio. The whole rig was a hunk of junk, but I was touched.

That night, I couldn't put it down—the concept of holding an instrument yet having the sound come from another place was mesmerizing. It gave a sense of power. Finally my father knocked on my door and told me to get to sleep. Clearly my parents weren't going to be buying me a Les Paul, the way they had for him. It was as though we lived in music squalor and this was my brother's act of charity.

In retrospect, passing on the cheap guitar to me may have been a possible ploy to have an ally in the family for his own misguided musical battle against our parents. But whatever his motives, it set the tone for a few years where we were close, like brothers should be.

In a few years, while our parents would be away for the weekend, my brother would snatch away a girl I liked whom I'd invited over from my 8th grade class (she'd be my age, he'd be twenty-one), plying her with alcohol and sleeping with her while I'd be within earshot. The next night, he'd barge into my room at 3am, hijack my newly purchased custom guitar (a white starbody, later to be used on my first recordings), pass it around to a roomful of drugged out deadbeats he'd invited over, then argue with me for demanding it back. Then, when our parents would return and notice a few things missing, he'd deny throwing a party and choose to place blame on a bandmember of mine who'd come over briefly, nearly causing our parents to make me quit my new band. These disturbing incidents would leave lasting scars, taking our period of brotherly friendship and smashing it to pieces.

But before then, my brother would begrudgingly provide one other act for which I'd be deeply appreciative: driving me to my first Kiss concert.

*

It had begun on a Sunday, as we were having breakfast in typical silence, reading the papers. I was looking through the arts & entertainment section of the *San Francisco Chronicle,* known as the "Pink Section." There in the music listings, I saw it clear as day.

KISS
LIVE IN CONCERT
NOVEMBER 25, 1979
THE COW PALACE, SAN FRANCISCO

"Oh my god!" I couldn't help saying. "What?" both my parents asked. I showed them the ad, courtesy of Bill Graham Presents—an organization with which I'd do business one day.

There was some discussion. It was decided that I couldn't go. I was too young to go on my own. My brother didn't want to go—he didn't like Kiss.

For several days, I was in tears. At that point, nothing meant more to me than Kiss. I had to find a way to go. It was as if my life depended on it. I prayed. Not to God or anyone in particular, just to the universe or whatever else was out there.

A few days later, my brother's friend Danny Gill, a local guitarist he'd been jamming with, talked my brother into going. Danny needed a ride and my brother agreed that if he could use the car to drive himself and Danny, he'd take me. Our parents at first said he could go, but not me. I was too young for a "crazy thing" like that.

"It's not fair," I cried. I cried and cried.

Finally, it was agreed upon—Michael would drive me and Danny, then come straight home afterwards and drop me off.

*

The Cow Palace was like a distant planet in our backyard—a convergence of youth from all over the Bay Area, uniting for the cause of rock 'n' roll. It was the big leagues—the Madison Square Garden of the Bay Area.

Although Kiss was the only concert I'd attend there with my brother, within a couple years, I'd have friends with older brothers who'd take us to concerts. I'd see The Police and Van Halen, both in 1982. Then there'd be the first concert I attended without supervision in 1984: Dio, the band headed by the former frontman of Black Sabbath (post Ozzy), Ronnie James Dio, someone I'd cross paths with over the years. In 1992, I'd finally get my time on that stage, as the support act to Iron Maiden. I'd feel as though I was on sacred ground.

In 2010, I'd return to the Cow Palace on a tour with Slayer/Megadeth/Testament. The seats, signs and general decor would feel exactly the same. I'd look over in the corner to exactly where I sat at eleven years old.

*

November 1979, The Cow Palace, San Francisco

The lights go down and smoke pours onto the stage as the deafening screams of 14,000 people fill the air. I can barely hear myself think over my own screaming. I don't believe I'm actually going to see them. I won't believe it 'til they come out.

Like a giant magic trick, four separate pillars of fluorescent smoke appear on individual platforms on the stage—one red, one purple, one blue and one green. The sound of the audience grows even louder as the four figures float up from below the stage into the smoke. No longer are these just faces from magazines and album covers, they're right here in person, each one standing motionlessly in the pile of smoke coordinated to his costume.

In the red cloud is Gene, "The Demon," bassist/vocalist with his red cape and seven inch platform shoes with tiny gargoyle faces. A painted black widow's peak extends to his nose, his eyes surrounded by black flames, the rest of his face white. He flashes his pointy tongue—his trademark. I've figured out how to do that with my own tongue, to the response of "Eew!" "Yuk!" and "That's gross!" by the girls in my sixth grade class. I don't know this yet, but as an adult, this tongue trick will get a very different reaction from grown women—smiles, giggles and playful comments like, "Will you marry me?"

In the purple cloud is Paul, "The Lover" with his purple cape, black platform shoes, and feathered jumpsuit—it reveals his hairy chest to the estrogen-filled female portion of the audience. Paul plays rhythm guitar and sings. His face is painted white with a black star over his right eye, the simplicity having enabled me to dress like him for Halloween a year ago— I'd cut the face out of my Planet of the Apes mask, painted my own and used the hair for the wig.

In the blue cloud is Ace, "The Spaceman." His costume is mostly chrome, with shoulders that make him look like a futuristic football player. His makeup is closer to Gene's, with both eyes surrounded by color against his white face paint, only his color is silver and the pattern is more pointy, like a galactic explosion. He plays lead guitar, so I either want to be like him or Paul, I'm not sure yet.

In the green cloud is Peter, "The Cat." His face is the most elaborate—green and black circles around his eyes, whiskers and a silver button nose, all against white face paint. At the same time, his costume is black and green, the least elaborate, probably so he can play his drum kit without too much discomfort. I don't know this at the time, nor does anyone else, but this is going to be Peter's last tour with the band. I would cry if I knew this. Who knows, one day, I may have to disappoint my own fans by leaving a band...

All of a sudden, a thunderous voice takes over the arena. It's like the announcer's voice I've heard at Ringling Bros. Circus, only much more forceful and aggressive: "You wanted the best and you've got it. The hottest band in the land: KISS!!!!"

With a flash of lights and an explosion, they launch into "Deuce." The most exciting moment of my young life has just begun. The giant KISS logo lights up, blinks and moves forward, backward and every possible configuration like the neon of a Las Vegas casino. It will be the only concert I ever see where I know every word to every song.

*

Before the performance, my brother and Danny had left their seats so they could go up to the front row, and I was left in charge of the seats. They were gone for quite a long time. I didn't mind being left alone, I was actually enjoying watching everyone—all different ages, mostly teenagers and young adults, a select few kids my age. Everyone seemed to be in black. Black t-shirts, black leather jackets. Some were in Kiss makeup.

Then a couple in their twenties sat down in the seats. I told them with all the authority I could muster up that the seats were taken. They told me that the concert was sold out, people can't just ditch their seats to go watch the concert somewhere else; then they sat down. I started crying and they ignored me. I just didn't have it in me to confront them. I didn't know how, and had no idea what else to say. When Mike and Danny came finally back, Danny, seeing the people in their seats, said, "Alex, we told you to save our seats."

"I told them," I said. Being eleven, nobody was taking me seriously. I felt like a spineless blob.

I heard Danny talking to the couple and they worked out a deal. These people would stay in their seats while Mike and Danny were up front and move when they came back midway through the concert. When they moved back to their seats as agreed upon, Mike and Danny were covered in sweat, their clothes ruffled and their hair frazzled.

The first few rows had consisted of teens and twenty-somethings encompassing all of the Bay Area—North Bay, South Bay, East Bay, San Francisco and all points in between. Most had spent their lives in their own regions, never giving thought to the fact that there were so many other Kiss fans from surrounding parts of the Bay. Here they were united under one roof, battling to get closer to the front row like a Darwinian "Survival of the fittest." The further up you got, the tougher you had to be. Only the strong survived.

One figure alone stood out among the carnage, someone so large, he could push his way through anyone else in that crowd. With a height of six-foot-four, wild black hair and a chest like a gladiator, he stood out. Slithering to the front row, he ruthlessly pushed aside anyone who stood in his way. Beers were knocked over, their contents spilling out, while ribs were elbowed. The victims, no slouches themselves, would turn around to confront this aggressor, anticipating physical confrontation. But as soon as they got a closer look, they'd turn the other direction, walk away, politely wave or smile like a commuter showing courtesy to another driver on the Bay Bridge. This was not someone to be messed with.

Who was this fearless rock 'n' roll combatant?

He was an eighteen-year-old Native American Indian, raised in the East Bay suburb of Dublin, California. Dressed in a black "Thin Lizzy" t-shirt and leather jacket, he might as well have dressed for a war dance and hunting ceremony. This Indian warrior who'd fought his way up front was soon spitting on Gene Simmons, aggressively challenging the fire breathing God of Thunder himself. The Native American warrior from Dublin was one of the toughest out of the crowd of thousands. I, the eleven-year-old Jewish kid from Berkeley, was one of the weakest.

In exactly seven years, he and I would be in the same band.

9. MAY THE FORCE BE WITH YOU

Having come of age during the Great Depression and having two children late in life, our father and mother behaved more like neurotic grandparents than parents. This was especially true compared to the easygoing behavior of the Woodstock generation parents many of my friends had. With doctorates from Yale, their status as Berkeley academics masked their roots as New York Jews from working class immigrant families of the 1930s and '40s. But their behavior at home couldn't hide their roots.

The pressures of having a family sometimes brought out the worst in them—my father would regularly fly off the handle, forcing my mother out of her silent shell and bearing claws in the face of danger. It sent my brother and me scampering upstairs like frightened animals, with irreparable damage being inflicted. Torn between the awkward silences and the shouting, life in our home became a quagmire of unspoken feelings, unrealized dreams and unacknowledged reality. All the while, they published textbooks, including a series on statistical trends of the American Family.

During this time, I would very rarely, but on occasion, encounter other types of parents who seemed to be able to treat their children with dignity as well as discipline, reinforcing confidence, individuality and self-esteem. They were younger than my parents and had more modern concepts of child-rearing and family interaction. They encouraged group activities and open communication, were able to have a sense of humor and allowed their children to have one too.

I couldn't understand why our family was so different or why our parents seemed to not know how to communicate with us or other kids. In these other households, anytime the kids needed to talk to the parents or the other way around, there was usually a calm sit down or a heart to heart talk in which issues were resolved. Sure, there would be occasional blowups and misunderstandings, but that was the exception to the rule. For the most part, these other families I came into contact with communicated functionally. In our house, it was the other way around: unnecessary yelling or cold silence was the norm.

Adding to my pain was the glee of these select peers who were actually able to have fun with their families. They got taken to amusement parks such as Disneyland and Great America, and other places that were fun for kids. I remember asking to go to Disneyland for years and being told, "We took you there…when you were two."

Our main recreational activity, ski trips, where blotted by the yelling, screaming (usually my dad), crying (on my part) and chilly silence that blanketed any sense of enjoyment like powdered snow upon the mountain. Even the simple recreational activity of going to the movies was something bungled by my parents.

While other kids I knew got to see light comedies, holiday films and other family friendly fare, I'd be taken to about one film a year. It was almost always one strictly for adults and painful to sit through. For example, I can remember being seven years old and bored to tears by *All The President's Men,* the 1976 Watergate movie starring Robert Redford and Dustin Hoffman. The next year, there was the Woody Allen film *Annie Hall.* I couldn't understand the situations and didn't see why the grown-ups thought it was funny. A couple of years later, we saw two films that gave me nightmares. I'll never forget the scenes of Jake La Motta, played by Robert De Niro, beating his wife to a pulp in *Raging Bull* or Francis Ford Coppola's Vietnam War epic *Apocalypse Now* with its scenes of helicopters being blown to bits, villages demolished and women and children being gunned down and butchered in a hail of bullets and blood. I was ten.

These are great films which I now have a tremendous appreciation for as an adult. But for the life of me, I can't comprehend how anyone could drag along a young child. One of the deals of having kids is making choices such as going to films and doing activities that you might not do as a couple without children. Incidents like this left me with a feeling my parents must be the dumbest people in the world. I couldn't believe it anytime someone would tell me they were "very smart people."

Even as a young adult, I would not be able to escape my father's idiotic choice of movies. There was this one Christmas Day, for example, where we'd got dragged to see *Amistad,* Steven Spielberg's film about the slave trade. I can understand we're Jewish, don't celebrate Christmas blah, blah, blah.... But for God's sake, Christmas is still a *holiday.* I don't care if it's Kwanzaa, Thanksgiving or Bangladesh Solidarity Day. We deserve to enjoy a holiday as much as anyone and I don't care if it's not endorsed by our background and traditions, which we've never practiced anyway. I'm not saying we need a Christmas tree and eggnog, just a day of enjoyment and fun. The last thing I need on any celebratory holiday is to see a film about a slave ship and watching men being whipped, chained together, thrown overboard, dragged underwater and drowned to their deaths.

Another parenting disaster took place with a film I desperately wanted to see as a child: *Star Wars.* My parents flat out refused to take me. For months on end, I would hear the other kids raving about *Star Wars* and sadly watch them bonding with each other and even their own parents over the film. Every day I would ask my parents, "When are we going to see *Star Wars*?" The answer was always the same:

"The lines are too long."

Months and months went by. Each day on the schoolyard, I would overhear new details and plot twists, despite my best attempts to change the subject, not listen or plug my ears.

By not seeing *Star Wars,* I became an even bigger outcast than I already was, even less desirable to play with. By the time I finally saw the film, everyone else had seen it, I knew exactly what was going to happen and the entire experience was ruined.

In my twenties, I had a girlfriend who couldn't believe that as a child, my parents had never shown me the great Disney movies *Fantasia, Alice In Wonderland,* and *Peter Pan,* as well as other classic family movies that would come on TV every year.

"What do you remember watching with your parents you when you were a kid?" she asked.

"*Washington Week in Review*," I answered.

A stillborn expression took over her face. "Are you serious?"

"Also MacNeil Lehrer Report. And Walter Cronkite."

Our primary link with the outside word was *The New York Times, Sixty Minutes* and PBS. My parents would sit and watch in silence, with all reactions limited to my father, who controlled the atmosphere. Once in a while, they would have guests over. The wine and hors d'oeuvres, which usually consisted of French cheese, fresh olives from the gourmet market and baguettes from the local bakery, were delicious. But they failed to numb the pain as they'd sit and pontificate over politics and academics. The guests were these fellow academic couples or families who either didn't have children or had children who were grown up and moved away. There was no acknowledgement or inclusion for my brother and me, even when my brother had reached "adult" age. We'd sit there mostly in grinding silence, sometimes spoken about in the third person as if we weren't even there. I suppose in many ways, we weren't.

It somehow never occurred to our father and mother that they were products of the Jewish neighborhoods of old New York in the '30s and '40s and were raising us in the public school system of Berkeley in the '70s and '80s. Somehow they expected us to develop into the same types of people they were and couldn't understand why we were having problems. That's like growing up on a cornfield in Iowa, moving to the South Bronx, and scratching your head wondering why your kids are having trouble adjusting.

All this was terrible preparation for the pop culture fueled cliques and herd mentality found in junior high and high school, especially in Berkeley, where I suddenly found myself surrounded by future frat boys and sorority girls, stoners and acidheads, and an entire region in a perpetual hangover from the Sixties.

Part III

SOUND CHECK 6:00 PM

*"It felt as though we got to adolescence and just stopped dead;
we drew up the map and left the boundaries exactly as they
were."*

-Nick Hornby

10. DAZED AND CONFUSED

Junior high, for lack of a better word, sucked.

For the first semester or so, instigated by a kid from the neighborhood (who'd later be caught lifting money from my mother's stray purse), I would smoke pot on the way to school every day. I was stoned pretty much through most of seventh grade.

Just about everyone else I knew from our upper middle class neighborhood, if they were in junior high or high school, was doing the same thing. In fact, I was considered a lightweight since so many of my peers were taking mushrooms, LSD and other hallucinogens. What was it about Berkeley that caused so many of us to want to deny reality at such an impressionable age?

When I think about this now, I can't believe the absurdity of it. Only when I'd meet people from outside of Berkeley would I realize that there are many who don't take their first hit of marijuana until they're in their late teens. By the time I'd reach that age myself, I'd be quitting pot for the first time.

*

Sexual tension became this invisible pulsating undercurrent that you had to pretend didn't exist. I'd never been one of those boys who thought girls were 'yucky'; I'd always appreciated the prettiness of the opposite sex. But I'd never felt such a sense of being controlled by their presence—it was as if, all of a sudden, their bodies were pulling me like a magnet. I was tantalized and tormented by the sight of these girls walking around campus with their smooth round butts barely covered by silky shorts, their tight tank tops exposing tan arms and highlighting newly formed breasts. My once tiny puddle of desire was becoming an overflowing reservoir, a damn ready to burst. Meanwhile, you were supposed to just act "normal" and concentrate on your books—Algebra, English, Biology... Oh, it was Biology alright—Biology 101. We were living it. All these male and female specimens thrown into the same enclosed environment, as if being watched under a microscope by giant scientists we couldn't see.

None of the girls wanted to talk to me, except to borrow change for a soda—a favor they'd return with a smile colder than the can of coke from the vending machine. I'd soon be guilty of looking at them inappropriately, standing too close to them, approaching them ineffectively and many other things that I'd later learn are huge turnoffs for girls. I just didn't know any better, and there was no one to teach me. My isolated family comprised of all males except for our introverted mother, who was disconnected from any sense of social dynamics in the real world. I had no sisters, no cousins and no other females I was close with to help or advise me.

Yet in just five years, I'd find myself on tour for the first time, and things couldn't be more different than they'd been in Junior High. It would be mostly guys at the concert (a disadvantage of the thrash genre), but of the few girls in attendance, some would actually come up and talk to me. Some of them I'd even be able to kiss and gain access to their precious bodies. At first, I'd be like a kid in a candy store, making up for lost time with any girl I could. But while the eighth grade loser in me could have only dreamed about this, the eighteen year old that I'd become would have a sobering realization: *To these girls, I'm just a guy in a band, the same as the last guy that came through town, and the next one as well.* I'd suddenly feel as though being in a band was a lame crutch. I'd understand what women meant when they complained of feeling like an object.

But back in Junior High, it was a sense of desperation. It wasn't just a physical desire—I was starved for connection. I wanted one of them to love me, physically and emotionally. I was sure I would never have a girlfriend. I'd be wrong about that of course. But I was in for years of such longing and loneliness, to the point where some of my early relationships would be catastrophically ill chosen.

*

With the change from Elementary to Junior High came many changes in friendships.

First, I drifted apart from my former best friend from Camp Kee Tov, Peter. There'd been many reasons. Although we'd had some great times together bonding over Kiss records and scary movies, he'd taken to complaining about my guitar playing. He said it was drawing attention away from him at camp, making him feel insignificant.

He'd also begun staking his claim on girls he liked as if they were plots of land—I was not to trespass. It didn't matter that these girls he was placing off limits weren't interested in him. I'd never even kissed a girl, but realized I'd missed a couple of rare opportunities because of pressure from him. Finally, there was a sense that as uncool as I was, being around him made me even less cool. I told him I wanted to move on to cooler friends.

Admittedly this wasn't very nice of me. In fact, it was behavior that I would describe today as extremely douche-like. I was right to move on from him; he'd become stifling, controlling and a negative influence. But I handled it really badly and caused things to be more awkward between than they needed to be.

Unfortunately, some of the new "friends" I moved on to were certainly not the answer.

*

I began hanging around a group of guys who were considered to be "cool" kids at Willard Jr. High. Our friendship mainly consisted of them ridiculing me and my lack of social skills for their own amusement, imitating the tone of my voice and quoting anything I said that they found funny.

I'd taken a job bagging groceries at the neighborhood store, Star Grocery. These guys were evil to me at school, but whenever they'd come around the store, they'd act really nice, sharing jokes with me, acting like I was their buddy. Since the store was very lenient about employees helping themselves to snacks, I didn't think twice about slipping these guys packs of gum, bags of beef jerky and candy bars whenever they'd come in. I didn't realize what was in play: they were shamelessly taking advantage of me.

I thought their supposed coolness would somehow rub off on me. It didn't. It shouldn't have mattered since they weren't my friends at all. They weren't even cool—it was just an illusion created in the context of certain mis-educational facilities: overcrowded, underfunded public city schools

54

which subliminally instilled mediocrity and the social elevation of covert bullies.

*

One of the supposed cool kids had a locker that was placed right above mine. Running into him at the locker, we got a chance to talk one on one. Away from the crowd, he was a bit more open. He started being nicer to me and it seemed, for a minute anyway, like we might actually become friends. But it all changed for some reason, probably pressure from the other kids who hated me (there were many).

One day, as I reached into my locker to grab a textbook, he lightly shut his own locker against my head, innocently saying, "Sorry, man!" A week or so later he did it again. I couldn't confront him—I didn't know how to deal with confrontation. My family shied away from it like helpless animals, except for our father on occasion, when he'd lose his temper. I didn't think much of it. I just let it go.

About a week later, as a couple other guys looked on, he slammed his locker against my head as hard as he could. I just sat there crouched down in pain, the books inside my locker a fuzzy blur. I could see stars. "Sorry, man" was followed by laughter as they walked away, the sounds coming to me as if I were underwater. I didn't know what to do. I didn't move for a few minutes, not even turning around. I just crouched helplessly as the bell rang, telling me I was late for class. I'd been violated.

To this day I have fantasies about taking a bottle, smashing it over this kid's head and gouging it into his face. Fortunately for both of us, I found music, particularly heavy metal, as a healthy outlet for the violent urges that have been unfairly inflicted upon me by jerks like him.

*

I fared a bit better in the friend department with Stefan, who lived down the street. He had been a horrendous hyperactive troublemaker when we were toddlers—the only neighborhood kid I'd ever been forbidden from playing with. This had been most curious, since his father was head of Child Psychiatric Services at UCSF Medical Center. His mother, a successful novelist, was someone I would deeply value talking to today as a writer myself, but back then I only knew her as the stressed-out mother of my hyperactive friend. But by Junior High, he had not only calmed down enough to put my parents at ease about my hanging around him again, he had found the perfect outlet for any hyperactive youth—the drums.

Stefan was the first drummer I played with. We jammed on the Led Zeppelin classic "Stairway To Heaven," "Ain't Talkin' Bout Love" by Van Halen and "Back In Black" by AC/DC. They weren't great versions—there are kids today on YouTube and in the "School of Rock" who could blow us away—but the experience of jamming with another person was invaluable.

Stefan and his buddy would make fun of me on the way to school. It was annoying, I didn't know how to defend myself, but at least it wasn't the ruthless taunting of the other guys. And one on one, Stefan and I seemed to have a real friendship, talking music, girls, and life in general.

In the future, Stefan and I would drift apart, almost as soon as we got to high school. He wouldn't relate to my growing metal interests, insisting that we both start listening to jazz and other more sophisticated music—advice that I could not relate to at the time. Furthermore, as I'd begin to grow my hair, wear metal t-shirts, start going to metal shows and hanging around metal people, I'd feel an increasing isolation from him.

This would be very ironic for two reasons. One, of course, was that, I would one day wise up and find myself doing exactly what Stefan had been telling me to do all along—get into jazz.

The other was that it was Stefan himself who steered me towards metal—by playing me one of the most important albums I'd ever hear as a guitarist and as a metal fan: Ozzy Osbourne's *Diary of a Madman*.

One morning before our walk to school, as we munched cereal in his family's kitchen, Stefan made me listen to Ozzy for the first time. As the final instrumental interlude to "Mr. Crowley" blared through the tiny boombox speakers, Stefan was insistent I pay attention to the guitar solo. "Listen to that! Isn't that amazing? Isn't it? C'mon! Don't tell me you don't think so!" He wasn't sure if I liked it since I didn't say much. That's because I was speechless.

It was only a month or so later that this incredible guitarist, Randy Rhoads, tragically passed away in a freak plane crash while on tour with Ozzy. I'd always think of Randy and his thirst for knowledge on the guitar— he'd plan to one day take a break from metal to study music at the University level—I'd one day do the same.

Almost overnight, it seemed everyone at school was into Ozzy. Ozzy was cool.

Taunted by the others at school because I couldn't name more Ozzy songs, I bought *Diary of a Madman* and *Blizzard of Oz*. These albums became the soundtrack to my days at Willard. I'd eventually learn most of the guitar parts.

Within a couple of years, these same peers who tried to single me out for not being a "real" Ozzy fan would trade in their Ozzy albums for those by pop/ska groups like The English Beat and Madness, since that was popular in school now. They followed the trends like blind sheep, unaware of their individual musical taste, if they even had any.

I wouldn't understand this. Sure, Ozzy's popularity at school was what had gotten Stefan into it, and that's what had led me to discover those great albums. But what my peers would not seem to understand was that I listened because I honestly liked the *music*—not because they liked it. Soon I'd become even more of an outcast for still listening to Ozzy when it was no longer "cool" to like his music.

And nearly thirteen years later to the day, I'd find myself on a stage in Nottingham, England, playing guitar for Ozzy Osbourne himself.

*

Working with me at Star Grocery was a guy I would occasionally take guitar lessons from, Bob Coons. Bob was the second-born son of my father's colleague Jack and brother to Mike Coons—the singer of a band that would very soon play an important role in the Bay Area metal scene, Lääz Rockit. Bob was very outgoing, personable and humorous. Every other line was a pun, some of them really bad. He also had a fluent talent for speaking backwards.

Bob had an incredible guitar technique—his right hand looked like a humming bird. There would be shows with his instrumental prog-rock band, Risk, where his hyperkinetic lead lines would get the crowd cheering right out of the gate. But soon, his lack of melody, dynamics and expression would be a detriment and after about four or five songs, that same crowd that had so enthusiastically embraced him would start booing. He also had no career direction. His quirky instrumental rock fusion was sophisticated on some level, but he seemed unable to play in any band with a hint of accessibility or commercial potential.

Despite his awe-inspiring technique, good nature and humor, I'd ultimately learn more from Bob about how not to play than how to play.

*

By now, there were other kids playing guitar too.

One of them was a former bully from up the street that I'd been scared of, Ben Netick. Somehow, Ben would become one of my closest friends and still is to this day. In fact, on the night of my first ever tour, he and I, in a surge of separation anxiety, would come up with a secret plan to stow him away in the equipment truck *(see chapter 20)*.

Ben didn't practice a lot and would eventually let the guitar go. But he wasn't a bad player. He may not have known as many chords or songs as me, but his lead guitar lick vocabulary was actually a bit further along. This prompted me to move on from Gary, much as I liked him, and start taking lessons from Ben's own teacher, a local rock/blues player, Mark Strandberg.

Ben had been a bit of a tough guy until one day when he got in a scuffle with a mob of tough black kids on the Willard Jr. High campus. The mob had won. Ever since, for reasons unknown, he'd come to school every day wearing a sweatshirt with the hood over his head.

Soon no one would remember what he looked like underneath. For this reason, he'd become known as "The Hood." This would continue through the ninth and tenth grade. As if I wasn't odd enough, I would now be seen hanging around a guy who always wore a hood.

"The Hood" would turn back into Ben again one night when we'd attend a Lääz Rockit show together—he'd arrive hoodless. At first no one would recognize him except the one person who'd known him since his pre-hood days—our mutual neighbor, Lääz Rockit singer Mike Coons.

The trigger for Ben's motivation to lose the hood had been an article in *The BHS Underground,* Berkeley High School's anonymously published alternative newspaper. The piece was entitled "What's Under His Hood?" and the question was fictitiously posed to random students on campus. The answers were divided by percentages, as in a public opinion poll. For example, "30% : 'An antfarm,' 20% : 'His lunch.' There were several other answers among those polled, but the final one was this: 1%: 'Fuck you, none of your goddamn business!'"

*

As odd as Ben was with his hood wearing, his argumentative nature made him even more of an outcast. He enjoyed nothing more than getting a rise out of peers, teachers, parents and typical Berkeley ideologues. To do this, he'd defend Ronald Reagan and even Richard Nixon quite eloquently and convincingly. I'd always think Ben was kidding about his Republican leanings until years later, when he'd become a loyal viewer of Fox News and a fan of Bill O'Reilly—passions of his that I'd never share nor comprehend, despite appreciating the strong statement he'd be making as a recovering Berkeley resident.

Ben's brother, a year younger, several inches taller and quite imposing, made Ben seem normal by comparison. His name was Alex, but we all called him "Bood" (rhymes with "hood"). Fighting, cutting class, drugs, vandalism, you name it, Bood had done it all. He'd been suspended more times in one school year than most kids were their entire K through 12 education. He would aggressively insult everyone within earshot. I'd even gotten in a minor skirmish with him on the sixth grade school bus when he told me "Kiss sucks."

Bood would spend the Junior High semesters at Provo Canyon in Utah, a well-known school that doubles as a treatment center for "troubled youth." He'd return during the summers, then remain in Berkeley for high school.

Yet, for all his troubles—with the law, with his family and with his own emotions—Bood was beginning to play guitar and was showing dedication and potential. Anytime I'd be over at the Netick house visiting Ben, Bood would corner me. "C'mon, Skolnick!" as if it we were back on that school bus and he was about to challenge me to a fight. Then he'd pick up his guitar, turn on the stereo and show me what he was working on— Cream's "White Room" and Jimi Hendrix's "Voodoo Chile (Slight Return)."

Sometimes he'd take LSD and play along with these records all day, convinced that the acid trip would put him in touch with the playing of Clapton and Hendrix in 1968. I'd have to credit Bood with inspiring me to learn a lot of Cream and Hendrix material as well. But I'd choose to do so without the acid.

Unfortunately, Bood's aggressive, antisocial behavior would prevent him from ever being part of a gigging band. In the future, he and my brother would try starting their own group—it would be a comedy of errors. Their rehearsals mainly consisted of dropping acid.

Perhaps one of the reasons Ben and I bonded is that we both had these troubled brothers that were so out there they made the two of us seem very normal (not an easy thing to accomplish). When I think about the amount of LSD our brothers must have taken collectively while living in Berkeley, it is quite astounding.

I would only try LSD once and it would be disastrous, one of the most awful experiences in my life—I'd injure my leg jumping off a docked boat into a pier (spurred on by Ben, of course). While I'd regret never experiencing a supposed "enlightenment" raved about by the deadheads, Merry Pranksters and my musical heroes like Jimi Hendrix and John Lennon, I'd be grateful that I was quickly turned off acid, seeing what it did to guys like my brother and Bood.

*

Peter Keyes was yet another kid that had started playing guitar. He was the first kid I came across who was better than me at the time. So how come you've heard of me but not him?

I honestly don't know.

I'm not sure what ever happened to him and never knew him well. Unlike most, there is virtually no information about him on the internet. He certainly had developed his talent at a young age, more so than I had at that time. And there's no reason that he shouldn't have been one of the better known guitarists from Berkeley.

Peter had taken his guitar playing much further in less time than me. He could play the solo to "Stairway to Heaven" while I was still grasping the first few sets of licks. He also had some Hendrix stuff down, knew how to use a Wah Wah pedal and even had bellbottoms to match. I'd just started to get into lead guitar, but he'd been absorbing Led Zeppelin records and already had a feel for the instrument. Peter had an advantage—his parents were Summer of Love hippies who embraced his musical aspirations, while mine were old school academics who tried to stifle mine.

I would meet one more peer who'd be a better guitar player within the Berkeley School System. His name was Jeff Tyson.

Like Peter, Jeff only played a couple years and seemed to go twice as far as me in half the time—a natural. Our mutual teacher, Joe Satriani (see Chapter 15), would cite Jeff as one of his best students ever, eventually graduating him, making him one of two students ever to be told there was nothing left to teach them (the other was Steve Vai).

Jeff would play for two bands on major labels, T-Ride and Snake River Conspiracy, both of which have toured with national acts. These bands eventually fell apart amidst plenty of personal drama.

Jeff has been able to maintain his high level of guitar playing, earning a living mostly on his considerable music production skills. As of this writing, Jeff's left the US, its failing music industry and taken up in Prague, Czech Republic, where he's earning a living as producer and guitarist. He also seems to be living a bit of a hedonistic lifestyle, surrounded by lovely young Czech women, and documenting his stories in YouTube videos. It will be interesting to see where he goes with his career from now, and I commend him for doing something different.

Whenever my tours bring me to Prague, we meet up, hang out and laugh about old times.

*

Meeting young guitarists who were better was like being kicked out of my Garden of Eden. I was no longer the lone young guitarist in town. There were faster guns in the West.

According to the logic subtly conveyed by my family—I should have given up. After all, here was somebody better. And unless you were the best in your field, it wasn't worth sticking with. I imagined them saying something like, *"You know if there's someone better, maybe this isn't for you. Perhaps it's time you think about something else."*

Obviously, this is utter nonsense, but when it is drilled in your head year after year, it is difficult to overcome.

I refused to listen. I couldn't imagine quitting or slowing down just because someone better had come along. If anything, it only made me work harder. Just because there were guys developing on guitar at a faster rate, there was no reason to slow down or stop. Even at that young age, I somehow knew that in the grand scheme of things, the other guitar player, no matter how good he or she was, couldn't take away everything I'd worked so hard on. To quit then would have been really stupid. I just had to stick with it and not be discouraged.

I'm really glad I didn't let the Peters, Jeffs and other better players of the world throw me off and chose to stay on course with guitar no matter who else came along. I really had no other choice. All the pain I was feeling in Junior High—ridiculed by guys, rejected by girls, patronized by my parents, chastised by my teachers, engulfed in loneliness, alienation and despair—was all going into my guitar playing.

11. BREAKIN' THE LAW

The City of Berkeley, in an effort to avoid overcrowding at Berkeley High School, which already had more than 2,000 students, combined all the incoming freshmen from the city's several Junior High Schools and placed them in a separate location, known as West Campus. My class would be the last at West Campus, for a year later, they'd end up just stuffing everyone, incoming freshmen included, into the main campus. So by the time I'd finally attend Berkeley High, the overcrowding would be at an all-time high, the funding at an all-time low. There would be close to forty kids in every classroom and over three thousand students scattered throughout, including a disproportionate amount of truants, delinquents and future criminals.

My year at West Campus felt like purgatory. As we morphed with the students of the Junior Highs across town, King Jr. High and Longfellow Junior High, I had no friends on campus. Stefan and I had drifted apart. Ben was already over at Berkeley High so I didn't have him to hang out with.

I'd occasionally run into people I'd known at Camp Kee Tov, including some girls I'd liked. But now we didn't know what to say to each other—we were like hollow teenage shells of the children we'd been. I avoided those pricks from the eighth grade who'd tormented me and pretty much everyone else I'd known at Willard. I gave up on making new friends. Trying to be social had resulted in mock, scorn and embarrassment, and I'd had enough. For most of the first semester, I was a complete loner.

That all changed as I found a group of fellow misfits: the metalheads.

*

The metalheads of Berkeley didn't give a fuck if you were awkward. Although not meek like I was, they fit into the general population no better than I did. Like me, they were sneered at by the cool kids; the jocks, the preppies and other social groups. And unlike them, the metalheads didn't discriminate or judge you unfairly. You didn't have to pass a litmus test to hang out with them, as long as you made the effort to get to know their music.

Of course, they still listened to Ozzy too; they'd never stopped. They also listened to groups I hadn't heard of yet, such as Iron Maiden, Scorpions and Judas Priest. They even displayed their allegiance by wearing t-shirts of Ozzy and the others.

As a fan of Kiss, and Van Halen, I'd already been indoctrinated into hard rock, but had never considered metal before. I'd already begun growing my hair as a result of my father more or less forcing me into a barbershop for the worst haircut imaginable (causing untold psychological damage). Soon, I'd take revenge on him by wearing shirts with slogans such as "Motörhead" and "Venom." He'd throw his hands up in the air and accuse me of having a motor in my "goddamn head."

Metal provided a form of rebellion against Berkeley, which by this time had become so rooted in being anti-establishment, that it had created its own oppressive establishment. We were, in our very small way, dangerous. Being a part of the metal scene helped provide the sense of belonging and social needs that I was not getting anywhere else. The fact that it was feared by those outside of it brought along something many of us had never felt before: a sense of power.

Metal also provided relief from a lifetime of left leaning, hippie-ish culture and the propaganda that surrounded it—slogans, petitions, bumper stickers of Greenpeace, Earth Day, No Nukes, No War, Save The Whales, and so forth. You were not to question the belief system imposed on you as a resident. This is one of the ironies about Berkeley, of which there are many, including the fact that Berkeley, a center for the anti-war movement of the '60s, is the birthplace of the atomic bombs that landed on Hiroshima and Nagasaki.[13] Like a dog chasing its tail, Berkeley has on more than one occasion been the very source of what it is supposedly fighting against.

---

[13] It was UC Berkeley's own science department that, under contract from the US Dept of Defense, had developed the bombs that eventually destroyed parts of Japan and many lives along with it, out of its laboratories in suburban Livermore (strategically far enough away from San Francisco to be safe in the event of a Japanese attack on the Bay Area).

Heavy metal shined a light on the grimier side of life, the things we weren't supposed to hear about: corruption, excess, hypocrisy, greed, decadence, alienation and domination, sexual and otherwise. With metal, it was okay to be angry and pissed off. The songs provided escapism in the form of extreme fantasy, other times hardcore grit and realism.

I related to the working class-like simplicity and directness of metal. It provided desperately needed refuge from what I perceived as the pretentiousness and bizarre social etiquette at cocktail parties and dinners forced upon me by my parents. As if held captive, my brother and I would sit in silence at these events, painfully enduring the laborious lectures of our parents' fellow East Coast Ivy League expatriates from generations past. They'd speak as if they were some sort of higher power looking down upon the society in which they were forced to co-exist.

Metal also went against all the folk-based music that had been forced upon us by the culture of Berkeley. The sound was fast, loud and in your face. Though I'd one day develop a deep appreciation for some of what I thought of as Berkeley music—Crosby Stills, Nash & Young, Joni Mitchell, Bob Dylan and their peers (ironically, not one of them from Berkeley), it was not what I needed as a teen. While much of the popular music of the '60s and '70s, even the protest songs, had always seemed to be peaceful, politically correct and polite, metal removed all pretenses and self-consciousness. Metal told it like it was. With all I'd been through in my household and in the school system, metal would provide a desperately needed outlet for my internal anger and seething aggression.

But with my immersion into the realms of the metal world would come the discovery of its dark side, a side in which I would one day have to go up against with all my inner strength.

The signs were there from the very beginning…

1982 Berkeley High School, 9th Grade, West Campus

I'm sitting on a corner of University Avenue across from the Foster's Freeze with a bunch of other kids who don't seem to fit in with the rest of the school. None of us know each other well, but we're all connected by the fact that we're awkward outcasts. One of them brings his ghetto Blaster. Every day and today, he's blasting a Judas Priest album, British Steel.

As the song "Breakin' the Law" blares in the background, I'm noticing a kid I haven't seen before. He's new around here, seems a year or so older than me. We look sort of alike—shoulder length brown hair, Levi's, black t-shirt. Must have just been transferred to West Campus.

There is a truck double parked next to the Foster Freeze, a medium sized one with a small sign on the side in the shape of a diamond symbol—it can be flipped back and forth to reveal several different images and messages. Right now there is a yellow image of an animated smiley face, like those "Have A Nice Day" buttons. Underneath the face is the message "Drive Carefully."

This new kid starts flipping the sign, to reveal several options. A white sign says "Flammable" with a picture of a red flame. A yellow and black sign says "Hazardous Waste" next to the international symbol for radioactive material (which came about right here at the UC Berkeley Radiation Lab in the forties). I come up to him, unhesitatingly and say "That one's cool!" As if we've known each other for years, he nods and says, "Yeah, Hazardous Waste. Bad ass."

"This other one's cool too. Flammable, with the flames."

"Let's pick the best one."

"Whoa!" we both say in unison. The sign is now black with a white skull and crossbones, like a pirate ship or secret society. Beneath this symbol, block letters spell out "POISON." (In a few years, this word will lose all its foreboding connotations forever, to be associated with a sleazy LA glam metal band that wears too much makeup and whose pretty blond singer, Brett Michaels, will one day become a reality TV star). But at this moment the word adorning the black sign with the white skull and cross bones is nothing less than metal—its letters sound a warning for all who come within reach that this is not a truck to be messed with. We have taken over the truck.

A voice that appears out of nowhere and sounds part human, part pit-bull: "Hey! Hey! What the hell do you think you're doing? You stop right there! God damn it! Stupid idiots!" We take off like Olympic runners in the hundred yard dash. "Get back here!" He chases after us.

In a minute we have dodged traffic across University Avenue, and our pursuer is foiled by a wave of approaching automobiles. Next we fly through the grounds of West Campus across the field toward the Swimming Pool, where two years ago, I would be taken to swim along with the other Jewish kids from Camp Kee Tov. Suddenly those days seem like another life entirely.

We slow down as soon as we realize the truck driver, waving his fist, has given up and gone back to his truck, cursing. I'm the first to speak. "I think we lost him." We both look at my watch and realize I'm almost late for *class. "See ya around." "Sure thing," he says. "Oh yeah, I'm Alexis." "My name's Alex." We dart off in different directions.*

*

At first, my friendship with Alexis mostly consisted of usual Berkeley teenage boy stuff—roaming around Telegraph Avenue, hitting the Silver Ball Arcade to play pinball, Pac Man, Galaga and Defender, wrapping up with a slice of Blondie's pizza, then heading over to mine the racks at Tower and Rasputin's Records.[14] Although not very book smart, he did seem to have street smarts, confidence and toughness. In fact, several times, I remember him being in fights at school. Being around someone who wasn't afraid of anything was a bolster to my own confidence.

I never would have messed with that sign on that truck, but Alexis wasn't afraid of any consequences—he would cut class with no hesitation, insisting that no one, not his divorced construction worker father, not the City of Berkeley and not the State of California could force him to sit in a class he didn't want to be in. Usually these excursions involved such harmless practices as picking up a burrito at the taqueria on University and MLK ("Ay Caramba!"), where a friend of ours, Mike Maung, worked and could sometimes hook us up. But other times, Alexis and some degenerate friends would descend upon a parked beer truck like mice to cheese. As soon as the driver would begin loading into the store, they'd flee with cases of beer, which they would in turn spend the rest of the afternoon drinking.

They'd try to get me to come along, but I'd refuse. I'd already been caught stealing twice as a young kid—once a toy space ship, another time a candy bar. The disappointment I'd felt when my parents were called was mortifying. That had been the extent of my criminal career. Ripping off beer trucks was a line I wouldn't cross.

This criminal activity would set the foundation for Alexis' career in the music industry. He'd become a protégé with certain movers and shakers at the local level of the Bay Area music scene who were rumored to be involved in various questionable activities.

One year after our first meeting, we were in tenth grade, attending the main campus of Berkeley High. It was during this time that we began attending local concerts, helping carry the amplifiers of local bands in order to gain admission despite being underage. This would lead to me joining my very first band, the one I would be forever associated with.

---

[14] Amoeba Music, which would eclipse both the other two stores, then expand to San Francisco and LA, hadn't shown up yet.

FREAKY EXECUTIVES

D a v i d   R o b i n s o n

JOHN COOPER TALENT AGENCY
(415) 845-0377

12. THE ROACH MOTEL

For every well-known musician, there are usually dozens, if not hundreds of others whom you've never heard of. Ask any national and internationally known musician—he or she can recite a lengthy list of names from their time rising up through the ranks, names that had once been considered peers. The list includes individuals who were said to be the ones to watch out for and bands who, despite becoming as big as ever in one metropolitan region, in some cases outdrawing new national acts, never managed to make it past the county line.

San Francisco and the East Bay are crawling with members of bands who at one time seemed destined for success, but most people outside of the Bay Area have probably never heard of. For example, we had hard rock/metal bands such as Anvil Chorus, Blind Illusion, Hans Naughty, Head On, Flame, Ruffians and Vain. We had ska/funk/rap bands like Freaky Executives, The Uptones, Fungo Mungo, The Broun Fellinis, The MoFessionals and many more. Some of these bands had so much potential that it's hard to believe they never made it out of the Bay.

The music biz is territory rife with hazard—among the biggest being the fact that musicians by nature are troubled individuals (just look at what you've read of my life, so far). How one band member's troubles are channeled can often be the difference between success and failure for an entire group. If one band member's inner pain is channeled constructively—put into the art of creation and music, reflected upon as life lessons learned, then it benefits everyone. By the same token, one person's issues can be turned into power trips, drug and alcohol abuse and other negative actions—this can sink the ship and everyone on board.

The ones that don't rise above the local level aren't necessarily not as good as the ones that do (in some cases, they are better). It's just that they've been overtaken by bad decision-making, negative behavior and sometimes bad luck and ill timing. The ones who rise above the fray have had enough positive, constructive channeling of energy to override the negativity. They are ready for luck and timing if and when it comes around.

Some bands make the difficult transition from local to national, only to crash and burn after one or two albums. In the '90s, Seattle's Mother Love Bone released a great, critically acclaimed, fan approved album and was on its way up, only to have its lead singer, Andrew Wood, die from a drug overdose (two remaining members formed a new band, Pearl Jam, that did just fine). An earlier example would be '70s girl group The Runaways, who broke up in the midst of tremendous early success due to substance abuse and personal differences.

Keeping a band together is a lot like keeping a marriage together. A band like Rush, for example, is like a very successful marriage—they've survived several decades with the same members (drummer Neil Peart is still the "new" member—since 1975) through individual personal challenges and changes in the music industry, their fan base intact.

While there are far too many local Bay Area musicians, managers, promoters and others in the local scene to mention (and much has been written about already), there are a select few that, while maybe not the most important, had a big impact on me.

Mike Skolnick: If we're going to talk about local musicians who had an impact on me, we have to start with Mike Skolnick.

From about 1980 to 1982, I'd accompany my brother to his gigs at clubs like Mabuhay Gardens, Keystone Berkeley and The Stone, San Francisco, with the competent new wave group Mr. Clean and later, the terrific ska/funk band Freaky Executives. Watching his gigs, I'd learn a lot, patiently waiting for my turn on the stage. It's hard to imagine now, but back then I was best known for being Mike's brother. I remember being asked "What's up, Skolnick's Brother! Where's Mike?"

While never the best bassist on the scene, Mike Skolnick was a very good player on a basic level. Everyone who played with him liked him.

Some, like the members of the Freaky Executives, credit him with inspiring their direction, despite their eventually having to let him go. If he'd only had more focus, discipline, introspection, acceptance of reality, the ability to learn from mistakes, resistance to temptation (in the form of hallucinogens) and eagerness to learn more and grow, there's no telling where he might have gone.

While I've been highly critical of his personal choices, I have to credit Mike with at least getting himself out there and becoming a fixture on the Bay Area scene at that time—not easy considering our background. He was the first musician I saw playing up close and being in proximity to his musical activity absolutely helped me formulate my own plans.

The Roach Motel: Littered with empty beer cans—Budweiser, Shaefer and Burgie—not to mention ashtrays overflowing with marijuana roaches, their smell competing with the stench of flat beer, the two neighboring apartments dominated the one-story building on MLK Jr. Way, which we affectionately dubbed "The Roach Motel."

It was an ideal meeting place to drink and get high before going to see a show, hitting a nearby party or, for those of us underage to get someone to score beer for you. Nearly anytime day or night, there would be a crowd, big or small.

Two of the guys that lived there, Mike Maung and Adam Segan, were inseparable and omnipresent in the Bay Area music scene. I originally met them through my brother but soon was hanging out at their place with my new friend from school, Alexis. In the roach motel, life boiled down to just a few things: rock music, drinking beer, smoking weed and, for its occupants at least, getting laid.

Adam Segen: When Adam Segen spoke, he at first brought to mind the California surfer/stoner dude in *Fast Times at Ridgemont High,* played by Sean Penn. Had he made it to the higher levels of the entertainment industry, he might have been an archetypical sleazy Hollywood agent or manager. He spoke with a mock sincerity that somehow, though you knew he was lying, caused you to listen and appreciate the fact that he was talking to you.

Underneath his long straight hair (he'd been a complete preppy only a year or so earlier) was a slightly puffy leering face, exuding more confidence than any human should have had. Like many of Berkeley's self-appointed band managers, Adam was rumored to be a pot dealer, and seemed to be at every concert and party. He had occasional run-ins with scary Berkeley characters who shall remain unnamed—notorious players in the local drug trade, who'd turn up at parties in between stints in jail.

Within a few years Adam would disappear from the Bay Area music scene without a trace. Years later, early social media such as MySpace yielded no clues to his whereabouts causing rumors of his death to circulate. He'd eventually resurface in Los Angeles and on Facebook—fresh-faced, clean-cut and many years sober with a burgeoning acting career.

Todd Crew: Another presence at the Roach Motel was Todd Crew. He looked like a rock star. So much so, that I went to his haircutter, a mutual female friend of ours and told her to shape my hair just like his (after that disastrous haircut forced upon me by my father, my hair had become rather important to me). Todd was an institution at the shows, part of our Berkeley scene.

One time, Todd pulled up in a pick-up truck as I was riding my bike up the giant hill on Euclid Avenue. Although we didn't know each other well, he kindly insisted he give me a ride, and he was just one of the nicest, most genuine people I'd met from the music scene. It also turned out he'd had some of the same teachers at Berkeley High that I did.

A short time later, I ran into him at Berkeley High—he was there visiting a biology teacher that he'd always liked and stayed in touch with. It was that day that he told me about the band he was forming. They had a name I didn't like: Jetboy. Eventually I saw them play. Their sound was hard rock but the songs were too happy. On stage, they wore more spandex, makeup and hairspray than I'd ever seen on guys. I was baffled that Todd— such a down-to-earth Berkeley guy—was part of a band that looked and sounded so... I didn't know how to describe it. Later, I'd learn the word was glam. Eighties glam just wasn't my thing.

Soon Jetboy would move to LA and be signed to Electra Records. I'd be in complete shock several years later, hearing what fate had bestowed upon Todd. Apparently, he'd spent his first few years in LA growing close with a great but troubled band called Guns N' Roses. Todd had been doing heroin with Guns for some time, especially their guitarist, someone we'd all soon hear of, an odd character in a top hat, known only as Slash.

One morning, after an all-night heroin binge, Todd OD'd and was found dead in an LA hotel room.

Paul Baloff: One Friday night, everyone was dropping by the Roach Motel to drink and get high before going off to some party nearby. Fast metal music was blasting in the background.

There in the crowd of mostly skinny, tall people, was this little guy, close to thirty, wearing a leather jacket and Motörhead pin. With puffy hair and a face like a JRR Tolkien character, he looked like he hadn't showered in a day or so. He was like a heavy metal version of those Berkeley street characters and had a presence that stood out among all the others.

He turned out to be the singer for the band Adam Segan had just started managing. The music we were hearing was their demo. Adam was talking right into my ear, raising his voice to be heard above the music. "They're the heaviest band of all time, bro! We got Maung playing guitar. We're goin' all the way dude. We're gonna be major, ya know? It's like...what's up, Paul!" he called.

The hobbit-like creature walked over and took the joint from Adam. "Skol, Paul Baloff. Bay, Alex Skolnick." Paul shook my hand while inhaling the joint. Then he handed it to me and in his natural voice, which sounded like someone clearing his throat, said "What's up." A waft of smoke poured out his nose as if from a miniature dragon.

"What's the name of the band?" I asked.

They answered in unison: "Exodus."

Exodus shows were the most intense, high energy, adrenaline inspiring experiences of my teens. (There is plenty documented about Exodus and not enough room to go into detail here.) Soon the band, with Paul Baloff on vocals, would record a classic thrash record: *Bonded By Blood*. Despite Paul's tremendous contribution, he'd had a hard time in the studio, not helped by meth use and binge drinking, which would only get worse. Never able to get control of his addictions, Paul would one day succumb to a stroke while riding his bicycle, dying at the age of 41.

It is amazing to think of these three larger than life presences in the Berkeley music scene during the mid-'80s: Paul Baloff, Todd Crew and Adam Segan. Two are dead and one was wrongly presumed dead.

Mike Maung: The person most synonymous with the Roach Motel was without a doubt Mike Maung.

When we first met, Mike had recently replaced Exodus's guitarist Kirk Hammett, whom he seemed to resemble, both guys being part Asian with long curly hair. Kirk had recently departed to join a band called Metallica, who had a buzz about them bigger than any other local band. Metallica was rumored to be recording an album and soon touring the world, but only time would tell.

With his black curly hair just past his shoulders, light brown skin, muscular arms and black clad attire, Mike Maung at first, appeared Mediterranean; Italian or Turkish. Or was he Brazilian or Argentinean? Upon closer inspection, he looked part African-American, like those famous Jimi Hendrix studio photos, where Jimi looks more bi-racial than black. In truth, he was half Chinese.

His clothes were a perfect blend of street and flash: parachute pants, which were the rage back then, and fashionable ripped t-shirts, some with Hendrix's face on them, mostly black but well fitting, like a mannequin in a rock clothing store. He was too glam to be a thrasher, but too street to be glam. He was once mobbed outside a Prince concert, so similar was his look to the pop star during the Purple Rain era.

Maung was a fixture at all the Berkeley shows, metal, ska and pop alike. Like his idol, Prince, he had a high speaking voice and soft timbre and was distinctly feminine. There were questions of him being gay, but he seemed to be clearly drawn toward attractive women, never indicating any evidence of ambiguity.

As a player, Mike Maung never stood out as one of the best. However, he had a good sound and feel and, most wisely, didn't try to play beyond his ability (which is the downfall of many a guitar player). As a result, he developed a reputation as someone who may not command the attention of a Bob Coons or a Danny Gill (who you'll read more about in chapter 14), but someone who delivered. As a result, he seemed able to be in any band of his choosing. I often wondered if Mike would have been a better guitar player had he not had his image to fall back on. I, on the other hand, was going to have to work a lot harder on image, given that I had the presence of a flea and the confidence of an ostrich.

Although Mike was said to sound very good playing metal, his tenure in Exodus would last no longer than a few gigs. He needed a band that had more of the element of his hero, Prince. He found it in a new band some friends were putting together. It was to be a combination of dance and ska music, with horns and multiple vocalists, a cross between The English Beat and Morris Day and The Time. It was to be a very integrated group, with white, Hispanic and African-American members. They had almost all the elements, except a bassist. Mike Maung said he knew a bassist that might work out, a friend of his named Mike Skolnick. This band would be known as Freaky Executives.

Freaky Executives: The Freaky Executives might not have had the direct musical influence on me in the way the local hard rock and metal artists did, but their presence on the scene was profound. They deserve more print time than I can give them here, and I hope their full story is told one day.

Affectionately nicknamed "The Freakies" by fans, FE invaded the scene with a new brand of high-energy pop/dance/ska. There hadn't been a band like that around, at least not in our clubs and in our scene, like a miniature big band. They were ten guys onstage, combining large back-up vocal sections, horns, dance moves and timbales. Unlike most other bands, they were an international collective of race, creed and color. There was room for everyone and their audiences reflected this: black, white, Latino, preppies, ska-punks, metalheads, rappers. Everyone loved The Freakies. For the first few years, they had my brother Mike on bass, so I'd go to many of their shows. At the Keystone Berkeley, Ruthie's Inn, Ashkenaz, The Berkeley Square and all other relevant venues, Freaky Executives were an institution fronted by a guy who was an institution himself.

Peo: Known as the "Mayor of Berkeley," Pierro "Peo" Ornelas, had the look and charm of a fellow Cuban American, one who'd been a cultural icon in the 1950s: band leader and TV star, Desi Arnez. At night, he seemed to be at every show in the Bay whether it was inner city blues at Eli's Mile High Club in West Oakland or an Exodus show at The Keystone. During the day, he could usually be found on Telegraph ("The Ave") but you could run into him in the Latin populated Mission District in San Francisco or on the urban enclaves of Downtown Oakland.

Wherever he was, he knew people and was always high-fiving, shaking hands and waving. Even my parents' insular world of the upper class Ivy League intellectuals wasn't off limits—his name would come up at dinner parties, usually courtesy of the thirty-something daughter of my parents' friends—she had an ex-husband that somehow knew Peo. He had the charisma, charm and personality for political activism. Had he moved in that direction, he might have had a future in politics. Instead, Peo's unique skills manifested on the stage in the form of powerful, politically charged performances.

The Freakies got to the point of selling out every show, supporting some national acts, and getting a development deal from a major label before disbanding. In the '90s almost the same thing would happen with Los Angelitos (which was like a Latin version of Freaky Executives). Both bands were unquestionably good, but fell apart, just as they got to the point where they could have moved to the next level—creative differences would rear their heads once in the studio, amidst lots of finger pointing.

No one was sure where Peo lived—he mostly crashed on peoples couches. Somehow, you were always able to get a message to him, through word of mouth, and he'd call you back on a pay phone or find you on the street. No one was sure how he made money—although he would sometimes borrow money, he always paid it back and most of the time, seemed to have enough to get by. He never owned a vehicle but had no problem getting rides on mopeds, motorcycles and in cars, with each simple request of "Shoot me up to The Ave?" (Translation: "Could I get a ride to Telegraph Avenue?").

With his balance of charm and street toughness, Peo always created good energy—he made everyone laugh. But you wouldn't ever want to be on his bad side!

This was made clear by a scene I witnessed one day between classes, having a cup of coffee just across from Berkeley High in MLK Park —a haven for students, former students, dropouts, stoners and homeless people who populated the park like stray pets and raccoons.

1984 MLK Jr. Park, Berkeley

A crowd is gathering over by the benches. Like spectators at a Roman gladiator match, they're edging on two kids who are pushing and shoving one another. I recognize one of them from my biology class. People are running towards them from all points of the park, joining the onlookers and instigators while others like myself, do our best to idly continue their day. The growing chaos is becoming unavoidable, so I decide to leave the park. As I get up to go, I see a familiar face sitting a few benches away from the fight.

It's Peo. Getting ready to unwrap a sandwich, he looks over at the gathering crowd, notices punches being thrown and then shrugs his shoulders.

He goes back to the sandwich as though it's just another day in the park. But before he can unwrap the white paper, he is bumped into and stepped on by spectators who continue running over to watch the action. He stands up and, like a gavel wielding judge calling for order, flings the still unwrapped sandwich down on the ground and yells, "What the fuck?"

A moment later, he is swimming into the eye of the storm, tossing spectators out of his way, a Cuban bull charging a herd of rodeo clowns. The two battling students are separated like Siamese twins, ripped apart by sheer brute force, simultaneously flung to opposite sides of the pavement like two useless traffic pylons.

Instinctively, the surrounding crowd approaches Peo like a pack of zombies. He spins around wearing a facial expression like a Latin Rambo, waving a fist, causing all of them to back up nervously. "You wanna fuck with me?!! C'mon!!" The predators stop in their tracks.

Peo looks at the disgraced young fighters, lying pathetically on the ground. He addresses one of them: "You still want to fight, motherfucker? You gotta fight me first!" The kid shakes his head as Peo turns to the other: "How 'bout you? Huh?" The second kid shakes his head while being helped up by his buddies.

Peo surveys the crowd. "Any of you other motherfuckers wanna fight? Let's go right now!" No takers. "Alright then." His voice echoes as if at the top of a mountain. It's like that episode of the Twilight Zone, where everyone is frozen in stop motion. All eyes are on him; leadership has been established. He addresses the crowd:

"Now listen up! I am having a very bad day. I got a relative, she's sick in the hospital. I just came from a visit, she's not doin' too good. Then I find out my buddy, who's puttin' me up, just got a fuckin' eviction notice. Now I gotta find a new place to live. Now, there's a bunch of other shit goin' on y'all don't need to hear about, okay? Just take my word, alright?" A few nods, many blank stares. "So here's the thing: this here's a public park. Y'all got any concept what that means? It means this shit belongs to all of us." (Looking at each person one by one.) "Me. You. Him. Him. Her. Him. You got that?" Silence. "So I come over to this public park and all I wanna do is sit here on this motherfuckin' bench and eat my motherfuckin' lunch in peace. Now y'all come along and fuck my shit all up. Someone better give me a god damn reason. Anyone?"

Silence.

"Alright then. Now here's what's gonna happen. I'm going back to my motherfuckin' bench to eat my motherfuckin' lunch and enjoy my motherfuckin' day. You're all gonna go on and we're gonna forget this shit ever happened. I hear anything 'bout any more fights, I'm comin' back here and kickin' ALL your asses."

Shamefully, the crowd scatters like flies shooed away.

Peo sits back down on the bench, sees me passing by and waves. "What's up, young Skolnick?" he says, taking a bite of sandwich.

"Damn Peo. I've never seen anything like that. Good job."

"Ah...fuck these stupid motherfuckers, man. These bitches just gotta learn," he laughs. "How ya doin' man? You off to class? How's your brother?"

13. KNOW YOUR ENEMY

Lääz Rockit ruled the the Bay Area metal scene with a show that made a four hundred capacity club feel like the Cow Palace Arena—they were our local Judas Priest. Named after the powerful M-72 LAW (Light Anti-tank Weapon) featured in the Clint Eastwood film *The Enforcer,* the five-man power metal band showed up armed with long hair, flying V guitars, studded wristbands and song titles like "Prelude to Death," "City's Gonna Burn" and the self-portrait, "Boys in Black Leather."

Lääz was a regular presence at the Keystone Berkeley, The Stone in San Francisco and the Keystone Palo Alto—the trio of small but important venues run by a grizzled, heavy-set, somewhat feared local promoter named Bobby Corona, better known as "Big Bob." On the national scene, everyone passed through the doors of the three Keystone venues on their way up, but Lääz was one of the few acts that always made Big Bob happy, nearly always selling out.

A Lääz gig was the perfect showcase for out of town bands making their debut in the Bay Area. Some of these bands would go on to become household names. There was the scary, face-painted band from LA that entered into horror movie music (the *Halloween* theme) before launching into the fastest metal any of us had heard—they were called Slayer. Another time, Big Bob brought in a band to co-headline with Lääz Rockit—a recently signed commercial hard rock band from New Jersey called Bon Jovi. Most notably, there exists a flyer for a 1982 show at The Stone in San Francisco. It announces the following:

Lääz Rockit,
With Very Special Guests: Metallica.

*

I discovered Lääz Rockit early on, having grown up just down the street from the singer, Michael Coons.

The Coons family had five kids, all of them several years older than me (Mike's older brother Bob would become one of my guitar teachers). Their father, Jack Coons, was a colleague of my own father at UC Berkeley's Boalt Hall School of Law. The two professors would one day share their grief about having wayward sons who forsook scholastics in favor of loud, indecipherable music.

One of my earliest memories is a ski trip to Lake Tahoe with the Coons family; I must have been four or five. Though our families would always remain good neighbors, this would be our only vacation together. There'd been no problems, it was just an odd match for several reasons, primarily that the Coonses were a large, jovial, outgoing Irish-American family with a very strong sense of community, fully connected to their Irish heritage, involved with their church and active in local elections. On the flipside was my tiny Jewish-American family, unsure of where we stood as Jews and as Americans: never attending synagogue, our sole Judaic custom was an informal Passover meal. Although maintaining an expert level of awareness and interest in current affairs, our parents' political activities took place mostly in isolation: monitoring elections from NPR, PBS, and the *New York Times*. And unlike the Coons family, we had very few communal gatherings and went through life constrained and inhibited—especially around others who were different from us (which was almost everybody). It must have been strange for our parents to be in a cabin with such a different kind of family for a whole weekend.

The differences didn't stop there. The Coonses communicated comfortably and laughed a lot, while my family didn't have much to say, ate many meals in silence and was generally humorless. Their family kept a grand piano in their living room for all to play as they pleased; my own parents would begrudgingly rent me a piano, then complain about the noise. The Coons kids were encouraged to be assertive and expressive—my brother and I would be shot down whenever we'd try to assert ourselves or express our own opinions.

Yet, this picture of two contrasting families was not as clear as I'd envisioned it. Years later, I'd realize that, despite seeming like the ideal family, the Coons clan was not without problems of their own. Their high spirits would not be limited to their joviality—in other words, the stereotype of alcohol affecting certain Irish-American families would hit painfully close to home.

*

Mike Coons and I would become the two most visible guys in the Bay Area metal scene with intellectual parents and prep school vocabularies. With our long history as neighbors, we would always get along well. However, we couldn't have been more different growing up.

Mike had always been charming and outgoing enough to brighten a room whenever he walked in. I, meanwhile, had been a sullen loner who, had I not been such a pathetic pushover, might have fit the profile for a future serial killer. He loved the competitive camaraderie of sports and was good at football, baseball, basketball and soccer. I'd always been more or less inept at team sports, occasionally trying, embarrassingly failing.

Mike was such a good athlete, in fact, that he was offered a full university scholarship for soccer. He promptly turned it down to devote his time to Lääz Rockit. Disappointed with his decision, his parents nonetheless lovingly supported him.

Unfortunately, his talent on the mic was no match for his natural talent on the field; there was no shortage of stage charisma and frontman skill, but he lacked a great voice. With classical training, he might have improved—yet he'd inexplicably decided against it. Had he been the singer of a punk, indie-rock or folk band, this might not have mattered, but for power metal, classical training was more or less essential—you needed all the help you could get. The bands who'd been the blueprint for Lääz Rockit, Judas Priest and Iron Maiden, were propelled by vocalists who were extremely talented, one of whom was classically trained (Judas Priest's Rob Halford), the other that very rare breed who sounded classically trained on his own (Iron Maiden's Bruce Dickinson) and both of whom ranked among the best singers in metal and arguably in hard rock, period.

*

Sadly, Coons' voice would be far from his biggest liability—his time in the band would be marred by relentless binge drinking that would only get more frequent as time went on. After Lääz Rockit's break up in the late '90s, his alcohol abuse would become downright uncontrollable with DUI's, revoked licenses and many failed attempts at sobriety.

I never could have imagined this.

Mike had been "most likely to succeed" in our neighborhood, adored by parents and admired by young children, never judging anyone, exchanging high fives with all, comfortable hanging with the preppy lacrosse players as much as the denim clad, scroungy headbangers. He'd had a magnetic personality, movie star looks, athletic ability, effortless people skills and a close-knit supportive family.

I, on the other hand, had been interminably shy, alienated at school, unable to throw and catch a ball, plagued by self-consciousness, insecurity, low self-esteem and desperate for emotional support that I was unable to receive from my emotionally withdrawn, non-communicative and reclusive family.

Yet it would be me who'd go on to find international acclaim in music and end up with a strong sense of dignity and personal responsibility. There would be no AA, no "tough love" or "interventions" in my future. I'd keep my vices in check, my own drinking never affecting my work and my life. My own family wouldn't have to endure being woken up on a regular basis by late night emergency phone calls: the police, the hospital, worried friends and fellow partygoers concerned for their son's safety and well-being.

After several stints in rehab, Mike would make a new start in his forties, finally getting an upper hand on the bottle. He'd experience some success as a part-time actor in LA and do part-time work in the concert industry. Although the years of abuse would take a toll—he'd become permanently weathered, losing the youthful zeal he'd once had—he'd still have his charm, good looks, good nature and unconditional love and support of family and friends, always careful to keep an eye on him.

If someone back then could have correctly predicted how each of our lives would turn out, they'd have been committed to where it once felt like I was headed: the psych ward.

*

Lääz Rockit's manager was a bit of a controversial figure in the Bay Area music scene. With his black leather jacket and long dark hair, he looked just like a sixth member of the band. Although charming to The Coons' parents who'd have him over for dinner and refer to him as a "nice young man," he was, unbeknownst to them, a high ranking unofficial in Berkeley's hidden underworld of activities best described as "illegal." He had the personality of a pool hustler, a card shark, a con man, the type you could imagine challenging unsuspecting tourists to "three card monte".

He was very effective at helping the band create an arena-like club show, incorporating flash pots, dry ice, smoke machines and a massive backline.[15] But as Lääz tried to graduate to the next level, things would start to go sour—he would coordinate three elements that would lead to the eventual undoing of the band: a bad record deal, a bad first record and an even worse album cover.

The cover of Lääz Rockit's debut album, *City's Gonna Burn,* can only be described as god awful. Lime green windows on badly drawn buildings flicker with candy-corn colored flames overlooking a street engulfed in a fluorescent explosion, looked over by a tiny pencil-drawn villain with a dynamite pump—he looks as though he were cut and pasted out of a cheap black and white comic. Hanging overhead, a budget cartoon-like Lääz Rockit logo in yellow and black overlooks the scene.

The image is on par with the fluorescent artwork of Rick Derringer's debut album *All American Boy,* regarded by some to be the worst album cover in rock history and which, had it not been for the hit song, "Rock 'N' Roll Hoochie Koo," might surely have put Rick Derringer out of business for good. The moral? *Never have fluorescent cartoon-like images on your album cover.*

The recording itself wasn't much better—it sounded like it was done in a tin can. Those of us who had faithfully attended Lääz Rockit concerts couldn't have been more disappointed—this was the first *Lääz* album! On stage, this band had always been an unstoppable assault unit. Now it was being taken down in a hail of gunfire, as though the recording studio had become the very high caliber weapon for which the band was named.

Their follow-up album was better, had a catchier title, *No Stranger to Danger,* and was wisely void of fluorescent cartoon artwork. Sadly, however, the logo hadn't improved. Even more troubling, the cover photograph revealed yet another problem for the band (as if a disreputable manager, a lackluster debut album and an alcoholic singer weren't enough): *it was unclear what kind of band they were.* To the uninitiated, were they glam? Thrash? LA? Bay Area? Who knew?!

The cover photo magnifies a clear-cut image problem: the two band members on the left, Aaron and Vick, are dressed in glam leather concoctions suitable for a gig on LA's Sunset Strip, minus hairspray and makeup. Mike, in the center, is wearing an ill-chosen outfit that resembles a ski jacket with the sleeves cut off. On his left (our right) is Phil, who mostly looks good—black leather vest, Terminator shirt (many years before Schwarzenegger was Governor), studded belt and black pants—he's almost

---

[15] "Backline" refers to a band's on-stage set up, including but not limited to amplifiers and drum kit

pulling off a true metal look, but wait...why is there a shredded red bandana around his leg? Most guilty of all is Willie, the bassist. His thundering bass playing and unrelenting stage presence make him the most metal of all (in a couple of years, he'll be on the short list of bassists tapped to try out for Metallica). But in this photo, he's wearing a decidedly un-metal beige colored vest, his giant mane of hair enhanced by various bushy tails—fox, beaver, leopard and coonskin—he appears to have been outfitted by a fur trader.

*

The third Lääz album, *Know Your Enemy,* would be their best yet. Unfortunately, the cover marked a return to juvenile comic book art (although an improvement over the first one). And by this time the band had decided to define itself as thrash, but wouldn't be fast or brutal enough for the true thrash fans.

The band accepted a small club tour supporting LA Guns, who had a name due to the fact that a couple of its members had gone on to form the now famous Guns 'N' Roses. But the glam metal crowd was not the target audience for Lääz, especially with their new heavier direction. And soon it didn't matter: with three weeks left to go, an altercation with LA Guns' tour manager would result in the Lääz guys locking him in a road case, getting themselves kicked off the tour midway through.

Lääz's own tours became grueling with no signs of ever rising to a higher level. Still, they partied on a level that would rival Guns and Mötley Crüe (minus the heroin).

Had *Know Your Enemy* been the band's first album, the band might have entered the international scene with a promising debut. They might have gotten away with dropping their glam image (a feat which would be successfully pulled off by a later band, Pantera). But after two disappointing efforts and many years on the horizon, the magic was disappearing and the band knew it. Even in the Bay Area, the once exalted kingdom, their fans had moved on, their draw dissipating—they'd never gain back the momentum that they'd once had.

As much of an improvement as *Know Your Enemy* was, it just didn't have the impact needed to create a strong presence at the higher levels of the music business. Meanwhile, Lääz's former support acts were making names for themselves, including my own band, now called Testament, and especially Metallica, who by this time, were on the verge of headlining arenas.

After one more Lääz album, three members would leave to enter civilian life, the bassist choosing to work alongside his father, who'd gotten rich founding one of California's largest trucking companies, the drummer returning to medical school (he'd go on to become a successful pediatrician), and the guitarist, Phil, becoming a bearded mountain man doing maintenance in Yosemite park. The manager would follow soon after, becoming an Ultimate Fighting manager until, after a shady fight deal reminiscent of the film *Pulp Fiction,* he'd disappear, pursued by fight promoters calling for his head on a platter.

Lääz would continue with just two original members, becoming a C-List band that had once been on the cusp of potential greatness, until finally breaking up.

*

Before then, there would be one day when, on break from my own tour, I'd walk past the Coons' house on my way to Peet's Coffee a few more blocks up the street. There'd be a Winnebago parked in front— Lääz Rockit's makeshift tour bus. Lingering outside would be Phil, one of the band's guitarists. He'd say hi and explain that the band was about to leave for tour, they'd stopped to pick up Mike and that the others were still in the house saying goodbye to Mike's family.

Phil would give me a tour of their vehicle. Once inside, I'd look around at the sleeping bags on the floor, the stray luggage, sweats and t-shirts scattered about. I'd say "cool," repeatedly, trying to sound impressed. I'd look at the tiny bathroom, soon to plague their long drives with the smell of urine. "Cool," I'd say, yet again. But we'd both know the truth: it was *not cool.* Lääz fucking Rockit, seven years and three albums in, touring in a motor home?!

By then, I'd be touring full time, supporting groups like Megadeth and Anthrax with my own band who'd recently made the jump from vans to a full-sized tour bus.

"So, bro," he'd whisper. "I gotta ask: what d'ya think's goin' wrong here? I mean, I'm so happy for you guys and all. But shouldn't we be farther along than we are? It's like, we're stuck. What do you think it is?"

Just a few years ago, I'd been a pesky kid at his shows, eagerly asking questions about guitars, thrilled that he'd even give me the time of day. Now he was confiding in me, asking for my advice.

By then, there'd been many clear reasons why things hadn't happened for Lääz. But as I'd pause to think about how to answer, one thing especially would firmly cross my mind...Granted our managers would turn out to be less than a perfect fit (which you'll read more about later) but at least they conducted themselves as *adults,* which was crucial to how we were represented in the music industry at the national level. They were older, wiser and educated—not the type who dressed and behaved as though they were *in the band,* like the manager we'd just let go a year or so ago. I'd clear my throat and say in a whisper. "Phil, I really think you have to look at how the band is managed. It helps to have someone older, professional and..." No sooner would I say that than Lääz's manager would burst in screaming about some club promoter cancelling a show and how he's going to *"whoop his fuckin' ass!!"* before punching the walls of the Winnebago. *"That fuckin' punk ass motherfucker! Fuck him, man!"* Punch punch.

I'd look Phil straight in the eye and whisper, "Nice talkin' to ya, Phil. You guys have a good tour."

14. BLACK DIAMOND

By 1981, my brother had decided to go New Wave. He and Danny Gill, the young guitarist, while still friendly, were no longer playing music together. While Mike had become a solid, if no longer developing bassist, Danny had become a more dedicated musician, studying with a teacher said to be the best in the Bay Area, someone by the name of Joe Satriani. The studies with Joe and many hours spent with Van Halen records and a guitar were beginning to result in heads turning every time Danny played. I realized this one night at a party at the Berkeley home of Ms. Holsing, a wonderful eighth grade English teacher (one of the few I liked in the Berkeley Public School System).

Although she was librarian-like and appeared to be my mother's age, Ms. Holsing defied stereotypes. For example, on the first day of class, our task was to guess what type of music we thought she liked and why, and write that down. She wouldn't give us any clues, only letting us know that we'd find out the next day. Sure enough, we walked into class the next day to find, adorning the walls of her classroom, posters of Led Zeppelin, The Who and Jimi Hendrix.

Ms. Holsing had a teenage son, Hans, who played electric guitar. They had the type of parent/sibling relationship I could only dream of—sharing musical tastes and getting along well. She'd allow him to have parties, totally supervised and in control, but still fun. She'd invite students from the school. At the party I went to, there were mostly young people, Hans' friends and a few of my classmates. There was Ms. Holsing hanging out, with everyone else, having a great time. It was the first time I'd seen a parent or teacher that could relate to young people in this manner.

My friend Stefan and I had taken a bus to the party, which was on the other side of Berkeley, North of the University. My brother and Danny dropped by later, just as a plugged-in guitar was being passed around between Hans, a few others and me.

When the guitar got passed to Danny, the entire room took notice. I recognized some of the sounds from Van Halen albums but I'd never seen anyone do that up close before—his hands looked like flesh colored spiders effortlessly racing up and down the white maple neck of the Fender Stratocaster. It had never occurred to me that it was possible for someone else to play like Eddie Van Halen, but Danny was doing it.

I decided right there and then to study with Danny. I'd leave my current teacher, Mark Strandberg, who had shown me some great licks by guys like Dave Gilmour of Pink Floyd and Mark Knopfler of the Dire Straits, but was a bit out of his element when it came to the styles of Van Halen and Randy Rhoads. A year earlier, I'd had to tell Gary Lapow I was changing teachers—it was hard to leave someone who'd helped me so much but Gary had understood, even agreed with me—a true gentleman. Mark was going to have to understand—now it was time to move on again.

I'd study with Danny for the next two years. It was fortuitous that this was someone I already knew from childhood—he'd been one of my brother's oldest friends, someone he'd jammed with for years and who'd attended the Kiss concert with us. But I'd never heard Danny sound like he did at the party that night. He'd gotten really good.

*

We all knew Diamond was going to make it. How could they not? They had it all: Danny Gill—the best up and coming guitarist in the Bay Area; a strong front man—Rick Ratto—who was like a cross between Paul Stanley and Sylvester Stallone; a drummer with a massive drum kit and a massive sound, reminiscent of Alex Van Halen, and a bass player like Michael Anthony of Van Halen—not a star in his own right, but someone that filled out the picture perfectly. They were our Van Halen.

Even Diamond's roadies were impressive; the most professional road crew we'd ever seen. One of the roadies had actually worked with the mighty Van Halen in LA and wore his crew jacket to prove it. Then there was a guitar tech with wild blond hair just like Danny who would dive out to the stage to fix a cord or investigate a problem like his life depended on it. I hoped to have a guitar tech like that someday. In five years this guy, Troy Boyer, would become my own guitar tech.

Diamond played neither hard metal nor glam metal. The name sounded glam but the music wasn't. It was just good hard rock in the style of Van Halen, Y&T, Sammy Hagar, Ratt, Scorpions and Ozzy, without sounding like anyone in particular. It was similar to the way Gov't Mule, the blues/rock band of today, sounds classic and familiar but not entirely like any one group.

Danny's effect pedal board was a hollowed-out bomb casing. I later found out Eddie Van Halen had already done this, but at the time, I thought it was the coolest thing ever. He also had a small model of H.R. Giger's Alien snarling from on top of his Marshall stack. WWII bombs? The Alien? That was metal!

Diamond also had the best posters and flyers, black paper with fluorescent lettering highlighting their awesome logo,[16] plus a silhouette of the band members. No faces, just blank images but a clear sketch of tight pants, leather jackets and long "big" hair, before that was considered a derogatory term. It all combined into a magnetic atmosphere.

That is, before it all unraveled.

*

Danny was a great guy, but unfortunately, he'd built up some bad karma. Now, whether you believe in Karma spiritually or not is completely beside the point. If you get too many people to dislike you, it's going to come back to haunt you due to human nature, if nothing else.

Being so much younger than everyone else in the scene, I wasn't sure what was going on—I'd heard some complaints about Danny and how he dealt with other people, but I didn't care. I was so focused on what I was learning at the lessons—and he was nice enough to me. I always walked out of his place in North Berkeley inspired.

Yet I had to admit, I was surprised at how he'd handled one certain situation with me…

"Maybe he didn't know," I kept telling myself. Of course he knew. How do you not know that you're selling a kid an amplifier and it's a total lemon?

Several sources told me that Danny had pissed off a rival band at a gig who'd responded by pulling the old "wrapping tin foil around the fuse" trick on his Marshall amp. This causes the amp to blow up and sustain

---

[16] When Testament would need a logo, I'd think of Diamond's. Looked at it this way— DiaMonD you notice the same consonant for the first and last letter and an even number of letters on each side of the middle 'M.' We had the fortunate advantage of having the same situation with 'T' instead of 'D' and an 'A' in the middle. TestAmenT. We connected the T's and we had our logo.

irreparable damage. Without telling me, Danny turned around and sold it to me for five hundred of my very hard earned dollars, earned over many months bagging groceries.

I could never imagine doing something like that—selling a faulty piece of gear—to a friend (or anyone else for that matter). I supposed this was the way things were done in the Bay Area music scene. A bunch of petty bullshit—one guy screws over another who gets back at him, then he passes it on to someone else, an innocent bystander like me who then screws over someone else, continuing the cycle of negativity. I made a vow to myself that when I got my chance, I would never try to get one over on a person because of what was done to me by someone else. If someone did me wrong, I would simply no longer trust the person anymore and place even more value on those I could trust.

I believe that maintaining this attitude is a big part of why I'd eventually become successful.

*

When we heard Danny's guitars had been stolen, it was as though a couple of neighborhood children had been abducted. He'd had the coolest guitars: a custom V with a graphite neck and a blue starbody with black clouds and a maple Charvel neck. They had the inventiveness of Van Halen's guitars without copying Eddie in the slightest. Everyone felt bad for him, to the point where any personal issues became water under the Bay Bridge. We didn't want to see our local hero go down in flames.

Danny's instruments went missing on the day he was participating in a guitar competition at the Stone in San Francisco, The Guitar Grudge Match. Looking back, this event was a bit silly: two guitarists on stage try to each outplay each other while being overseen by a guy in the middle in a black and white referee shirt and whistle. The Ref happened to be the organizer of the event, Mike Varney, who'd start his own shred guitar record label (Shrapnel Records) and eventually be co-president of Magna Carta Records, with whom I'd end up releasing some instrumental albums in the distant future.

But that day, Mike Varney was just this bossy guy in a referee's shirt. He wouldn't let me and my friend Ben come backstage to talk to Danny. But he briefed us on what had happened: Bo, the tech who'd worked for Van Halen (and, we later realized, had been fired), had left the trunk of his car unlocked and gone into a store for cigarettes. When he came out, the guitars were gone. Terry, the guitarist from Hans Naughty (and Danny's biggest competition), had very graciously loaned Danny a guitar to use, a flashy yellow guitar in the shape of a Gibson Explorer.

Danny tried his hardest on stage that night. We all cheered him on and chanted his name like it was the best soloing he'd ever done. But the magic wasn't there. It was like a samurai losing his prized, custom sword just before the ultimate battle. His fingers just went through the motions. We were witnessing the fall of a great warrior.

*

Danny Gill's rising guitar status and career momentum was slowed down by his understandably low spirits in the wake of the theft of his instruments. The downfall of Diamond took place soon thereafter and could be blamed on something else entirely: Los Angeles. His entire band had moved there and had begun to make a mistake I'd see many bands make: "going commercial," abandoning everything that was great about the band in the first place.[17]

During Diamond's first visit to the Keystone Berkeley since moving to LA, my buddy Ben, who despite quitting guitar, never lost his ear for good music, looked at me incredulously. I looked back at him, then we both said the same thing in unison: *"What happened?"* While based in Berkeley, Diamond had introduced hard hitting, fast driving songs with titles like "Goin' Over the Edge" and "Danger Zone." Now visiting from LA, the band had replaced these songs for ones with lame limp-dick titles like "Won't You Look My Way" and "She Bites."

*

I no longer studied with Danny. Although I'd valued my lessons with him, I'd realized that as far ahead of me as he was in technique, there'd been something missing.

One day, before my lesson, I'd been killing some time on Telegraph Avenue. While browsing the records in Amoeba Music, a great song by James Brown come on, from his '70s funk period. Sure, it wasn't Dio, Ozzy or Scorpions, but there was something mesmerizing about it. It just resonated with me; I couldn't imagine going through life not having a knowledge of that cool, funky rhythm guitar lick. When I asked Danny if he could show me the tune (I think it was "Soul Power,") he told me he didn't know it. In fact, he'd never even heard James Brown before!

How could he not know about James Brown, who'd been one of the biggest influences on music, period? Even hard rock and heavy metal's most influential act, Led Zeppelin, had openly cited James Brown as an influence,

---

[17] I'd later witness this happening to other bands that were further along, releasing albums that were blatantly commercial, alienating their fans and permanently derailing their momentum. Examples: Y&T *Summertime Girls,* Savatage *Fight for the Rock,* Raven *The Pack Is Back* and even the mighty Judas Priest *Turbo.*

quoting his famous catchphrase "Take it to the bridge" in their funky tribute to him "The Crunge."

Another time, I was warming up for our lesson with some Rolling Stones riffs. He asked what it was I was playing, then told me he didn't recognize any of it and had never even owned a Rolling Stones album. This seemed bizarre to me—how could you attempt a career as a rock guitarist without at least some knowledge of one of the most influential acts in rock?

Danny responded that it wasn't the music of his generation and that today, if you're going to succeed in hard rock, you have to only focus on what's current. We agreed to disagree.

When the next wave of successful rock bands hit, the torchbearer would be Guns 'N' Roses, a band who'd cite as its biggest influence none other than, you guessed it, The Rolling Stones. They'd be followed by a band that combined rock and funk very effectively, Red Hot Chili Peppers, whose influences included, of course, James Brown.

*

Danny would move back to Berkeley and form a band closer to the sound Diamond had started out with: Guilt. On vocals he'd have the Native American Indian who'd been at the Kiss concert, Chuck Billy, now a regular part of the Bay Area hard rock scene.

Meanwhile Diamond's former singer, Rick Ratto, had been going around bad mouthing Chuck, who'd gotten word of it. One night, Chuck grabbed Rick, a big guy himself, got him in a headlock and cut off a huge chunk of his hair. Chuck then told him to watch his mouth or he'd come back and cut the rest of it. The incident was forever known as "the scalping." Years later, Rick would thank Chuck for teaching him a lesson.

Guilt would do just a few gigs before Danny decided to leave his own band and move back down to LA. He'd form several other bands, all of them stereotypical "big hair" bands which sounded like a cross between Quiet Riot and Warrant. One of them did a record for Atlantic Records and a short tour cycle before being dropped. He'd become a guitar teacher at the Musician's Institute—I'd see him there when brought in as a guest artist in the mid-'90s.

Eventually, he'd fall in love with a female student from Sweden and the two of them would move to Sweden, where to this day, he earns a comfortable living teaching guitar, performing on television and playing in tribute bands. Berkeley's former leading light of hard rock guitar may have made some mistakes along the way, but he came out of it, if not a well-known name, a good guy who seems happy with his life. These days, he's always in great spirits, free of any baggage from the past.

Part IV

DOORS 7:00 PM

"Everyone has talent. What is rare is the courage to follow the talent to the dark place where it leads."

- Erica Jong

15. "SATCH"

In the mid-1980s, Berkeley resident Joe Satriani was our very own "local legend," a musician in our own backyard that ranked among the best anywhere. Already in his late twenties (*no spring chicken,* as they say), with no national recordings on his resume and no touring experience yet, Joe was frequently cited as an example of why we should all give up on the music business. After all, if someone this good hadn't "made it" by now, then what hope was there for the rest of us?

The absurdity of this logic would be proven by the fact that today, if you made a list of guitar players who've received the most coverage in guitar magazines during the last twenty years, Joe Satriani would probably be in the top five. But back then, Joe was just a very good musician earning a living teaching guitar in a broom closet located within a tiny music store in North Berkeley.

Second Hand Guitars was a virtual waiting room—in addition to the regular customers, there were always a few teen and twenty-something students fiddling with their unamplified electric guitars, nervously awaiting their turn to get called into the office by Dr. "Satch."

The streets of Berkeley, meanwhile, were littered with former Joe students who, unable to handle his high expectations, had stopped showing up after just a few weeks. Many, not heeding his warnings to practice harder or start showing up on time, had been fired or expelled. One of them described Joe as being "as serious as cancer."

Needless to say, I was a bit nervous to start my lessons.

Among Joe's disgruntled pupils had been two of my own teachers, Danny Gill and Bob Coons (older brother of Lääz Rockit vocalist Mike Coons). Both had reputations of being among Berkeley's finest guitarists in the local rock scene. Bob and Danny told me in no uncertain terms not to study with Joe. Like many others, they'd grown tired of walking into Joe's little room feeling like the best on the block, only to come out with their egos smashed like one of Pete Townsend's guitars after a Who concert.

"What' dya wanna do that for?" Bob asked. *"He's kind of a dick,"* Danny told me.

How could anyone tell a young guitar student *not* to study with Joe Satriani?

This was an example of what I'd learn again and again upon entering the music world. Those I'd initially look up to—musicians, producers, publicists, A&R reps, attorneys and others—would often turn out to be people who, because of their inflated egos or other self-imposed limitations, had stopped moving forward and hit their peak of achievement. Unable to rise above their own insecurities, they would impart ill advice, however well intentioned.

These experiences would cause me to not only keep my own ego in check but to keep in mind the following lesson:

Take any advice with a grain of salt, peppered with your own instincts.

By ignoring the advice of my two former guitar teachers, I'd be making one of the best decisions of my career.

*

Having two of Berkeley's best guitar players giving me bad advice wasn't enough: even my own mother, no doubt scarred from her aborted artistic inclinations at New York's High School of Music and Art, would do everything she could to subtly derail my musical ambitions. A perfect example would be the day she tried to kill my lessons with Joe Satriani...

1984 Berkeley, CA. I'm standing with my mother in a large crowd at a political rally for the presidential nominee Gary Hart. I don't even want to be here—she's pressured me into it. I look at my watch. He was supposed to arrive at 11 am. Now it's after 12, and we've been here almost two hours. I have very limited time because at 1 pm, I'm supposed to have a guitar lesson, my first with a new teacher, Joe Satriani. I explain this to my mother. She tells me to reschedule the lesson. I tell her I can't. She asks why.

"Because it took months to get scheduled for this lesson. He's the best in the Bay Area, and has a long waiting list. If I cancel at the last minute he may not want to teach me."

"Just wait a little longer. Senator Hart is going to show up soon. This is a very important event, Alex." I can't understand why she's imposing this on me. It's as though she thinks a passion for politics will suddenly take over my passion for music. She doesn't know how wrong she is.

We wait.

We wait some more.

I look at my watch again.

The longer we stand here, the more resentful I am of her and this annoying politician, both of whom are threatening my musicianship—my sole purpose on this Earth. I tell her that's it, if he doesn't show up in five minutes, I'm leaving.

"But Alex, I really want you to watch Gary Hart speak. The man may be the next president. This is a very important thing to experience."

"I've been experiencing it for two hours and this jerk isn't even here!" We wait some more.

At some point, a switch in by brain goes off—I start walking away, very angry, unable to believe she would do this to me. My mother follows behind.

"No! Alex please. Make your lesson another time. This is important."

"No! THIS is important!"

I yell in one of my first acts of all-out defiance (there will be many more). I've disagreed with a lot of parental rules and decisions, but this is the first time that, knowing I'm right, I'm taking matters into my own hands.

Noticing a bus pulling up to the stop about half a block away, I realize that if I run very fast, I'll just barely make it. With my mother calling after me, I make a break for it. I make my lesson and end up studying with my new teacher for the next two years.

Joe Satriani will turn out to be one of the most respected guitarists of all time. Studying with him will turn out to be a valuable credential—like the private guitar lesson equivalent of the Julliard School of Music.

Gary Hart, meanwhile, will turn out to be a political has-been, someone whose career at the national level ends before it begins. A few months from now, a photo will circulate of him with a moderately attractive young woman on his lap (not his wife) aboard a boat. The boat is aptly named: "Monkey Business."

*

Arriving at Second Hand Guitars about ten minutes late, I introduced myself and explained to Joe what happened. He told me that since it's the first day, it's okay, but it can't happen again. "It won't," I assured him, hurriedly taking my guitar out of the case, apologizing again for being late.

Right away, I noticed that he didn't waste any time. There was no excess banter and little small talk. He asked me to "just play," as if I'd picked up a guitar to try out off the wall in the store. I was nervous. Playing unaccompanied can be really hard to do in front of anyone, let alone a guitarist with such a lofty reputation who is about to evaluate you.

I played some riffs, Ozzy, Scorpions and Dio before launching into some licks—quotes of Randy Rhoads and Eddie Van Halen and some arpeggios inspired by this new guy from Sweden, Yngwie Malmsteen. I sounded a bit sloppy—trying to blend everything together but not being very cohesive.

I was sure Joe would say I wasn't fast enough and needed more work on my technique. But when he signaled it was okay to stop, he told me the opposite of what I expected: "You should stop concentrating so much on speed. You're going to be a fast player—that's the last thing you have to worry about. Let's work on your musical knowledge. How much do you know about intervals?"

"What's an interval?"

"Hand me your notebook, please."

I passed Joe the little graph paper composition book, the same type I brought to math class. As he began silently scribbling his ballpoint pearls of wisdom, I sat there, not knowing if I should play my guitar (was that rude?) or sit quietly while he wrote… I chose to sit quietly.

There was a special energy in the room, of someone who meant business. I'd never been around a master musician before. Still out of breath from running for the bus, a tiny bead of sweat inched its way down my forehead.

Joe placed my notebook on the music stand and launched into an explanation of what he'd just written down: the names of each interval along with a diagram of where they fell on the lowest string. Next week, we'd cover the fifth string, the following week the fourth and so on until I'd memorized the names of the intervals and the notes on all six strings, all the way up and down the neck.

I thought about the mission I was embarking upon...Joe was right. I'd been playing as fast as I could without a solid understanding of one of the most basic elements of music: intervals (the distances between one note and another).

There was a lot to learn. There always is.

*

My lesson that day lasted exactly twenty-five minutes—I'd lost ten and Joe mercifully tacked on an extra five (despite there being a student right after me). Despite the short amount of time, it seemed as though I'd learned more in that one lesson than I had in all my previous guitar lessons combined. This included these two invaluable tidbits of information:

1. Licks too strongly identified with certain players are best avoided.

For example, the famous triplet guitar lick from Eddie Van Halen's solo "Eruption," which I'd just played during my quick evaluation. It was okay to learn a lick like this and use it to inspire your own ideas, as long as it was left out of your own playing. But that exact pattern would always be too closely linked to Eddie Van Halen.

2. The ones who stand out among the crowd are the ones who don't get too caught up in the hype surrounding the player of the moment.

Joe brought this up in reference to Yngwie Malmsteen, who had just made the cover of *Guitar Player* magazine (the youngest player ever to do so at the time) and who guitarists around the world, myself included, were studying with religious fervor. Joe said it was okay to learn a few of his licks, but not copy everything about him—especially his vibrato and other expressive details.

He also mentioned that for most of the '80s, Eddie Van Halen had been *that one guy*[18]—the one it seemed everyone else was listening to and imitating until Texas blues guitarist Stevie Ray Vaughn had come along and grabbed some of the spotlight away. Right now it was Yngwie Malmsteen, but he wouldn't be there forever. Having just replaced Yngwie in the band Alcatraz, Joe's former student Steve Vai was starting to get lots of attention and was looking to be next.

---

[18] "That One Guy" would also be the stage name of a young, funny, brilliant, underrated multi-instrumentalist who would be a huge local influence on me in the '90s, Mike Silverman.

My new teacher explained all this matter-of-factly, without a hint of speculation, presumption or knowingness that in exactly three years, it would be he himself, Joe Satriani, who would be *that one guy.*

*

The kid who'd had his lesson after mine, was very understanding any time we'd run a few minutes over—his name was Larry. Unbeknownst to either of us, he and I would both be frequently mentioned in a list of noteworthy students of Joe's.[19] Larry played in a thrash/death metal band Possessed, whose first album Joe would produce (odd pairing as that would seem to be). Larry's girlfriend at the time was Julie Abono, the daughter of Possessed's manager Debbie Abono.[20]

Larry would eventually leave Possessed for Primus, a band that seemed very weird and quirky at the time, but would ultimately be hugely successful in the '90s, touring the world and eventually providing the theme music to the animated TV series *South Park*.

A year or so after my first lesson, I would find myself briefly dating Debbie's other daughter, Gina. This would lead to one Saturday when Larry and I would both find ourselves at the Abono household in Pinole, CA, and planning to take public transportation to our lessons, about a fifteen minute ride on the freeway. Instead, Debbie would offer to give us a lift.

Only many years later would it dawn on me—here was the Bay Area's metal matriarch, giving the future guitarists of Primus and Testament a ride to their guitar lessons with the future superstar of instrumental rock, Joe Satriani.

*

Joe had spent a few formative years isolated in Kyoto, Japan, simply to develop his craft as a guitar player. Berkeley's own future eight-string jazz guitar wizard (and fellow "Satch" student), Charlie Hunter, had followed

---

[19] Joe's other students included Metallica's Kirk Hammett, Steve Vai, Charlie Hunter and guitarists from pop bands like The Counting Crows and Third Eye Blind.

[20] Debbie Abono passed away in May 2010 at age 80. I contributed the following words for her Eulogy: *"In the mid-1980s, when most folks over forty were afraid of metal, there was Debbie Abono, a kind, sophisticated woman in her 50s. She saw right through the pentagrams, upside-down crosses, leather and spikes and recognized that some kind souls lay underneath the anger reflected by this imagery. She opened her door, her heart and her ears to the much-younger, often-misunderstood group of metalheads and become manager to some of the heaviest bands. By doing so, she helped helped us realize that older people weren't so bad either. The fact that she passed on the same day as the great Ronnie James Dio is almost not a surprise."*

Joe's lead, devoting several years to playing anonymously on the streets of Paris. I'd later read about the great tenor saxophonist Sonny Rollins, a leading light of jazz in the late 1950s, who felt the need to step away from the spotlight in order to develop his craft further—he spent the better part of three years in New York's Lower East Side blowing his horn under the Williamsburg Bridge.

Having joined a band at such a young age, I'd realize that I'd never been able to set aside the years for reflection, self-discovery and true musical development. In 1998, I would move to New York City, earn a BFA degree from New School University's Jazz and Contemporary Music Department and keep a low profile for several years before emerging with the ability to play jazz guitar—not rivaling the best in the world (as some of my self-appointed critics would point out), but at a level that was, few could argue, *professional.* Later, I'd step back into rock and metal, with renewed vigor and enthusiasm.

My years studying in a university jazz program in New York would represent to me what Kyoto was to Joe Satriani, Paris was to Charlie Hunter and what the Williamsburg Bridge was to Sonny Rollins.

*

I don't pretend to have been one of Satch's best students.

I'd show a remarkable improvement in my playing, practice hard and always remain in good standing with Joe, which was more than some others could say. But by the time Joe stopped teaching to make a serious go at touring and recording, I still didn't have the confidence, nor the focus to take on everything he'd shown me.

Steve Vai was someone who had a reputation as being one of Joe's best from their days back in Long Island. Charlie Hunter was another one, someone who took to the most advanced theory right away. Another fast learner was my new friend from school, Jeff Tyson (see chapter 10). We'd exchange ideas on the steps of Berkeley High, passing a cheap nylon acoustic back and forth. I wasn't sure how Jeff did it—he had just played whatever Joe wrote down, even some of the more theoretical concepts, which had felt to me like advanced quantum physics.

Years later, unfulfilled with my own playing, approaching twenty years old and experiencing an early "mid-life crisis," I would finally smash through the barriers of the limitations that had been set by those little voices in my head, the ones which had always told me:

"That's too hard for you."

"You don't need to learn that."

"There are plenty of guitar players who don't know this stuff."

"You're not that type of guitar player."

I'd imagine these voices of doubt as evil little creatures whose eyes I'd gouge out with my low E string, then wrap it around their throats and suffocate them till they died. I'd break out that pad of white graph paper and glue myself to Joe's notes, determined to understand every chord, scale, mode, triad, arpeggio, pentatonic and other pattern and how they all related to one another.

Failure was no longer an option. I'd given up on taking my playing to the next level so many times before, but no longer. It didn't matter how long it took. I was learning the art of perseverance: try, try again, take a break—get some air and inspiration, come back and try some more. Repeat the whole process if needed. It would be difficult, but I'd push through. And eventually, I'd learn to not just persevere but to have fun doing so.

It would all start with tackling those Satch lessons from a few years earlier that I hadn't absorbed properly. Soon, it all would begin to really take hold; a whole new world of sound. I'd connect each concept to music I knew by ear.

How did I know I was really on my way? It all became clear as soon as I grasped the one concept I never thought I'd get: the modes.

*

I'm not sure of the exact moment the modes started to make sense to me. It may have been when I noticed songs whose chord patterns moved *backwards* through the modes. There are many popular songs that do this.

For example, though I wasn't exactly a fan of Billy Joel, I didn't mind hearing his songs on the radio, including his early hit, "Piano Man." One day it occurred to me: this song (which has a 3/4 waltz feel) was a great example of the backwards modal cycle through one key.

Later, I'd notice the exact same chordal motion on the chorus of "I Want You Back" by The Jackson 5. It was a bit harder to find a metal song like this, but soon I found one: Ozzy Osbourne's power ballad "Goodbye to Romance."[21]

I'd realize that a key only has seven basic chords. In the key of C, for example:
I C II Dm III Em IV F V G VI Am VII G/B.[22] You can very easily play basic, three-note versions of these chords on a piano, playing every other note starting at C, then moving the pattern up through the key.

---

[21] I'd later arrange "Goodbye to Romance" for jazz guitar, and make it the title track of the first album by Alex Skolnick Trio.

[22] A G/B is a G chord with a B as the lowest note, usually played as a passing chord, not held very long.

Soon, I'd figure out several popular rock/pop tunes, all of them in the key of C, each one of them bringing out a different mode:

C Ionian "Let It Be" (The Beatles) Chord progression: |C G| Am F |

D Dorian "Another Brick in the Wall" (Pink Floyd) Chord progression: |Dm |G |

E Phrygian "Space Oddity" (David Bowie) Chord progression: |F |Em |

F Lydian "Over the Hills & Far Away" (Led Zeppelin), "Jane Says" (Jane's Addiction)

Chord progression: | F | G | (actual relative key of these songs is D, not C)

G Mixolydian "Paradise City" (Guns 'N' Roses) Chord progression: | G | C | F | (actual relative key is B, not C, because the guitars are tuned down one half step)

A Aeolin "Stairway to Heaven" (Led Zeppelin) finale Chord progression: | Am G | F |

B locrian "Stairway to Heaven" passing chord on twelve-string guitar interlude ("There's a feeling I get...") Chord progression: |C G/B| Am |

Even a scale that I couldn't imagine using, the melodic minor scale, made sense as soon as I connected it to that "strange sounding" chord in the Pink Floyd song, "Us and Them."

The modes and scales weren't so intimidating once you *heard* them. The problem had been that I'd been copying them off the page, but wasn't *hearing* them. You just had to hear the sound to understand the theory. Connecting the theory to actual music had been the missing ingredient. [23]

Soon I'd come up with my own metal rhythm that went through all the modes in order to practice them. This piece would later find its way into a Testament song and become one of my signature solos. The song's title would be very fitting: "Practice What You Preach."

*

Joe would often refer to his own teacher, a haunting disciplinarian, as his "blind piano teacher." This was the man who'd set the standard for Joe's own teaching and taught many others before passing away in the late '70s. Joe would describe the lessons as very daunting—his teacher would play all the fundamentals on piano, then instruct Joe to do the same on guitar—scales, modes and arpeggios in all twelve keys. At the time I couldn't imagine studying on such a challenging level.

---

[23] A much later teacher of mine, jazz pianist Mark Levine, would impart the following bit of wisdom: *"Music Theory" came along after music—it exists for the sole purpose of making sense of music and isn't even 100% accurate—if it were, then it would be called "Music Truth."*

That would all change in the '90s, as soon as I'd begin correspondence lessons with the teacher that would have the greatest impact on me, Charlie Banacos.[24] I'd be inspired to do so by one of my favorite jazz guitarists, Mike Stern, who, despite becoming an elite in the world of jazz and "knighted" by the king of improvisation, Miles Davis, never stopped studying with Charlie. Charlie's methods would remind me more and more of Joe's mysterious "blind piano teacher." Both had systems of covering concepts in all twelve keys, which Charlie credited to his own late teacher, who'd also been a strict blind pianist, Lennie Tristano. An important, yet often overlooked figure in the world of jazz (a household name, among musicians and jazz aficionados only), Lenny Tristano had been part of an ultra-sophisticated clique of players, including Lee Konitz and Wayne Marsh. I'd hear his name often while studying at New School and would be the proud owner of several of his albums.

Could it be that Joe Satriani's blind piano teacher was the same person who'd taught my own teacher, Boston pianist and renowned jazz guru, Charlie Banacos? Besides being blind, the only other thing I'd recall about Joe's teacher was that he had a very Italian sounding last name, like Satriani, but different. I began to connect the dots… Suddenly it all made sense: Joe and Charlie had both studied with Lennie Tristano.

Via two very different pupils of his, Lennie Tristano had indirectly become my teacher as well. He was like Socrates, who'd passed on his wisdom to Plato, who'd passed it on to Aristotle (and so forth). Joe Satriani and Charlie Banacos were both like Plato, and I had the great fortune to study with them, as well as the wisdom to realize this fortune and seize the opportunity.

Having come from Long Island, and gone into New York City every week to study with someone of the highest standards, the great Lennie Tristano, Joe had brought a little piece of New York out West with him. That's why so many young guitar students in Berkeley couldn't handle him.

---

[24]My own lessons with Charlie would last more than ten years, until he'd sadly lose a battle with cancer in 2009. At a Mike Stern gig at New York's 55 Bar (where he'd played a weekly residence for nearly three decades), we would briefly remember Charlie and commiserate about, for the first time in many years, not having a teacher. Charlie's other students included sax greats George Garzone and Jerry Bergonzi, as well as several of my teachers at the New School—pianists Gerard D'Angelo, Gary Dial and underrated jazz guitarist Vic Juris, with whom I'd study privately. Like me, Vic had never met Charlie, and only knew his voice from a cassette tape, referring to him as the "man in the box."

Joe's New York work ethic and high standards enabled him to not be dragged down by Berkeley's contagious disease of mediocrity—the illness which caused most bands to not get anywhere—showing up to rehearsals with a bag of pot, a six-pack of beer and a posse of friends. Or, like my brother, they'd spent too much time frying on acid and not enough working on their craft and learning about the entertainment industry. It was why so many individual musicians didn't rise above the herd.

I can't tell you the number of times over the years I'd hear the following: "Music's supposed to be fun. Don't take it so seriously."

Bullshit.

Music is serious business. It requires focus, discipline and a strong work ethic. But that doesn't mean it can't be fun. Practicing and working hard is fun. Rising to the challenge and setting high standards is fun. Sure, it's hard sometimes, and there are many setbacks, but it can really be fun if you allow it to be.

In New York, I'd take a philosophy class and read about the Protestant Work Ethic. Right then I'd realize that I'd gotten out from under something I thought of as the "Berkeley Work Ethic."

The Berkeley Work Ethic is like an invisible toxic fume spewing forth from a UC laboratory infecting the entire Bay Area, causing people to slow down and, in many cases, aspire to do nothing. Its mantra can pretty much be summed up as follows: *"Just chill, man."* Whenever a memory pops up of a Berkeley deadbeat saying, "Just chill, man," I want to take my guitar and smash it over his head.

16. SKULLWRECKER

Alexis and I started traveling in a small, motley group of friends. Our circle included Ben—still wearing the hood—soon to grow out of it, Ben's brother Bood, borderline antisocial but amusing, Fish, our red-headed friend, still piggish and overweight but soon to transform into good looks along the lines of Boris Becker, and Liz, our cute, giggly, blonde female friend who somehow we were able to be platonic with.

We saw everyone: Exodus, Lääz Rockit, Diamond, The Freaky Executives, Ruffians. Even Metallica, who was coming through on their first album, *Kill 'Em All.*

Alexis and I were too young to get into some of these shows. But the bands, especially Lääz and Exodus, were always cool about letting us carry speaker cabinets and amplifier heads into the venues for them. The door guys just accepted each of us as crew or someone's little brother. Eventually, some of them knew us and just let us in.

After a few months, it became clear that Alexis had plans to channel this into a career. He could go on tour with a band, and it would not matter if he finished his homework or even finished high school.

Meanwhile, I was avoiding college like the plague, but somehow the thought of not graduating from high school was horrifying. I felt that if I didn't at least finish high school and dropped out, I'd be a fucking loser. Dropouts seemed to be the most troubled people.

Soon I'd be in a band with several of them.

In order to get me to go to shows with him, Alexis would apply guilt and pressure—something that would continue as time went on and our relationship became more complicated. If I went to all the shows he wanted me to go to, I'd never get any homework done and would start missing an absurd amount of classes. Of course that's what he wanted. He started attending concerts every week, whether they were in San Francisco or the East Bay. And there was one such concert that he would not stop rubbing in my face about missing.

"It was the heaviest band, ever! They blew Exodus away."

"What?" I said.

"Not really. But they were heavy."

"I'll have to check 'em out."

"They're at Ruthie's next month. You're going."

"That good, huh?"

"Dude, I'm most this band[25]" he said. "I might try and manage 'em."

"Cool. What are they called?"

"Legacy."

*

Ruthie's Inn was a former R&B club, run by a fifty-something African-American guy named Wes Robinson. Wes had somehow become the number-one promoter of Bay Area metal. Like so many other members of the scene, Wes had a substance abuse issue, mainly speed, and would bond with the younger scraggily haired teens wearing Motörhead shirts.

We would pester Wes to let us in for free. It was a ritual, no matter who was playing—Freaky Executives, Death Angel, Exodus, whoever. "C'mon, Wes," we'd beg, until finally he said, "Alright, just this once." Usually once you gigged there, you had carte blanche, and I was a short time away from achieving that status, and hanging out in Wes's office drinking Kamikazes. The most famous musicians to go there were the Metallica guys, but it was only a matter of time before they'd be whisked off to the upper levels of the music biz and no longer be seen at the grand dive that was Ruthie's.

*

It was at Ruthie's that I first saw Legacy. I remember the song "Curse of the Legions of Death." Later it would be one of my least favorite songs, just because it wasn't that interesting to play, but at the time, I felt it had a very strong chorus, very memorable. The other songs sounded messy,

---

[25] East Bay metal scene slang circa Mid-'80s: *I'm most* = I like. *I'm least* = I don't like

like scrambled eggs. It was hard to tell what was going on, but there seemed to be potential.

The thought of actually joining this band never crossed my mind until one day at school, when Alexis said to me, "Legacy's guitar player is quitting the band. I told them about you."

"What about me?"

"Maybe you could play guitar for them."

"I don't know. Those guys sound like Venom and Slayer. I don't play like that. I'm more into Ozzy and Dio." That was what I really wanted. A single guitar band that was heavy, yet melodic.

"Well, I already set it up. You're coming to a rehearsal."

"What for?"

"So you can try out."

"I don't think they'll want me. And I'm not sure I want them either."

"Just try it."

"Alright," I said.

*

The following week, I was at my weekly guitar lesson where I consulted my teacher, Joe. At this point I'd been studying with Joe for over a year and felt comfortable asking him what he thought about me joining this band.

"I think it's probably a good idea," Joe said. "You'll get experience. You can work on your stage presence and develop as a performer."

"Really?" I asked. "But it's this really noisy music. It's hard to tell what's going on. The guitar player they have now is so sloppy, it's like he's in Venom. I don't want to play like that."

"You don't have to. Play like you. Try to bring what you listen to." Hmm. I hadn't thought about it that way before.

It seemed most of the super heavy bands had guitar solos that were punk-like and trashy, built off the Motörhead and Venom model. There were a few that were a bit more polished, such as Metallica, Megadeth, and Accept (which wasn't a thrash band, but had written one song, "Fast as a Shark," that became a thrash anthem). But it was the glam rock bands from LA that had the great guitarists, such as Warren De Martini of Ratt, George Lynch of Dokken—guys that were disciples of the late great Randy Rhoads and, of course, the godfather of modern hard rock guitar, Eddie Van Halen.

I was well on my way towards being a player with those standards. And it seemed like all the other advanced players were looking to join glam bands or not to play metal at all—none of them would take on music like this. If I pulled it off, applying the standards of the best hard rock guitarists to thrash metal, I could really make a statement in the music.

I was going to give it a shot.

*

Legacy's rehearsal space was in downtown Oakland. Zet and Greg would come in from Dublin/Pleasanton, about a half hour away, while the other guys, Eric, Lou and Derek, who had just left the band to work full-time, came from the island of Alameda, the next town over from Oakland.

Eric picked me up on the first night I tried out. He wasn't what I expected. He was older, around twenty or twenty-one, but looked younger than me. He was slightly pudgy, not very rock-looking but with a look that could work for speed metal, I supposed. I was very nervous and didn't know what to say. Him being a few years older, I thought he'd know what to say, but he didn't either. We got into his red El Camino.

"What's up?" he said, not looking me in the eye.

"What's up?" I answered back in a near whisper.

When we got to the rehearsal spot, he pulled out his guitar, a red BC Rich. He immediately started moving his fingers up and down the neck like Yngwie. *What do these guys need me for?* I remember thinking. *Look how he moves his fingers up and down the neck.* It turned out that was all for show, it sounded like a wall of noise as soon as he plugged in. However, once he began playing riffs, he sounded clean, with the consistency of a great drummer—one of the best rhythm players I'd heard.

He handed me the guitar. One by one the other guys walked in. Louie, who was shy like Eric. Greg who was just as shy. Finally, in walked Steve Souza who, for reasons unbeknownst to me, they all called "Zet."

*

I'd never met anyone like Zet before—he was on stage as soon as he walked into the room, grabbing everyone's attention, shaking hands and taunting each guy, a Vegas act with the appearance of a heavy-set, denim-wearing biker (although not a Harley owner himself, his father was a bona fide, card carrying member of the one and only Hells Angels). Although he was as far from Jewish as you could get, his demeanor at once reminded me of two famous Jewish entertainers: Van Halen front man David Lee Roth and comedian Don Rickles. He was like a suburban, white trash version of a Borsht Belt comic. "Greggy, you look like a fuckin' pencil, gain some weight kid. How the fuck are ya?! Louie, what the hell's going on? *(Pats him on the stomach)* You don't have that problem, do ya? How 'bout losin' a few pounds…so Greggy can find 'em, ha ha ha! Eric, ya silly fuck, what d'ya say!"

Eric was about to introduce me but before he could, Zet turned and looked at me. I tried to speak first. "Hi, I'm Alex Sko…"

"Oh I know exactly who YOU are, dude! How do you DO, my young son?! You don't mind if I call ya my young son do ya? Good! Because I understand that YOU, my young son, are a fuckin' KILLER guitar player!"

My voice was a squeak. "I'm okay, I guess.."

"Well, let's hear ya!"

I started playing some licks I'd recently learned, triplet hammer ons. They were kind of Van Halen-like and helped get my hands moving. After about a minute, I stopped and noticed they were all looking at me in silence. "Fuck yeah, bro!" said Zet.

Eric said nothing. The rest nodded in approval. We ended up playing a few songs together. I followed Eric's hands. The songs were so fast I was laughing. Later, Alexis would tell me I should stop smiling when I'm playing, it doesn't look right. About an hour later Zet announced: "Sounds good to me! What d'ya boys say?" Everyone nodded.

"Dude, can you start rehearsals next week?"

"I have to check with my parents, but it should be okay."

"Well, you do that. We rehearse once a week. Twice if there's a gig coming up. We've got one at Ruthie's with Death Angel. You know Death Angel, my young son? They've got a young punk like you in that band, the drummer. If they can do it, we can." I nodded, like he was my dad. "So we're all set then? We'll see you next Tuesday."

"Ok," I said.

I shook hands with each of them, Eric, Greg, Lou and Zet. I walked out with Eric and Alexis, Eric was driving us back. I heard a yell in the back, it was Zet.

"Hey wait up! One more thing…" We turned around. "Skolnick, eh? We might think about changing your name. Don't get me wrong, it's a good name. But I'm thinking, if ya don't mind…" he raised his voice and pitch to a gargly sound, like a male version of the Wicked Witch from the Wizard of Oz, saying, *"I'll get you my pretty."* In that voice, he said, "We're going to call you…" he paused for dramatic effect:

"Skullwreckerrrrrrr!!!!"

17. CRASH COURSE IN COINCIDENCE

1984 would turn out to be a pivotal year with events that would have lasting repercussions for the rest of my life. Key among them would be joining my first band, losing my virginity and learning to drive.

None of these events would turn out exactly as I'd imagined them—in each case, new freedoms would be presented and with them, new challenges. The first two would open the doors to the worlds of heavy metal music and females—both would lead to years of disillusion. The third would be comparatively simple—I'd learn the skills I needed and be on my way, never thinking twice about it, save for one very early mishap that many years later, would take on a rather mysterious meaning…

October, 1984, Oakland, CA.

I'm driving my parents' car away from Legacy's practice space in Downtown Oakland. With me are Alexis and another friend who came down and watched our rehearsal. We're listening to "Sirens," the title track of an album by a band called Savatage.

The tape we're listening to is a third generation cassette. Like everyone else, we can't seem to locate the actual album. If it were available, they'd easily sell millions—all the metalheads I know like it. But because you can't find it anywhere, everyone is forced to make a copy of someone else's tape.

How can this band, which sounds so good, be so unknown? It makes no sense. Nobody seems to know anything about them, other than that they're from Florida.

Now, hang on a second—at this moment, if you told me what was going to happen, I would do two things: question your sanity and drive more carefully...

We pull up to an intersection in Alameda, the urban island that functions as a suburb of Oakland. Just as the light turns from red to green, we notice Legacy's singer, "Zet" (Steve Souza) with some friends in a car, turning in the intersection across from us. He's just made a left turn on a yellow light. They don't notice that it's us in the car facing them, my parents' blue Toyota Tercel. In a few seconds, Alexis, certain they are on their way to a party that we'll miss if we lose them, will tell me to follow them.

Instinctually, I will do so. I've become accustomed to doing what he says without question. In this sense, Alexis develops power over other people, taking shameless advantage of them. He's incredibly persistent; saying no to him becomes more trouble than it's worth. You end up just picking him up and giving him a lift, taking him on errands and doing whatever he says, simply because he won't stop.

What is about to happen will cause me to become aware of this and stop being subservient to him. Eventually he will be fired as the band's manager, a move I'll support 100%. But right now, when Alexis says, "Follow them," I automatically do what he says without processing the fact that I am in the left hand lane at the light and need to make an illegal right turn in order to head in the direction they're going.

Zet and Co. are already down the block and still unaware of our presence when they notice a collision taking place in their rear view mirror. I've attempted to make the turn without realizing we're not in the proper lane and without looking at the blind spot (like they warned us about in Drivers Ed). We're struck by an oncoming minivan.

As the glass shatters, the body of our vehicle crushes as if at a junkyard. A second later, the front door of the car is smashed in and Alexis is almost in my lap. We spin out and the car stalls. Miraculously, none of us including those in the minivan, are hurt (chalk one up for the Toyota Tercel).

Once the police have taken everyone's information, they'll let us go. I haven't been drinking, and it was a very stupid mistake on my part. The car will be totaled although, another testament to Toyota's knack for making practical automobiles, it is drivable. Facing my parents is something I'll *dread more than getting my wisdom teeth removed the year before. But that's all in the near future.*

Right now, as the car lies in the street like a smashed toy, our bodies safe but covered in shattered glass, the evening (like the car) has come to an abrupt halt. Most eerily, the stereo is unaffected and playing even louder, now that the engine is off. The music becomes the soundtrack to the scene of the accident, courtesy of this enigmatic band Savatage. Blaring from the speakers:

"Sirens... Sirens...Hungry for man tonight..."

I reach over to turn off the music. As my finger touches the car stereo button, all is quiet, save for the wails of approaching emergency vehicles. Sirens.

Shaken up but unscathed, I drive the car back, a mangled hunk of scrap metal on wheels.

I would drive much more carefully from then on and, knock on wood, haven't ever had a crash since. I'd have to give my parents credit for their handling of this one—they'd keep their cool (surprising, since tempers would flare at the most mundane things). At least no one had been hurt, and it was obviously an accident—wrecking the family car is one of those typical boneheaded teenage things that unfortunately happen more often than not.

But this event would become more than that. In fact, this would go on to represent one of the strangest occurrences of my life. Here's why:

In 1994, nearly ten years to the day of the crash, I would find myself in a Florida recording studio, playing guitar for Savatage, replacing their guitarist, Criss Oliva, who had just tragically passed away in an automobile accident.

*

The connection between Savatage and the car crash would cause me to do something scarier to my parents than the crash itself and more perturbing than my decision to pursue music as a career: seriously consider the notion that there might be mysterious forces that guide us.

Now before going on, let me explain something: I'll always remain a pragmatist, a skeptic with an open mind, more skeptical than not. If you can't give me scientific proof, I'm not going to believe in it. I'm an educated, critical thinker and am quick to debunk religious and conspiracy theories of any kind. On the other hand, it feels wrong to be a purely scientific atheist, strict in the notion that there is no connection between mysterious events.

So call me crazy, but I've come to believe that the universe, nature, chance, coincidence or some other forces we don't understand might, *might* be at work. I don't feel any organized religion can provide the answers—

calling these forces "God" and giving them a face and name just distorts it. I believe it's important to feel spiritual while avoiding organized religion. Sometimes things make no scientific sense but you have to go against conventional logic and follow your faith—and I'm not talking about religious faith. I'm talking about faith in yourself, your destiny and the fact that certain courses of action are right for you, despite what everyone else says.

In my own case, there have been situations where most people around me—family, friends, musicians—all thought I was nuts. Admittedly it took a bit of gall, but I decided that *they* were nuts and I was the only one who was sane. A few examples: joining a thrash band despite being an advanced melodic guitarist (unheard of at the time), studying jazz guitar despite being a metal player, returning to school despite being a professional musician and leaving Berkeley for New York City despite being brainwashed into thinking that the Bay Area was the best place on Earth.

In each case, although it would take years to pan out, I'd be proven right. These would be the best decisions I'd ever make and I would be grateful I'd gone against conventional logic and listened to a mysterious force I didn't quite understand. Intuition, instinct and inclinations are not scientifically explained in black and white. Does that make them wrong?

*

Certain events that have taken place in my life, like the car crash, have seemingly foreshadowed events many years in the future. I'm not saying that this is actually what happened, only that the pragmatist skeptic in me has to take a backseat and say, "You're right. That's pretty fucking weird."

While I admit, like most honest writers, to making tiny literary embellishments, none of these strange occurrences are made up. Had I the capacity to invent fiction on that level, I'd become a writer of fantasy. And while the car crash has been one of the weirdest, seemingly prophetic events, it's far from the only one.

You've already read about the Gibson doubleneck SG on the wall that caught my attention as a child, foreshadowing one I would surprisingly be given years later to play high atop a platform in front of thousands with TSO. In a later chapter, you'll read about a song coming on the radio after I'd been woodshedding it all day—Wes Montgomery's version of "Round Midnight," the most recorded jazz tune *of all time*.

While these are highly memorable incidents, I've had countless little ones as well. For example: I'll think I see someone whom I haven't seen in years, but it turns out to be someone else—later that same day, I'll run into the actual person I'd thought it was. Other times, I'll be thinking of a phrase or thing and it suddenly appears—coming from the radio, TV, spoken by another person or posted on a sign or billboard. And I've had several incidents where I've been out and about, listening to music on my headphones and had external noises become eerily synchronized with the music I'm listening to. This has happened with random street noise, as well as overhead music in supermarkets, coffeehouses, restaurants, etc....music blending in perfect harmony with the music on my headphones. Once it happened with a jazz saxophone solo on my headphones and a voice singing on the overhead speakers in a store—they held the same long, crying note, in harmony, for the *exact duration*. I know it sounds weird, and I can never prove it. But if you were there it, it would freak you out.

None of these coincidental events surprise me anymore—they happen far too often for me to keep track of.

Occasionally there are events that occur in public with a similar strangeness. Although a connection is impossible to prove, the fact that the event happened is irrefutable.

The first example that comes to mind is the 1989 World Series—the only World Series between the Bay Area's two Major League Baseball teams, the San Francisco Giants and the Oakland A's. On October 17, at 5:04 pm, shortly before Game 3 was scheduled to start, a magnitude 7.1 earthquake struck which, except for the 1906 San Francisco earthquake, was the largest ever to hit the region. Had this happened any other time than when most residents were home glued to TV's or in the open air of Candlestick Park in San Francisco, casualties would have been enormously higher.

My final example is one in which, though they probably don't remember, my family was present. It took place in late 1984, the night before my first ever gig—the one that would launch my music career, while we were out to dinner at our local Chinese restaurants on College Ave. in Berkeley.

After the meal, the waiter brought over the check, along with orange slices and a plate of fortune cookies. As my father, mother and brother each routinely read their fortunes aloud, I cracked open a bright, triangular cookie, unfolded the tiny white slip of paper and observed a fortune I hadn't seen before (and haven't seen since): *"It's your turn to shine in the spotlight."*

*

You can't plan on coincidence to happen. That's one of the things that make it so difficult for many to attach any sense or reality or validity to it, especially dogmatic skeptics. And of course, many events that seem connected *are* just strange random coincidences, which can even be explained by statistical models, I'm sure of that. *All of them*? I'm not so sure.

I've come to believe in a creative (or destructive) energy that is connected to at least some of these occurrences. I can't explain it scientifically and to do so would defeat the purpose; some things are better left unexplained. But somehow, tapping into this energy helps create great art—denying it suppresses the creative process.

It is up to the individual to interpret this energy however he or she sees fit. Johann Sebastian Bach composed every note for what he interpreted as God. Many Eastern artists attribute the force to Nature and man's connection to it. The builders of the Parthenon interpreted this force in the form of Greek gods. While certain western European philosophers attribute this force of inspiration to the power of man's Will.

They are all correct. Whatever label one chooses to attach to it is fine as long as it's not forced upon others. If you're going to be an artist/creative person on any level, what is important is to believe in *something*.

Looking for connections and signs and using them as guidance has not exactly hurt my life, my art, or my career—it's only helped. I don't care if any of this sounds crazy. Being a little bit "crazy" is what has enabled me to find myself and reshape a life that used to be appallingly depressing into one that has joy, purpose, fulfillment and meaning.

"But we're never gonna survive unless we get a little crazy."
Lyrics by Seal.

18. FOR WHOM THE BELL TOLLS

By the close of 1984, three unregulated random rites of passage had brought my innocence to a screeching halt: my first and (knock on wood) last automobile accident, which had closely followed my joining a metal band, which in turn had followed my first sexual encounter. Up until then, life had been proceeding at a painfully slow pace, as though attempting to maneuver its way out of a parking lot.

But by 1985, time is whizzing by as if seen through the windows on a freeway. Soon I'll be on the Autobahn (literally).

Metallica's recently released sophomore album *Ride the Lightning* provides the soundtrack to our young lives. It marks the first time my friends and I are listening to music that isn't several years or decades old, giving us pride that this rising band Metallica is poised for greatness and based here in the Bay Area. We run into Metallica at shows—The Kabuki Theater, The Stone, even Ruthie's in Berkeley, and we are star-struck. Nothing could make us forget about *Ride the Lightning* until 1986, when they release an album whose title would throw everyone off guard at first, before becoming an instant classic: *Master of Puppets*.

Most notable on *Ride the Lightning* is the track "For Whom the Bell Tolls." It proves that thrash metal doesn't have to be all about speed, giving me faith in the possibilities of this music. I'm more drawn to the bass parts of the great Cliff Burton, particularly in that song, than I am to Kirk Hammett's lead guitar parts, which, while they have great personality are a bit more punk rockish in execution. It is Cliff who provides the melodic virtuosity to the band. And tragically, it will be Cliff himself to whom the title of the song applies.

*

I play my first gig at Ruthie's Inn in Berkeley. I don't remember much about it, other than I have no control—it's as though my hand is an independent creature, like Thing from the Adams Family. But afterwards, everyone is cheering and high fiving—it's a triumphant moment. *I can do this.*

The next gig, also at Ruthie's, is a little better. At my third gig, at the Stone in San Francisco, I learn not to drink coffee before I play—I'm too excited as it is—my hands shake even more. Only by the fourth gig, back at Ruthie's, do I start to feel like I can play with a hint of control. It dawns on me that I won't be able to rely on sounding "good for my age," forever. I'm playing alongside other bands with older, very good guitarists—I want to sound good *now*.

As hard as I've worked on guitar, I'm going to have to work a lot harder, especially since we're planning our first demo in a few months.

*

At Berkeley High School, old challenges fade and new ones begin.

Socially it's better. I'm still afraid of everyone and feel vastly inferior, but at least there's no more bullying or being taken advantage of. The so-called "cool kids" from tiny Willard Junior High are suffering a wake-up call: they're no longer cool. And with three thousand students, it's easier to blend in; anyone can find someone less cool than him or herself (even me).

While I'll never find the high school girlfriend I dream of, I manage to have a couple of flings, including that oft-remembered loss of virginity. But with each encounter I realize it will take dozens of experiences before I have any confidence. A couple of girls completely scold me, like a child— *Why don't you touch me more? You haven't gone down on a girl before? Don't you know about going slow? What's your problem?* (Excuse me, but no, I didn't know any of those things, okay? I had no way of knowing. I appreciate you telling me, but you didn't have to get so angry, jeez…sorry.)

Academically, things are worse. At BHS, you're forced to take UC Berkeley level courses, where just to get a C so much study is required that I can't practice guitar. The only alternative is being demoted to classes so simple and lame they're bordering on special ed. I re-register for these lower level courses and bump into my friend and, for now, band manager, Alexis and other "educationally challenged" acquaintances there—it feels all wrong. I may not be like our buddy Ben, with his 4.0 average and engineer-like information processing skills, but surely I'm smarter than these dopes in the lower rung of classes.

I have three choices:

1.Take the overwhelming classes and suffer poor grades and/or weakening guitar skills (probably both).

2. Take the lame classes, don't learn anything, waste my time and feel demeaned or…

3. Find an alternative solution.

As will be the case with the majority of big decisions in my life, I will opt for #3: *Find an alternative solution.*

*

I switch schools. My new school, Independent Learning School, is one in which you learn at your own pace, only moving on when you've passed with good grades. In other words, they let you take the tests over, which, in reality, it is a bit of a scam—it would be easy to cheat the system and not learn anything. Because of this, I don't know it at the time, there are some universities that will refuse to recognize a diploma from ILS.

Nonetheless, because I actually do want to learn, I end up learning a lot more than I did at BHS. I also write a couple of papers and for the first time, enjoy it. My favorite one is on this annoying group of Washington Housewives, the PMRC. Leading the battle is a musician I've known mostly for humorous songs, but is a brilliant innovator and social commentator whose work I'll appreciate in greater scope in the future: Frank Zappa. One day I'd like to be like him—a musician who is an independent thinker.

Most of the kids at ILS are from upper middle class families. Many are troubled in some way (I suppose I'm no exception). However, some of these kids are full-on delinquents, not showing up, doing hard drugs, suffering petty arrests, etc.

However, I do meet one really sweet, nice girl there, Chandra, whom I'll break up with for stupid reasons—I feel we don't communicate well enough (it's really my fault), and I don't feel challenged enough—why? Because she liked me *first*. It's just like Woody Allen says in *Annie Hall*: "I never want to join any club that would have a guy like me as a member." I'll regret not staying with her, but before I can approach her about getting back together, I'll find out she and her friend ran into Alexis, who took them home—Alexis hooked up with her friend, she hooked up with his friend. Alexis describes watching her and his friend in graphic detail. I'm crushed.

Heartbreak aside, ILS is the perfect situation for me. I show up, do the work and leave. It is much lighter than Berkeley High's upper level courses but not as demoralizing as their lower level ones. I'm able to practice my guitar and begin showing a marked improvement. Although it ultimately makes sense to have left Berkeley High for ILS, I'll be haunted by a sense of running away. I'll even have nightmares as a result. Only when I'll return to college many years later will these nightmares go away.

*

Zet becomes the drill sergeant of the band, giving regular lectures at the top of his lungs. To each of us, he drills his mission statement into our heads: *the band comes first, no matter what!* Zet points to Louie as an example of true "commitment" to the band "This guy over here has a baby on. the way, but even he knows the band is the most important thing, right, Louie?"

At one point Zet yells at Eric for showing up hours late. "You think life is real easy, don't you? Ya get up! Ya eat a bowl of fuckin' cereal. Ya go to the beach. Ya go drink beers at someone's house, eh? Well fuck you! I work every day. And I still show up on time ready to practice! The rest of you fucks hearin' this?" We all nod. Eric says nothing.

Zet continues: "Commitment! Commitment to excellence, just like the fuckin' Raiders. Any of you can't give full commitment to this band? We'll find people that will."[26]

*

The demo recording takes place at Prairie Sun Studios, north of San Francisco during a midsummer weekend. We spend the night in sleeping bags on bunk beds, our meals consisting of canned food and packaged snacks that we've brought—a glamorous entry into the music business.

The singer of an LA glam metal band, London, originally formed with Mötley Crüe bassist Nikki Sixx (and unbeknownst to us, contains members of a future super-group Guns N' Roses) is putting final touches on an album in the next room. He invites us in to contribute back-up vocals— our first contribution to an actual record. The album comes out, but we are never credited.

Our demo has been financed by a plan coordinated by Alexis, in which everyone in the band has sold drugs to raise the money. A failure as a drug dealer, I've sold mine back to Alexis and owe him the profits, which I'll earn from teaching guitar lessons to kids at school.

*

For the rest of 1985, the Legacy Demo gets reviewed in American and European metal "fanzines," increasing our profile. We'll continue to play gigs at Ruthie's and The Stone

By early 1986, we have garnered interest from a tiny European record label, Music For Nations, who distributes Metallica's albums. MFN sends over an actual recording contract, the first I've ever seen. I show the contract to my father who, though he is an expert on criminal law, doesn't know the first thing about entertainment law. He knows one thing: never sign a contract without the consent of a proper lawyer. He asks that we don't sign anything without having a lawyer look at it. He puts in a call to his former student turned entertainment attorney, Elliot Cahn—a former member of Woodstock performers Sha Na Na, (a fifties musical revue that went on to have a successful TV variety show).

---

[26] Louie will soon stop coming to rehearsals. We'll find a new drummer, through a friend of a friend. A guy in Hayward, whom we'll never get to know well: Mike Ronchette. We'll do our demo tape with Mike, but Louie, at Eric's urging, will be brought back in less than a year. Mike will leave us each a message, saying, "Thanks for the stab in the back!"

Elliot has bad news and potential good news…First the bad news: the Music For Nations contract is abysmal, not to be signed at any cost. While this is nearly always the case with first draft record label proposals, in this case, he doesn't see any point even trying to negotiate with them.

Now the good news: there is potential interest from Megaforce Records, the label who had initially signed Metallica and is on the verge of a distribution deal with Atlantic Records.

How?

Unbeknownst to us, Eliot placed a call to an acquaintance, legendary East Coast label exec, John Zazula, known in the industry as "Johnny Z." Johnny, the head of Megaforce, already had the tape sitting on his desk, along with a tower of other cassettes. Elliot asked Johnny if, as a favor to him, he wouldn't mind giving a quick listen to our tape. Johnny took a listen. Elliot called him back and Johnny said there's something "holy" about our tape. Unsure exactly what that meant, Elliot asked, "Holey? Like their underwear?"

Elliot wisely makes it clear we aren't to get overexcited. Johnny could change his mind about us—it's not unheard of. Johnny is bound to propose an unfair deal, as all labels do, and we just have to hope that this is one that can be negotiated into a fair one (Johnny's not exactly known for being easy to negotiate with). However, Johnny is hinting that down the line, there may be possibilities. He wants to stay in the loop on our activities and at some point, possibly fly out from New Jersey to hear us play in person.

In the meantime, he's in the midst of negotiating a distribution deal with Atlantic Records which, if it goes through, assuming he still wants to work with us at that point, would mean we have a possibility of being on Megaforce, still a tiny indie label, but with major distribution from Atlantic. A deal like that could be worth signing. Again, that could fall through at any time, so we can't start planning our futures around any of this.

Regardless, the fact is, we've gotten some positive feedback from an important figure in the emerging thrash metal industry. That's incentive for us to keep working hard, to be proud of what we've accomplished so far. We are officially on Johnny Z's radar.

And no sooner do we hear this news than we are faced with a difficult and unpredictable setback from out of left field.

*

April, 1986 Oakland, CA. The whole band is gathered in the hallway outside our rehearsal studio—any band friends that came along are waiting inside our room. Zet wants to talk to us alone, no one else around, no interruptions. I know what he's going to say…

It was just the other day that I heard the rumor: Exodus had fired Paul Baloff, was looking for a singer and had their eye on our singer. It sounded too crazy to be true. But now Zet's looking down at the floor. He gives a big sigh, then looks up. He's ready to speak.

"How ya doin', guys?" he says quietly, unheard of, for him. The big tough guy, son of a Hell's Angel, looks nervous. He tries to speak but the words don't come out. I decide to do him a favor. "So it's true then?" I mumble. He nods.

"Guys, you may know by now. I got an opportunity. Opportunities don't come around every day. I'm gonna be the new singer for Exodus." Our jaws drop. "Now guys—I've thought it over and over. I haven't had a night of sleep since I can remember. It's the hardest fuckin' thing I've ever had to do. But I gotta do it."

Silence.

"I'm sorry dudes. I'm so fuckin' sorry!" I can't believe it. Legacy's drill sergeant! The one who hammers into our heads terms like "commitment" and "loyalty!" Et tu, Zetro? He begins sobbing. "You guys have been like (sniff) brothers to me. Since fuckin' '83 when we started Eric…Greggy…Lou…You too Skullwrecker, it's barely been a year, but you're like a little bro to me to ya know? I love all you fuckin' guys. But I gotta do this."

Eric speaks next: "But Zet—that's Exodus's trip. What about our trip?"

"Exodus is signing with Capitol and going on tour with Maiden. Iron fuckin' Maiden (sniff, sniff). I'm fuckin' sorry!" He hugs each of us, then walks out of our rehearsal room for the last time. [27]

*

We needed a new singer. Great. Just fucking great.

Hiring Paul Baloff was out of the question. Poor Paul. Everyone knew he had trouble keeping it going in the studio and on the road. There were substance and stamina issues. But still—couldn't something have been done? Paul was the face of that band! A true personality. So perfect for Exodus. Unfortunately, he could never work singing our stuff, especially

---

[27] Exodus will release their first album with with Zet, *Pleasures of the Flesh,* finishing out their contract with their current label before moving over to Capitol. Suffering from mediocre songs and not helped by the bands collective addiction to meth, sales are lackluster and Exodus will be dropped from Capitol after two records. Their tour with Iron Maiden never happens.

melodic songs like the first one I had written on my own, "Alone in the Dark."

The first thought was to do what Exodus did, steal someone from another band. But there were a couple problems with that. First of all, who wanted to put another band through what we'd just gone through? Second, the choices were so few.

There was Death Angel, but their singer Mark didn't really fit our style. Besides, as far as we knew, he was related to the other guys in the band (weren't they all cousins or something?). There was Forbidden, whose singer, Russ, had arguably the best voice of any of the local thrash singers. Unfortunately—he looked too normal—a typical oversized guy who didn't move much. Zet had been far from a photogenic lead singer, but at least he had the crucial ingredient for this type of metal—intensity. We needed someone like that, only more so. Someone a little bit... *scary*.

There was one interesting possibility: that big guy from the suburb of Dublin, CA, whom Zet and others in that scene called "Cheese" (after the pizza parlor Chuck E. Cheese), Chuck Billy.

*

The story of Chuck and his fellow gargantuan marauders getting into fights, always emerging victorious, were legendary. Their unofficial gang of roving mid-twenty-something suburbanites, known as the Dublin Death Patrol, had struck fear into the hearts of many a Bay Area partygoer. But inexplicably, the band we all knew him from, Guilt, had a sound more like Ratt's *Out of the Cellar* than Metallica's *Kill 'Em All.* Onstage, he wore colorful scarves and bandanas, like Aerosmith's Steven Tyler and sang like Ratt's Stephen Pearcy. Would he even be able to sing thrash?

No sooner had the guys and I brought it up than my phone rang that night. I heard this strange voice, a bit gruff but very surprisingly mellow, telling me he'd heard we might need a singer. I hadn't quite gotten his name at first, but as we spoke, it became clear: it was Chuck.

Ironically, he'd gotten my number from Zet. No one had mentioned to Zet that we were even considering Chuck as a possibility. We hadn't even seen Zet since the fateful meeting.

So now, the meek Berkeley kid and the feared suburban Native American, both of whom had been at that San Francisco Kiss concert some seven years earlier, had connected.

Today, choosing Chuck Billy to sing for the band probably looks like a no-brainer decision, but truth be told, that wasn't the case at the time. It's easy to look at him now as someone with a style of his own, one that has influenced countless other bands that followed, some of whom have gone on to do what we never managed to do: sell millions. But in 1986, his potential was still untapped. Had the timing been different, there may have been a longer search for another singer. But at that moment, we needed someone fast. There was record company interest and we didn't want to lose that. Here was someone with undeniable presence who could potentially develop into the right voice for the band. Everyone agreed: we had to make a move, now—this would be our guy.

I was still intimidated communicating to anyone, let alone this member of the Dublin Death Patrol (who had essentially scalped the former singer of Diamond, Rick Ratto, who himself used to pick on me when he was in a band with my brother). But I did my best to explain to Chuck our plans: first, we rehearse and do some Ruthie's gigs. Then, we record another demo as soon as possible.[28] We send it to the label and, hopefully, they'll like it. If they do, then the president, Johnny Z, and his wife Marsha, would fly out to see us perform in person. If they like us live, we could be recording our first album by the end of this year, early next year at the latest. Then we'd go on tour.

Chuck was fine with all that, except the part about going on a tour. For over a year, he'd been working at Lucky—a Northern California supermarket chain. He'd just been bumped up to assistant manager. Going on tour was out of the question. With that, I began the daunting task of explaining to a six foot four Native American giant that we would be expecting him to quit his job at the grocery store.

*

We record our second demo at a small studio on College Ave, in North Oakland, near our attorney's office and not far from where I live in Berkeley. Musically, it is far beyond the first tape. With songs like "The Haunting" and "Apocalyptic City" (fiercely resisted by Eric at first because they had more harmony, which he'll later grow to appreciate), all the tightness that we've gained from playing live is there. And we have our original drummer back who, while not the best on a purely musical level, re-energizes the band—Eric's rhythms just sound better with Lou and my layer on top of his—rhythms and leads sound better as a result. Most of all, we have a new singer, who, while different, has a style that somehow seems better suited for the band.

---

[28] By now, from the gigs and sales of the demo, there was enough money put away for us to record a demo without the band having to sell drugs to fund it.

Johnny Z agrees. He immediately makes plans to come to the Bay Area, meet us in person and watch a rehearsal. But the day he arrives is marred by tragic news from very far away.

*

Sep. 27, 1986. I'm walking into the studio building with Eric. We're excited to meet and perform for Johnny and his wife Marsha. They're at their hotel and will be arriving later.

A few other rock and metal bands are rehearsing, but everyone is milling around looking depressed. We bump into Greg who himself looks somber. We ask if everything's all right and he says, "You guys didn't hear what happened last night?" We shake our heads. This doesn't sound good.

"Metallica's tour bus crashed last night. I think it was Denmark or Sweden, I'm not sure. But I do know one thing for sure: Cliff Burton died."

Eric laughs nervously—not because he thinks it's funny but because it sounds like it must be a joke. He doesn't know how to react. I'm not sure myself but I try saying, "Are you serious?"

"I may talk a lotta shit, yeah, but trust me, I wouldn't joke about something like that."

*

Meeting Johnny and Marsha for the first time is like being introduced to someone at a funeral. They have a long history with Cliff, as Metallica's original record label before they were bought out by Electra. By all accounts, Cliff was the one that was the most down to earth, and whom Johnny and Marsha never lost their friendship with, even when things got rocky between Megaforce and Metallica.

Months later, we will hear a story from Cliff's actual funeral—Zet spinning donuts in his car, cheerfully yelling to acquaintances as though he were at a party, showing no respect, to the disgust of James and the other Metallica guys. Maybe we're better off without him.

For now, we proceed to run through our set. It goes well enough, but the shadow of Cliff's passing engulfs any sense of enthusiasm.

*

Negotiations begin between our camp and the Megaforce camp.

Twenty years in the future, a humorous document will circulate via a modern electronic form of communication known as e-mail, entitled "36 Rules for Bands." It will include anecdotes that are true more often than not, such as "Never start a trio with a married couple" and "Never name your band after a song" and "Never name a song after your band" But there is one "rule" on the list that is unequivocally true: "Look up the word 'recoupable' in the dictionary." Another such rule should be added: "Look up the term 'trademark search.'"

"You guys have done a trademark search on the name Legacy right?" Elliot asks us during our band meeting following Johnny and Marsha's visit.

Eric answers for us. "Huh? What kinda trip's that?"

"Every band has to do an official 'Trademark Search' just to make sure no one else has registered the name of your band."

"Legacy's *our* trip!"

"Sure it is. But if some other band owns the trademark, even if it's some local band in some small town, if they've registered the name, it's theirs."

"We're Legacy!"

"Look, guys, it's probably nothing to worry about, but I'm going to have to run a Trademark Search, just in case. You can search for three names, a first, second and third choice. Think about what other names you guys want to run through the search."

We have no other names. There *are* no other names…

A week later, we meet with Elliot again. The results of the search are in. "Guys, I'm afraid I've got some bad news…" An R&B cover band at a hotel in New Orleans has trademarked the name Legacy. They've had it for years.

*

Word goes out that we've lost our name and, like a search for a lost kitten, all within reach, East Coast and West Coast, are asked for help coming up with a new one.

I try coming up with names—it is the hardest thing I've ever tried to do. *Mystery?* That sounds so lame. *Nemesis?* That sounds alright, but it turns out there's already a band (not a good one) with that name. What about the band I tried to start at Berkeley High, *Black Rose?* That's a Thin Lizzy album. *Fuck…*

Eric comes up with some names, but they all sound like characters from the fantasy board game Dungeons & Dragons. Johnny Z comes up with some names but they're all forgettable. Even my father suggests a name he thinks will be great for a band: *Hardball.* (God help us…)

It is Billy Milano, singer of SOD—a great side project with members of the band Anthrax (and produced by Alex Periales, our soon-to-be producer)—who comes up with the name *Testament.* It has a similar phonetic sound as Legacy and, as alluded to in an earlier chapter, has a lettering scheme similar to Diamond (DiaMonD) who, by now, has long since broken up. If we make use of the letters T and A (no relation to the salacious term "T & A"), it actually makes for a powerful logo: TestAmenT. We'll try living with that for a while.

My father, someone who has been completely against my career and with very little to offer in terms of useful advice, actually surprises me by being on the money with a theory about band names. He points out that The Beatles is really not a great name for a band. He likes The Bee Gees better — not musically, but phonetically. I see his point. Obviously, The Beatles' greatness made up for any discrepancy in their band name. But it is those names that have a slight rhyme to them that are really catchy: Rolling Stones, Led Zeppelin, Black Sabbath, Bee Gees, U2. (Many years later: White Stripes). Testament may be one word, but it has that double syllable rhyme scheme.

Testament will take some time to get used to. Some will make fun of the name, calling it "Testicles." (We'll respond by printing up a t-shirt saying, Testicles: Metal With Balls). We'll hear that Metallica's James Hetfield, upon hearing it responded, "It sounds like a toothpaste." But none of that that matters, or like James will sing in five years: "Nothing else matters."

We need a new name. Testament is the best we've got. It's *all* we've got. Testament it is.

*

The Oakland studio closes down for some reason and we begin rehearsing at a just-opened rehearsal studio in Hayward, a couple of towns East of Oakland. With two industrial storage buildings and multiple sized rooms, it is perfect for many different levels of bands. It's owned by a hard-edged, slightly militant, middle-aged former Hayward cop.

The ex-cop studio owner has a brother who is his polar opposite: an easygoing, smiling, laid back aging hippie/stoner who helps him run the studio. He's the embodiment of *Freedom Rock,* a compilation album of mid-'70s American rock that gets advertised on TV late at night with a 1-800 number and is fun to make fun of (*"Is that Freedom Rock man?" "Well, crank it up, man!"*). The brother, like the owner himself, doesn't get the thrash metal thing. But listening to me warm up from the hallway, he hears a musical quality he recognizes. After making some positive comments on my playing, he encourages me to check out the guitar players from the '70s: The Allman Brothers, Johnny Winter, Leslie West & Mountain, Tommy Bolin, Steve Gaines of Lynyrd Skynyrd, etc…

One day, he comes to work with a stack of records to loan me. I take them home and transcribe a lot of the licks. The next week, when he pops into our room and asks if I got a chance to check out those records, I play some of my recently learned licks on my guitar. He decides right there and then that those records, which he's had since the '70s, are more useful in (and for) my hands than his. He tells me to keep 'em. I say no, but polite resistance is futile—he insists. I'm grateful as these albums open up a chapter in rock history I wasn't aware of and expose me to new guitar players, especially Leslie West on Mountain's "Flowers of Evil." It not only strengthens the feel of my playing, but helps me get a better grip on the work of UFO, MSG guitarist Michael Schenker, who has cited Leslie West as an influence. This wayward brother to a hard ass Hayward ex-cop, the Billy Carter to his Jimmy Carter, has selflessly become a mentor in my unofficial education.

Unfortunately, the band's relationship with his brother, the studio owner, is less than jovial. Eventually, we'll try to move out and he'll confiscate some of the bands equipment because of a disagreement over the bill. We'll end up getting Elliot, our attorney, to go after him. After Elliot threatens him with an injunction, forcing his hand, the guys will see Elliot as a hero and ask him to take over as band manager.

*

For the year or so the Hayward studio is in operation, it becomes *the* place to practice. Being closer to Dublin, it is more convenient for Chuck, who often commutes to practice with members of Violence or Willie from Lääz Rockit, as both bands have started rehearsing there as well. Surprisingly, even the mighty Metallica, along with a team of production managers and techs, has set up camp there to audition bass players in search of Cliff Burton's replacement.

An all-points bulletin has gone out to the bass community of the Bay Area metal scene to try out for Metallica. At every rehearsal, we bump into bass players lining up to audition. The stories add up—Dean from Terminal Shock, our own bassist's roommate and a friend of Cliff's from Castro Valley, comes to his audition methed out, white powder hanging from his nose, tramping around the rehearsal room like he's on an arena stage. Les Claypool from Primus auditions, horrifying James Hetfield (and blowing the gig), by suggesting they jam on a tune by '70s funk/soul band the Isley Brothers. Willie from Lääz Rockit becomes a finalist. Needing a strap, he has gone to our rehearsal room where Chuck, his childhood friend, loans him my strap covered in Madballs (popular rubber balls with creature faces) which I don't mind except when it comes time to rehearse. Chuck tells me to go in and get it. I barge in on Metallica and Willy, apologize that I need my strap back, and promise not to tell anyone.

And for about two weeks in a row, our bass player Greg has been missing—he's not returning calls, not coming to rehearsals, and is being very vague all of a sudden. We're pretty sure he is locked away, preparing for a Metallica audition, but he won't admit it to us.

We've lost a singer, almost lost a record deal, are close to back on track but now we might lose a bass player! Eric and I finally catch Greg on the phone and start yelling at him into the receiver. We're forced to remind him that whether he lands the Metallica gig or not, he's still our bass player and there are just four months till we're slated to go into the studio. Greg auditions and doesn't get chosen. He's back with us, as though he never left.

*

One of the last to audition for Metallica is a guy who flies in from Arizona. I bump into him in the hallway, tell him about my band and he's thrilled to meet me. He says he knows who I am because the guitarists from his own band, Flotsam & Jetsam, have heard our demo tape and are fans of my playing. He seems eager-eyed, enthusiastic, not knowing what to expect but just excited to be in California and having this experience. He shakes my hand eagerly and tells me his name: Jason Newsted.

Jason gets chosen. When I see him a few days later and walk up to congratulate him, he acts like we never met. He nods, makes some comment about the weather and walks away. *Is that the same guy?!* I wonder. He is like a caricature of a nose in the air star. I don't know what could compel him to act like that. Before his audition he was my new friend. Afterwards, I'm not worthy of his acknowledgement? I can't imagine behaving like that and vow never to do so, even if I were to land a gig as big as that. A few years later, he'll remember me and, despite the band's meteoric rise in popularity, his behavior will seem more like the guy I met before the audition. I'll later find out that he'd been the recipient of much ruthless fraternity-like hazing from the other Metallica guys in order to bring him back down to earth.

*

In December of 1986, my brother and I are dragged in typical fashion to a dinner party thrown by an Ivy League couple, academic friends of our parents who teach at Stanford. At the table, one of the hosts asks me, as everyone else listens, what my plans are for next year. I explain what I hadn't had a chance to tell my family yet—that plane tickets have just been bought, hotel rooms reserved and studio time booked in Upstate New York first thing next month, in January.

"Congratulations," they all say, except for my brother, who looks like someone has jammed the serving spoon of yams down his throat. I

126

downplay it, saying the contract was still being negotiated, several more things have to happen before we're touring professionally, but that it looks like, if all goes well, the album will come out next year and we'll be touring soon thereafter.

It is difficult to look over at my brother. The reality is setting in. He's been unable to stay on track at college, fired from nearly every one of his bands, unable to hold down a worthwhile job, is still living at home and unbeknownst to our parents, consuming almost daily doses of marijuana and LSD. He's turned his life into an embarrassment. I refuse to be dragged down by him any longer.

Upon first hearing that I had a possible recording contract in the works, my brother, only half-kiddingly had said, "Maybe I need to join one of these thrash bands!" To him, we'd just gotten lucky—that's all it was. He'd also dismissed my practice and hard work as part of a new "athletic" type of guitar playing that was just a fad. The concepts of music as a vehicle of self-expression, being a true artist and simply appreciating music for its potential to improve the lives of people were nonexistent to him. All he understood was the formula he'd worked out in his head: *Getting signed = no work, no responsibility!* Now, his worst nightmare was coming true: his own little brother, whom he'd taunted and derided from the day he was brought home from Alta Bates hospital, is within arm's length of his mythical holy grail, his ticket to freedom: the record deal.

Even at seventeen years old, I know the truth: that this record deal, assuming it even goes through (we haven't put pen to paper yet), is only a small step. Then the hard work *really* begins. I'm also reticent about the whole thing, never discussing it unless someone brought it up first. But now it's unavoidable.

Next year, it will sink in that I've moved on with my life and he's still stuck at home living like a child. He'll play his bass less and less. He'll find various frivolous excuses to "go away," simply because I'm "going away" (our family therapist will point this out). For example, he'll get involved with volunteer (i.e. unpaid) organization helping build a biosphere-like urban planning project in Yuma, Arizona, only to have the funds cut and the entire project halted before it can be completed. The following year, 1988, he'll travel to Europe with no aim or purpose and, not knowing what to do with himself, catch up with our tour, tag along, doing nothing but getting in everyone's way, not volunteering to help out and scarfing all the food in our dressing room like a starving homeless refugee, until finally I'm asked by the bus driver, the tour manager and others to please ask him to leave (see chapter 27).

But back at that candlelit dinner, a regular ritual where any warm feelings brought upon by the gourmet food and wine are regularly shot down by the scar-inducing judgment and covertly dismissive behavior of our parents and their hyper-academic colleagues, I finally have something to show for all the hard work I've been putting in since I was ten. No, it's not a PhD. No, it doesn't necessarily mean I'll be rich and famous like Kiss or Van Halen, but it's *something.*

For the first time, I am truly excited about the future. And unfortunately it comes at the cost of putting a bullet in the delusions that have been driving my brother for ten years now. Out of the corner of my eye, I can see him sinking into a depression, one from which he'll never recover.

*

There is a brilliant scene at the end of *Boogie Nights*, where actor Mark Wahlberg, playing down-on-his-luck porn star Dirk Diggler, has just recorded a certifiably awful demo tape. He pathetically pleads at the top of his lungs with a recording studio owner who is holding the recording hostage until he gets paid: "We'll give you the money when we get the record deal! How can we get the record deal if you won't give us the tapes?!"

Dirk Diggler and my brother both suffered from the same syndrome: a drug induced delusional idea that signing a piece of paper with a record company will be the ticket to easy street—the answer to all of life's challenges. It never is.

In the late '90s, while studying jazz at New School University in New York, I'd see the whole syndrome of bad signings from a new perspective. More than one of my teachers would be the victim of bad record deals from the '70s or '80s. No longer owning the rights to their master tapes, they'd be forced to sit and watch as their record labels folded, their former owners not releasing the rights to the music. One such teacher/musician would be selling copies of his critically acclaimed but commercially unavailable album on cassette tapes to his students, the original cover copied like a black and white promotional flyer. My father had been right about one thing: never sign anything without the consent of an attorney.

In most cases, signing that record deal, even a half-decent one like we were signing, is where the challenges of being in a band really begin. And during a frozen January in Upstate New York, the recordings for the first Testament album would be no exception.

Part V

SHOWTIME 8:00 PM

"It's a long way to the top (if you wanna rock 'n' roll)."

-Song by AC/DC (Lyrics by Bon Scott)

"Fame is something that must be won. Honor is something that must not be lost."

-Arthur Schopenhauer

19. WINTER FRESHMEN

The small plane touched down on the frozen runway, slowing down as a warm voice came on the overhead speakers. We'd all been taken aback by the mild blizzard outside the windows, but it was obviously a routine landing—the pilot welcomed us to Ithaca as though it were a clear spring day rather than a snowy winter night. Outside, the ground was blanketed white, the sky resembling a just shaken snow-globe.

As we exited the plane, descending upon the tarmac, we could all see our breath in the cold. A couple of guys were wearing Bermuda shorts, very popular at the time, (the next day they'd be picking up some warmer clothes from the local Woolworths). As the shivers began, the reality dawned upon all of us: we were no longer in the San Francisco Bay Area.

Though we'd been flying all day, first to JFK, then to Ithaca Regional Airport, it was still hard to believe this was actually happening. I'd never flown cross-country without my parents. Now here I was with this thrash metal band I'd somehow found my way into, along with our first manager. As with my real family, I was the baby of the group. But unlike my biological family, when it came to this new "family" of mine, it often felt as though I were older than some of the others.

As more and more drinks had been ordered from the beverage carts, the behavior had become increasingly unruly. Two guys in particular, Eric and Lou, both of them short, slightly pudgy with the same long straight hair styles and matching sneakers (we called them "Heckle and Jekyll" or "Frick and Frack"), had been causing scenes the whole way. Oblivious to the stares of the other passengers, they'd been pushing and taunting each other from their adjoining seats: *"Fuck you Lou, you're trippin!" "Uh uh, Eric, fuck YOU, you're trippin." "No, you're trippin." "No, you are." "Uh uh." "Uh huh! "Nah uh!" "Uh huh!"* at which point, they'd start tickling each other and giggling profusely. It was strange to fly with guys who were less mature than I'd been as a ten year old.

Waiting inside the terminal was our first ever producer, Alex Perialas, his wife, and their librarian-like studio receptionist. The three Ithacans welcomed us as though we were long lost kin—their shy, scraggily distant cousins from another land. Introductions were made as the luggage arrived on the conveyor belt. Then we walked through the bitter cold of the parking lot, got into three vehicles with snow tires, and off we drove to check into the Ramada Inn—our home for the next six weeks.

*

With his wire rim spectacles, shiny bald head, thick black sideburns and mustache, Alex Perialas had the aura of someone in his fifties. In truth, he was just in his early thirties. He would become an uncle-figure to our group, taking us under his wing with advice, lectures and in some cases, parental discipline. Alex had opened Pyramid Sound studios with help from his father, the town's local real estate mogul, said to literally own half of Ithaca. Pyramid was bigger than both our previous recording studios combined.

Upon first entering, there was a waiting room with leather couches, coffee tables and stacks of music industry magazines—*Billboard, Mix* and *Rolling Stone*. On the walls in the hallway were displays of all the records that had been done there, including a few we were familiar with: Overkill, Anthrax, SOD, Nuclear Assault. That hallway led to the control room, which was dominated by a giant mixing console; it looked like the controls of an ocean liner. Two elegant office chairs on wheels faced the board and behind them, in the back of the room, was a plush leather couch. All of this looked into the main recording room, which featured a grand piano and a drum kit. The entire place had natural wood paneling, giving it the feel of a ski cabin.

Next to the grand piano in the main room, was a stack of cardboard boxes of various sizes, some of them practically life size. "What's all that stuff?" we asked Alex P. He explained: this was our brand new equipment that had arrived the previous day. *"Ours?"* we asked incredulously.

Somehow, in the chaos of rehearsals and preparing for the trip, we'd completely forgotten: we'd ordered all new amps, pedals, effects racks, cables and other equipment, paid for out of our recording budget ($25,000, not great, but not bad). This had been necessary—our gear at home had been primitive, the result of trades with friends, garage sale acquisitions, some of it borrowed, much of it not working properly. In my case, after getting stuck with so many lemons over the years, I'd finally have my dream rig: a brand new, state-of-the-art Marshall Stack.

Like toddlers, we scampered into the big room and began ravenously tearing open the boxes. It was Christmas in January, a feeling only enhanced by the ski cabin-like feel of the studio and the snow outside.

*

For the next few days, the routine was more or less like this: we'd wake up, call the other guys (there were two of us per room), and whoever was up by then would have breakfast at a diner and drop by Pyramid. Any late risers would show up eventually.

At that point, most of us weren't needed yet in the studio except for Lou, as the activity was limited to the drum kit: changing the heads, miking the drums, dialing in sounds, etc. This gave the rest of us the chance to walk around and take in our new surroundings.

The irony of being in Ithaca hit me right away; the similarities to Berkeley were uncanny. Ithaca was a host to Cornell University in the same way that Berkeley was to the University of California. Ithaca was about the same size as Berkeley and had the same odd dynamic of a constantly shifting population, the majority of whom were there to attend university and leave. Among the permanent residents were, as in Berkeley, an unusually large subgroup of aging hippies, younger hippies who'd taken up after them and an upper middle class of university faculty removed from the rest of the population. Underneath was a downtrodden lower class that resided permanently in the shadow of the university and its prosperousness.

Like Berkeley, Ithaca was a pleasant place to explore. There were many sophisticated stores that sold books, art, gifts and designer furniture, as well as many coffee houses, ethnic food establishments and a number of upscale restaurants, including one that had shot to international fame: Moosewood Restaurant, which felt like Ithaca's counterpart to Berkeley's Chez Panisse.

Yet despite the similarities, Ithaca had certain qualities that were unique to Upstate New York. It was here we'd experience a new form of spicy bar food: Buffalo Wings (then unheard of outside New York), the magic ingredient being Frank's Red Hot sauce, which I began adding to everything: omelets, pizza, deli sandwiches. The beer of choice came in a small green bottle—it was one I'd never encountered on the West Coast but that everyone seemed to drink in Upstate New York: Rolling Rock.

The local taverns, meanwhile, had a warm energy that was influenced by the people of the region—it was easier to talk to people, even strangers, than it was in the Bay Area. Everyone did shots together, including oyster shooters, which I'd never had before, and this liqueur from Greece, ouzo, which I couldn't stand the taste of but participated in nonetheless. Ithaca had a pace that, although slow compared to its famous neighbor several hours south named after the state, was leagues beyond the SF Bay Area. People moved faster and cut through nonsense quicker.

I liked being in Ithaca—the new flavors and slightly faster pace were exciting to me. Most surprisingly, I even liked the cold and the snow. Something just felt very natural about the changing of the seasons—I wasn't allergic to cold weather like some of the other guys. I didn't know it at the time, but the first inklings that I belonged on the East Coast were beginning right there and then.

*

A few of these bars would become second homes to us.[29] There was a tiny corner bar right across from our hotel called The Ritz.

About a fifteen minute walk to the other side of town was a large nightclub we'd end up going to most weekends: Captain Joe's Reef. Captain Joe's had live music and the best hot wings in town. One of the bartenders there, Gordy, had been immortalized on the SOD album in a track that was just a couple seconds long, its only lyric being "Hey, Gordy, Gimme a Shot!"

Now for one moment, let's be completely honest about something: everyone was young, undisciplined, consuming lots of alcohol, far away from home and male. In other words, most of us had girlfriends, but the reality was this: all bets were off.

Chuck strikes up a friendship with one of the bartenders at the Ritz, Terri. She's a non-metal chick, curly haired, freckled Irish/Italian girl from Long Island, listens to Springsteen. They like each other but nothing ever happens—she's too hung up on this married cop. Nonetheless, we begin seeing a lot more of Terri and like having her around.

One day, Terri stops by the studio and brings her roommate, Cindy. Cindy's tall and beautiful, like Julia Roberts with dark hair and large boobs, not that it matters (ok, maybe a little). Void of all the trappings of so many

---

[29] At the time, the legal drinking age in New York State was 18 years old. I was able to get into the bars legally.

metal girls I know—drugs, promiscuity and superficiality—she listens to James Taylor and Carly Simon. We hit it off right away.

The following night, we're all at the Ritz while Cindy is tending bar there. Alexis, our manager and friend from the ninth grade (to whom by now I'm no longer close to), tries to hand his hotel room key to her. She throws it back in his face. I'm impressed.

I begin going to The Ritz by myself, sitting and talking to Cindy while she works the bar. I could be wrong, but she seems to like having me there. At one point, I'm surprised to receive a beautiful handwritten poem slipped under my hotel room door – it's from Cindy. Towards the end of our stay, my friendship with Cindy will culminate into a passionate affair. One night after she closes up The Ritz, we'll make love on the bowling machine. For the first time I experience a relationship where there is a connection, along with chemistry and mutual appreciation. She helps me realize how much better I deserve than the abysmal relationship I'm stuck in back home (more on that later).

Over the next few years, we'll have many secret long distance phone calls (the days before Facebook and Skype), and eventually move in together in the early nineties. Unfortunately, by then, I'll realize my former dream girl and I are completely incompatible. We'll break up two years later.

*

One night, we're all having wings and beers at Captain Joe's. The place is packed and everyone is getting drunk as this really cool ZZ Top tribute band is playing.

Alex P walks up to the stage and has some words with the singer/guitarist who, just like the real singer/guitarist of ZZ Top, Billy Gibbons, has a big bushy beard down to his belly. Suddenly, I notice them pointing at me. It turns out Alex is insisting that they let me sit in, but the singer is resisting. Alex goes so far as to get on the mic and announce, "I've got a kid here that can play a mean guitar. He'll rock the house. How many of you want to get your socks rocked off?" The crowd cheers, especially our table. Alex pushes and pushes, debating the singer over the PA system until finally he relents.

I end up jamming with the band on ZZ's classic "Tush." They give me an extended solo which gets a good response from the crowd. Suddenly, "Billy Gibbons" cues the band to quiet down, challenging me by addressing the crowd: "Alright. This kid's pretty good. But I'll bet he don't know no Hendrix!" I respond by quoting Jimi Hendrix's "Purple Haze," with the key and time feel adjusted to fit over the rhythm. The crowd cheers even louder as the singer interrupts and says, "Hang on, hang on! Alright, the kid got me

GEEK TO GUITAR HERO

there. But hey—if anyone knows one Hendrix tune, it's that one! I'll bet this kid don't know no other Hendrix tune!" I launch into "Voodoo Chile (Slight Return)," which surprisingly fits well with the timing. The band adjusts its groove to that of the original Hendrix track, and I start playing the screaming guitar solos, which at this point, I know in my sleep, having studied "Voodoo Chile" on three albums: *Electric Ladyland, The Jimi Hendrix Concerts* and *Couldn't Stand Weather* by Stevie Ray Vaughn. As though we'd rehearsed it, we launch right back into "Tush" without missing a beat.

The crowd goes berserk. The confounded singer gives it up to me, and I receive several ovations from the crowd. It is a triumphant moment. Afterwards, everyone shakes my hand, we all hang out and talk over drinks. I'm proud to have earned their respect.

*

A few nights later, the same band is playing again at Captain Joe's. I go down by myself, bright-eyed and eager to get to know my new friends better. The singer sees me, looks away and goes to talk to someone else. His band-mates don't say a word to me; a few of them glance over, then look away. One of their girlfriends walks up to me and says "Well, look who it is! You come down to steal the show again?"

I'm in shock. I walk out of the bar, choking on my inability to respond, then head back to the hotel through the snow. Only years later will I be able to reflect upon the experience with a proper perspective.

They didn't seem like bad people. Sure, they could have been nicer to me when I came back around. But I can't imagine they'd have snubbed me like that had they known where I was coming from.

How could they possibly have known how paralyzed I was by my own feelings of worthlessness and inadequacy? From their vantage point, I was no different than those obnoxious students from nearby Cornell and Ithaca College—the ones who'd come into town, take over all the bars, act like they owned the place, look down on the locals, then disappear forever.

They saw me as this young "hot shot" guitarist who'd soon be gone, off to wherever my life and music career would take me. Meanwhile, they'd still be in that little town, working their day jobs, paying bills and looking forward to the one thing that gave their lives meaning: that gig. I would have never agreed to play if I'd had any clue that it would be like crashing their party.

Alex P had meant no harm dragging me up there to play with them, but I realized that I shouldn't allow myself to be pushed into a situation like that. In the future, I'd be more sensitive to other musicians at all levels,

135

especially hard working guys like this, whose sole existence revolves around their local gig.

The lesson learned: *If a band invites you to come up and sit in with them, then by all means, do so. But never push yourself or allow yourself to be pushed upon someone else's gig by sitting in uninvited.*

*

Throughout the recording sessions, the band would receive many lectures from Alex P about not staying out too late, mostly unheeded. Many times, the guys, particularly Eric and Greg, would come in dreadfully ill from hangovers, sometimes barely able to play.

One evening, my roommate, Greg, came back from the Ritz more drunk than I'd ever seen him. It was amazing he'd found his way back to our room. Lying on his belly, he began vomiting in his sleep. With images of Bon Scott and John Bonham in my head (late hard rock legends who'd choked on their own vomit), I turned him on his side and checked to make sure he was still breathing throughout the night.

Cindy, who'd been working the bar, not realizing he'd already been drinking heavily when he'd stopped in for one last nightcap, served him as he'd ordered multiple shots of ouzo. She was extremely regretful.

*

Despite the alcohol-induced insanity taking place on the town at night, during the day it was all business, at least over at Pyramid.

Alex's work ethic was unblemished by any partying. He would join us for beers after a long day, or on the weekends, but always remained in control (I suppose someone had to). In addition to being the producer, Alex was engineering, assisted by various interns who'd come down from Ithaca College's recording department. It was fascinating watching them work from the ground up: patching cables, designating tracks, mapping out a calendar and goals for each day and week, etc.

One of the things I liked best about being "in the studio" was that suddenly we were interacting with people who were smart—creative, analytical thinkers—no longer limited to the social limitations and lack of professionalism in our local scene. After so many years where being a musician had been synonymous with being *laid back* and not taking things seriously, it was refreshing to be in a place where creating music meant showing up to work on time and working hard. Being "in the studio" at this level gave an air of legitimacy to our music and combated the image unfairly projected upon me by my parents and teachers—that "music people" are flakey, incompetent deadbeats.

There were, however, a few things about the recording process itself that I didn't like, at least in the early phase of these particular sessions.

For example, during the tracking of the drums, we'd have to play along by laying down "scratch tracks" that were for reference only and sounded absolutely god-awful. The reason for this was that we couldn't use our overpowering amplifiers without bleeding into the drum tracks. With terrible guitar sounds like this, it was difficult to get inspired, and difficult to inspire our drummer to play his best.

Today, things are different—there are microprocessors and computer plug-ins which sound much closer to a real amp without speakers. This way there's no bleeding—they plug directly into the console. Sometimes these processed tracks are even usable in the final mix. But back then, with the way Pyramid was set up, the only way to track drums was to play guitar through a direct, partially distorted signal that sounded more or less like a fart.

*

About midway through the first week, the drums were miked, the headphones dialed in, and it was time to start recording. On we slogged for days and days until we had usable drum tracks. Then came the bass, which really should have been recorded with the guitar for maximum tightness.

When Eric and I finally recorded our rhythms, we had to adjust to Greg's bass. This made little sense—in reality, he should have been adjusting to us, but there'd been no way for him to do so with our muddy scratch tracks. Another thing we realized—Eric and I had been doing many of the rhythms slightly differently from one another. There were different "chug" patterns and in some cases, different single note patterns—it had been hard to tell, playing full blast in rehearsals. Now, all the parts had to be broken down, examined, tightened up and the permanent patterns agreed upon. We'd never looked at our music under a microscope like this before. Essentially, that's what the studio was: a giant microscope.

*

On the day I was scheduled to begin recording guitar solos, the studio lounge felt like the waiting room of a doctor's office, and I was the patient.

Eric and Lou were teasing me and for good reason: I was shaking all over. Asking them to leave so I could practice, I'd been reduced to a quivering bundle of melodrama. They left, and I turned off the TV, which had been permanently set on MTV, repeatedly playing videos of songs I'd forever associate with this time period: Genesis: "Land of Confusion," Bon Jovi: "Livin' on a Prayer" and Def Leppard: "Rockit." Although we'd never have a hit on this level, we would soon find ourselves on MTV, via the newly created metal show known as *Headbangers Ball.*

After a half hour or so of fretboard gymnastics, I was called into the control room.

At first, every time Alex P pressed the red "record" button, I felt like I was stepping up to do a high dive in the Olympics. But eventually, I adjusted to the feel of playing along with a recorded track. I was finally getting my feet wet.

Alex gave good guidance: he'd let me know whenever he thought a solo was worth keeping or if parts of it were. He could also hear slight discrepancies and tuning issues that I couldn't hear yet. Occasionally he'd stop me unexpectedly, but it was always for a good reason. I'd do several takes before I found an idea I remotely liked. Then, I'd develop this take into something more solid. I still work this way when recording metal solos, but it takes a lot less time these days. Also, today, you have the option of keeping as many solos as you want. But back then, you quickly began running out of tracks and had to erase previous solos.

I was learning that much of recording, especially guitar solos, is creating illusion. Hard rock and metal solos are rarely played all the way through—they're usually done section by section, even by the most acclaimed players. There's just no other way—the potential for excess noise is too great, much more so than with jazz or blues guitar tone. But the larger sections you pull off at a time, the better your solo will sound. Occasionally you'll get lucky on a first take all the way through (as I would two years later on "Practice What You Preach"), but most often you do the best you can and then fix it.

As my ears developed over time, I would be able to hear solos on albums that were obviously not done in a solid take.

Some of Eddie Van Halen's early solos are exceptions, which is why I'm such a fan of those initial Van Halen albums (all the ones with David Lee Roth on vocals). But if you listen to Eddie's solo on Michael Jackson's "Beat It," there are slight glitches between the two-bar sections. I'm not saying it's not a great solo, or even that this makes it less worthy, only that it was obviously pieced together. This conflicts with producer Quincy Jones' famous story about Eddie coming in one night and knocking out the solo in a single take. It's a perfect example of those words that were mentioned in an earlier chapter: *If the legend sounds better than the truth, go with the legend.*

*

In the days before it was time to do my solos, I'd be locked away in the Ramada Inn all day, practicing as hard as I ever have. This had been my plan all along, but I'd been pushed even harder by two other factors.

One was the fact that while tracking the drums, Chuck had been harping on me about how bad the solos sounded. He was totally right, of course, but the problem hadn't been any lack of preparation on my part. Not to make excuses, but the issue was this atrocious scratch guitar tone that we'd been using. His haranguing caused me to practice much harder, which wasn't a bad thing. I knew the solos would sound good once I was no longer forced to play with that 'fart' sound.

Another thing that pushed me to practice harder: during the rhythm guitar tracking, Eric had been having trouble playing this one clean part I'd written, the intro for a track, "Apocalyptic City." It utilized these crazy, stretchy chord voicings that Joe Satriani had taught me. Alex P asked me to come in and play it, but I wasn't pulling it off either—it still lacked the precision necessary for the studio.

That's when Alex P brought up the idea of bringing in a local session guitarist to play the part, a guy whom he referred to only as the great "Chad." Supposedly Chad was one of the best in the business; according to Alex, this guy woke up every morning and practiced guitar "before taking a piss." "Let's just bring in Chad," he said. It would save time and money. Besides, there were other albums he'd produced (not to be named here) where this guy was brought in to play certain parts. Alex told me to relax—it was nothing to be ashamed of.

I timidly told Alex P that I could play it if I just had a little bit of time to work on it. But inside I was thinking: *No fucking way am I going to have an outside guitarist come in and play a part on my album because I "can't do it."* Alex made a deal with me: we could hold off for now, but if I couldn't pull it off within a week, we'd risk being behind schedule, in which

case, we'd have to consider bringing in Chad. I woke up every day and (admittedly after taking a piss), practiced the part religiously. It took several days, but it became very natural to play, and the hard work I was putting into it carried over into my practicing for the guitar solos.

A few days later, I came into the studio to give it another try. I nailed the part.

Some fifteen years later, in New York City, I'd meet a young jazz vibraphonist who'd hire me for some gigs. During rehearsals, he'd mention this other guitarist he's been working with recently, saying we remind him of each other—both of us are proficient in jazz and rock. He'd add that while he likes this other guitarist, he prefers my playing to his.

"Who is he?" I'd ask.

"You probably wouldn't know him. The guy just moved to the City this year, after getting a divorce. He's been one of the top session guitarists Upstate for years."

"Where's he from?"

"Ithaca."

"Uh, his name wouldn't happen to be Chad, would it?"

"Yeah, that's the guy! You know him?"

*

While there was minimal band drama during this recording (there would be plenty of that later), there were increasing problems with our manager, Alexis.

It was a difficult dilemma: he'd been my friend since we were high school freshman, had introduced me to the band and had been around, albeit contentiously, every step of the way. But now, as we were recording our first album, the issues with him were stacking up like a pile of unpaid parking tickets. There were missed conference calls with our lawyer and the record label's lawyer. He'd misunderstand the time, forget to write it down, or most often, after a night of carousing, he'd simply oversleep. Inexperienced with contract negotiation, he'd been instructing our attorney to cave in on key issues, compromising our negotiating positions and damaging our future leverage with the label. Hampering the process even further, a lot of basic grammar had to be explained to him. Remember, he'd been in those low-level classes at Berkeley High (see chapter 18), so when it came to sophisticated legal terms, he was completely lost. Our manager's incompetence was the one thing the two opposing attorneys solidly agreed upon.

Then there was the matter of his phone diction—he had a deep, indecipherable voice, like Johnny Cash on qualudes. Back when Zet was the singer, he'd warned us about this, holding out the phone with a loud whisper: "What the hell is this guy saying? He's our manager and we can't even fucking understand him on the phone?!" The low mumbling had reminded me of the teacher in the Peanuts cartoons, Ms. Othmar, which was voiced by a muted trumpet or trombone. "Wa WA wa WA WA WA." The others laughed when I mentioned this.

From then on, we'd privately refer to him as "Othmar."

*

Things came to a head about mid-way through *The Legacy* sessions, as Alexis was scheduled to fly home from Ithaca a few weeks before the rest of us.

Shortly before his flight, he arrived at the studio with a special thanks list in his hand which he presented as though he'd just created the Mona Lisa or the Brandenburg Concertos: it was his masterpiece. Unable to type, he'd spent untold hours of time writing it out by hand in pen (time which could have, and should have, been more productively spent). Though legible, it had inexcusable misspellings and looked as though it had been written by a third-grader. More troubling was the amount of names—they outnumbered all of ours combined and would have taken up most of the entire back cover of the album (and these were the days of vinyl).

The list began with a mini love poem and dedication to someone named "Naomi" (not her real name). *"Who the hell is she?"* the guys wanted to know. I was the one other person who knew: she was this girl from Berkeley High who was supposedly heir to a fortune that he'd somehow convinced himself he would one day marry (no doubt for her money). She had nothing to do with the band, had never even been to a show and most of us had never even met her. From what I'd seen, he wasn't even dating this girl; meanwhile he was hitting on everything which had a vagina. Now he wanted our album dedicated to his *"fiancé*?!"

The problems with him and girls hadn't been limited to this incident. Over the years, he'd frequently stake claim on a girl, telling all his friends, myself included, to stay away. Most of the time, these girls wanted nothing to do with him—any initial interest was quickly dissipated by his obsessive, aggressive behavior. One time, this had happened with a girl, let's call her "Denise," who'd suddenly developed an interest in me. Unable to say no to a girl (which would cause me even worse problems, as you'll soon see), I hooked up with Denise. He stopped speaking to me and stopped managing the band unofficially.

Showing up at rehearsal a month or so later, he ignored me but said to the others he'd found it in his heart to do them the favor of managing them again, despite the fact that I, now his enemy, was in the band. It was Zet who confronted him, aggressively announcing "If you're gonna manage us, Alexis, you're gonna get over this little problem you're having with *our* guitar player." It felt good to be stood up for. Zet made him shake my hand, which he did awkwardly. Alexis agreed to try to put the "Denise incident" behind him.

But he never would.

*

When asked about the size of his special thanks list, Alexis told the rest of us that we'd simply have to shorten our own lists to make room for all his names; they were important. When confronted about the dedication, he claimed to be deeply hurt that we'd question his feelings for his "fiancé." He flew back to the Bay Area barely speaking to us.

Months later, at the guys' urging, our lawyer, Elliot Cahn, would become the manager of the band. He'd recruit his friend and fellow lawyer, a rail thin man with a falsetto voice, Jeff Saltzman, as his partner, the two of them forming a management company Cahn-Man.

Alexis would hire another Bay Area attorney, Barry Simon[30], to negotiate a settlement with us, which none of us had a problem with—after all, despite everything, he had played a role in where we'd come thus far.

Meanwhile, being fired from Testament would cause his self-inflicted wounds from the Denise incident to be reopened. He would harp to all within earshot about how the band, and especially me, had screwed him. He'd mark me as an all-out, hands down, no holds barred enemy (I'd take some comfort in the fact that he had many enemies). He'd try framing me at a party, telling a severely drunk and distraught Paul Baloff that I'd been badmouthing Paul's recently deceased wolf (excuse me?), then take credit for diffusing the situation. Others at the party would call him out on this right there, and he'd suffer a loss of credibility from the incident.

Any hopes I'd have that he and I would salvage our friendship would be gone forever. That day we'd met in the ninth grade, changed the signs on that truck and gotten chased by the driver would forever be relegated to that of a mere distant memory.

But before all that, Chuck, Eric, Lou, Greg and I would fly home from Ithaca together, having just completed our very first album. A few days later, we'd meet at Eric's to have a conference call with our manager Alexis, firing him on the spot. Immediately afterwards, we'd drink heavily, then find a parlor close to the Alameda Naval Base where we'd get matching skull tattoos.

*

When I look back upon flying across the US to record *The Legacy*, I can't help but think of it as a major "coming of age" event both for the band and for myself personally.

As an album, *The Legacy* is good for what it is. There are some really strong moments—it's a very young thrash band touching on some interesting ideas, not quite finding them yet, but showing enough potential to justify making a next album when the time came (touring behind each album

---

[30] Ironically, Barry Simon would join my e-mail list and send me friendly messages of support in the 2000s.

would make us a much better band). We would do better recordings in the future.

The album isn't the triumphant debut that I'd dreamed of *à la* Van Halen and Led Zeppelin. Then again, that's an impossible comparison. Those were major label debuts by bands with many years of experience, forerunners of their genres, led by guitarists in their twenties who'd already found themselves (and weren't sharing the sonic air with another guitarist, let alone one who insisted on being louder in the mix).

My solos were nowhere near the level I'd reach in a few years. So while I'm pleased with my work on the album for being eighteen years old, I'm happy it's not the only thing I'll be remembered by. In several years, I might have honed in on a stronger musical and personal identity, or not, but in 1987, I was fresh out of high school and pretty lost in life. I didn't have five years or so to toil in the music scene and find myself on the local scene, or do what other young aspiring guitarists were doing: moving to LA, New York or Boston, auditioning for bands, starting their own and/or attending music college. I didn't even have the confidence to pull off something like that.

Despite creating this opportunity to do an actual record, my parents were continuing to express pessimism whenever the subject of my future arose. Their endless hostility, dismay and disgust that I was planning music as a long-term career left me with no choice but to put the resulting emotional baggage into my guitar playing and hope the music would take me as far away from Berkeley and my strange upbringing as possible.

These were the cards I'd been dealt and this album was the shot I'd been given—I had to take it. It would be many years before I'd adequately be able to process, digest and reflect upon all I'd experienced during January of 1987 in Ithaca, New York.

20. BLUE VAN TOUR

There's nothing like being thrown into your first tour. Suddenly you find yourself in front of an audience every single night, not just once every couple of months. Every note you play matters, so you'd better make it count. Unlike the rehearsal room, there's no room for stopping and starting and no place for self-consciousness on that stage. Just getting out there and going for it night after night takes you to another level, separating you from your neighbors in the practice spot: the locals, part-timers and day jobbers.

The machinery, momentum and motion of the constant shows and travel can cause some bands to become stronger and others to become damaged. For us, it would be a little bit of both.

While we'd never done a full-blown tour before, there had been a couple of road trips. The previous year, there'd been a show in LA followed by one in nearby Corona, CA, about 50 miles away, both supporting Anthrax, whom we'd be joining up with on this tour. Seeing Anthrax had been a bit of a wake-up call. We weren't sure about the vocals at first—it was as though the singer of Journey was singing thrash—but it grew on us. The lead guitar wasn't too exciting—it blended in. But they had one of the best rhythm sections we'd seen—Charlie Benante, whose drum tone and groove was and is so good that he could back up anyone; Scott Ian, who gave the rhythm guitar more character and personality than most soloists; and

Frank Bello as a solid player whose presence could rival any lead singer. We'd also realized how perverted some road crew members could be when one of Anthrax's techs, let's just call him 'Al,' showed us a photo scrapbook that was like a homemade *Hustler* magazine. All of it was shot in the back of the Anthrax tour bus—Polaroid close-ups of female fans' breasts, rear ends, vaginas, you name it. Somehow Al's photographic endeavors were much more odd and bizarre than erotic.

And in the months between returning from Ithaca and leaving for this tour, we'd gotten a last minute offer to fly in and out of New York to open for Slayer at L'amour. That had been an interesting trip.

*

L'amour was located in Borough Park in Brooklyn. The show was on a Saturday evening. Essentially, this meant that we'd be arriving right at sundown, the end of Shabbat (the Jewish Sabbath), in the middle of an enclave of ultra-Orthodox, Hasidic Jews.

Pulling up to the venue just as the synagogues were letting out, the streets were paraded with long black-coated men with bushy beards, hats and yarmulkes. Looking out the windows of our shuttle van, the others started asking me, the sole Jew of the band, what the deal was. Who were they? Why the outfits? What were they all doing?

I honestly didn't know the answers. I'd never seen anything like this spectacle in California. I could only guess that those toy-soldier-like figures were like my people's strange distant relatives who kept to themselves and clung to archaic traditions. I'd pretty much been right about that.

Interspersed among the Hasidim were small pockets of equally striking individuals. These people looked like a different religious sect, also dressed in mostly black, but with scary t-shirts and arms with whole sleeves of tattoos—these were the Slayer fans. Out there on the sidewalk, the Slayer fans were peacefully coexisting with their Hasidic neighbors, as though they were en route to their own black sabbath. But that would all change once they arrived at the venue.

Slayer fans in New York had a reputation for being especially ruthless. If they didn't like the support act (and they rarely did), they'd make it known, chewing up and spitting out opening bands alive. Our first album hadn't come out yet, so we were marked for death.

I'll never forget the heckling, as we launched into our first song. It was as though we were members of the Boston Red Sox crashing a rally for the New York Yankees:

Booooooooooo!! You guyz suck!!! Ya hear me? You SUCK!!! Where's Slayeh?!!

Soon, they began to chant: *Slay yeh! Slay-yeh! Slay-yeh!*

As we played on, the hecklers continued their assault but midway through our set, it was clear we weren't going to buckle; they began losing their spirit. A few rowdies in the front row tried to spit on our singer but unbeknownst to them, they'd met their match. Chuck one-upped them by spitting on Eric, Lou, Greg and myself. *Spitting on his own band?!* They froze in disbelief as Chuck launched into his next trick: spitting up into the air and catching it in his own mouth; the front row helplessly stared, bug-eyed. As we launched into our "mosh-inducing" anthem "Apocalyptic City," Chuck began his grand finale—spitting on the spitters in the front row like one of those tennis ball machines. They began cheering uncontrollably.

Soon, no one was heckling anymore—the cheers throughout L'Amour blasted out the few remaining boos. We played our last notes and left. Backstage, Johnny Z and the rest of the Megaforce entourage congratulated us. Everyone said that if we could survive a Slayer crowd in New York, we could survive anything.

*

With the gear packed into a yellow Ryder Truck and the band crammed into a blue van, we set off for nearly two months.

The van had no back seats and was fitted with makeshift Styrofoam mattresses. In order to get any rest on overnight drives, our legs would have to be lifted, our feet placed upon the walls of the van. After seven weeks of this, it would feel strange to lie down on a bed normally.

A lot of activity would take place in that van: travelling, eating, sleeping, changing clothes, arguing, drinking, pot smoking, romps with female fans (including a few group sex escapades), and going for days without showers. I can still smell the scent of beer bottles, fast food containers, empty soda cans, condom wrappers and marijuana roaches competing with the foul stench of stray sneakers and dirty socks.

Needless to say, any glamorous notions about the entry level of the music business were quickly dispelled.

*

Some bands are able to fall into touring mode quite easily—they just have the instincts to automatically adjust and be comfortable on the road, play a great show every night, take care of business, meet the fans and have a good time in the process. We were not that band.

Since I was just eighteen and everyone else was several years older than me, I'd secretly been counting on their seniority for guidance—the role models I never had. I couldn't have been more wrong—these guys, in their own individual ways, were as lost and confused as I was. We were all

146

wrestling with some of the same internal questions. How were we supposed to interact with people? With the fans? With the other bands? With each other?

Like my older brother who'd never been "the older brother" I'd needed—the one who's been around the block a few times, the one who shows you the ropes and to whom you can turn to for advice—my band mates and crew seemed trapped in adolescence. They didn't seem to know how to communicate with anyone outside our immediate circle (not that I was any help—I didn't know how to communicate with anyone *inside* our circle, let alone out).

From the get-go, they were drowning themselves in herb and alcohol, not appearing to attain any pleasure out of it, as though they were partying away the day simply because they didn't know what else to do with themselves when we weren't onstage. The result was too little focus on the music and too much focus on trying to get laid and rounding up the next bag of weed.

In all fairness, I was no choirboy myself. In an effort to fit in with them, I'd find myself drinking too much, smoking too much, trying to curse and using the same juvenile expressions as part of my vocabulary—a type of slang pretty much exclusive to the white lower class suburban youth of the Northern California East Bay *(Fuck yeah, man. Got some hella bad herb? Fire that shit up!)*. Yet as hard as I tried to fit in, I could never get past the fact that, compared to the others, I was more like a nerdy prep school student. And when it came to partying, I was an embarrassment, a lightweight. My post-show beers and acceptance of a bong hit or even, on occasion, a line of coke, would be no match for any of them—these guys could put away beer, pot and other drugs with reckless abandon.

At least I was learning my limits, which would be a good thing. Whenever my stage performance felt compromised from too much partying the night before, I'd cut back. Still, I partied a lot more than was necessary on that first tour. And if the drugs and alcohol weren't distracting enough, there were the girls.

*

For what had seemed like a thousand endless years, I'd been an untouchable leper, socially stratified to the lowest rungs of the unwritten caste system of Willard Junior High and Berkeley High School. Now here I was, a few years later, being approached by musician-hungry girls who viewed me as the shy, cute one. It was a mindfuck, to say the least.

On a night off in Columbus, Ohio, an attractive girl stopped me as I was walking out of our motel. After a nervous "hello," she took out a rock magazine, opened it up and pointed to a band photo where I was wearing shorts. "This is you, right?" she asked, looking me over like a piece of merchandise (not that I'd minded). Then she asked, "Can I get together with you?" I told her to wait right there, dashed back to the motel room and told the guys I needed to get the keys to our tour vehicle, making up some excuse or another. She and I spent a lovely ten minutes in the blue van.

Another time, in Atlanta, GA, a couple of girls were invited backstage and plied with drinks. As the band looked on, some of the crew guys tried to entice them to show their boobs. One of them said flat out, "Y'all can quit tryin' cause I ain't liftin' my shirt for y'all and I ain't getting with none of y'all." Then, seeing me quietly nursing a beer in the corner, she pointed my direction and said, giggling "'Cept for him! That one!" Everyone groaned in disappointment as she came over, took my hand and the two of us headed towards a rendezvous in the graffiti-covered bathroom down the hall.

It's not that stuff like this happened all the time. For the entire seven weeks, I probably had about a half dozen affairs or so. Although that was a lot for me, it was very little compared with others. There were some on our tour, crew especially, who seemed to be on the prowl at every show like animals in heat.

And truth be told, the majority of us were frustrated and disappointed most of the time—there just weren't that many girls at our shows. Females, at least back then, just didn't seem to be into thrash music. On a typical night, we'd look out into the crowd and there'd be a sea of sausage.

I confess to feeling a bit cheated by this. Despite my infrequent triumphs, for the most part, my delusions of unlimited sexual escapades were being squashed—crumpled like the pages of a cheap porno mag. I dreamed of what it would be like to tour in a Van Halen, a Mötley Crue, a Def Leppard, one of those super groups that seemed to draw an endless amount of women, all of them looking like those '80s' video vixens that I'd been lusting after since the ninth grade.

On the other hand, who was I kidding? How could I ever be like a Nikki Sixx or David Lee Roth, a full-on rock star bedding groupies with relentless abandon? I was still too shy to even approach a girl! For my first few years of touring, every single sexual encounter I ever had would be instigated not by me, but by the girls themselves, bless their hearts. Outside of the gigs, I was still a shy loser.

I'd soon realize that there was something shallow, hollow and emotionally unhealthy about all this. I'd grow to hate the idea that fame, even very microscopic fame like I was experiencing at this time, was a prerequisite for being considered attractive by a female.

Yet at the same time, these early road flings would be invaluable—just the corrective experiences I needed. After so many years of being ignored, snickered at and taken advantage of by young women insensitive to my crippling insecurities, it was quite therapeutic and empowering to finally receive a little bit of positive female attention, superficial or otherwise.

*

Further eroding my adolescent rock star sexual fantasies was the fact that for the most part, there was no way to hook up with a girl without everyone knowing about it. Each fling would be inevitably followed by probing questions from the band and crew, usually in front of everyone. *How big were her tits? Did she give good head? Did you eat her pussy?*

I realized that as much as I loved finally being able to occasionally experience what I'd fantasized about for so long—sexual intimacy with a girl—I hated discussing it and sharing with everyone else. It seemed like such a violation of the girl's privacy, sanctity and dignity, not to mention my own. To me, sex was this deeply personal experience to be shared with one other person: your sexual partner. And okay, maybe a friend that you tell in private. But not the whole van! In the future, I'd do my best to keep all my flings a secret.

I'd also realize early on that if I didn't at least have a friendship with the girl, then it really wasn't worth the physical encounter. On a basic level, I had to like the girl personally to have sex with her, no matter what she looked like. Of course, if I were to meet someone like my favorite actress at the time, the stunning Jamie Gertz (from the films *Crossroads* and *Lost Boys*), I'd go straight to bed with her even if she'd turned out to be an annoying, clingy bitch.

For the most part, I'd have lasting friendships with my lovers and potential future lovers. I'd give them all the address of my parents' house in case they wanted to keep in touch. After the tour, there'd be a stack of letters there, all of them handwritten in feminine ink and neat, elegant curvaceous characters. My parents would uncomfortably hand me the pile of letters and say that I should probably keep them to myself.

I'd already made the colossal mistake of moving into an apartment with a girl I shouldn't have (see chapter 22). Now that I was meeting new girls on tour, I was not about to be loyal to someone I'd never been in love with and hadn't even liked that much in the first place. It's not like anyone else on tour could be loyal to any of their girlfriends either, at least not at that time.

Some of these girls I would remain friends with for years. Most are now married with kids, working in offices and leading extremely normal lives. You'd never know that a couple decades ago, they were the token hotties at thrash metal concerts.

*

It would be on this tour that I'd begin to question the virtues of incessant marijuana use.

Growing up in Berkeley, I'd been a veteran, having smoked pot since Junior High. But I'd never seen anyone smoke it the way these guys would, especially Chuck and his buddy from Dublin High School, my new guitar tech, Troy, the same Troy I'd watched all those years ago tech-ing for Danny Gill (see chapter 14).

Upon getting up in the morning, everyone's brains would be immediately susceptible to their "Wake and Bake." Barely an hour would go by without another joint or bong passed around. This continued throughout the day and even more so at night, when the smoke was mixed with the beer, Jack Daniels and other alcohol provided in the dressing room. During long drives, the blue van would become filled with smoke like the van in the Sean Penn movie *Fast Times at Ridgemont High.* You couldn't avoid getting high from the second-hand smoke.

It was as though clarity was something to be avoided at all costs. I could understand the virtues of unwinding from a hard day's work at the end of the day with a drink or two and, if weed is your thing (it's no longer mine), then that's fine too. But why would you need to cloud your judgment and escape reality first thing in the morning?

I'd always be thankful that unlike other hard rock bands, we never had any members dabbling in heroin or other hard drugs. Yet I'd soon question whether their incessant marijuana use wasn't just as bad. This was especially true during the second half of this tour, after we'd linked up with the New York metal band Overkill.

*

Overkill had once hired our then tour manager/soundman, Kerry Whitig, and somehow our guys, overtaken by pot paranoia, had the seed planted in their brains that Kerry was making us sound bad on purpose. Their theory basically went like this: *Kerry secretly wishes he was working for Overkill again. Overkill and Kerry are plotting to ruin our show every night, run us into the ground and make Overkill look better.* Kerry, naturally sensing the hostility directed towards him, would soon begin hanging out more and more with his old cronies in Overkill, further agitating the tension.

The whole idea was quite preposterous—Kerry's name was attached to our show, not Overkill's, so why would he purposely make himself look bad and damage his credibility by trying to do a bad job on our sound?

There'd be no logic to these fears, only marijuana-infused madness. It would rob the band of the necessary energy to put on a great show and focus on rising to new levels of the music biz. Making things worse was the fact that anytime there was a shortage of weed, the crankiness and irritability factor would rise, making it an even more unpleasant environment to be around.

I started cutting down on how often I'd accept a joint, despite getting disapproving glances with each refusal. A year or so later, I'd quit for good, focusing all my energy on practicing guitar and being a better musician. This would make me something of a pariah, but by then, I'd no longer care.

I'd realized the truth—all that fucking weed was keeping me trapped in the very shell I'd been trying to break out of all my life.

*

So what do you think was the music most listened to in the Blue Van? Something cool like Black Sabbath? Judas Priest? Metallica? AC/DC?

Try this: an offbeat comedic British punk rock trio called the Toy Dolls.

The Toy Dolls' music sounded like, depending on your point of view, drinking songs for children or children's music for stoners. Their songs made no sense and were just all out silliness: "Nellie the Elephant," "The Spider Song," "Dig That Groove, Baby" and "Firey Jack," with the lyrics "Firey Jack, Firey Jack, It's red hot, on your back."

The two deranged children in our band, Eric and Louie (aka Frick and Frack) were endlessly amused by the Toy Dolls. They seemed to think they were God's gift to music. They'd listen to that Toy Dolls tape over and over and over, laughing more hysterically with each listen, refusing to turn it off when asked, and turning it on just to aggravate everyone else in the van. Our annoyance with their Toy Dolls obsession caused them to laugh even harder.

It got to be so annoying that at one point, Chuck Billy told them to either shut it off right fucking now, or he would pull the van over and throw the tape out the window. Still, they wouldn't shut it off. So what do you think happened?

Let's just say that somewhere underneath the New Jersey turnpike, near the PA border, lies the remains of Eric and Lou's Toy Dolls cassette tape.

*

There would be many other adventures.

In Washington, the guys would get in trouble for sneaking into Anthrax's dressing room and stealing their beer. At the Sundance Club in Long Island, there'd be fistfights in the crowd throughout our entire set. We'd get fed tubs of cheap, flavorless ziti pasta and served endless kamikaze cocktails in plastic cups. We'd get trashed, totally wrecking ourselves for the next day in New York City. There would be big bags under our eyes for our photo shoots with *Hit Parader, Metal Edge* and *Guitar World*.

In Manhattan, a convention would render it impossible to find a hotel room, so I'd make a last ditch call to my uncle and aunt, who lived in a Hell's Kitchen co-op. The entire band would end up crashing on their floor. When we'd ask if it was safe for us to walk around outside at night, my uncle would laugh, *"Look at you guys and your leather jackets. And this one (points at Chuck), what is he, seven feet tall? They're all going to be scared of YOU!"* We'd walk around the garment district, grab food and stop in a few bars, all without incident.

The next day, "Metal" Maria Ferarro, our pitbull-like, petite, plus-sized, blond mohawked A&R rep would take us around Greenwich Village. We'd stop in a record shop, where she'd proudly show us copies of our album for sale. Then she'd notice a hole punched out in the corner of each, indicating that they were promotional copies, not for resale. She'd snatch them up out of the bin, walk to the register, confront the salesman and announce that she's taking them all. He'd start screaming, threatening to call the police if she walked out with the albums. Her response? "Fuck you, call the police. I'll have you arrested for selling illegal promo copies. Let's go boys." *"You can't do this! Come back here! Stop that woman!!"* he'd yell, following us down the street.

In Allentown, PA, we'd meet a group of young women, forever to be referred to as the "Allentown Girls." They'd be regulars at our shows in the Pennsylvania and Jersey areas for the next few years. The Allentown Girls would bring us cookies as well as invite us over for barbeques whenever we passed through. I'd date one of them, Jani, generally agreed upon to be the prettiest; the next year, I'd lose her to some local guy who supposedly looked just like me. Greg would date another, Trixy, but things would get awkward—she'd start coming to too many shows, cramping his style as he tried to hit on other girls. There'd be two Greek sisters, both pretty, one of whom my guitar tech would end up marrying (and divorcing) in the distant future. In Cleveland, OH, at Peabody's Down Under, I'd come down with the flu and barely remember the gig.

Yet for all these adventures, perhaps none would measure up to those that took place during the first few days of the tour.

*

On the first day we headed all the way down the state of California, to Orange County just south of LA., for a mini thrash event at a club with about ten bands or so. After the gig, the plan was to drive across the US, day and night for the next several days, inching our way towards the mysterious mecca that awaited us: Pensacola, FL, site of our first gig with Anthrax.

The Orange County show was an all-day metal affair that spilled late into the evening; we finally played a short set around midnight. The place was very dimly lit. At about 2 am, bands were still playing, and the floor full of pitch dark figures: tired, drunk revelers who'd chosen to lie down rather than miss any of the bands. Many of these kids had fallen asleep. A few young couples had fallen asleep cuddling including one or two who'd had their pants down and their butts blanketed only by a sweatshirt—they'd been slowly gyrating in the dark on the floor.

Just then, Troy, my tech, who along with our new soundman, Kerry Whitig, was one of the designated drivers for the trip, came up, and announced that we'd soon have to start rounding everyone up to get into the van and head out.

I'd been hanging out, watching it all in the darkness with my old friend Ben who'd come down during his college Spring Break to check out the show and see us off. We'd each had a lot to drink.

Like me, Ben came from an academic family that was socially dysfunctional (but in his case, more of an offensive, argumentative way, rather than an introverted one like mine). Ben grew up a few blocks away, just up the hill from Mike Coons of Lääz Rockit, and he and I had started hanging out in Junior High, while he was still wearing his hood.

Stepping outside of the club and into the moonlit parking lot, Ben and I started talking about how absurd it all was: after his break, he'd resume classes at UC Berkeley, and go on to become a CPA and CFO. I was about to tour the US for seven weeks with a speed metal band I'd only hooked up with a couple years ago while we'd both been attending Berkeley High School.

Now I didn't realize this at the time, but Ben had inadvertently become like my umbilical cord between the small world I'd known and the big world I was heading into. I'd come to represent that for him as well. Many years later, I would hear a psychological term that would offer the perfect explanation for what we were both feeling: *separation anxiety*.

"Al, I just had the craziest idea," he said.

153

"Yeah? What?"

"I could so easily sneak in the cab of that Ryder truck and join you guys."

"That'd be awesome! How'd you get back?"

"I'll just get my dad to wire me money for a flight or train. It's crazy. I kind of want to do it." We both laughed.

"You should," I said.

"No, I shouldn't. It's a stupid idea."

"I guess you're right."

"Should I do it, Al?"

"Yeah, do it!"

"Nah, it's crazy."

"You're right. Don't do it. I'll get in trouble."

"Then again, it'd be fun! And so easy."

"Yeah! C'mon, do it."

"It's insane, Al."

"You're right Ben, We're drunk. I don't know what we were thinking."

After going back and forth like this for a few more minutes, we reached a drunken conclusion: with my blessing and encouragement, Ben crept into the backseat of the truck's cab, where he went to sleep under a bunch of jackets.

*

The next day, as the morning sun crept down upon the cactuses and desert mountains, shining upon our mini-caravan, a mysterious yawn was heard coming from the behind the driver's seat in the yellow Ryder truck. The occupant of the front seat, Kerry, jumped a foot, his head nearly hitting the roof of the cab as Troy, at the wheel, swerved the truck from side to side. Just then, both noticed a pair of glasses attached to a tired pale face with scraggily hair. It was Ben's head protruding forth, his eyes squinting, his mouth opening up to say... *"What's up?"*

*

Threats to put Ben on the next Greyhound bus we could find began as soon as he started arguing vigilantly about the best way to change the oil in the truck. I had to talk to Ben and tell him to keep his mouth shut, something he was very bad at. I fessed up to everyone that he and I had been in a drunken stupor the night before, somehow deciding it would be a good idea to have Ben stow away.

Nerves were calmed as I assured everyone that he'd only go as far as the first or second gig, then be on his way. And soon all bickering was put on the backburner as we drove through the most vicious rains and dazzling lightning storms any of us had seen. Welcome to the South.

We arrived in Pensacola and checked into a hotel the night before the first gig with Anthrax. Ben slept in the Ryder truck. We were all exhausted from the trip.

Eric and Lou were muttering about going to find hookers. They tried to recruit me. I steadfastly refused. As sex-starved as I'd been all through adolescence, the thought of paying to get laid was revolting to me. They tried to recruit Greg, who was sharing the room—he was exhausted from the trip and had fallen asleep instantly. They asked him, he shook his head, half asleep. But they wouldn't take no for an answer. "C'mon, Greg," Lou continued, shaking him awake. "Be a man! C'mon, Greg!"

"Get outta here. I'm fuckin' sleepin'."

"C'mon, Greg!"

Just then, Greg had the first meltdown of the tour (it wouldn't be the last): *"Fuck you, Lou! Just fuck you!"* He reached for a shoe and threw it at him. "You wanna be a man?! Go be a fuckin' man, then! Fuck you." He flipped him off, and hid under the covers.

Eric and Lou ran out of the room giggling. They never did get hookers—they'd been winding us up the whole time.

*

The next day was the first gig of the tour.

I don't remember much about the gig other than meeting two young groupies, one of whom was more or less wearing a homemade Anthrax flag, draped as a dress. During Anthrax's set, they wandered backstage, not knowing where they were going, where they ran into Ben and me. We asked them what they were doing there. It turned out Anthrax's tech, Al, had given them passes earlier, in hopes of a post-show photo shoot. Ben and I had just made an interception…

Soon, Ben and I were in the shower with them. Never had it been so easy. He and I, who had been rejected at so many parties, looked down upon by 99.9% of the girls in the Berkeley Public School system, suddenly found ourselves naked in the shower with these girls. It was like a prerequisite to one of those *Girls Gone Wild* videos that became popular in the early '00s.

My girl was very quickly on her knees taking care of me, while Ben ended up in a long, drawn-out erotic tangle with his. It was fun to be sharing a full-on groupie rock 'n' roll experience with a fellow Berkeley nerd from my neighborhood.

By the time I walked out with the girl, Ben was still in there with his. They were taking a long time. Eric and Lou kept peeking in, giggling and giving play-by-play reports to the rest of us. Just then, Chuck came up and needed to take a post-show shower. He was told he couldn't because Ben was in there with some chick. Every few minutes Chuck would open the door, call out, "C'mon Ben. Hurry the fuck up or I'm coming in there." Finally twenty minutes went by, and Chuck went in. By this time, the guys in Anthrax had finished their set and were gathered around to watch as well. The girl reached for a towel and came out to applause. Chuck pulled Ben out of the shower, naked, a glistening hard-on protruding from his body. More applause.

For the rest of the tour, for good reason, my friend from up the street would be referred to as "Big Ben."

*

By the end of the night Testament had done its first tour date, and Ben, dried off and flaccid, phoned his father and more or less demanded money for a flight home. Ben's dad just didn't have the energy to argue or inquire what kind of mess he'd gotten himself into.

I'd be sorry to see him go and agreed his stowing away may have been careless, crass and stupidly irresponsible on both our parts, an alcohol-induced moment of inspiration. But hey, he'd gotten to see me off in style, sharing in my first dalliance with groupies, something I'd experience again here and there, and he wasn't likely to see much in the accounting world. We high-fived and called it a successful adventure.

But no sooner had arrangements been made to get Ben on his way, than the Testament tour was faced with another parasite straggler, someone whose sudden, haunting appearance would cast a shadow upon the band for years to come.

21. THE FUGITIVE

In general, it is probably never a good idea to invite a stranger to join your tour, especially when said stranger is a convicted felon on the run from US Federal Authorities. Somehow this thought never occurred to Chuck Billy, who'd just met a new friend in the crowd at our very first tour date in Pensacola.

Several years later, a movie would come out starring Robert De Niro as a tattooed ex-convict reminiscent of this stranger, whom we'd refer to as "Tattoo Rob." While Tattoo Rob had a slightly less menacing personality than the character portrayed in *Cape Fear,* his bodily appearance made De Niro's fictional felon look like a cute, cuddly kitten. Shirtless most of the time, Rob's tattoos were never-ending: on his arms, the sleeves were so thick the images formed giant clouds of black ink. On his neck, a hissing snake wrapped all the way around several times, appearing to choke him. Under his eye, a permanent black tear, dripping from his face. Meanwhile, his chest, stomach and back were like a museum of ink, displaying various symbols related to prison gangs: roman numerals, gothic lettering, knives, skulls, eagles with wings spread across his chest and back and, most disturbingly, several giant swastikas.

During Anthrax's set, Tattoo Rob and Chuck had stood next to each other at the bar, where Rob complimented him on our set. Over beers, they'd gotten to talking, bonding over their shared Native American heritage. Rob claimed to be half Indian and chalked up his swastika tattoos as ancient Native American symbols of good luck rather than representing Nazis or White Supremacy. While his brief description was somewhat accurate (true of India, not Native American Indians), it was little consolation to someone of Jewish descent like myself.

*

Chuck seemed to be coming from a charitable, if misguided place. He insisted on helping out Rob, who probably reminded him of some of his friends from back home in Dublin, CA. While none of Chuck's friends were heavily tattooed ex-cons like Rob, several had criminal records. One guy, whom Chuck brought to practice often, had done hard time for holding up a convenience store. In a low gargly, muppet-like voice, he'd recite the line that had caused him to be found guilty of armed robbery: *"Put the money in the bag, bitch."*

I could only reason that, just as I'd allowed my childhood friend Ben to stow away in the truck the night before, Chuck was now feeling a bout of separation anxiety—clinging to his own past through this new friend of his. So enamored was Chuck that it never occurred to him that there might be anything odd or uncomfortable about Tattoo Rob joining our tour, indefinitely.

After all, Chuck reasoned, Rob happened to be on the road, like us (*on the run was more like it*), the poor guy was out there all alone (*that's because he was scary-looking and dangerous*) and why not help him out, put him to work for the band and take him with us? (*How about the fact that he made us all uncomfortable and we'd potentially be put in the position of harboring, aiding and abetting a fugitive from justice?*)

After giving us a few minutes to think about it, Chuck approached us again to see what we thought of the idea. Tattoo Rob was by his side. The conversation went something like this:

Chuck: So...you guys cool with givin' him a lift?

Tattoo Rob: You guys kick some fuckin' ass! Did I tell ya that?! Fuckin' kick ass!! Whoooo!!!

Chuck: He's headin' that direction.

Tattoo Rob: Just for a day, couple days, whatever. It's all good my brothas. Did I say you kick fuckin' ass?!! Fuckin' Testament! Yeahhhh!

Chuck: It'd be cool. This guy's out here all alone, needs a lift.

Tattoo Rob: That's cool, Chuck. Whatever you guys want! If I can tag along, lift shit and help out a fuckin' great band like this, well GOD FUCKIN' DAMN! I'M IN! But hey, whatever, it's cool. Been on my own, got this far. Fuck yeah, brothas!!!

We look at Chuck, a six foot four Native American with a chest the size of Cleveland and no shortage of tattoos himself. Then we look at Rob, shirt off and full display of knives, eagles and Aryan Brotherhood symbols, the one person on Earth scarier than Chuck. Unsure what to say or do, we all speak at the same time:

"Sure," "No problem," "It's cool," "Welcome aboard."

*

Tattoo Rob is in the van with us for the duration of our Florida shows (about three days). Then, after pleas from our managers, and members of Anthrax, a couple of whom are Jewish like myself and uncomfortable looking at a guy with swastika tattoos, Rob is dropped off on a pitch-black endless highway in the middle of the night. Within a few weeks he'll be apprehended by law enforcement and brought back to jail. Eventually, he'll reappear in the Bay Area. He'll track down Chuck, who befriends him once again.

Tattoo Rob has grown his hair out and decided he wants to be a singer. Chuck loans him money for a PA system, showing him how to use it. Rob is better groomed now, wearing long-sleeve button down shirts (hiding his most disturbing tattoos), cologne and snakeskin boots. He seems to have his life together. Or so it appears.

Rob accompanies us to the "Practice What You Preach" video shoot in Houston, Texas. At about 2 am, he and Chuck, back from drinking and armed with two large buckets of water, have the bright idea to descend upon the video crew, sound asleep in neighboring motel rooms and wake them up with a splash. The video crew, not amused, vows to call off the shoot the next day. After apologies from Chuck and Rob, they relent.

A month or so later, at a concert at the Omni in Oakland, Chuck spots a pretty blond girl with large boobs and sends Rob over to speak for him. "Hey, Babydoll. See that big guy over there? That's my man, Chuck Billy, singer of Testament. He wants to meet you."

The girl answers with unyielding sassiness, "You go tell Chuck Billy that if he's really a 'big boy,' he can come over here and talk to me for himself."

Chuck and the girl, Tiffany, will start dating, move in together, and eventually get married. To this day, they are forever linked by Tattoo Rob.

*

Stories begin to circulate about Rob offering rides to girls from the shows and then pulling to the side of the road and committing the crime of rape. Two girls pressed charges against him.

Even back in Florida, two years earlier, we'd heard that Rob had offered to walk a girl home, then forced himself on her. He had denied it, saying it was consensual, they were both drunk and that the girl was making up a story. That had only added to the reasons to get him off the tour at once. But now there was no question that the rape stories were true.

Despite believing in the inner goodness of Tattoo Rob from the beginning, Chuck recognizes that an accused rapist is not a good person to have attached to our band in any way, shape or form. He attempts to contact Rob, tell him that he can't hang around the band any longer and advises him to turn himself in. But it's too late, Rob has fled without a trace.

By now, the Federal, State and local authorities are all looking for him. Soon they'll come knocking on our door.

1989 Oakland CA. Jackson Street Studios

Rob Lombardo (a distant cousin of Slayer drummer Dave Lombardo) is doing some work on Eric's guitar rig, prepping for the upcoming tour. Shy even by my standards, he barely says a word other than "dude," and for this reason, has earned the nickname "Robbie Dude." What Robbie doesn't realize is that outside, the place is swarming with police cars. A commando team stands by in a nearby van.

An undercover agent has just walked in and approached the front desk. The studio owner, Al Luchessi, a fixture on the East Bay music scene (and coincidentally, my former math tutor), realizes this suit-clad fellow is not a musician. He's too business-like. Perhaps it's someone from the City of Oakland? Last he checked, the building was up to code. "What do they want now?" he wonders to himself. He says hello to the stranger.

"How ya doin'? I'm detective O'Malley, Oakland Police Department." He holds up his badge then shakes Al's hand. "Nice place you got here."

"Thanks," Al says nervously "Is there something I can help you with?"

"Perhaps you can. I'm lookin' for someone. Matter of fact, our whole department is looking for someone. We heard he hangs out here."

"Well, we have a lot of bands that rehearse and a lot of guys hanging out here."

"There is this one fellow that hangs out with one of the bands. Band by the name of uh, let's see…" He reads his notes, "Testament. Yeah, that's it."

"What's his name? The guy you're looking for?"

"We're not sure his full name. But he goes by 'Rob.'"

"Rob? Oh, you must mean Robbie. Of course. He's a guitar tech for the band. He's in there right now, doing some work on some guitars."

"In where?"

"In the big room over there." (points) "It's just through that door."

"Listen, I'm going to need you to step outside for a minute. My guys need to go and talk to this guy, Rob. This could get ugly. Stand back."

The detective gets on the walkie talkie and starts issuing commands. Al gets up from behind the desk and steps out of the front door, wondering what the cops could possibly want with little Robbie Dude.

Within moments, a commando raid unit is storming the building. They kick open the door to where Robbie Dude is changing strings on Eric's BC Rich guitar and point an array of pistols and high-powered assault rifles straight at him.

160

"THIS IS THE POLICE! GET DOWN ON THE GROUND AND PUT YOUR HANDS ON TOP OF YOUR HEAD! NOW!" Too startled to move, Robbie just stands there and practically urinates in his Levis. *"I SAID GET DOWN! NOW!"* He falls to the ground face first. The police move in on him, one of them points a pistol straight at his head. They check his ID, realize that Rob Lombardo aka Robbie Dude is not Tattoo Rob.

The cops apologize and help him up. Robbie Dude will be shaking all day from the experience.

Detective Calahan on his way out, says to Al. "Guess that's the wrong 'Rob.'" He thanks him for his help, apologizes for any convenience.

Then he says, "In case you hear anything, here's my card. Then he says with a smile. "And one more thing..."

"Yes?"

"We'd REALLY like to find this guy. You have a good day, now."

A few weeks later, Tattoo Rob was apprehended on the run in the Southwest somewhere. He was sentenced to life in a federal penitentiary.

We never saw him again.

22. FATAL ATTRACTION

I was only seventeen when it started. During our year and a half long relationship (in which I'd been away recording and on tour for much of it), she'd had no life of her own, no interests beyond daytime television dramas and a slithering descent into the throes of methamphetamine addiction. Eventually, I finally got the courage to break up with her.

First, she caused scenes in public—at parties and local concerts—telling everyone what a bastard I was, succumbing to tear-drenched emotional meltdowns and hurling profane insults my direction, such as *"Nice knowing you, you fucking dick!"* As if that would somehow make me want to come back...

Then, for years, she'd tell everyone I was a cruel monster who'd broken her heart, neglecting to mention that, five years older than me, she'd been a brash, clingy, controlling, delusional, emotionally unstable, jealous, unemployed , psychologically abusive and unaspiring parasite.

I'd thought that was the worst of it, but I couldn't have known how wrong I was.

At every gig I would ever play from then on, not to mention every event she knew I might attend—parties, concerts, awards shows—she was there, a ghastly apparition, lurking around corners, looking longingly at me and glaring menacingly at every girl I talked to, even scaring a few off in the process. All the while, her meth use was causing her to decay, growing more and more unrecognizable by the day. Soon she'd morph into a hideous ghost—a lump in a formerly human shell, stalking me for the better part of ten years.

This was Edie, my first long-term girlfriend.

*

Edie would get wind of my activities through the girlfriends of my band members. She used them for access to me, and they used her for drugs and other favors. It worked like this: the girlfriends always made sure Edie was backstage. They conspired to keep her in the loop on everywhere I went, every girl I went out with and every other detail they could get of my private life. In return, Edie would provide them with companionship, an endless supply of meth and, on occasion, concert tickets.

The tickets came courtesy of Edie's new best friend, the girlfriend of Metallica front man James Hetfield—the one for whom he'd write the song,

"Nothing Else Matters." She had unlimited access to tickets for all the major rock concerts. Unlike Edie, she was pretty and thin, but she shared the affliction of being a severe meth addict desperately in need of therapy. Eventually, her increasingly famous boyfriend would get wind of her drug-addled behavior and she'd be dropped as if by a major record label.

*

Anytime I separated from a subsequent relationship with a girl, my band's girlfriends would give Edie the heads up. That's when Edie's obsessive love letters would start pouring in, my phone ringing incessantly with her calls. One time she even convinced her poor mother, bedridden after a heart attack, to call me in a wretched attempt to gain my sympathy and use it as bait to try to lure me back. Encouraged and aided by my band's flock of infuriating females, Edie's stalking continued.

My own band members' tolerance of this situation was shocking, hurtful and dismaying. Their sycophantic other halves were unable to shut their mouths or mind their own business, chastising me with such challenges as *"What is your problem, Alex?" "Why can't you just be nice to her?" "She has as much right to be here as anyone else!"*

One time, they even invited Edie to tag along on their trip to visit us on tour. They saw nothing wrong with it. I put my foot down and said, "Absolutely not." At the behest of their girlfriends, my band members told me that I was being unfair. I told them either tell your girlfriends "No" or consider finding another guitar player.

*

If I'd had any clue about addictive and borderline personalities, I never would have associated with this person, let alone entered any kind of relationship with her. But at seventeen, desperate for companionship, torn apart by the bloody battles at home over my musical aspirations and with no one else to talk to, I'd allowed it to happen. It would the worst mistake of my life.

It hadn't even been her that I liked. I'd preferred her friend, Karen. Even more so, I liked her other friend Donna. At first, we'd referred to them as the "Lääz Rockit girls." Lääz was still ruling the metal club scene, and we'd always see these girls at their gigs and sometimes at rehearsals, which were right down the hall from ours. Donna was bona fide hot, a stunner, swimsuit-model quality; she was in a tumultuous on-again, off-again relationship. Karen was a bit overweight but had a face so pretty it made up for it. Edie was, well, average, at least before her decay.

In 1986, Edie and I moved in with Karen and one of my band members in a tiny apartment in Oakland. Karen would borrow things without asking, help herself to the groceries I'd buy, then label hers off limits, play weird psychological games (even once brazenly touching me inappropriately in plain view of Edie, who didn't know how to react). As difficult as Edie was, Karen was worse to live with and I'd be thankful not to have dated her.

Karen was so manipulative and passive aggressive, in fact, that Edie and I would be driven to move into our own place. Secretly I knew it was all a mistake—I should have just moved back home, getting away from all of them. But things had gotten so bad with my parents that we couldn't even have a civilized conversation—they'd just scream me out of the house, about my hair, my clothes and what I was doing with my life. I couldn't go back there.

I was trapped.

*

Years later, while styling my hair, Donna, the hot one, would divulge to me that Karen had liked me too, but Edie had staked her claim first, so Karen had backed off and ended up with my band mate instead. Karen was resentful of Edie for getting me, hence her brash behavior. Donna seemed to indicate that during one of her and her boyfriend's off-again periods, she herself—the hottest girl of them all—might even have gone out with me, had I only made a move...*Made a move?!* I hadn't even known how to make a move. I couldn't even carry on a conversation with a girl. I'd been paralyzed, limited to the girls who would approach me.

Unfortunately, the one that did was Edie—a living nightmare just a few steps away from those portrayed in movies like *Fatal Attraction, Play Misty for Me* and the films of David Lynch.

A subsequent girlfriend of mine, Cindy, the bartender I'd met in Ithaca, would cause Edie to keep a bit of distance by confronting her and saying if she didn't stop following us she'd *"fucking kill her."*

But only after I'd moved 3,000 miles away would I feel totally safe and out of reach from this creature whom many, after witnessing her public spectacles, had long since referred to as "Fatal Attraction[31]."

*

In the mid-'90s, I would run into a pretty girl at my gym named Jean. She'd approach me cautiously, then look me deep in the eyes and say, "Hi, Alex." When I asked how she knew my name, she'd say, "I'm going to bring up a name you probably don't want to hear: Edie. I was her roommate

---

[31] Decades later in the 2010s, Edie would resurface on Facebook, sending repeated 'friend requests'. My assistant, not knowing her past, accepted her on my friend list on my public page. It was nearly a year later I saw her on the list and realized she was now continuing "online stalking" at which point my assistant "blocked" her.

for two years." I'd wince. "Don't worry. I'm no longer in contact with her. In fact, she's the only person I can think of that I wish I'd never met."

"I guess we have something in common, then."

"Yes. Now, please don't be afraid when I tell you this—ok? Edie and I used to case your house. We'd follow you in her car. It's all really creepy, I know. I'm really embarrassed about it. She's like a cult leader—she had me so far on drugs I didn't realize the level to which I'd sunk. She did this to others too. She's not only self-destructive but she brings down people around her as well. I don't look anything like I did before. I was malnourished."

"Oh my god…"

"I've wanted to talk to you about this for a long time, let you know I feel your pain and how terrible I feel. I was going to look you up but didn't want you to think I was stalking you too. Then, I saw you here at the gym and just had to tell you."

Since coming clean, Jean had become a personal trainer.

For a few weeks, we'd bond very closely over our shared agony, having long talks and even going out on dates, kissing passionately and almost sleeping together, knowing how much that would drive our mutual antagonist nuts.

But outside of our shared trauma with Edie, Jean and I would have little in common. I went to the gym regularly, but Jean worked out obsessively, sometimes twice a day. She mostly talked about cardio, weights, amino acids and protein shakes. She'd essentially replaced one addiction with another, albeit a healthier one.

Jean would tell me all about how Edie fluctuated from conspiring to win me back to plotting to ruin my reputation; how she'd lured Jean into friendship, then moved into her formerly well-kept apartment, turning it into a rundown drug den and how she and Edie would be awake for days straight on speed binges.

Most memorably, there were stories about their visits to a meth lab in Oakland run by this creepy, reclusive, paraplegic, fifty-something wheelchair-bound Vietnam War veteran. He accepted no money from them and only asked, in exchange for his illegal chemical product, to take a Polaroid photo of their naked breasts—his walls were a collage of cleavage belonging to female meth addicts from all over the Bay Area.

The last experience had been so demeaning it caused Jean to abruptly run away, leave her home, abandon all her possessions and promptly check herself into rehab. She'd heard through the grapevine that

Edie had gotten stuck with the excess rent charges after she'd left, had been looking for her and threatening to come after her.

Jean had since taken an assumed name, changed her hair color, started dressing different and was essentially living like a member of the US Federal Witness Protection Program.

*

Dating Edie should have been a long-forgotten relationship, a minor mistake, insignificant and easily left in the past. Instead, she would cast a shadow over the entire time I was in my band, whose insensitivity to the situation and allowing their own girlfriends to perpetuate it only made things worse. It would take years of soul-searching to apply meaning to the situation and finally, learn to see a bright side.

Bright side? you may ask. *How can there be a bright side?!*

I'm happy to report that there is one, although it is more like the silver lining on the cloud of a tornado: I'd gone into this situation as a seventeen-year-old leper. The thought of saying "no" to a girl, *any girl*, had been unimaginable—I'd embrace whoever would take me. I'd thus allowed myself to get involved with a woman at the lowest level—a bottom feeder— a deeply troubled, out of shape and undesirable wretch who, during our short relationship, used psychological manipulation in order to try to keep me, then afterwards, turned into an unceasing stalker whose obsession with me had been matched only by that of the venomous powder she'd snort up her nose.

I came out of it, with a huge annoyance that would plague me for years, but also an understanding that I was deserving of someone who treated me with respect, someone with ambitions beyond just being the girlfriend of a guy in a band, someone that takes care of herself physically and emotionally and, should things not work out, someone who keeps a healthy distance. I'd also learned that most of the girls in the metal scene, at least at that time[32], were to be avoided at all costs. Too many of them were unambitious, superficial, illiterate, backstabbing, petty and manipulative.

I realized I was going to have to become appealing to women outside the metal scene, who had more to offer and liked me for not just who I was but who I was becoming. With no one else to believe in me, I was going to have to start believing in myself. This would take some work on my part, including a regular diet of self-improvement books and explorations of various life management systems.

---

[32] Today, things are very different. There exists the once unthinkable—beautiful young women metal fans with class, depth, culture and sophistication. They are in the minority but they exist. I also later discovered that metal is/was very popular among highly educated engineering and architecture students.

My self-esteem had been so low that I'd allowed myself to get dragged into a nightmare right out of a psychological thriller. Only when I'd get as far away from Berkeley as I could, thousands of miles away, would it feel over.

TESTAMENT
DYNAMO OPEN
AIR '87

ALEX
Backstage Pass
ACCESS
ALL AREAS

23. EINDHOVEN

Playing in Europe for the first time is like losing your virginity. You get nervous with anticipation. You imagine it vividly, but no matter what you do, nothing can fully prepare you for it. Eventually, when that moment arrives, you just have to overcome your fears and do it. Such was the case when we flew to Eindhoven in 1987 to perform in front of 30,000 metalheads at the annual Dynamo Open Air Festival.

I'd been to Europe seven years earlier with my family. But here I was, eighteen, out of the house and no longer the little boy under the watchful eye of mom and dad. As the van shuttled us in from Amsterdam International Airport, I looked out upon the peaceful serenity of The Netherlands, better known by its unofficial nickname "Holland." It was a lot like I'd remembered it: life-sized gingerbread houses, rolling green hills, windmills, tiny cars and people on bicycles. Could this fairy tale-like country really be into metal?

All doubts were quickly cast aside when, the night before the festival, we performed a warm-up gig at the Dynamo Club to hundreds of sweaty fans. The intensity of the mosh pits and stage-diving rivaled that of any crowd we'd seen before.

Already, it felt like we'd reached a new level. We weren't playing for the local metal scene back home. These were total strangers across the ocean who spoke a different language and asked us for our autographs. Tonight there were hundreds, tomorrow there would be thousands.

After the warm-up show, several of our new fans became gracious hosts, buying us drinks and showing us around town.

With its endless array of nightclubs, sex shops and hashish houses, Eindhoven was like an adult playground. We bounced from bar to bar in a beer-and hash-induced haze. Soon it was 3 am, and the bars were still open. I'm not sure how I got back to the hotel, but I made it. Eventually, everyone else did as well.

At around noon the next day, we were driven to the festival site, a giant airfield with a stage and PA system. The crowd was a sea of leather and denim. Everywhere you looked there were people with band logos on their patches and t-shirts. MOTÖRHEAD. VENOM. IRON MAIDEN. SLAYER. I'd never known this many metal fans existed let alone expected to see them in one place.

Headlining the festival was Stryper, a Christian rock band from LA, who had developed a big presence on American radio and MTV. They wore black and yellow stripes, had huge eighties hair and sang commercial hard rock songs for Jesus.

We didn't know Stryper, and had nothing against them, but it seemed especially weird to have us on the same bill, for several reasons:

1. Our music was fast, intense speed metal. Theirs was easy listening by comparison.

2. Our songs were about darkness and violence. Theirs were about the virtues of Christianity.

3. We indulged in alcohol and other vices. They indulged in the Holy Bible.

How ironic that the name of our band was "Testament."

In keeping with their pious lifestyle, Stryper had imposed these three rules for backstage etiquette: *No drinking, no smoking and no cursing.*

All the other bands were instructed to observe these rules while in their presence.

When the time came for us to walk out and perform, the guys from Stryper were just arriving backstage. Our vocalist, Chuck, decided to greet them by letting them know just what he thought of their rules. "Where's my pot?" he yelled. "Let's smoke some pot! I can't go on without my goddamn pot!" The members of Stryper turned their heads and looked perplexed.

They didn't know what to say. Chuck looked straight at them and didn't miss a beat.

"You guys got any fucking beer?" he asked.

We all started giggling like naughty school children and headed outside into the damp cloudy air to take the stage. The show was a total rush. It was cold out there. My hands felt frozen. It started raining. The sound onstage was terrible. But we were pulling it off.

For the first time, we were playing in front of thousands of people. And in the blink of an eye, it was done. I don't remember much else except that it was followed by a lot of celebrating and another night on the town in Eindhoven.

The next day, as we were driven back across the Dutch landscape towards the Amsterdam airport, we awaited our flight back home to the USA. Mixed in with our hangovers was an overwhelming sensation of relief that it was over. We had done our first big European gig.

Like a first time sexual encounter, it was far from perfect, but with repeated experience, it would get better. Nothing would capture the excitement of that first European show. For now, we had done it. We had lost our virginity and were no longer a "local" band. We had just stepped out of the Bay Area and onto the world stage.

24. SOPHOMORE JINX

As 1987 skidded to a halt, we were faced with the daunting task of following up our first album. Suddenly, we had to come up with an equal amount of material in a fraction of the time.

Since I'd come aboard three years earlier, we'd been able to work out a new tune every few months or so with no pressure. There'd already been close to a half-hour or so of the band's early material and we'd had the next two years to add new songs. But what we hadn't taken into consideration was that we'd had the luxury of taking our time and writing with ease. And with 1988 quickly approaching and the band scheduled to return to Ithaca for another go in the studio, we found ourselves with a desperate shortage of new material.

This problem was not helped by something that would prove to be a serious hindrance to the band's progress in the future: a lack of leadership.

With his Indian Warrior-like quietude, Chuck, being the singer, as well as the oldest and the biggest, seemed a natural fit to lead; we were all intimidated by him. But in reality, he was a shy person—a shy person that could kill a man with his bare hands, but shy nonetheless. Like "Chief" Broman, the silent six foot seven Native American portrayed in *One Flew Over the Cuckoo's Nest*, Chuck caused unease in others simply by his size, though in truth, as long as you didn't start a fight with him, he was mostly a gentle giant. Having been in the band less than two years, Chuck was still

171

finding his place in the music. Giving musical direction to the rest of us just didn't come naturally.

Having formed the group, Eric was naturally entitled to a leadership position. But like myself, he was an awkward communicator void of self-confidence, although in a much different way. Unable to form a complete sentence, he almost never spoke without using the words *fuckin, hella* (hell of) or *trip*. For example, when showing an idea for a riff, he'd say something like: *"My new trip, check it out, it's fuckin' hella bad."* He also had the giggles. In truth, this was symptomatic of his own insecurity—he couldn't keep from laughing. But he'd often use this to turn the tables on others, snickering uncontrollably and pointing maliciously, as though you were the source of some inside joke of his, one he'd never let you in on. Needless to say, Eric wasn't cut out to lead the band.

Greg was the easiest going guy in the band and a good enough bassist, but far from a leader. In younger days, Greg had skipped a lot of school, but whenever he'd shown up, he'd paid close attention to subjects of interest to him, such as history, geography, insects and reptiles, which he'd cite facts on as though he were a contestant on *Jeopardy*. Unfortunately, his keen aptitude for these subjects was nonexistent when it came to his own life. He'd make terrible decisions, such as smoking multiple packs of Marlboros a day, drinking far too many Jack Daniels, snorting methamphetamine, being served eviction notices by landlords and running up a growing pile of parking tickets courtesy of the City of Oakland. Greg could barely direct himself out of bed in the morning, let alone direct the rest of us.

Then there was Louie, our drummer who was musically struggling to keep up. Although that never stopped certain other metal drummers from directing their bands (case in point—Lars Ulrich of Metallica), Lou's biggest hang-up wasn't musical but personal: he was always in cahoots with Eric. Whenever Eric went on one his giggle fits, he'd get Lou to play along, the two of them chuckling like hyenas, often at others' expense.[33] It was hard to know who Louie was or where he stood outside of their two-man team, which by now had earned yet another nickname: "The Gremlins" (Eric was "Gremlin One," Lou was "Gremlin Two"). They'd been named after the Gremlins because they were reminiscent of those evil little monsters from the film of the same name that, in much the same manner, pointed, covered their

---

[33] Eric and Lou had once shown up at my house while my parents were away to hang out with me and a girlfriend I had over. Both had taken LSD without telling us. As the night wore on, they became more and more obnoxious, giggling between themselves, never saying what was funny. It became so awkward, embarrassing and uncomfortable that finally, I had to ask them to leave.

mouths and snickered. Because of this, and the fact that whatever Eric pushed for, Lou nodded in agreement, there was no way Louie could ever to lead the band.

That left me. At nineteen years old, I was timid, psychologically traumatized and self-conscious about every word I said. It was difficult for me to talk to anyone, let alone this stubborn group of suburban bad boys, all of whom were several years older than I was. It felt like everything I said sounded stupid (much of it probably did), and I couldn't get a point across without cracking a nervous smile. Though I may have been a strong guitar player for my age, I was a very weak personality, just as I'd been in school, which, truth be told, hadn't been that long ago. I sure as hell couldn't lead this band.

We were a hodgepodge of insecure, stubborn personalities, radically different in nature. We all had difficulty expressing ourselves as individuals. It was even more challenging for us to achieve any sort of focus as a group.

Yet, if we were going to survive as a band, we had to get past all these hurdles and come up with a new album, fast.

*

The first riff I'd contributed to the band had become a song called "Burnt Offerings." It was based on a scale I'd first heard in Jewish songs, such as "Hava Nagila." In technical terms, it's the 5th mode of the Harmonic Minor scale. Joe Satriani had shown me how to play the scale on guitar, calling it Phrygian Dominant. My future jazz instructor, Charlie Banacos, would call it Mixolydian b2 b6. But technical jargon and fancy names aside, I'd always thought of this pattern simply as the "Middle Eastern scale." The "Burnt Offerings" riff was simply the first five notes of this pattern, ascending and descending.[34] Though I'd heard it in Middle Eastern flavored hard rock, such as Led Zeppelin's "Kashmir" or Rainbow's "Gates of Babylon" (with the late Ronnie James Dio on vocals), I'd never heard it used in speed metal.

So to begin writing for this second album, it only made sense to turn to my old friend, the Harmonic Minor 5th mode, or Middle Eastern scale. It seemed to be something that was a bit of a signature for us that no one else in our genre was using at the time. The only other example was Exodus, who'd

---

[34] In the '90s, while listening to the radio I'd hear the exact same sequence used by the modern rock/punk group The Offspring for the hit "Keep 'Em Separated." Although the rest of the song couldn't be more different, that riff is nearly identical.

just released their first album with Zet. Its title track, "Pleasures of the Flesh," featured a single note line similar to the one I'd written for "Burnt Offerings."

I found this a bit odd.

In high school, I'd been a big fan of Exodus, one of many followers. But now, they'd not only run off with our band's singer, they were attempting a sound that we'd clearly brought to the thrash table first. In Exodus' hands, this type of riff just didn't seem to work. Many of their own fans agreed—it was too far removed from the type of non-modal riffs that had been Exodus' signature—strong brutal, unpredictable chordal riffs like "No Love" and "Bonded by Blood." So with all due respect to the great band Exodus had been, Harmonic Minor thrash felt like our territory. A sense of competition was aroused—I was not going to let them have it.

Diligently, I set out to come up with a new harmonic minor part that would eclipse not only Exodus' new song, but our own "Burnt Offerings" as well. This riff would become our title track: "The New Order."

The Harmonic Minor line in "The New Order" is very similar to the one in "Burnt Offerings," yet it sounds completely different. The main reason is that the riff starts on an upbeat, rather than a down beat. I didn't know it at the time, but I'd just stumbled upon a trick that would come in very handy in the future.

Here's the trick: take any chordal riff or single note line and try moving it forwards or backwards one eighth note. Maybe change the pitch of a note or two. The result is a variation that sounds very different from the original part. In the early '00s, I'd be taught this same concept as applied to jazz improvisation, with the fancy name of "rhythmic displacement." It was exactly what I'd unwittingly done with metal riffs all those years earlier.

Following my Harmonic Minor riff in "The New Order" was a great fast thrash riff that Eric had brought in. Although it was very different in style from my melodic single note riff, it worked somehow. By putting our ideas together like this, despite our formidable differences in guitar styles, musical tastes, mannerisms and direction, Eric and I were managing to find a sound.

Over the course of a couple of months, we came up with a series of basic song structures this way. On "The Preacher" I came up with an intro and arpeggio riff, Eric came up with a verse chugging pattern. On "Disciples of the Watch" I came up with a rhythmically tricky intro/chorus riff (a six-bar phrase followed by an eight-bar phrase), he came up with the verses. On "Into The Pit," I came up with a half-time single note line (using the

Harmonic Minor once again), and he came up with a complimentary thrash part.

Soon, we had more than half a dozen of these "sketches," and for a brief moment, it appeared that everything was going to be okay. That's when we realized that we were a ship in danger of sinking with barely a voyage out of San Francisco Bay. There was an iceberg straight ahead: *the lyrics.*

*

Zet had always written the lyrics. We'd never had to think about them before. We'd recorded our rehearsals on a crappy cassette tape[35] and he'd take the sketches home, always coming back with words. They weren't necessarily the most sophisticated:

> *Armies of witches are called in from the North,*
> *Murders of elders occur*
> *The high priest of evil has lowered his iron fist,*
> *Thousands of people will die.*

But hey, we weren't U2 or Leonard Cohen.

If Zet wanted to write about witches and evil priests, so be it. At least we had lyrics. Zet considered his story telling, Dungeons & Dragons imagery and all, as important as his singing and stage performance. It had made things very easy for us. Zet had suspiciously begun slacking on his lyric duties in 1986. This was what had first tipped us off that he was bailing out to join Exodus.

By the time Chuck came aboard, most of the lyrics for the first album had been done. Eric had finished what Zet started on "The Haunting," and he and I together barked out lyrics that seemed acceptable for "Apocalyptic City," making it about an arsonist simply to fit the title. The final song, "Do or Die" happened in much the same manner, with Eric and I barking out lyrics out of desperation, with a few words thrown in by Chuck.

It became clear that while we'd made the right move bringing in Chuck as vocalist and front man, the role of lyricist wasn't coming naturally yet. I remember one lyric writing session with Chuck, Eric and I that just didn't go anywhere. Everyone was stuck in a box, all of us tossing out "evil sounding" words aimlessly, none of it making sense and none of it fitting the music. Not that I'd been much help—I just couldn't come up with any lyrics while working in a group. It felt like trying to urinate in front of someone else.

---

[35] Today, thanks to MP3 recorders and laptops, it's possible to get much better quality rehearsal tapes.

It was time to take matters into my own hands. I'd never thought of myself as a lyricist before. I was sure the lyrics I'd thrown together for the first album would be my last. But this was an emergency. Our careers hung in the balance. I was also tired of lyrics about priests, witches and demons, simply because they seemed so *juvenile*. Enough already. Perhaps there was a way we could write about something deeper.

But how? Heavy metal words just weren't in my head. I needed to get some source of inspiration, then turn them into lyrics. That's when I thought: *Why not turn to books?*

*

Once upon a time, as a little boy, I'd enjoyed reading. But things had changed. The process of reading had been all but ruined for me by the crumbling Berkeley Public School System and my family's sterile intellectualism.

The message sent at home was that books weren't to be viewed as "works of art," only as mediums for the storage of information such as studies and statistics. There were thousands upon thousands of books in our home—mostly textbooks. These scholastic abysses of academia contained little poetry or modern fiction. It was as though the world was to be understood through the information in these books, never through actual living. None of the books were fit for a child (I had very few children's books as a kid, except *Where the Wild Things Are,* which I love to this day) and none were ever explained, shared or given a purpose. What wonders it would have done for my reading had either parent said, *"Here is a novel that I feel passionate about. This book changed my life. I want to share it with you."*

School hadn't been much better; the novels that were assigned were read solely for the purpose of attempting to understand the work's historical significance. While I could see some virtues in this, it seemed as though most of the works presented had little relevance in the modern world, and the curriculum was severely void of works that did. There had been, however, a couple of exceptions. And it were these exceptions that I was able to look back upon as a source of lyrical inspiration for our new album.

How ironic that this impending crisis—desperately needing lyrics for heavy metal songs—would bring me back to reading.

I suddenly remembered that while in junior high, in between all the clutter of forced subjects, being bullied and adolescent angst, there'd been one book that had shone through and spoken to me—a grim forecast of the future: George Orwell's *1984*. This story, about a government taking over its citizens and stripping them of all their individual civil rights and liberties and watching over their every move, was something I related to. I understood the dark world inhabited by the main character, Winston Smith, who is keeping his true feelings hidden from the Thought Police.

That was how I'd felt growing up, hiding my inner self from everyone in Berkeley.

I picked up a copy of Orwell's *1984* and started rereading it. I imagined a battle between the resistance movement Smith secretly belongs to and the rulers who are in control, known only as The Party and led by a mysterious figure known as Big Brother. That night, while brushing my teeth, I heard some lyrics in my head for that "New Order" riff, inspired by Orwell's story:

> *Takers of humanity, elders paranoid,*
> *The time is now—give up this world you once destroyed.*
> *Society vs. the underground. The battle is fought and lost.*
> *The time has come to rule this world, at any cost.*

While the guys in the band didn't quite understand the meaning and had never heard of George Orwell, they really liked the sound of these lyrics.

Since the Orwellian influence was working so well, I thought of another author I'd enjoyed while in school, a poet known for his dark, sinister imagery: Edgar Allen Poe. I read Poe lines out loud to Chuck and Eric and they picked out ones that sounded "cool."

> *Foul plays of passion at twilight's dim*
> *In joy of woe, of good and sin*
> *Now winter storms and fates overcast.*
> *Darkly my presence is now your past.*

These words, which would find their way into our new song "Into The Pit," were more or less variations of Poe verses.

Hearing that I was getting into books, our manager, Elliot, passed on a bunch more books he'd read decades earlier that he felt I'd enjoy—Tom Wolfe, Hunter S. Thompson, Jack Kerouac. I'd later get turned on to authors like Kurt Vonnegut, Erica Jong, Tom Robbins, Charles Bukowski and more. I'd never read stuff like this in school—it wasn't about long gone eras, it was about relevant situations and life today. In school, you weren't supposed to *like* reading, it was something you *had* to do. But these books were so relevant, so passionate, so alive, I was hooked. I devoured them like fresh baked cookies, my passion for reading reignited after all these years, never to wane again.

And thanks to my newfound love of books, books that represented how I felt, and were read on my own terms, many more lyrics were forthcoming, the majority on "The New Order." Little did these authors know that they were now inadvertently and unknowingly inspiring heavy metal lyrics.

Chuck, Eric and I soon found an unspoken system: I'd bring in some lines inspired by my books, Chuck would change a few around so he'd be more comfortable singing, I'd make suggestions to fit his new patterns, Eric would contribute by bringing in words he'd heard in a horror movie or comic book. [36]

Eventually, we had enough music and even lyrics for a whole album. Or so we thought.

Upon completion of the recording, *The New Order* would be promptly rejected by our record label, sent back like a steak that was cooked too rare.

*

1988 Pyramid Sound, Ithaca New York, Emergency Conference Call with Megaforce Records.

The entire band and our producer are crowded around the small table next to the mixing console as Johnny Z's voice distorts through the speaker-phone.

"I gotta tell ya, I heard the album, guys. You're sounding great but...listen—we got a big problem here. You know that right? Anyone checked the time of the record?"

Everyone speaks at the same time: "No," "Nah uh," "What is it, Johnny?"

"Thirty-one minute, boys! That's not good! Thirty-one minutes?! I'm listenin', I'm groovin' along, and the thing ends. I say, 'You gotta be fuckin' kiddin' me!'"

We're all too stunned to respond.

"Don't get me wrong, guys, I like what I'm hearin', but c'mon already! Where the fuck's the rest of it? You guys keep callin' up talkin' about the cover, how we gotta work on getting' the cover right, blah, blah, blah... But what about what's underneath the damn cover?!"

We look to our producer, Alex. "Uh, Johnny. It's Alex here, Alex Perialas. I'm sorry, I have to take some responsibility here, I..."

"You're goddamn right! Now look, Perialas, you're the one in charge, do something. You're in deep shit. I'm in deep shit. We're all in deep

---

[36] Eric was the main contributor on some songs such as "Disciples of the Watch," lyrics about the horror movie *Children of the Corn*.

shit. *You don't know to time the fuckin' album? Look at the fuckin' record deal for Christ's sake! Guys—it's your own fuckin' record deal. Whatcha don't read your own contracts?"*

Louie tries to speak—"Johnny, we fucked up. We seen it but we forgot. Whatsit s'posed to be?"

"Forty fuckin' minutes, guys. Minimum. And that's the goddamn MINIMUM! And ya know what?! Nobody's doin' the fuckin' minimum no more! Metallica "Master Of Fuckin' Puppets"—fifty-four minutes. The new Anthrax that's comin' out next month[37]? Fifty fuckin' minutes. Pretty soon all the albums are gonna be an hour long! Whatsa matter with youse guys?"

Alex P: "You're totally right Johnny. I have to say, in our defense, that I think this new record is really great. It's so good that we all just got caught up in it and didn't realize that it came in a few minutes under, it feels complete. At the same time, we understand that..."

Johnny Z: "I don't wanna fuckin' hear about it, Perialas! Now what are we gonna do here, huh? We got big problems. This fucks me! It fucks me on pushing the album! It fucks me on getting the press behind it. And it fucks me on the publishing. And another thing..."

(Greg gives the phone the finger and whispers about how Johnny swindled half our publishing for the album. He's right, but it's no consolation.)

Johnny rants for a few more minutes, tossing out ideas for a possible solution: Leftover tracks from last time? A guitar solo from me? Write some new songs?

"Like I was sayin', I don't know what the fuck we're gonna do here, fellahs. But we gotta do somethin'! Now getcha heads together and figure this shit out!"

Johnny hangs up the phone, hard. The ensuing silence is deafening.

*

Alright, we fucked up.

But in fairness, Megadeth's latest, *So Far, So Good, So What,* was just a few minutes longer than ours, at thirty-four minutes. And Slayer's album from the year before, *Reign in Blood* (still considered their most essential album), was only twenty-eight minutes long! Then again, the length of *Reign in Blood* was part of its character. No other band could get away with an album that short.

---

[37] Anthrax *Among the Living* (Island,1987).

The bottom line was this: Johnny was right. For metal, the template was being set by Metallica, who were following the lead of mainstream hard rock artists, like Def Leppard, by releasing albums that were close to an hour long.[38] And with compact discs quickly replacing vinyl and cassettes as the new medium for recorded music, there was more room for content—the fans were expecting it. Johnny Z, besides being our label president, was Anthrax's manager, so he'd made sure that those guys had enough material to compete.

Ultimately, there were many to blame for our predicament. We certainly hadn't helped ourselves simply by not coming up with more music. And not to shirk responsibility, but as our producer, Alex P really should have been keeping track of the minutes, not just assuming the songs would all add up to an acceptable length for an album.

And then there was Elliot, our manager and attorney—he'd negotiated the damn contract. To his credit, he'd gone through great effort to explain everything to us, much of which had still gone over our heads. Yet somewhere in that mountain of paragraphs, articles, items, provisions and clauses, the part about the minimum amount of recorded material had been overlooked. Elliot had dropped the ball as much as Alex P and the rest of us.

But ultimately, to quote our lone cover on the album (by Aersosmith), it was "Nobody's Fault." Everyone was to blame. Somehow it had failed to translate to everyone's mind that anything less than forty minutes of recorded music for this album would constitute Breach of Contract. We had a big problem on our hands.

*

One of Johnny Z's ideas had been to have me play an open guitar solo, like Van Halen's "Eruption," or Jimmy Page's cadenza from Led Zeppelin's "Whole Lotta Love." During the conference call, he'd said: *"You guyz got this freakin' whiz kid guitah playah there. That'll buy ya three or four minutes right there. Do one a those goddamn guitah solos!"*

A conference call with Elliot followed, where he seconded Johnny Z's idea: *"Gentlemen, we all have to take responsibility and I apologize for my role in this. But the fact is, we have a situation on our hands. Mr. Skolnick is just going to have to do an open guitar solo."* No one else had responded. They just shrugged and sat stone faced.

I really didn't want to do an open solo. It wasn't just because the guys didn't seem into it, but because I didn't feel ready—I was still finding myself on the instrument. Maybe in a few years I could pull it off and feel

---

[38] Metallica's next album *And Justice for All,* would be their longest yet at sixty-five minutes.

proud of it, but not at this time and especially with this kind of pressure. Van Halen's "Eruption" had been a musical piece Eddie had been playing live with the band for years, not something he'd had to come up with on the spot.

Besides, those types of things worked for one guitar bands, like Van Halen and Led Zeppelin. I'd joined a two guitar band, formed by another guitar player with a sensitive ego. I could see the pain that the mention of it caused Eric. There'd already been some hints of tension—he hated the idea of me becoming like a Van Halen/Randy Rhoads of thrash, while he was viewed as more of a rhythm guitarist. He hadn't started this band to have another guitarist receive more attention. Doing an open guitar solo on our album was out of the question.

So what could we do?

The drums had been broken down already, so there was no way to rebuild the kit, mic everything up again and get the exact same drum sounds we'd had. The guitar rigs were still up, so the only choice was to come up with some music using just the two guitars.

In the end it was decided that we'd drop in several instrumental guitar pieces with no drums. First, the album's opening track, "Erie Inhabitants," was given a long harmonized clean guitar intro, which I soloed over using these cool diminished arpeggio patterns that I'd heard Randy Rhoads use. This intro bought us two minutes. Then, an instrumental of just two guitars, "Hypnosis" added a couple more minutes. Finally, there was a full instrumental track "Musical Death: A Dirge," which we'd already recorded with drums, but hadn't been planning to use. Now we were not only using it, we were adding to it—the whole piece was doubled in length.

With all the little interludes completed, our music now totaled 39 minutes, 22 seconds. With the gaps between songs, the total time amounted to (just barely) forty minutes.

We breathed a collective sigh of relief.

Fans have told me they love the little instrumentals—that they're what sets *The New Order* apart and gives the album its character. But the only reason those pieces exist at all is because we'd been flying by the seat of our pants to avoid being in breach of contract.

*

I couldn't be too mad at Johnny Z for this. Sure, the stress had been hyperkinetic. But because of it, we actually had a better album than we'd had before. Less easy to forgive him for was the fact that, as alluded to earlier, he'd screwed us on our future royalties for this album.

Here's what had happened: as per the record deal, we'd been allotted a certain amount of tour support, theoretically enough money to get us through the album cycle. But along the way, there'd been these last minute, unexpected support slots such as the Slayer show in Brooklyn and the Dynamo Open Air in Eindhoven. While these had been great opportunities, there'd been too many expenses—flights, hotels and other costs. Then, we'd done our seven-week US tour, which had led to van repairs and numerous other unforeseen costs.

And as helpful as it had been to support bigger acts like Anthrax and Overkill, the shows really didn't pay enough to support the tour—it was like paying for advertisement.[39] So by the time we'd gone back to Europe, again to support Anthrax, on a two-month tour, there'd been very little tour support money left over and we ran out of funds midway through the tour.

In the future, we'd get business managers to keep a close eye on the incoming and outgoing funds and make sure something like this never happened again. But for the time being, we were in a bad position.

Our choices were as follows:

1. Cancel the remaining shows and head home.
2. Approach Johnny Z and work out a deal for additional tour support.

The good news was that Johnny was more than happy to help us out of our predicament. The bad news? He would do so only in exchange for the rights to half our publishing royalties on the next album.

Ouch.

*

Admittedly, this situation had presented a bit of a moral dilemma for me. How was I to now think about Johnny Z?

What had happened was *inexcusable*, the type of shady, morally reprehensible, backhanded, getting over on someone in need that I could never in the wildest depths of my good conscience imagine partaking in. Yet at the same time, this was the guy we owed everything too! Because of him, we were launching careers in the music business. Who knows where I, or the rest of the band, would be without him?

Yes, he had taken shameless advantage of us in our time of desperation. On the other hand, our band had gotten *itself* in the situation! Johnny had never gone out of his way to try and make this happen. Sure he

---

[39] Even today, most support tours don't pay enough to earn a profit. In fact, there are some acts who pay headliners in order to tour in the support slots. Sharon Osbourne deserves some of the credit for this by charging young bands' record labels to get a slot at Ozzfest, money which, of course, would have to be recouped by the musicians, making it that much tougher to ever earn a profit from their music.

may not have been nice about it and I'd like to think I'd have handled the situation differently—then again, who knows how I'd think had I been his age, with his life experiences and having risen to his position as the head of a heavy metal record label in the '80s?

I decided I still liked Johnny. I was learning that, in this business, one has to learn to swim with the sharks. And just because someone's a shark in business doesn't mean they can't be your friend (maybe not a close friend). Just as there are personal friends to whom you probably shouldn't tell a secret, or loan your car or money, there are friends in business who you just shouldn't approach to bail you out or borrow money *from.* Instead of harboring a grudge, it seemed best to just learn from this experience and move on.

If you limit your personal friends and your business associates to include only those whose moral compass and sense of right and wrong is on par with your own, then I've got news for you: you're going to be very lonely and you'll miss out on a lot of business opportunities. Being able to swim with the sharks doesn't mean you have to become one yourself. Just make sure you don't go into the water without protective diving gear. It also helps to have a good cage.

So far I was learning many valuable lessons, including the following two, which the whole band had learned collectively:

1. Never find yourself in the position of begging your label for tour support.

2. Never enter the studio without having at least enough material to complete the album as required by your contract.

*

Recording the bulk of *The New Order* had been a bit different than recording *The Legacy.*

For one thing, we'd been through the process already, so we had a better idea of what to expect. For another, we tried having Eric play all the rhythms. We'd heard that's how Metallica did it—James played all the rhythms, Kirk played most of the solos. This made sense for the sake of getting the music as tight as possible. However, it would be generally agreed upon once the album came out that something was missing.

The first album may have been noisier but the sound of both guitars playing the rhythms gave it more personality. *The New Order* would have a darker, more box-like sound. But in fairness to Eric, a big part of the problem was that Alex P insisted on using these tiny little condenser mics to capture his guitar sound, as well as mine.

When we questioned Alex P's decision, we got a lecture about how these mics represent the future of recording. *We want the album to sound current, don't we? Then let's move forward not backwards.* Alex then reminded us that *he* was producing this album, not *us*.

This had been strange.

Alex had been, up to then, our source of guidance, a great "coach" for each of us in the studio, and would certainly rise to the occasion when it came to the crisis of needing more recorded material. But here we all felt his choice of guitar mic was glaringly wrong. He blamed the tone on Eric's rig which, truth be told, could have stood some improvement, but certainly would have sounded light years better with a good quality mic. It increasingly seemed like Alex P was committing errors yet unable to admit any fault.

Someone like Lars Ulrich or Dave Mustaine probably would have gotten the hell out of there, phoned the record company and demanded a new producer. But at that time, we didn't have the foresight to realize that this uncle-figure we'd been looking up to could possibly be wrong about anything and didn't know how to go about challenging him or replacing him.

To this day, *The New Order* is frequently written up as having some of the best songs of our career, but an album that sadly suffers from very poor production.

*

On a brighter note, Alex P had recently taken on a great assistant engineer: Rob Hunter. I immediately recognized him as "Wacko," the great drummer from Raven, who'd always dressed in sports jerseys and had worn a hockey mask. I was a bit star-struck.

Rob was in a new phase of his life, having left Raven, settled down and married to a very nice woman, the receptionist at the studio. They'd recently had a baby. He turned out to be very funny, easygoing and down-to-earth.

I'd been a big fan of Raven. They'd been the other band on Metallica's first tour of the US. Not just the support act but the co-headliner. In fact the whole tour had been named after both of their albums. Metallica's album was *Kill 'Em All,* while Raven's was *All for One.* Both albums had been released by Johnny Z,[40] who'd cleverly put the two titles together, resulting in the "Kill 'Em All for One" tour.

It was widely believed that Raven was the band with more commer-

---

[40] Metallica was subsequently bought out of their contract with Johnny Z by Electra Records.

cial potential of the two. Obviously that sounds preposterous now, with Metallica one of the top-selling acts ever to come out of the US, but no one saw that coming. Metallica was big, loud, ugly and scary. Raven was more polished, less gritty, and with shorter, simpler song structures. And while I loved both bands, I admit to actually liking Raven a bit more, at least at the time. I've read interviews with others, including Buzz Osborne, from the Melvins, who've said the exact same thing.

After *All for One,* Raven attempted to go commercial, a move that worked for some bands but, more often than not, was career suicide, especially for hard rock/metal bands like Raven. Other bands that had committed this faux pas, never to recover, included Y&T and Savatage. In each case, the band would try to get back on track by releasing subsequent albums closer to their original sounds. But all it takes is one really bad commercial album to completely derail a career.

On our next tour, Raven (minus Rob Hunter), would actually support Testament. It would be strange to see a band that I'd looked up to and listened to religiously in high school, one that had co-headlined with Metallica, suddenly in the position of opening up for us.

Rob was and still is an excellent engineer. He'd go on to work with many different producers. Many years later, I'd find myself listening to an album by jazz saxophonist Branford Marsalis. I'd notice the credits, Rob "Wackamas" Hunter. Sure enough, Rob had gone on to work for Branford and become his good friend and permanent drum engineer, live and in the studio. It would be good to see that I wasn't the only one who'd had a foot in both metal and jazz.

*

With the *New Order* mixes done and the filler instrumental tracks almost finished, all was well again in Ithaca.

Just as they'd done the year before, Johnny Z, Marsha and Maria flew up from Jersey to hang out with us, listen to the mixes and take the band out to dinner. Johnny was like our surrogate papa once again, as though all the drama surrounding the tour support and length of the album had never occurred.

Arriving late on Saturday afternoon, they took us out to a great meal at a local seafood restaurant that featured all you can eat crab. Afterwards, they went to their hotel to call it a night and meet up with us at the studio the next day. Since it would be Sunday, they told us to take our time—they were going to take it easy, go out for brunch and meet us later in the day.

As for the rest of us, we were ready to party. I had a few more last-minute guitar parts to add to the instrumentals. But other than that, the bulk of the album was pretty much mixed and we were ahead of schedule. It was Saturday night and after the stress of the previous week, we all needed an evening to unwind. Greg and Chuck headed to Captain Joe's Reef to drink and check out a local band as Alex P opened up the studio for Eric and Lou and I to mess around, drink beers and have fun.

At the studio, we got drunk and laughed ourselves silly, recording embarrassingly goofy songs (which are probably still on tape somewhere). One of these songs had started because Greg, the skinniest of all, had eaten more all-you-can-eat crab than anyone else, even startling the restaurant staff. So the song began with the refrain "Go go Greggy! Eat that crab!" This led to a series of verses describing each member of the group, followed by a chorus.

"First there's Eric, he's all you can stand. He is the one who started the band. He'll do anything so he can have fun. That's why we call him "Gremlin One." Then the chorus, very loud repeated four times: *"Go go Eric! Gremlin one!"* Then there was a verse about each of the rest of us.

With its subtle, quiet verses and screaming choruses, our "Go Go" song had the dynamics of Nirvana's hit "Smells Like Teen Spirit," five years earlier. It's a shame the song was just a private goof; it probably had the most commercial potential of anything we've ever come up with.

*

On the way back, we stopped at a couple different bars. With each drink, things got more and more fuzzy. Finally I decided to stop. Eric and Lou kept going.

I barely remember us getting back to the motel. Since the Ramada had been under construction, our new home was the Meadow Court Motel, which we referred to as the "Metal Court." It was about a mile down the road.

Greg had already come back and was asleep in the room, so I knew it was late. Eric and Lou had stopped at a liquor store and tried to get me to go to their room, where they planned to smoke and continue drinking throughout the night. Fortunately, I had a good excuse not to go, since I did have those last-minute parts to play the next day.

At about 4:30 am or so, I woke up to what sounded like the smashing of a thousand wine glasses all at once, coming from across the motel courtyard. Greg didn't wake up—he kept on snoring.

Had I imagined it? Couldn't be. The noise had caused a car alarm to go off in the parking lot.

I looked outside my window, and there, in front of Eric and Lou's room, was shattered glass all over the walkway and an upside down table in the midst of it all. Eric, in a moment of delusion, had decided he was Axl Rose or Elvis, taking the wooden table in his motel room and using it to smash his window before tossing the table outside. Now he was standing in their doorway giggling and shouting: *"I'm a rock star! Yeahhhh!"*

I called Alex P in a panic, woke him up, and told him what had happened. "I'll be right there," he said. Interestingly, Alex P was calm and seemed to know exactly what to do—perhaps this wasn't the first time he'd had to deal with a drunk band member trashing a hotel room. He talked Eric into bed, and straightened everything out with the motel clerks, who knew him (everyone in town knew Alex).

The cost of a new window and table was well over a thousand dollars. It would be paid for immediately by the studio, who would then later be reimbursed by the band. The band would take the money out of Eric's future salary and per diems. When asked if he had any regrets about this, Eric would respond, *"No fuckin' way! I had fun!"* Still, it would be the last hotel room he'd trash.

*

The next day, I was back at the studio with Alex P to record my final parts. Johnny, Marsha and Metal Maria were due to stop by any moment. He and I agreed it was best to keep quiet about Eric's room trashing the night before.

They arrived a short time later. With them was, Elliot's co-manager Jeff Saltzman. He'd flown into Ithaca a few days prior, and had joined us for dinner the night before but being recently sober, had avoided partying with any of us afterwards.

Jeff, a bald, skinny attorney with a high voice who looked like the comedian Steven Wright, had met with Johnny and co. over brunch. He was off to catch a flight in order to be in the office on Monday morning and had come to say a quick goodbye. Seeing that I was the only one at the studio, he asked me to give his best to the rest of the guys whenever I saw them. Just then, a cab came and whisked him off to nearby Ithaca airport.

For the next hour or so, Johnny, Marsha and Maria just hung out on the sofa behind the mixing console listening to me adding my last minute guitar overdubs to the instrumentals. They'd offered to go to the next room, but I didn't want to be rude. Though I'd always shied away from having anyone else in the studio while I recorded, I was finding that I was surprisingly comfortable with them there. Unlike the guys in the band, who seemed to nitpick at everything I played, Johnny and Marsha were encouraging and supportive, like my middle-aged Italian/Jewish cheerleaders from Jersey (Johnny Z is of mixed Italian and Jewish descent). It was the most relaxed I'd ever been while in the studio. I was enjoying recording for the first time. It was a calm, pleasant Sunday afternoon.

Until…

Jeff Saltzman, who by this time is waiting for his flight at Ithaca airport, decides that rather than sitting around, he'll make use of his time by taking care of some business. He walks to an airport payphone intent on tracking down Johnny Z. His goal? To negotiate a minor point of dispute in the contract.

The phone rings. Alex P picks it up "Oh, hi Jeff. At the airport? Everything alright? Great. What's that? You need Johnny? Okay, hang on a sec…"

"Johnny, it's Jeff Saltzman on line one." Johnny picks up the phone, presses button one.

"Yeah? Mmm hmm. Yeah? Okay. Uh huh….Yeah…Ok, now hang on a second. You listen to me close now, ya hear me? You been dealin' with our attorney on shit like this, right? Yeah? Alright so listen—you do me a big faveh, alright? You call my god damn attorney first thing Monday morning! What the fuck is this Sunday shit anyway?!"

He brings the phone down, a judge smashing down the gavel. CLICK! Johnny then explodes: *"THAT SKINNY FUCKIN' WEASEL!! SON OF A BITCH!!! CALLIN' ON SUNDAY TO SHAKE ME DOWN FOR PROMO BUDGETS OR SOME SHIT! YA KNOW WHAT? FUCK HIM!! WHO THE FUCK DOES HE THINK….?!"*

He marches out of the control room into the lounge. Marsha runs after him hesitantly. She whispers with a smile that she's sorry about this, as though it happens all the time.

"Honey? Honey? Calm down, sweetheart, he don't know, he's just a jackass attorney, neveh managed before. He don't know, hon. He's bein' a shmuck. But he don' mean nothin'."

Johnny and Marsha's voices fade as the door closes to the lounge but I can still hear him:

"That muthafuckin' weasel. God damn him. The nerve o' that goddamn skinny, bald pencilnecked… "

The phone rings again. It's Jeff calling to apologize. Alex P tells him it's really not a good idea to speak to Johnny right now. Metal Maria stays in the room with us, smiles cheerfully and says with a hearty laugh: "Guys, you've just witnessed my world. Welcome to Megaforce!"

Alex P looks ultra-serious, as though I'm a child who's just witnessed a dark family secret. He addresses Maria and points towards me: "He really shouldn't have to see things like this."

I shrug, disinterestedly. "It's reality." I say. "Let's get back to work. Now, where were we?"

*

Johnny apologizes to me later and I tell him not to worry. I'm honestly fine with it.

I saw his point. Sure he overreacted. But Jeff shouldn't have bothered him, especially on a relaxing Sunday when he's hanging out with us informally, to nag him about some contractual detail that is best discussed with Johnny's attorney.

Jeff's intention, to make use of time, was good. But his tact was anything but. And good relations in the music biz are all about tact. It's hard for many musicians, especially metal musicians, to have tact—that's partly why we need representation. Even at nineteen, I realize this. That's one of the reasons I'll later decide that, with a few exceptions, attorneys shouldn't manage bands.

Yes, Johnny Z is intense and can be ruthless. He's someone that says whatever comes to mind with no hesitation, self-consciousness or socio-political correctness. If you're not careful, he might just steal the shirt off your back.

But on the flipside, he's got a sense of endearing familial affection as manifested by how important it was for us to spend quality time together on that peaceful Sunday afternoon. It's hard not to admire convictions, even though he occasionally bumps up against some of your own deep-rooted values and norms.

In about ten years, a memorable television character will be created with similar complexities. Like Johnny Z, he will be family-oriented, of Italian-American descent and from New Jersey. He too will have a dark side, albeit one far more dangerous. And like Johnny, no matter what he does, you somehow sense that at his core, he really means well, so as a result, you just have to cut him a little extra slack. His name? Tony Soprano.

There is something appealing about ultra-assertive characters like this, even though you might not agree with all of their actions. This is especially true for someone like me, who has been trying so hard to break out of a shell. After growing up in a social environment of forced politeness and having been trained never to express my true feelings, seeing things through the eyes of the Johnny Zs of the world is a breath of fresh air.

189

25. EXPANDING HORIZONS

Being the best musician you can be requires a strict sense of independence and the ability to look inward, to not go with the crowd. That inner spirit of independence, not to mention a general disapproval of life as it had been presented to me in Berkeley, had caused me to break ranks with family and peers, which was how I'd wound up in the band in the first place. But now, that same sense of independence was forcing me to ponder whether there might be more to life than what was now in my immediate surroundings.

So with the *New Order* sessions coming to a close, I was beginning to feel a little bit, shall we say, stifled. There was no doubt I would be in this band for a long time, yet I was seriously questioning the virtues of being a guitarist who was limited to just metal.

It's not that I expected the other guys to be the type of musician I was—it just wasn't in their nature and I had no problem with this. There was no reason why we couldn't find some musical common ground. For the most part, we had. However, it was now beginning to present challenges, musically and socially.

On a musical level, I was getting bored playing in E minor all the time, the lowest key on the guitar. On the previous album, I'd managed to push through one song that was in the key of A ("Alone in the Dark"), but it was becoming clear that this was never going to happen again. I knew that with a little more open-mindedness, we could explore territory that no one else had explored yet—but it was no use. It was very hard for the band to grasp the idea of different keys and time signatures, even though Metallica had already broken out of E. Adding to the challenge, Eric was becoming a bit resistant to my solos. He said they were too long, too "American-sounding" and that I should play more "European" (whatever the hell that meant). Meanwhile, it was difficult to get him to play parts that supported my solos—he preferred to play overactive riffing, often rendering my licks indecipherable to the ear.

On a social level, everyone's priorities were elsewhere: constant partying and hanging out in their own little clique. I was quickly losing interest in the whole stoner scene—it just struck me as *really lame*. And whenever I'd opt to stay in my room and practice guitar for an evening, I'd receive odd glances and other hints of disapproval.

This reaction was very bizarre to me.

I was all for having a good time whenever there was something to celebrate—being done with tracks, finishing the mixes or whatever. But to get high and get drunk, day in and day out, seemed to defeat the purpose of partying in the first place. Guitar was something I'd dedicated my entire life to. Why on Earth should I throw it all away in order to waste time getting drunk, stoned and engaging in silly banter every single night?

By refusing to go along with everyone else in this manner, I was becoming the weirdo. I kept overhearing murmurs from the band such as *Alex doesn't wanna hang out. What's his trip? I don't know, he's just trippin'*. Even Alex Perialas began expressing concern, asking me repeatedly, *"Is everything okay?"*

Alex P meant well, but just didn't get it. Having mostly worked with bad boy rock bands, it was difficult for him to get the concept of someone young, with long hair and a tattoo, focusing all his energy on developing a craft with the same level of dedication as a concert pianist. When Eric had trashed his hotel room, Alex P had shown barely any surprise at all, as though he'd been expecting that kind of thing from one of us sooner or later. He seemed to derive great pleasure recounting the tale afterwards, gently ribbing Eric and getting laughs for his storytelling.

Somehow, Eric drunkenly throwing a table through his motel room window at 4 am was perfectly acceptable behavior, while my becoming a more serious, focused person was cause for alarm. What the hell was going on here?

In hindsight, it was very simple. While I was expected to act according to the pre-conceived cliché of the "metal dude" knucklehead, I was displaying a more disciplined and sensitive temperament like that expected from a ballet dancer, classical musician or introverted poet. Like *Billy Elliot*, the miner's son from a rough Northern Britain neighborhood born with a passion for dance who'd go on to join the Royal Ballet, I was in surroundings nonconducive to serious artistic development.

So, as had been the case growing up in Berkeley, I felt out of place, not fitting in. Once again, I became a pariah. I'd fought so hard to get here, just to be able to play music as a profession. Yet now, in order to play it with higher standards and dignity, I had a whole new fight ahead of me. Having already faced aggressive hostility and opposition at home and at school, I'd basically gone from one totally unsupportive environment straight into another.

In order to keep from going crazy, there was no choice but to tell myself that nothing was wrong with me, but something was wrong with everyone else. I realize it probably sounds a bit elitist, when put that way. But as it turned out, I couldn't have been more right.

*

This new level of drive and focus had begun midway through the *New Order* sessions.

I'd been rooming with Greg, who'd usually go next door to Chuck's room to get stoned, then come back and veg out in front of the TV while I'd sit on my bed and practice my guitar unplugged. He'd often watch those animal documentaries—you know, the ones that show close-up scenes of nature with a gentle voiceover commentary. (*"Here the orangutan is seen in his native habitat happily eating a banana...."*) His favorites were the ones about insects. Whether he had my attention or not, he'd offer his own running commentary. *"That spider's gonna fuck that fly up...yeah! Die, motherfucker, die! Dead fly! Go spider! Suck his blood!"* His behavior was Beavis & Butthead incarnate, a few years early.

Greg's actual knowledge on the subject was uncanny—he seemed to know the exact species and habits of each insect. With a bit more maturity and focus, he might have been able to channel these interests into a second career involving entomology (much like Slayer's Kerry King would go on to establish a second career as a respected herpetologist). Alas, maturity, focus and Greg wouldn't find each other.

During the last two weeks in Ithaca, Greg flipped the channel past the most incredible music I'd ever heard. I asked him to turn it back, which he politely did, watching with me for about a minute disinterestedly before going next door to smoke more pot. I watched the rest of the program.

It would change my life.

*

The Ithaca PBS station had been broadcasting a live concert with trumpet, percussion, saxophone, keyboards and screaming electric guitar. At first, I wasn't even sure what kind of music this was—it went back and forth from rock, funk, swing and ethnic rhythms but with a driving energy. The guitar solos were incredible, bluesy, jazzy, whispering and screaming.[41] Yet great as they were, I was equally drawn in by the solos of the horns and other instruments. Even more surprising: the band's accompaniment behind each solo was as exciting as the solo itself. It became part of the solo. Each player was equally adept at every style, playing notes and patterns that seemed impossible, yet worked somehow. The dynamics would go from thunderous volume and delicate silence and back again seamlessly, all without missing a

---

[41] Most likely it was John Scofield, Mike Stern or Robben Ford on guitar.

beat. Whoever these people were, they had to be among the best in the world. I was transfixed.

I had to find out more about this music. It had spoken to me, in an almost mysterious way, as though it were reaching out and calling for me to come closer. Only during the end credits did I see a name I recognized: Miles Davis.

Although Miles was universally considered a jazz artist, what I'd just witnessed was not jazz, at least as I'd thought of it. This was one of his amplified electric projects from the '80s, with screaming guitar licks. Yet ironically, this music would eventually become my gateway to playing acoustic modern jazz. Soon I'd start collecting Miles' albums. His *Kind Of Blue* would become my all-time favorite album. I'd soon own more Miles Davis albums than any other artist (even Kiss).

When I was growing up, my friends and I had never thought it cool to like jazz. I remember one of the local record stores on Telegraph Avenue, Rasputin's, had a separate Soul and Jazz shop. We used to make fun of it as we'd walk past (how fucking stupid we'd been). I wish I'd been going into that Soul & Jazz shop, purchasing invaluable recordings from Blue Note, Verve and Impulse. They'd still be in my collection today.

*

I began to realize that the medium of television was very contradictory. On the one hand, it was this highly addictive, focus-killing medium of cheap entertainment—trashy soap opera reruns, gossip shows and in more recent years, bad reality shows. Yet there were occasional moments of pure art being captured and sent out to the world, like that Miles Davis concert, which helped me wake up, get out of my funk and get in touch with something deeper.

Besides Miles, there were other great public television performances that would occasionally flash across the TV screen. During a *Great Performances* series, I got drawn in by a classical pianist playing J.S. Bach's two and three part inventions. On *Austin City Limits,* I saw country pickers wailing on Fender Telecasters, making it look effortless. Once, on another channel, there was an acoustic jam session featuring the guitarist Al Di Meola playing tangos—I'd already taken an increasing interest in Al's music, but being able to watch him was a whole new experience. And most nights in the motel room, the David Letterman show would come on, highlighting the skill and versatility of his house band, led by keyboardist Paul Shaeffer and known as The World's Most Dangerous Band.

One night, Letterman's band was joined by jazz saxophonist Branford Marsalis (Rob Hunter's future boss). They jammed on a John

Coltrane tune.[42] I couldn't believe that this same house band, who'd just been cutting to commercials with great covers of Cream and Led Zeppelin songs, was now backing Branford on a Coltrane tune. Once again, I was completely blown away.

I made a comment to Greg along the lines of *"Wow! Listen to these guys —they can play anything!"* Having just returned from yet another weed session next door, he'd been staring at the TV with faraway blood shot eyes. He muttered something about how guys like that were *real musicians,* not guys like us.

This comment stung like one of those wasps on the nature channel. *Guys like us?!* I refused to be dragged down by anyone else's lack of drive and motivation. I liked Greg as a person and always would, but it was time to distance myself from this self-inflicted sense of inferiority. Over the years, I would occasionally try talking to him about self-improvement and having higher standards in music and in life. But most of the time, it would be like conversing with a stoned parrot.

I decided right there and then that nothing was going to stop me from becoming a "real musician," like those guys on TV.

*

The next day, armed with incentive from Miles, Al, Branford, Paul Schaeffer and his band, I rifled through my suitcase and dug out my old notebook from Joe Satriani. It had all the modes that he'd shown me but hadn't stuck. Those same learning blocks I'd always had in school had gotten in the way of my advancing to the next level of musicianship, and were now being reinforced by others around me. No more. It was time to break through these blocks.

I decided right then and there that I would learn these modes, once and for all, whatever it took. If I took time every single day and just worked with those diagrams on that page, something at some point had to make sense. A breakthrough would be inevitable. I just had to stick with it.

Sitting with my old "Joe" notebook, I practiced the seven modes of the major scale, over and over. I didn't see the point at first and the usual negative voices started appearing. *You don't need to know that stuff. You're not that kind of musician. That's not for guys like us.*

But I refused to be thrown off this time. I'd had enough of that bullshit. And after just a few days playing, taking a break when I got frustrated, and coming back to it undaunted, it all started to come together, conceptually and melodically. I was now hooked on something. Not

---

[42] A rare occurrence, as David Letterman is notoriously not a jazz fan.

something that led to a dead end like getting high and flipping channels. Something that felt positively invigorating and enriching.

Of course, spending all this time practicing and not choosing to get dragged into beer, pot and television with the others, opened up that whole scenario described earlier of everyone acting weird towards me. But it no longer mattered. I'd finally figured out what was really important. I no longer needed approval from anyone else.

*

Back in Berkeley, I immediately began making life changes.

On the day we landed, I got out of that bad relationship I'd been in. Trying to be as kind and gentle as I could, I explained that things weren't working for a number of reasons. She threw a fit, as I'd predicted. It was ugly. Yet, I never would have predicted the years of public meltdowns and stalking that would come.

Then, I showed up back at my mom and dad's with suitcases and boxes. My timing was not good—my father was in the middle of what my mother called *one of his moods.* He exploded—wasting no time hammering me about my hair, my clothes, what I was doing with my life and the usual screaming about why the hell don't I just go to school?!

It reminded me of the opening scene in the Cheech & Chong film *Up In Smoke* where Chong leaves home for good, his father following him out of the house yelling, *"You get a goddamn job before sundown or we're shippin' ya off to military school with that goddamn Finklestein shit kid!"* Then Chong flips him the bird on the way out. Only in my case, this wasn't a comedy—it was tragic. And worse, I wasn't walking out—I was moving back in.

I couldn't help but question where on Earth this kind of parenting came from. At what point was it ever decided that this type of all-out screaming was a *good* idea? How could you go through life with no control of your temper and no concept of the negative effect it has on the people you're supposed to love?

Clearly some kind of old school, misguided generational faux pas was at play. This was exactly the type of abuse that had kept me in the clutches of an emotionally disturbed female meth addict for more than a year. Now I was about to move back into a house with a father who made me feel like a new recruit in the United States Marine Corp.

Desperate, I tried to think if there was anyone else on Earth whom I could possibly live with. Sadly no one came to mind. For a moment, I pondered homelessness.

Then, I remembered a saying that I'd seen quoted recently, by Nietzsche: *"That which does not kill you makes you stronger."* Telling myself this over and over, I went straight to my room, vowing to put up with it as best I could and spend as much of my days out of the house as possible.

*

So miserable were both parents with my being a musician that over the years, I'd often wonder if they'd been happier had I been the Unibomber.

The Unibomber had been the youngest professor ever hired by UC Berkeley. Eventually he resigned, moved to Montana, went mad and engaged in a mail-bomb killing spree, eluding authorities for more than twenty years. I could imagine my folks on the day of my arrest, watching the drama unfold on TV as I was forcefully removed from my remote cabin in the woods by the FBI. Surrounded by friends and colleagues, they'd thank everyone for supporting them during this time of unspeakable tragedy. Then, barely able to suppress a smile, my father would add, *"Did we mention he went to Harvard and has a PhD in mathematics?"*

A few days after moving back in, my father caught me completely off guard by behaving kindly towards me. He was calm and rational. I could only guess that the gentle urging of my mother had gotten through to him. While I couldn't allow myself to feel too safe for fear that the calm winds were only temporary, it was a relief to feel as though a great storm had passed. Speaking to me like a civilized person, he asked how things were going with the band.

I told him that while I felt good about the second album and the upcoming tour dates, I was starting to make serious progress as a musican and that I felt there was more to me than just this type of music. No, I wasn't going back to school. But if it was any consolation, I'd been taking music very seriously. I told him what my plans were: taking private lessons, not just guitar, but general musicianship—composition, improvisation, jazz studies, classical theory, music history etc...in other words, a more educated approach.

That's when my father got up, went to the phone and started dialing. "Who are you calling?" I asked. He didn't answer. When he spoke into the phone, it became clear that he was calling his office. At first I thought he was being rude—here we're having a civilized conversation at last and he gets up in the middle to call the office. But these thoughts changed to curiosity as I heard him ask his assistant to look up the music department of the University. He then asked if there were any references to music professors who teach privately and if not, could she make a couple calls on his behalf?

It's for his son, the musician. *His son, the musician.* It was the first time I'd heard these words uttered without bitterness.

A few minutes later, he had the phone numbers of several UC Berkeley college music professors for me to call. "Well, kid..." he said to me, while he was waiting, "I guess I can't get you to go to the university. But at least maybe the university can be of some use to you."

Though there would be more bad days than good days living at home for the year or two, there'd be occasional moments like this, where shining through the dark curse of Depression-era instability was a thin beam of light, one which would appear a bit more frequently when I got much older: the light of a supportive father.

*

Thanks to my father's inquiry, I began studying with two UC Berkeley music professors, Laura, a classical pianist and a male composition teacher, Robert. They got me started with composition and advanced music theory. After a few weeks, Laura, referred me to her TA, Bill, a grad student seeking a PhD in music education who specialized in jazz. He'd become my main teacher for the next several months.

With his glasses and round face, Bill Evans reminded me of a favorite guitarist I'd recently discovered that had a similar look—a combination of nerdy and hip at the same time. Bill not only shared a first name and look with this guitarist, Bill Frisell, he also shared an exact name with a late jazz piano giant and Miles Davis collaborator who'd become a big influence of mine.

My lessons with Bill Evans took place once a week in the music department at UC Berkeley. The lessons were just what I needed. Bill introduced me to some very early jazz guitar, such as Charlie Christian and Django Rheinhardt. He also introduced me to bepop pioneer and tenor saxophonist Charlie Parker, whom I began listening to and studying voraciously. Studying the simplest licks of Charlie C., Django and Charlie P. was exactly what I needed to start getting basic jazz licks under my fingers.

It was a bit strange showing up on campus and being around all the students. Having grown up in the shadow of the university, I'd always viewed college students as much older. Now they were mostly around the same age as I was (I would have been a sophomore had I gone straight to college). On top of that, they all looked so much more "normal" with their short hair, preppy clothes and book bags. I had my own book bag, with notepads and a few books (*Sight-Singing, Rhythmic Training* and *Thesaurus of Scales and Melodic Patterns),* but couldn't help standing out with my long hair and electric guitar.

Still, I avoided wearing black leather jackets and concert t-shirts, especially ones of my own band. It wasn't that I was ashamed of looking metal or anything, I just preferred not to draw extra attention to myself. I was no superstar, but fans had started recognizing me at concerts, record stores and occasionally on the street. It's not that I minded being stopped for an autograph, but somehow going to these music lessons at UC Berkeley felt very personal and private. I just didn't want anyone to know.

Not that I had to worry. There was no way in hell anyone in the music department of UC Berkeley was ever going to recognize me. Or was there?

*

One day, on my way out of a lesson, I felt a tap on my shoulder followed by a very loud, friendly voice. I turned around and found myself face to face with something of a curiosity: he was about my age and with long straight hair all the way down his back, looking even more out of place than I did. He looked too proper to be a hard rocker. He was too clean to be a hippie. He was dressed in corduroys and a t-shirt promoting a dart tournament at a local British pub. I'd never seen anyone like him.

"Uh, pardon me!" He said. He sounded exaggeratingly upper class and well to do, reminding me of this TV commercial for Dijon mustard. In fact, I was sure he was going to ask *"Would you happen to have any Grey Poupon?"* And the more he spoke, the more he'd remind of another TV reference, Frasier, from the show *Cheers,* as played by Kelsey Grammar.

"If I may be so bold, I was wondering if it might be possible to grab one quick moment of your time for a question. I noticed your guitar and as you can see I'm a guitarist myself. Now funnily enough, while I happen to be doing my undergrad in classical guitar here at UC, I also play the electric guitar." I thought this has to be a drama student doing method acting. No one's like this in real life!

"Now, contrary to first impressions, I bear a familiarity with a whole multitude of musical varieties. Though you might not think so by looking at me, I have a musical palette that is as varied as it is discriminating. In fact, it was just the other day that I made a most worthwhile purchase of a brand new album by a metal band." Was he going where I thought he was going? "Now what I like best about this particular band is their fine guitarist of whom you bear a most striking resemblance. Now I've seen you here before, carrying in your hands a guitar-like case and I've said to myself, 'My god, it's impossible! Might this guitarist on that album be the one I've seen showing up here from time to time going in to see Bill Evans,' who, by the way, is a teacher of the most impeccable order, I've had him for my

198

Twentieth Century music history class... Anyhow, my good man, I implore you to pardon this most long-winded intrusion but I couldn't help wondering if you might happen to be this same fellow named Alex with a last name of..."

"Skolnick. Alex Skolnick. That's me, yes. Hi."

"I'm Niall" (pronounced Neil). "Some people call me Ni-all (pronounced Nile) Fordyce."

We shake hands. Neil/Niall asks what in God's name I'm doing in the music department of UC Berkeley. I tell him I'm taking music lessons in between tour dates. He commends me for allowing my horizons to expand and tells me that there is a lot of classical music he thinks I should listen to. He and his brother, a classical composition major (also named Alex), are having people over this weekend to drink beer and listen to CDs. Might I consider joining them?

The following weekend, I become the only member of a speed metal band (in all probability) to find himself mingling with a houseful of classical students and professors, discussing the virtues of Bartok, Holst, Stravinsky, etc.

Niall works in Tower Classics, the classical division of Tower Records on Telegraph Avenue. He offers to help me shop and help build my collection of classical CDs. He also makes me cassette tapes with collections of various music he thinks I might like, including Opera, Celtic reels, New Orleans jazz and prog rock. I like it all.

Thanks to Niall and Alex, I learn that classical music doesn't have to be the light background music I've associated for my parents' cocktail parties (Vivaldi, Pachelbel, etc.). It can be driving, intense, even disturbing. That's exactly what I like!

There will be many more parties at the Fordyce house. I'll get to know their parents, two Scottish doctors who are highly cultured and intellectual like my parents, yet most curiously, able to hang out with young people. Sometimes they drop by the party house, full of beer bottles, and Rubik's Cubes (all solved instantly by Alex, too brilliant for his own good). Sometimes they invite us over. There is never the stigma of being watched by the parents. They are part of the gang. The Fordyce family shows me that it is possible to be intellectually and culturally aware and still be able to party and have a good time.

Niall, that oddball character who snuck up on me that day in my moment of solitude, has been one of my closest friends ever since.

26. SERGEANT SLAUGHTER

Without a doubt, the most memorable and dominant personality in the history of the band is Mark Workman. It pretty much started on the day he took over as tour manager.

With a fierce directness, strict work ethic and leadership skills to match, Mark was the only one able to get us checked in and out of hotels, to interviews or wherever else we needed to be on time. As our first lighting director (LD), his demeanor had been that of an unassuming, discreet crewmember who kept to himself. But as tour manager, he transformed us from an out of control nursery school to an army barracks.

Anytime one of us ran minutes late to a lobby call, bus call or interview, there were apologies to Mark, who'd usually respond with a silent angry glare. Even Chuck Billy, our six foot four, tattooed, gladiator-chested lead singer was kept in line by Mark's militant demeanor, nicknaming him "Sergeant Slaughter."

After more than a decade in Los Angeles, Mark only had a hint of his former Southern drawl. Somewhere along the way, he'd picked up some sophisticated vocabulary words, such as "Utterly Horrific" a phrase he'd use to describe anything, a meal, a band or a venue. *"I've done this shithole before—the place is utterly horrific."*

"Blithering Imbecile" was a term he'd apply to anyone incompetent—caterers, runners, even our own managers: *"Jeff Saltzman is a blithering imbecile!"* Once, he declared this with such conviction that for a brief moment, I actually visualized our manager, an educated man and respected attorney, sitting at his desk playing with a pencil, his tongue sticking out and drool dripping to his desk.

"Veritable Plethora" was a phrase that, despite growing up in an educated family, I'd never heard before. *"No broads at this gig, gentleman. It's a veritable plethora of cock in there."* These shocking statements were delivered in a dry, deadpan tone, his conversations peppered with more profanity than I'd ever heard one person use.

There were many memorable moments. When anticipating lunch or dinner, he'd hold out his arms as wide as they would go and proclaim in with mock sincerity: *"I'm so hungry I could eat a whale schlong."* Knocking on my hotel room door one day to brief me on a schedule change: *"Hey, Al, hope I'm not catchin' ya wackin' off to donkey porn or anything."* Roaming through the bus at 5 am to wake up the band, calling out in a sweet high-pitched falsetto voice, *"Yoo hoo...oh girls...good morning, girls. Get up, you faggots."*

To Louie, always the last to get up, he'd turn his falsetto female imitation into a mock Italian accent: *"Luciano! Dis is your grandmother. Your pasta's ready."* Then in his regular voice: *"Get the fuck up!"* To a German bus driver, who didn't speak much English, he held up a Coke bottle: *"You ever have one of these shoved up your ass?"* Occasionally he'd catch me watching and say, *"What do you think about that, Al?"* I'd just shrug.

Fed up with the *"clueless morons"* in countries like Italy and Spain, who continually provided broken gear and a disregard for timely schedules, he once promised to kiss the ground once we arrived back in the US. As we walked down the ladder off the plane, he got down on his knees and gave the concrete of the runway a smooch that would have made the Pope proud.

*

The entire mannerisms and vocabulary of the tour changed as Mark introduced a lexicon of new sayings:

Walk the Hall of Shame— This came up whenever someone from the crew (and occasionally the band) would find themselves having sex in the back lounge of the bus after the show, causing a delay in departure. The bus would be poised to take off, everyone drinking beers, Slayer blasting from the speakers, the driver in place looking at his watch and shaking his head, the engine idling. At this point, Mark would walk through the hallway and pound on the back lounge door. *"Hey, get that broad outta here, we gotta haul ass!"* Then the lounge door would open and the girl would walk out embarrassed, the crew guy zipping himself up. Mark would look at the poor girl like a priest during an exorcism and as if she were the incarnate of Satan himself, following her through the hallway chanting like a man possessed: *"Walk the Hall of Shame! Walk the Hall of Shame!"*

The Eagle Has Landed—Named after a '70s' war film starring Robert Duvall, this was code to alert the rest of the crew that there were young women with a high alcohol content and a low sense of morals backstage. It usually happened during the crew's rare moment of free time— after the load out, and just before bus departure. As soon as one or two drunk metal chicks were there, the crew guys would make a beeline for the dressing room as Mark's voice blared over the walkie-talkie like a military commander: *"The Eagle Has Landed."*

Hire the Handicapped—Fed up with the occasional hapless, incapable crew member who really had no business being on a professional tour, he'd mimic the tone of a newspaper salesman chanting "Extra! Extra!"

"Hire the handicapped! That's right, Testament takes pity on the specially challenged and less fortunate—hire the handicapped!"

Excuse Me, Miss!—This was a prank that involved pulling down a guy's pants in public, then yelling to get the attention of a female passerby. I first witnessed it outside a motel in Jersey. As one of our crew guys crossed the parking lot back towards the bus, Mark snuck up behind him, pulled his shorts down to his ankles and called out, *"Excuse me, miss!"* Two Hispanic maids were pushing carts on different floors outside the motel room doors which faced the parking lot. They both looked over in time to see the tech standing there in his fire engine red briefs.

Another time, a different crew member snuck up on his colleague in the middle of a shopping mall parking lot. Several Macy's White Tag sale shoppers, mostly soccer moms, looked on in horror as this poor guy, who hadn't worn any underwear that day, just stood there with a defeated look of shame—his flaccid penis dangling in the wind.

*

In some ways, Mark Workman was a character on the level of a Johnny Z—both were shockingly forward and each had a temper like a time bomb. Mark would never have the gall to behave like Johnny when it came to business, being sneaky and backhanded in the name of profit. On the other hand, Johnny would never speak like Mark did, saying things so profane, it would cause a trucker or a Marine drill sergeant to blush.

Yet, Mark Workman and Johnny Z had one thing in common, which was the thing I'd always remember them for: *both refused to let anyone else walk all over them.* For someone like myself, who'd spent his entire life feeling like a cheap doormat to be spit and trampled on by anyone who wished, the education and inspiration these guys provided can only be described as immeasurable. Unlike most people I'd met, especially in the music world, Mark never once failed to do something he said he'd do. Sure, he exhibited depravity, at least as far as personal vice was concerned. But you could never fault him for not being honest, even if it was a bit too brutally for most people's taste.

He would, however, break vows and display lapses of responsibility when it came to just one person: himself. Promises to quit smoking and exercise were continually reneged on, resulting in his declining physical fitness. There were also personal issues and battles with drugs and alcohol. Yet, his passion for boxing led to a part-time second career as a sports writer for various boxing websites and even Fox Sports. And like fictional boxing legend Rocky Balboa, Mark never failed to get back in the game.

Ultimately what distinguished him most is that he always maintained an iron-clad sense of honor and responsibility when it came to his job. In this sense, he became somewhat of a role model. I'd grown up around a family who seemed so uncomfortable in their own skin, afraid of the world outside our walls, unsure how to express themselves and react, I'd escaped into a group of zombie-like band members with an entirely different set of hang-ups. For these reasons, it was extremely refreshing to be around someone who told it like it was, whether you wanted to hear it or not, and was quick to react to questions and challenges with no self-consciousness, a sense of certainty and a sense of black humor.

To this day, I am able to derive humor and inspiration from Mark's bus and dressing room announcements such as this one, which took place on a European festival date:

"Everyone listen up: we could be looking at no show tonight, thanks to this cocksucker promoter. The prick lost his ass on the show yesterday, now he can't pay the sound company up front. The sound guys just told him to go fuck himself, so this idiot is trying to offer the sound company the deed to his fucking house. They'll probably tell him to get fucked. I TOLD the prick he should've budgeted this shit out beforehand. So be ready to haul ass out of this clusterfuck and whatever happens, this cocksucker's gonna be shitcanned from the music biz. After tonight his whole career's goin' down the fuckin' tubes."

27. OVER THE HILLS AND FAR AWAY

When it was time to tour behind *The New Order,* we would have been best off touring the US with larger acts, as we had previously. But we were quickly running out of groups to play with. Having supported Anthrax and Overkill, we'd exhausted Megaforce Records for headliners. That left Metallica, Slayer and Megadeth.

Metallica was out of the question. Now in another stratosphere, they'd graduated from playing with heavy bands with large cult followings like Motörhead and Merciful Fate to international supergroups like Van Halen, Scorpions and others. Eventually they'd surpass even those groups in sales and status.

Metallica had also made the wise decision not to marginalize themselves, which I saw as a very wise career move. This involved choosing as their own support acts unique bands like Faith No More and Primus, avoiding any bands too closely aligned with Metallica's own sound, including us. While this decision didn't help our careers any, I couldn't agree with them more. I'd been growing totally frustrated by my own band's reliance on Metallica. In vain, I'd tried to explain to the guys that they were the last band we should be mimicking, but it was no use. Even Metallica's then most recent recording, the $5.98 EP, which contained covers released in jest to hold fans over until the next LP, was listened to and studied religiously by Eric as though it were *Sergeant Pepper.*

Since Slayer was off the road for the time being, holed up in the studio, that left one ideal band to support: Megadeth. However, Megadeth would be opening for Dio on their upcoming American summer tour and wouldn't headline the US as a result. All this meant we were totally out of luck for a good support slot in the US for *The New Order.* We'd have to headline tiny clubs across America, reaching far less people than we would supporting a bigger band.

There was one shred of good news, however: to warm up for their Dio tour, Megadeth was headed over to Europe for some headline shows and we were invited to be third on the bill along with them and Flotsam & Jetsam.

*

Flotsam & Jetsam was riding a bit of a wave since their bassist, Jason, had been the one chosen to replace the late, great Cliff Burton in Metallica during those auditions I'd witnessed a few years earlier. The bassist who had taken over for Jason, Troy Gregory, would become a good friend on tour—he'd be one of the best and smartest young metal musicians I'd meet, practicing his bass with the same dedication I had on guitar. He'd also speak eloquently about philosophy and other subjects, telling me I really ought to check out the works of Nietzsche.[43]

I always thought Troy would end up becoming one of the best known bassists in hard rock/metal. Similarly, I was sure Flotsam & Jetsam would become better known as a band since they were one degree of separation from the mighty Metallica. For some reason, it didn't turn out that way.

The headliner, Megadeth, of course, had an even more direct association to Metallica. The singer/guitarist/founder of the band, Dave Mustaine, had been Metallica's original lead guitarist. As every fan of the band knows, he'd been unceremoniously dumped while on tour and sent

---

[43] 19th Century German philosopher.

home on a Greyhound Bus just prior to Metallica recording their first album. That whole bus ride home, Dave plotted his revenge; Megadeth was born.

Dave was rumored to have personality issues compounded with substance and alcohol abuse. Nothing I'd see on that 1988 European tour would do anything to change my mind. There would be some drama involving him on this tour and later tours, causing us to refer to him in unfriendly terms. However, Dave would, many, many years later, get his life together and seriously make amends, so much that, despite his extreme right wing views, he'd be called something hard to imagine us ever calling him: a friend.

*

Sandwiched between the endless amounts of French bread, Dutch cheese, unfiltered German beer, hashish cans, sweat, lost sleep, hangovers and painfully loud volume, there would be many bizarre occurrences on that tour. One of my guitars, a flying V, would become victim to a curtain knocking it off stage. On another night, Greg would get so sick, he'd have to play sitting down and throwing up into a bucket, crying out: *"Just let me die!"* He'd gone on an early evening drinking binge, shortly after eating a dinner called the "seafood surprise." Recalling the incident days later, he'd say in a voice mimicking *Sanford & Son* star and comedian Redd Foxx: *"I got a surprise from the seafood surprise."*

A few days later, my amp went out during sound check. My tech borrowed a set from Megadeth guitarist Jeff Young, planning to replace them the next day off. Jeff later pulled me aside, and handed me several boxes of tubes, insisting I keep them all free of charge. I tried to refuse, but he wouldn't take no for an answer. Jeff's well-intentioned but misguided generosity drew the wrath of Mr. Mustaine, who gave him a frightening verbal lashing.

Megadeth's tour manager found me and directed me to Dave's dressing room for an urgent meeting. Feeling like I was back in school, getting called into the principal's office, I walked in to find myself alone with the infamous Mr. Mustaine. After a few seconds of intimidating silence, Dave said in a low rumbling growl, *"Your name's Alex, right? I'm here to help you, Alex. You know that, right? You need to borrow a set of tubes? No problem. I'll help ya. But Jeff playin' Santa Claus? Not his place to do that. You look like I can trust you, kid, so between you, me and the wall, that guy's been fuckin' up a lot lately. His days around here could be numbered. I know none of this is your fault, but do me a favor, alright? You need anything, you come straight to me, okay bud?"*

Yet, despite all the strange events of that tour, by far the strangest was the sudden appearance of my brother, Michael.

*

On a whim, my brother had decided to wander Europe aimlessly by himself, staying at youth hostels and living like a drifter. I knew he'd been abroad but was surprised when, all of a sudden, he turned up at one of our gigs unannounced. In the last year and a half, I'd been away so much, I hadn't seen much of him. Now, with his hair buzzed short and having packed on a few pounds, I barely recognized him.

At first, I was happy to see my brother, thinking we could find a new relationship safe from the ghosts of Berkeley and our shared trauma growing up. But I quickly realized that there was something odd about him, more so than usual. He seemed unable to hold a coherent conversation, bouncing from subject to subject, becoming totally withdrawn, then overly animated again. Every verbal exchange brought forth a shrug or a diatribe of endless rambling. When he got nervous speaking, he'd squint uncontrollably.

At least he'd become a very nice, friendly person—no longer the menacing, taunting teen that had laughed when I got hurt and forbid me from playing his guitars, or the young adult childishly rambling endlessly about getting stoned, getting laid and getting signed. But in many ways, his demeanor now was more troubling than it had been before, when it could at least be attributed to being young and stupid. Now, he was a grown man in his late twenties with disconcerting awkwardness and pre-teen social interactions. He had a lack of confidence, focus and awareness. He had no semblance of life direction, ambition or identity.

I didn't know how to answer all the questions I kept getting about him, both from the Testament camp and from Megadeth and Flotsam & Jetsam. Everyone kept asking things like, *What's his deal? Is he alright? He seems kind of....off.* And these were guys in metal bands—people not exactly known for their sense of stability.

Recently, he'd begun substituting yoga, Zen Buddhism and other Eastern practices in place of LSD and other narcotics, which was a hugely positive step. But while this may have spared him further corrosion, maybe even saved his life, he still had serious problems. In the two years I'd been away recording and touring, he'd no longer been playing his bass and had been caught up in a cycle of attending college, dropping out, going from odd job to odd job, re-registering for school, then dropping out again. Most of his friends from his teen years had moved away, gone off to college or were no longer in touch. His only close friend was an older guy who owned some property and seemed to be using his friendship for the sole purpose of exploiting him for manual labor.

Now, here he was out in Europe with no plans, no purpose, poor communication skills and totally alone—a vagabond void of direction or any semblance of future plans. When asked what his plan was, he'd answer, "I don't know" adding that there was nowhere else for him to go and nothing else for him to do.

The guys in my band took pity on him and invited him to ride to the next town. I couldn't say no. He was my *brother*, after all. He rode with us from Denmark to Belgium. Then from Belgium to Paris. From Paris to Milan. And the next gig and the next.

Now we had another straggler who, while not being dangerous at all, made me even more uncomfortable than Tattoo Rob, the menacing escaped convict who'd jumped on board the first tour. Tattoo Rob may have struck fear into the hearts of brave men, but at least he hadn't felt like my responsibility.

In a way this situation reminded me of the movie *Rain Man* with Dustin Hoffman and Tom Cruise. It's not an accurate comparison, since my own brother's issues were far less obvious than those of the severely debilitated character played by Hoffman in the film. And of course, I was nothing like the glamorous, outgoing, overly confident character played by Tom Cruise. But there was a huge similarity in the following sense: here I was in this new world of mine—concert venues, tour buses, trucks, guitars, fans, quirky characters—a strange world, no doubt, but one in which I was finding my own way. Out of the blue, along comes my brother, mentally trapped in our shared Berkeley past, dropping in on my new world and clinging to me simply because he had, in his own words, *nothing else to do and nowhere else to go.*

I wished I could help him, but it was no use. I felt powerless. He was like a houseguest who's been invited to stay over for a night or so, but has inexplicably moved in.

Soon, everyone began asking *how much longer?* This was a complete role reversal, as I became the older brother, in the uncomfortable position of having to lay down rules: *Mike, I'm getting complaints about you eating all the food in our dressing room. It's there for the musicians. It's okay for you to have some, but please be considerate of the fact that it's for everyone, okay? Mike, you really need to be out of the way when the crew is trying to set up. You're standing right in their path, understand? Mike, you can't travel with us forever. What are your plans? How long are you going to ride with us? And what exactly are you doing here and what are you planning to do when you get back?*

I was turning into our father, minus the temper. It was difficult to explain to him that, yes, it was nice to see him and no, he wasn't causing any serious problems but yes, it was time for him to move on. If I didn't have this talk, he'd never leave.

At least he wouldn't be let go like Tattoo Rob, dropped off in the middle the night, in the middle of nowhere, left to live off the land and run from law enforcement. My brother would be let off at the central train station of the next major city. He had cash and was in contact with our parents. He would continue his aimless journey of youth hostels before returning to Berkeley and continuing his cycle dropping out of school and taking odd jobs.

*

We were home for just a week or so before it was time to tour the US again for our first headlining tour.

We took Vio-lence, which consisted of a few of Chuck's buddies from Dublin and ex-members of the band Forbidden. Vio-lence was doing the van tour as we'd done the previous year, while we'd graduated to our first bus.

Vio-lence's guitarist, Rob Flynn, and I hung out a couple of times and he asked me to show him how I did my sweep picking. He was a bit shy, like I was, and seemed to look up to me. A year or so later, Rob would leave Vio-lence and form his own group and focus on being a singer. The next time I'd see him, he'd have a whole new persona, and I'd barely recognize him—no longer the eager-eyed kid who'd asked me to show him arpeggios on the back of our bus, he'd wear a fierce expression that created a striking resemblance to Charles Manson. His band, Machine Head, would become the biggest metal band from the Bay Area after Metallica. Decades later, in 2009, I'd see Machine Head open for Metallica in Newark, NJ, and we'd hang out afterwards, for the first time in years.

Today Rob's one of the most respected metal performers there is, not to mention one of the most ferocious looking. But I'll always remember him as that awkwardly, slightly insecure kid on tour with us and Vio-lence.

*

It was just before this tour that I began to receive my very first guitars via a "full endorsement," courtesy of Ibanez Guitars.

Artist endorsements are coordinated by a go-between for the manufacturing company, known as the artist rep. It's a unique position because, in order to understand the needs of musicians, an artist-rep needs to be a musician himself, or at least a hobbyist. At the same time, he must be able to communicate with corporate types and function in a business environment. It is a dual existence: going to concerts, drinking beer and hanging out backstage at night; showing up at an office, attending staff meetings and crunching numbers by day. Few are cut out for it. Many are former pro-musicians who have settled down (it's uncanny how often the transition from musician to artist rep coincides with getting married and/or having children). Some are much happier with this new life—they have stability, clarity and they still get to be around music and music equipment. Others are visibly tortured—they wish they were still playing professionally. You can hear it in their voices and see it in their faces.

In my case, I got really lucky. My Ibanez artist rep was a fellow from Austin named Chris Kelly, who was a musician but loved being an artist rep even more. He thus became one of the best in the business. Chris was and is one of those rare breeds—not only a business partner but a trusted friend of those he's worked with, a bit like a John Hammond or Clive Davis[44] of artist reps (Joe Satriani and the late Stevie Ray Vaughn would both speak highly of Chris). Chris would leave the rock world around the same time I would—both of us choosing to walk away with our integrity intact—and resurfacing years later.[45]

Receiving a guitar in exchange for nothing more than playing it seemed like the best deal known to man. In truth, there is a bit of a catch: you are no longer free to be photographed with competing brands of instruments. And should you wander into a music store on tour somewhere and see a guitar you like, you'd better think twice about buying it —you've made a commitment to the guitar you're currently playing. It's bad etiquette and, in some cases, breach of contract to play any other company's guitar.

In the future, I would become very particular about which guitars I played. I would leave Ibanez after the quality took a nosedive (guitar companies, like bands and TV shows, have good years and bad years). I would actually resist many high profile potential endorsements because the quality wouldn't meet my standards. I'd choose to buy guitars I liked rather than be tied to an endorsement. I'd also decide to play more high quality, timeless models like the Gibson Les Paul.[46]

---

[44] Producers and talent scouts Clive Davis and the late John Hammond have been cited as being that rare breed of loyal, trustworthy and highly effective friend and mentor by such people as Bob Dylan, Aretha Franklin, Bruce Springsteen, Whitney Houston and Carlos Santana.

[45] Today, he is my rep for Peavey/Budda Amplifiers.

[46] The guitar I play today, the Heritage "Alex Skolnick Signature" model, is close to a Les Paul and hand-built in the same factory where many of these early Les Pauls were built.

But at the time that red Ibanez Sabre guitar (later to be called to 540S) showed up at my door, I couldn't imagine ever playing another guitar. Like the time all that new gear showed up in the studio for the first album, it was Christmas all over again. I would forever be identified with that guitar, even though I played it for just a few years. Had I been smart, I would have thought about working out a deal for a signature model during this time, with royalties. It's frustrating to think how many of those stock instruments have been purchased over the years by people thinking of it as the "Alex Skolnick" model.

At first, the other guys in my band would tease and taunt me about the red guitar. *"It looks gay!" "Why not black?" "Lame!"* Blah, blah, blah. But it stood out, helping emphasize being different than the rest. In fact, when I used it in our video for the song "Trial By Fire," MTV picked up on it and began showing close-ups of the guitar in promotional spots alongside other quick clips from videos, most of which were by mainstream pop artists like Steve Winwood and Peter Gabriel. The color of my red guitar, like my solos juxtaposed against the rhythm tracks, added something that got the attention of the world outside our bubble.

Perhaps having a little color against the darkness wasn't such a bad thing?

*

When the Testament/Vio-lence tour reached the East Coast, we were dropped off to play our record label's 5th anniversary party in New York. Megaforce Records, which had started in 1983 with Metallica's *Kill 'Em All,* was hosting the event at The Ritz in Midtown Manhattan.

Our crew drove with Vio-lence, with whom we were sharing a truck, to the next gig. We planned to meet up the next day, since this event was backline with crew provided and we had hotel rooms. Our bus would swing by to pick us up in the morning.

The champagne was flowing from the time we walked in the door, and there was an open bar. There were more people wanting to talk to us than we could handle. Our rooms for the night were in the neighboring luxury hotel, so it was very easy to escape, get high, do shots of whiskey or vodka, then go back and brave the madness.

By the time we were rounded up to go on, I was stoned and buzzed from the champagne. Most of the other guys were barely coherent.

On stage, it was like a blurry dream gone wrong. Midway into the first song, Eric tripped over his cable and fell flat on his face. Louie's cymbal stand fell over with a crash and Chuck's voice was a gargle-like wash, drowning any semblance of rhythm—you couldn't hear any guitars. I soon realized why—the amps had gone out. I had no sound, and neither did Eric. At first I thought Eric might have damaged his amp when he fell, but mine was clearly not producing sound either.

It made no sense—Overkill had just played a successful set, minutes before us. We'd stopped and no one came to the rescue (remember our own road crew was en route to the next gig). Chuck, drunk and very stoned, began reliving last year's totally imagined rivalry with Overkill. It didn't help that Overkill, being from New York, had their own crew running the gig who, after the tension of last year's tour together, weren't eager to run out and help us.

An idea formulated in Chuck's mind: these amps must have been sabotaged – the old tin foil on the fuse trick (like that lemon of an amp I'd bought all those years ago). According to this logic, Overkill, their crew (which now included our previous soundman, Kerry) and for that matter our record label itself were all in on it. It was a conspiracy to *make us look bad*.

What happened next would only make us look worse.

*

1988 Onstage, Megaforce Records 5th Anniversary Party, The Ritz, New York, NY

Chuck: *"I'm gonna count to three. If no one comes out to fix these fuckin' amps, I'm pushin' em over. One..."*

No one comes over. I'm thinking the label must have techs or someone here to help out. We're screwed without our crew here. Damn.

"Two..."

C'mon. Someone help us out. This is embarrassing, we're all here on stage, in front of all these people, and we have no sound. We're all pleading with Chuck not to do it.

"Three...alright..."

I'm sure Chuck's bluffing. He wouldn't push all these amps over. That would be the stupidest...

BOOM! THUD! CRACK! POW! BOOM! THUD! CRACK! POW! BOOM! THUD! CRACK! POW!!!!!!!!!!

The crowd is silent. Gasps, oohs and whispers followed by commotion. Now the sound crew guys are running to the stage. They don't look very happy. Someone puts music on the PA system, Metallica's "Ride the Lightning."

Elliot and Jeff, our managers, come out yelling and screaming.

Elliot: "Chuck! Goddamn you! What the hell is this?"

Chuck: "They just left us hangin' there. What, we're supposed to stand there lookin' stupid? Fuck that."

Jeff: "Fuck that? Man, you've just fucked your career."

Chuck: "Whatever."

Elliot: "You see those people out there?! Half of them are journalists! You've just shown yourself to be arrogant and unprofessional in front of all the media!"

Chuck: "So? Fuck it, it's rock 'n' roll."

Jeff: "And this is a party for your own record label! Are you out of your mind?! You think this is going to earn you any favors?!"

Chuck walks away. Elliot and Jeff yell at me that this was the stupidest thing they've ever seen in the history of the music industry, that our singer is out of control, something must be done, he has no idea of the consequences. I nod and indicate I understand. Eric and Lou walk over in disarray, and Elliot and Jeff start yelling at all three of us.

Someone calls out to me, handing me my guitar in a gig bag, which I use as an excuse to get away from Elliot and Jeff. I leave the scene on stage and disappear toward the bar. In the hallway, I get a lot of strange looks and questions of "What happened up there?" "Why'd he do that?" I just answer that I don't know and need a drink. I run into Elliot and Jeff again, they bitch to me about "my singer." I avoid them the rest of the evening.

I see Johnny and Marsha and say how sorry I am, and I don't know what got into him. They are understanding towards me, say it is not my fault, give me a hug. I appreciate that, but it's clear they're pissed.

Could it all be over between us and Megaforce? Will they drop us? Are we finished? What has Chuck done? And why couldn't we just have announced that there's a problem with the equipment, we're going to walk off stage now and give the techs a chance to fix it, we'll see you guys in a few minutes?

In the future, I'll see many bands in this situation handle it accordingly. I'll never see one handle it as bad as this.

*

As that evening spiraled out of control, I never saw the rest of the band. Instead, I sought refuge with Heather Davidson.

Heather was about my age, worked at our record label, and had a very pretty face and a professional demeanor. She reminded me a bit of the actress Molly Ringwald. Finding each other in the chaos, we both agreed it was best to escape the escalating madness, head to the hotel next door and get the hell out of there.

We snuck off to her room a couple of floors below the one I was sharing with Greg. I planned to head back up to my own room at some point. She had a bottle of wine. We just sat in the silence of her hotel room, our ears ringing. There was too much to talk about; it had all been so overwhelming.

I'm not sure who kissed who first. The next thing I knew, her mini skirt was lifted, her polka dotted underwear was off and she became the first (and last) girl with whom I'd ignore a cardinal and often violated rule of the music biz: do not sleep with any girl who works for your record label. Fortunately, there would be no long-term consequences, other than some awkwardness between us.

But in the short term, there was one serious consequence—waking up in her bed late in the morning and finding the tour bus had left without me.

*

It was one of only two times in my career that I'd be left by the bus, or as it's known in the biz: *oil spotted.* And both times, a guitar in my bunk would be assumed to be me and only when the bus was far along en route was it realized that I was not on board.

Heather, being quite a resourceful woman, despite being only a year or so older than me, knew to reserve a commuter flight from New York to Boston and get me a shuttle to the airport. If the label found out about this, she'd be in bigger shit than I was.

I called Elliot in his room. He was due to fly back to California later in the day. It didn't even register to him that at that moment, I was supposed to be on the bus to Boston, and shouldn't be able to call him. He launched right into a diatribe about what a catastrophe the night before had been: *"I don't know what we're gonna do!"* blah blah blah *"We've got big problems!"* blah blah blah *"Your singer this!"* blah blah blah *"Your singer that!"* I headed him off at the pass.

"Elliot, listen. I missed the bus, it's my fault, I'm catching a flight to Boston, it's all set, I'll be there in time for sound check, yes I fucked up—I know, I'm sorry, I'll explain later, please get a hold of the crew and let 'em know. Yes, last night was a bummer, I've gotta go!" Click!

At sound check, I had to confess to everyone why I was late. But everyone was so shell-shocked from the night before, no one seemed to care.

*

A day or so later, we got word that Megadeth had cancelled their appearance at the upcoming "Monsters of Rock" shows at two soccer stadiums in Europe. The reason given was "personal illness," which could only refer to those addictive habits we'd witnessed in Europe.

The slot was ours if we wanted it. We'd have to cancel the last few dates of our US tour, but those were mostly smaller markets and could be easily rescheduled.

We immediately said yes and a week or so later, found ourselves on a plane bound for the German towns of Schweinfurt and Bochum to open for Iron Maiden, Kiss, David Lee Roth, Great White and our former tour mates Anthrax.

*

Being onstage in front of 60,000 people would be the biggest letdown of my life.

On the one hand, it would be incredible to look out at a sea of people stretching as far back as the stadium would go. Here we'd be, *living the dream*, playing for the largest crowd we'd ever played for. On the other hand, I'd feel a combination of exhilaration and disappointment. I'd play my heart out and attempt to communicate with all 60,000 people directly. But they wouldn't hear a note I was playing.

For that matter, I wouldn't even hear myself. The sound would be a wash of noise. No one would notice my solos and many wouldn't even comprehend the riffs.

For a crowd like this, you needed riffs that were clear and powerful and songs that held the groove long enough to translate to the large audience. Metallica had them, so did Megadeth. But we didn't have a "For Whom the Bell Tolls" or a "Peace Sells," a song with a steady beat and a powerful, memorable chorus. We had some great riffs alright, easily as good as those bands. But our problem was in the arrangements, the tempos and the vocal parts. When all was said and done, our songs were too busy and complicated. Not helping was the fact that in concert, we played them so fast that they sounded like gibberish.

Maybe the others were okay with this simply being a big moment we always talked about, one that would never happen again, like our manager Elliot's tales of playing Woodstock as a member of Sha Na Na. But I didn't want that—I wanted our first stadium gig to be the beginning of a whole new level of the music biz. Like when Metallica played Day on the Green in Oakland, a sold-out stadium show with Scorpions.

The few thousand fans who knew who we were would have their arms in the air and cheer politely. But the vast majority of the 60,000, while not hating us, would not be impressed either. I'd know in my heart that what we had to offer was not going to make a good enough impression to get us higher on the bill at stadium rock festivals in the future. If I was the promoter, I wouldn't have brought us back.

*

Backstage, in the sea of dressing room trailers, it was a crash course in rock star behavior. I had no idea how to behave in this environment. No one gave a fuck who I was. By far the worst, and the least impressive band, was Great White—I tried talking to the guitar player and he just looked at me like I was an annoying kid.

David Lee Roth's guitarist Steve Vai wasn't much better. I'd meet him years later under different circumstances, and he'd be much nicer. It was really hurtful to be blown off like this. It would help me be more conscious when fans met me.

David Lee Roth, despite being a superstar, was surprisingly one of the nicer people there. His demeanor was a bit cartoonish, much like his videos, but he was very friendly, unlike a lot of less important musicians. As Chuck, Eric and I nervously approached him, he was sitting in a lounge chair next to a tent, smoking a cigarette. He actually took the time to ask about our band and take a quick photo with Chuck, telling us a story of how he'd tried to take his Harley into his hotel and they wouldn't let him. A dedicated motorcycle man, he'd chosen to spend the night sleeping in the field with his Harley Davidson, rather than yield to the stuffy German hotel people. We laughed at his story and thanked Diamond Dave as he sent us on our way with a wave of his hand and a show business California smile: *"You guys have a gooooood show!"*

*

Meeting Kiss, something I'd dreamed of since childhood, was weird.

It really hadn't been long since I'd been a twelve year old totally obsessed with them. These guys where the reason I started playing guitar. I'd dreamed of this monumental meeting of the minds my whole life. But suddenly I realized that as important as this moment was for me, it was nothing for them. They met fans like me all the time, musicians and otherwise. Why should they remember me or even notice me? How could I ever relate to them as people?

They weren't bad guys, but I found their behavior a bit bizarre. They seemed to think it was still 1978 and they were on top of the world. Not so. In 1978, shortly before I discovered them, the most recent Kiss album, *Love Gun,* was an instant classic, selling millions and forever to be loved by fans like me. They sold out every arena they set foot in. But it was the '80s, the makeup off and the original lineup no longer intact. Kiss couldn't even sell out my high school.[47]

They'd just released *Smashed, Trashes and Hits* an unnecessary rehashing of classic songs with two new tracks, including one that I'd count as having the worst lyrics of all time: *"Baby, let's put the X in sex, Love's like a muscle and you make me want to flex"* (Way to go, Paul and Gene. You really made us Kiss fans proud with that one).

Paul Stanley was nice enough, a bit mechanical. He seemed to have a formulaic answer to every compliment I gave or question I asked.

Gene Simmons seemed exaggeratingly arrogant. Yet, I couldn't help feeling he knew that, and it was all part of an act, like a wrestling character. He shook my hand with an expression that said, *"Face it. You wish you were me."* Shannon Tweed, the recent Playmate and future Mrs. Simmons, was by his side. She seemed uncomfortable and insecure, much different than the confident, wise-cracking woman seen on their reality TV show twenty years later. She nervously asked if I had a spare cigarette as Gene posed for a horde of photographers. I suddenly wished I was a smoker, if only to accommodate the beautiful Shannon. During an awkward silence, I looked over at Gene and said sarcastically, "Isn't this fun?" He smirked. I knew he saw this whole thing as a game, not to be taken too seriously. I would try to remember that in the future.

By far the nicest person I met that day was Kiss's second drummer,[48] Eric Carr. His warm, outgoing New York Italian demeanor reminded me of the actor Tony Danza. He was the one guy who actually sat down to talk to me and made me feel like I was a person, not a pest. He asked me about myself, made me feel human again. As disappointing as the whole experience had been, meeting and hanging out with Eric Carr was a silver lining. I looked forward to meeting him again and thanking him one day.

Sadly, that day would never come.

A scant three years in the future, I would learn that Eric Carr had been diagnosed with advanced stages of cancer. He passed away a short time later.

*

As we left the Monsters of Rock Festival, I should have felt triumphant. Instead, I felt an overwhelming sense of letdown.

---

[47] The Berkeley Community Theater is the auditorium for Berkeley High School. Kiss played there in 1983.

[48] Eric Carr had replaced original Kiss drummer Peter Criss shortly after I'd seen my first Kiss concert.

I'd so looked forward to meeting, connecting with and being inspired by fellow musicians, especially those at the higher level of the biz, who'd been around the block a few times. Instead, I'd felt like a real peon, like I was back in Willard Junior High School again.

Looking back, I have to admit some of it was my own fault. Knowing what I know now, many of them acted that way out of insecurity. I hadn't known how to talk to any of them to put people at ease. Sure, a few may have been real assholes, like Great White, for example (as proven by their inexcusable arrogance in the wake of the deadly 2003 Station nightclub fire). But with most of the others, I think of something Erica Jong said about meeting a bunch of movie stars at a Hollywood cocktail party: *"I was terrified they were judging me. They were terrified I was judging them."*

More importantly, I was disappointed in my band. This should have been a chance to prove ourselves as worthy of the big leagues, but it wasn't going to happen. It's not that we had a bad show, it's just that our presentation was amateurish onstage and off.

What they saw as being "heavy" meant playing too fast, too busy, too noisy and without structure, a recipe for not moving to the next level of success. I'd been unable to convey to them that we didn't have to be more mainstream, just more professional. The guys couldn't seem to look beyond the Bay Area local scene.

On the flight home, I should have felt on top of the world. Instead, I felt let down. Our chances to rise above and move forward in the music biz were being squandered. And as frustrated as I was by the guys' inability to see us rising above the limitations of the Bay Area at that time, I was being held back even more by my own personal insecurities.

*

Immediately upon arriving home, I put on some music to unwind. It was an acoustic piano record by my new hero, jazz pianist Chick Corea. The music was soothing and inspiring. It made me feel better about myself and about music.

As Chick's colorful chords and cascades enveloped the room, I thought about how it was time to reconnect with that epiphany I'd had while recording *The New Order*. It was time to move to a place where I was happier personally, more fulfilled musically, more communicative and able to relate to the world beyond the self-inflicted borders of the band and the ghosts of my Berkeley past.

That's when I noticed the back cover of Chick's album, a little sentence in the corner. The sentence that grabbed me contained the words *"indispensable tools for improving my life."* That sounded like exactly what I needed!

These words would cause me to seek my first outside source of help to guide me on my new journey. In the short term, this exploration would turn out to be very fruitful. But in the long term, it would be far from what it was cracked up to be.

28. HE DROPPED HIS BODY

"*Stress? Anxiety? Unreasonable Emotions? Dianetics is the all-time self-help bestseller!*"

Such said the message on the book display case. Sounded good to me, I certainly had all those things and was in need of self-help. In early 1989, at twenty years old, I was confused and depressed, with a lot of baggage and issues to overcome. I'd sought answers and had found one on the back of that Chick Corea album: *"And once again, my deepest thanks to L. Ron Hubbard for providing me with some indispensable tools for improving my life."*

*Well...*I thought. *What have I got to lose?*

No one I knew personally had ever read *Dianetics*. I knew it was supposedly controversial, but I had no idea why. So I bought a copy and was determined to find out for myself. After all, if the great Chick Corea was endorsing it, how could I not at least check it out?

The very first part said that there were incidents in everyone's past that they may have forgotten consciously but not subconsciously. Every single memory was retained and affected the reactions of each individual. This seemed reasonable to me. I knew I was affected by some bad memories from my youth. As the book went on, it encouraged the reader to seek out one of many Dianetics Centers across the country.

Which is how I found myself at the Dianetics Center on Shattuck Avenue in Berkeley California, talking to a skinny, pony tailed, glossy eyed, hippie-like individual.

*

I explained to him why I was there: I'd seen Chick Corea's words on the back of an album and, being a big fan of his music, I was seeking a better understanding of it. I'd felt creatively and personally unfulfilled and had a big problem studying and retaining complex information. This was especially true when I tried to study advanced music theory and jazz improvisation; I would get only so far before becoming frustrated and giving up. I wasn't dumb and, for that matter, had very educated parents. But something was holding me back, and I needed help overcoming whatever blocks I was dealing with.

He told me that the center offered a week-long study course. I could get through the workbook on my own time and then come in twice a week for a written exam. After that was a week-long course in communication.

This sounded great to me, and I didn't see anything weird or unusual about it, except when he deferred to Ron. "You know, Ron says we all have these blocks caused by our past. And according to Ron, we all have the potential to move beyond these blocks and become 'clear.' With these initial courses, you'll be able to grasp Ron's ideas more effectively."

I couldn't help but ask, "By 'Ron' do you mean L. Ron Hubbard?" He nodded. "I could've sworn I heard he passed away, years ago."

As if I'd disrupted the quietude of a library, he put his fingers to his lips and said, "Shhhh." Then he glanced left and right, motioning with his finger for me to come closer and spoke in a whisper: "We prefer to say *he dropped his body.*"

*

I chose to ignore the weirdness of this incident and began the study course right away. It was simple, but very useful and I noticed improvements at once. There were a few key points, and the one I remember most involved the unfamiliar or misunderstood word—the more you skip over words that you don't know, the more frustrated and ready to give up you'll become. This sounds so obvious to me now, but really wasn't at the time. I learned to always keep a dictionary handy (much easier today with on-line dictionaries and phone apps) and look up every new word before moving on, applying this to musical concepts as well.

The communication course was equally helpful—I'd never had any guidance when it came to communicating or dealing with life's challenges. In my family, discussing ways to address anything remotely unpleasant or confrontational was avoided. Now I was learning that there were ways of confronting that were respectful to the person with whom you were communicating. I also learned to be a better listener and be a more direct talker as well. I had to admit that what I'd learned in these two basic courses was, despite their simplistic descriptions, very useful.

After I'd completed the two courses, I was introduced to Sylvia, a short, heavy-set, troll-like woman with a moustache. She gave me an evaluation that consisted of several questions about the course and how I was feeling about it. I felt pretty good. Then she said, "Ok, it's time to sign you up for your next course! Now, we're going to sign you up for membership and you're going to need the following materials." She brought out a half dozen or so books, some hardcover, some paperback, and more workbooks. "It'll be two hundred dollars. Will you be paying by personal check or credit card?"

I expressed concern that it was a big chunk of money. She pointed out that as one makes progress, more money comes. I supposed she had a point but told her I'd like to wait and think about it. She crowed gleefully: "But you liked the course, right?" She nodded as she spoke. I nodded back. "And you noticed some improvements, right?" I nodded again, in time with her nods. "And of course you want to continue the progress you've made so far, don't you?" We both nodded once more. "Then let's get you signed up for your next course! How will you be paying?"

"Check."

I was conflicted—on the one hand, I'd just been manipulated into shelling out a bunch of money for a course I hadn't decided to take. Yet, there was no denying I'd learned some invaluable things in those initial courses. So I thought I'd give the next course a shot.

*

The next course confirmed my nagging feelings of discomfort as they started sneaking in "Scientology" jargon—the church, past lives, space travel... And the behavior of the people at the center had gotten weirder. It wasn't just that L. Ron Hubbard, excuse me, *Ron*, had passed away, excuse me, *dropped his body,* and that they were all referring to him as if he was still alive and had just stepped outside for a smoke; it was that they viewed him as some sort of deity, never questioning any of his writings and giving him all the credit as the creator of these concepts.

Their study materials were clearly drawn from Eastern and Western philosophy, psychology and spirituality—then made easily digestible with elementary simplicity. This was all well and good, except that all credit was given to Ron, as though he was some genius, and no credit to any other sources. In fact, when it came to any other social sciences, religions or belief systems, the writings and consequently the followers, were dismissive at best, and severely critical at worst.

How could these people knock the original sources and make this guy into some sort of spiritual guru who could do no wrong? He was a science fiction writer! Could they not see it?

They also took the jargon too seriously, including a system for evaluating a person's mood (a scale of .5—apathy to 4.0—enthusiasm). I overheard one comment from a casual conversation—it went something like this: *"Oh yeah, the guy was a real 2.5, if you know what I mean."* They were like sheep unwilling to think for themselves. They reminded me of people in the local music scene who tried to be cool by copying the speech and actions of others. Even worse was the fact that the entire organization was now being run by some secretive collective of advanced disciples operating off a ship somewhere off the coast of Florida (no doubt so they could bypass certain US laws).

I quickly realized it was time to move on and continue my self-improvement studies elsewhere.

When I called to say I'd no longer be coming in, that same woman, Sylvia, tried to put pressure on me. She alternated between guilt trips and pleading with me to come in and just talk about what was troubling me. I refused to be manipulated again, and told her that just as I was following my own path in music, I was following my own path in personal growth. My experience at the center had yielded some great initial results but I didn't like where it was going and wasn't comfortable with the idea of membership or anything that resembled an organized religion. She kept pleading and scolding but I held my position and said goodbye to her for the last time. One of the most important lessons I'd learned in my studies at the Dianetics Center—facing confrontation head on—turned out to be quite useful when applied to the organization itself.

Ultimately, I look back on my brief flirtation with Dianetics like this: it was a valuable learning experience and I'm glad I took the initiative to find things out for myself, rather than being swayed by the hype surrounding it. The study and communication courses gave me some useful tools that I'd later find available through more reliable and less imposing sources. I never felt like there was anything dangerous about these people, they were just idiotic and bizarre.

Over the years, I wouldn't be surprised as Scientology became fodder for tabloids, late night comics, and the *South Park* series. While I was happy for Chick Corea, Tom Cruise and other celebrities who felt that becoming a member of this organization worked for them, I didn't need to go any further to realize that it wasn't going to work for me.

I came, I saw, I got out of it what I needed and left.

ALEX SKOLNICK

29. WORLD OF FANTASY

Going into the sessions for our next album, I was reinvigorated. I'd been taking better care of myself and had become more focused. I joined a gym and also became a runner. I was no longer smoking pot. Cocaine and other drugs were completely out of the question, never to be tried again. I was eating healthy and consciously, drinking in moderation and never doing either out of boredom.

In fact, I'd completely forgotten what it was like to be bored—there was always a creative project to work on, a book to read, mental planning to do, even while waiting in lines or stuck in traffic.

Meanwhile, I was progressing fast with my music lessons. I'd get up early every single day, often while it was still dark, go running or drive to the gym, return back home, have a good breakfast, and work hard on music all morning. At some point I'd give myself a break, walk up the street and grab a cup of Peet's Coffee before getting back to work with my guitar, my music books and/or instruction videos. A few hours later, I'd walk up the street for lunch, more Peet's, then work for the rest of the afternoon, or until it was time to leave for band practice.

It showed: I was making huge gains.

At the same time, it felt a bit weird, in one sense: my whole life, all I'd ever wanted to do was fit in, be like everybody else. Now I felt more isolated than ever. But at least this time, it wasn't because I'd been trying and failing to meet everyone else's approval. My new role models were people I'd never met: musicians, authors and other creative, inspirational figures.

I'd also figured that there were people my age—professional athletes, doctorate candidates and others—who were getting up early and devoting the necessary time, energy and focus their endeavors deserved. Why shouldn't I do the same for the guitar? Because of some expectation that musicians are supposed to be total fuck-ups? No thanks. I tried that, the excess partying, the not caring enough about being serious. It didn't work for me. This felt much better.

I mostly kept quiet about my activities. If asked, I'd give an answer. But I never brought it up to anyone. Talking about it only opens the door for others to discourage you and causes you to question your own motivations.

Besides, I'd realized there was a huge difference between talking about something and actually doing it. Guitar players were the worst offenders—so many of them were all talk, talk, talk and me, me, me; the new guitar they were getting (as though that was the missing ingredient to their playing), the new licks they got down (just play it, don't talk about it!) and whatever else they could think of to draw attention to themselves. I didn't want to be one of those guys. I'd realized that all truth lay not in the talk but only in the result. If you had to talk about it, you were a joke.

I suppose I could have been doing what I saw others in the scene doing—drinking beer all day, getting high constantly, staying up for days at a time, watching too much TV, never missing a party or local gig. Instead, here I was living healthy, expanding my knowledge, working hard on something I loved and looking forward to it each day.

*

At home, I'd been dissecting a substantial amount of music.

I'd bought a little Tascam Porta One multi-track cassette recorder. My father looked at it and said, "What the hell is that complicated…thing?!"

I recorded little instrumental versions of songs I liked, classic and current, starting with Sgt. Pepper-era Beatles songs. This opened up a good deal of understanding about production and composition. More current pop music, like Sting and Peter Gabriel, being less guitar-driven, took more time to understand. The same was true of progressive rock like King Crimson and Yes. But I was beginning to assimilate it all.

While you could easily point a finger at these activities and accuse them of being *not metal*, the truth was that listening to and dissecting sophisticated pop and prog music was breaking me out of the same old patterns and opening up new metal ideas.

I was also listening to and purchasing a lot of jazz. I liked how the music made me feel; it seemed to expand my consciousness and somehow felt "classy." I also loved the fact that recordings from the '40s', by artists such as Charlie Parker and Bud Powell, were as relevant as the latest recordings by Pat Metheny and Herbie Hancock. In fact, if you didn't have essential recordings from the periods of '40s Bebop, early '50s Cool Jazz and mid-'50s to mid-'60s hard bop, you were out of the loop. There seemed to be more appreciation of history than in the rock world, where so many felt music began with the '60s British Invasion bands. And many in the metal scene were unable or unwilling to recognize any music that existed pre-Black Sabbath.

One of my favorite activities was working with the Charlie Parker Omnibook, a comprehensive book of the bebop pioneer's alto sax solos and melodies. Reading the notes was painstaking, but I was able to dissect them slowly and learn sections from Parker's recordings. A few of these licks would even find their way onto the new album, at the tail end of a song, "Perilous Nation."

In between guitar practice, I'd write lyrics, certain most of them would never get used. Amazingly, most of them would, more out of desperation than approval of what I was writing about: current events. "Perilous Nation" was about *Satanic Verses* author Salman Rushdie and the recent Fatwa, or death sentence placed on him by Muslim fundamentalists. "The Greenhouse Effect" was about just that, the greenhouse effect, which artists like Sting and Peter Gabriel were bringing attention to. I figured why not raise a little environmental awareness ourselves?

The political, social and environmental awareness implied in these lyrics would get attention from journalists, especially mainstream newspapers. They'd also create some awkward moments as the other guys in the band, not being up on these issues, would frequently be asked to comment on them during interviews.

As far as playing jazz, that was just not coming together yet. I kept getting discouraged and giving up, then giving it another shot, then giving up again. Being a competent jazz artist would take many more years and several false starts.

At least now I finally had all those modes and scales fluidly under my fingers and in my ears. In fact, the new record would have the solo I referred to earlier, over a pattern I'd created simply for practicing the modes, on the title track of our new album: *Practice What You Preach*.

*

They say you find out who your true friends are whenever you need help moving. I say this: you find out who your true friends are when you begin to make healthy choices in your life.

It seemed that with each positive step I took, Eric would try to shoot it down. I don't bring this up out of bitterness or disrespect, only because it posed a serious challenge during rehearsals for the new album. It's a bit strange to write about now, because the Eric of today would never act like this.

In fact, before going any further I should point out that Eric deserves a lot of credit, not just for keeping the band going during the dark times of the '90s, after this book leaves off (1992), when the band had regressed to club level in the US, but also for becoming the most improved person in comparison to who he was. But back in those days, he was…let's say…..difficult to be in a band with, something it's hard to gloss over.

At practice, when it came up that I'd joined a gym, Greg said he'd been thinking about lifting weights himself. I told Greg it would be good for him. Chuck, overhearing us, mentioned that he had an old barbell set in his garage that he could bring on tour. At first I thought the positive steps I'd been taking in my own life might carry over to the rest of the group. But the momentary ray of sunshine was clouded over by Eric, who made a "tssss" sound, as though he were spitting. Looking down at the ground, he muttered: "So what the fuck's that s'posed to mean, we're all gonna get buffed, oiled up and have muscles like fuckin' Manowar[49] or some trip?!"

When I stopped smoking pot, I got some odd looks from the others, but they begrudgingly accepted it. Everyone, that is, except Eric, who continued trying to pass a joint to me. He became borderline aggressive each time I refused: "C'mon…. just take it….one hit! Why the fuck not? C'mon, just take a hit….It'll be cool. What's your problem? It's our fuckin' trip. C'mon!"

---

[49] Manowar, a power metal band from upstate New York, is famous for combining bodybuilder builder physiques with a Conan the Barbarian-like wardrobe. They were and still are superstars in Germany-the David Hasselhoffs of metal.

When he finally realized it was a lost cause, he'd looked as though I'd just murdered his pet. I'd seen him pull this on others, especially Lou. Whenever Lou didn't do what Eric wanted, he wouldn't acknowledge him, except with a scowl, sometimes for days at a time. Now, by not getting high with him, I was experiencing what became known as the "Wrath of Eric."

I could only figure that his reaction stemmed from a couple of things. One was a sense of needing to be in control. The other thing, I'm pretty sure, was that deep down inside, he must have known that becoming more health-conscious, not abusing substances (legal and otherwise), acting more mature and behaving more responsibly was the right thing to do. But for him, moving in that direction would have meant taking an honest assessment of his own life, something that was probably too painful for him at the time.

I could relate. Recognizing the need for change in my own life had not been easy. It had required a good amount of introspection, humility, acknowledgement of mistakes, and steps to correct those mistakes. The hardest thing to come to terms with was that I was still the same damaged person I'd been when I'd joined the band. I was modified, sure, but I had the same soul as the incompetent, insecure reject I thought I'd escaped from.

Joining a metal band had felt like turning into a comic book superhero. But what all superheroes have to reckon with, as the mighty Superman and Spiderman can attest to, is that we all have a Clark Kent or Peter Parker inside.

On the other hand, I'd really had nothing to lose by embarking upon, to quote the cover of a book I'd just read,[50] "a journey of a man in search of himself." My own failure fitting into peer groups, whether at school or in the band, had enabled me to embrace my own self-discovery. I may have still been shy, awkward and unconfident on the outside, but I was becoming a warrior on the inside. And I was now seeing that so many others, no matter how tough they acted on the outside, lacked that internal strength.

So while Eric's negative reactions to my positive choices were baffling to me and making my life increasingly difficult, all I could do was carry on and try my best to live with it. After all, being in this band, no matter how fucked up things would get, was like being in a family. And you know what they say: *You can choose your friends, not your family.*

*

---

[50] *Zen and the Art of Motorcycle Maintenance* by Robert M. Pirsig, 1974.

As we began rehearsing the new songs, the musical differences began to manifest.

It started when I brought in a song sketch with a pulsating groove, less influenced by Metallica or Slayer and inspired by Pink Floyd's "Run Like Hell." The song was met with fierce resistance from Eric, who kept saying it was *not our trip,* and trying to replace it with something more *old school.* Thankfully, friends of the band all told him to at least try it. And as soon as the fans would hear it, they'd make it very clear they were all on board with the song, which was called "Sins of Omission."

In the meantime, Eric and I managed to find a solid point of agreement: we both felt that the band needed a slow tune that crescendos into a heavy energetic finale, something along the lines of Metallica's "Fade to Black." Eric initiated some great clean rhythm parts that I added some color to and wrote additional parts for.

For the song's intro, I incorporated the influence of guitarist Al Di Meola's acoustic work. We rehearsed it with Greg and Lou, who were clearly in favor of the song. For once, we had a song that gave relief from the breakneck tempos, had substantial melodic color and gave me a nice chance to stretch out on some acoustic playing and over some key changes.

This one had serious potential—until Eric and I suddenly found ourselves aligned against a formidable opponent: Chuck. For some inexplicable reason, Chuck felt that slow songs were "lame" and "pussy-like." Still, we pieced together the slow song in hopes that he'd come around.

Knowing that Chuck was unlikely to come forward with lyrics, I went ahead and wrote a bunch on my own. Since I'd been going through so many personal changes, a collection of sad words, though ambiguous, had come naturally. Everyone seemed to respond to the lyrics except Chuck, who didn't react.

With the entire band and management pleading for Chuck to sing the song, he eventually relented. Unfortunately, it would be obvious that he never really liked the song. It was quite a different situation from "Fade to Black," which was written by the same guy who sang it, and delivered accordingly in concert.

In the future, while playing live, Chuck would often make fun of this tune with mock crying and sniffling. He'd refuse to let us call it anything else but "The Ballad" because, according to him, that's all it was—a song he was doing because the rest of us wanted a ballad. *The Ballad?!*

Oh well. While this felt super lame, we didn't have any other titles. Besides, it was better than not doing the song at all.

*

There was one other issue that would cast a shadow over my duration in the band: the issue of "leads." It was becoming a bit obvious to others and to me that with each compliment I got and each review that mentioned my guitar solos, Eric was becoming more and more uncomfortable.

His riffing was terrific—he had the consistency of a great drummer and could rival the best thrash rhythm players like Hetfield or Scott Ian of Anthrax. But his lead playing at this time had been suited for bands like Venom and Motörhead—punkish, raw, unpolished. Not that there was anything wrong with that (and not that it describes his playing today).

But here was the problem: since I was fifteen, I'd been inspired by players of advanced precision along the lines of Randy Rhoads, Eddie Van Halen, or Joe Satriani and more recently John McLaughlin and Al Di Meola. I'd been practically religious about studying their techniques and had been obsessed about developing a serious work ethic. Yet my solos, and the positive attention they were bringing to the band, from fans, other musicians and journalists, had become a touchy subject around Eric.

It was understandable that he didn't want to end up an unsung hero of rhythm guitar like Malcolm Young of AC/DC or Rudolf Schenker of Scorpions—guys who were the backbones of the bands they'd started but whose lead guitarists received most of the media and fan focus. To get more attention, his best bet would have been to develop a unique stage personality like Scott Ian (who has more presence and visibility than most lead players) or slowly ease his way into lead guitar with simple melodic parts.

Instead, there were attempts to mimic my own style, which wasn't working. He'd begun envisioning the band as a thrash version Iron Maiden— a twin guitar band with two guitarists of equal soloing ability—but his soloing next to mine sounded out of place, clashing rather than complementing, something the rest of the band and various producers would try to convey. This would be an increasing source of conflicts in the future. Meanwhile, he'd have total dominance of the sound in the live mixes, while I was often barely heard. He'd have his own side of the stage and his own tech, while I'd always have to share stage right with the bass.

But I wasn't complaining. Mainly because I didn't know how to.

This was beginning to feel like déjà vu: that experience with my brother competing with me when I first started tinkering on that toy guitar, happening all over again. But I was never competing with anyone; my brother nor with Eric. I just did what I did, for the sake of self-expression. It should always be about the music—never the attention that it may bring.

Focusing on this would help me get through the challenges of dealing with guitar-envy and sibling rivalry once again. It would cause me to work even harder.

*

Earlier in the year, Chuck, Eric and Lou had gained so much weight that our record label and management had to have a conference call with them about slimming down. All three went on one of those popular mega-diets, Nutrisystem, paid for by the band.

The problem with fad diets like Nutrisystem, Jenny Craig and more recently Atkins is that they offer quick fix solutions. Quick fixes don't last. So while the guys would look slim for the *Practice* photo shoot, all three would eventually, like many who endorse these diets, yo yo back to their original weight and more.

Maintaining a good physique, like playing advanced lead guitar, requires a series of many disciplined short steps with a focus on the long-term goal. Regular workouts, healthy food choices, cutting out late-night gorging, not abusing alcohol or marijuana (with its side effect known as the munchies) and other habits of wellness are what create real, lasting results. These short, healthy steps aren't easy and don't provide any instant gratification, but they make all the difference in the long run. And it is the long-term goals, whether physical or musical, which require humility, focus, acceptance, patience, respect (of self and of others) and most of all, depth.

Instant gratification is shallow. It is the release from the clutches of instant gratification that separates those who follow through on things from those that look at others with envy.

*

Despite our differences, there was one thing that Eric and I were totally agreeing upon: this album needed to be recorded differently. Different recording process, different studio and most likely, a different producer.

First, the process: all the great energy of our concerts was failing to be captured in the studio. I'd felt all along that I thought we should have been recording more "live." In other words, track the whole band at once, minus vocals, have great-sounding "scratch tracks" that could be kept if tightly played, replaceable if not. With better sounding scratch tracks, we'd all be much more inspired, than with that horrible rinky-dink guitar tone we'd been forced to track with in Ithaca. It seemed so obvious. Then again, recording live like this required an 'A List,' studio with multiple isolation rooms. And there just happened to be one right here in our backyard: Fantasy Studios.

Located in an industrial area on the west side of Berkeley, Fantasy had been the brainchild of Saul Zaenz, a hugely successful record exec who'd signed a rock group to his jazz label, Fantasy Records. The success of the group, legendary '60s' Bay Area band, Creedence Clearwater Revival, had helped provided Zaenz with the capital to build the studio and eventually fund and produce major motion pictures, all of which received post-production[51] at Fantasy.

Zaenz's legal battles with Creedence's principle songwriter, John Fogerty, over royalty rights and defamation, were legendary and controversial, seriously derailing Fogerty's career. While it was instinctual to side with the musician over the businessman, this case wasn't so clear cut: Fogerty's own brother and band mate, Tom,[52] had sided with Zaenz—the two brothers were barely speaking at the time of Tom's tragic death in the '90s. And Zaenz, I would soon find out, had not only overseen some of the best jazz music ever recorded, he was responsible for some of the greatest movies of all time. We're not talking typical Hollywood summer blockbuster fare, but invaluable, thought-provoking, Academy Award winning films such as *One Flew Over The Cuckoo's Nest, Amadeus* and *The English Patient.* So whatever Zaenz's situation was with Fogerty over CCR, it was hard to look at Zaenz as the villain he was being portrayed as by the John Fogerty camp.

Budget-wise, a place like Fantasy had been far out of our reach. However, one of our managers knew someone who knew someone that worked there. A call was made, and they were put in touch with the studio manager, Nina, who offered the "bro" deal. It was still expensive, but better than the usual rate charged to acts on major labels. And since our contract called for an additional $25k to our allotted recording budget with each album (recoupable of course, but who was counting?), not to mention that we'd be saving money by recording at home, we had a lot more to work with. So with the friends & family studio rate, the removal of flight and hotel costs for the band, and a contractual clause raising our budget to $75,000, a new budget was approved and a decision was made: we were recording the next album at home using Fantasy Studios.

This left one problem: who was going to produce the album?

*

By this time, Alex Perialas seemed to have cornered himself in a thrash ghetto. He'd recorded nothing noteworthy outside the genre, and it was presenting a huge problem. Metallica, Megadeth or Slayer had all found

---

[51] Post production usually refers to editing, effects, audio and anything that occurs after filming.

[52] Tom Fogerty's son, Jeff Fogerty, was a hard rock guitarist in the East Bay music scene who'd jammed with my brother. He could never escape the shadow of his famous Uncle John.

GEEK TO GUITAR HERO

success with producers who'd had an outside perspective. Even Anthrax, who'd become close with Alex, was moving on from him.

Another problem with Alex P was the fact that he'd made some serious miscalculations on our last album in terms of microphones, mixing, etc. Sure we hadn't made it any easier, hovering over him during mixes, everyone, myself included, saying, *"Turn me up!"* But the fact was, Alex felt like a B List producer and we were about to enter an A List studio.

Unfortunately, good thrash producers, at this time, were few and far between. Metallica's original producer, Mark Whitaker, had more or less disappeared off the face of the Earth. Shortly before, he'd produced an album for Lääz Rockit, which had sounded terrible (besides, it seemed to be Lars and James who'd really been producing Metallica anyway). Slayer's triumphant *Reign in Blood* had been produced by Rick Rubin, but there was no way we'd ever meet the standards of the world's most in-demand rock and hip-hop producer (who happened to love Slayer). Besides, Rubin was busy producing a new album called *Blood Sugar Sex Magik* by a unique up-and-coming band called Red Hot Chili Peppers. Megadeth, meanwhile, was being produced by its eccentric leader Dave, who didn't produce other bands. Mustaine's new production partner Mike Clink, who'd produced Guns 'N' Roses' triumphant debut *Appetite for Destruction,* was clearly out of our budgetary reach.

So the unfortunate fact was, we had barely any options besides Alex P who, when told that the band was considering other producers, immediately flew from Ithaca to Oakland to meet with us.

*

In our manager's law offices, Alex P pleaded his case for staying on as producer. He took the tactic of agreeing with most of what we had to say about *The New Order.* Sure, there had been sound problems, the tone sounded thin; in fact, the whole mix sounded muffled, like it was locked in a box. But (according to him) *that wasn't his fault!* There had been budgetary restrictions and miscommunications. Yes, Pyramid was his own studio, but it was designed around acts on a budget. Give him a studio like Fantasy, with bigger mixing consoles, better sounding rooms, more isolation, the ability for more instruments to track and a higher budget, and we'd see a whole new level of production.

Furthermore, he and the band really knew each other now: he'd been there from our first album, knew how we worked, knew how we'd come along, understood how to communicate with us better.

In other words, he took no responsibility for the problems with the previous recording and made the claim that now was the big chance for all of us: if we didn't seize this moment, we'd be missing out on a huge opportunity—the one that could put all our careers where they should be: in the big leagues.

We bought it, hook, line and sinker.

Alex P was going to produce the next Testament record. It would be his last.

*

Fantasy Studios lived up to its name. With its smooth walls worthy of a modern art gallery, shiny granite counters, numerous gold and platinum plaques, plush leather sofas and giant screen TVs, walking into Fantasy's rotating glass doors, it felt like you were entering the Emerald City.

Lining the hallway was a gallery of black and white photos, a who's who of clientele, from Bay Area rock stalwarts Journey, Grateful Dead, Santana, Bonnie Raitt, Chris Isaak, Sammy Hagar to jazz legends Joe Pass, Bill Evans and Sonny Rollins to blues artists BB King, John Lee Hooker and Robert Cray and everyone from all genres in between.

I loved the feeling of walking the same hallowed ground where so many great artists had set foot. Although we'd never sell anywhere near the number of albums of these multi-platinum rock bands or receive the respect of the jazz and blues greats, our picture would soon join them on the wall. I couldn't help but be inspired by this and hoped that the feeling of being in that company and reaching a higher level would rub off on the rest of the guys as well.

Instead of things often going amuck, the wrong people hired and kept on for years at a time, ridiculous Spinal Tap-like incidents all justified with the attitude: *"Well....you know...this is Testament,"* I wanted to see better decisions made. I wanted the band to feel a stronger sense of self, just as I was feeling individually. And then, when things started to go right, I wanted to see the band say, with pride: *"Damn right. This is Testament."*

It wouldn't happen.

*

Despite feeling alienated from the lifestyle of the band, despite Eric's increased frustration towards my rising status in the guitar community and despite Chuck's stubbornness about slow songs and other issues (such as his insistence on bringing in our live soundman, Dave Pigg, as vocal producer, only for Dave to be declared useless and sent home—a futile waste of time, energy and money), there was one challenge with this album that overtook all the others: the growing disconnect between the band and Alex P.

Alex seemed to have his own agenda and was as stubborn and close-minded as everyone else, in his own way. This band had enough communication troubles on its own—we needed someone to help the process, brighten the energy and lessen the aura of confrontation. While the blame certainly couldn't all be pinned on Alex, his being in the producer's chair seemed to be hampering the process even further. He treated all of us condescendingly, as though we were still the first-timers we'd been when we'd landed in Ithaca that snowy January night two years earlier.

But things were different now. No longer a baby band, this was a group with two years of touring under its belt and a fierce determination to rise above the primitive production of the first two albums. And while Alex had claimed to be the one to make this happen, I wasn't so sure. Fairly or unfairly, I couldn't help but feel he'd sold us up the river.

I felt conflicted about this. After all, Alex had been there from my first moment as a professional recording artist and had offered much valuable early guidance. For that, I was indebted to him. But now, he seemed plagued by his own frustration (at times justified, at other times not), trapped in his own self-righteousness and being out of his league running the massive 48-track digital recording system at Fantasy.

Keep in mind that this was the end of the '80s: we were in the dawn of a recording revolution. Fantasy was leading the charge, armed with all the latest digital technology and brand-new computerized recording systems. The paradigm was being shattered. Alex had attempted to keep up with the times by attending audio engineering conferences and reading trade publications, but he hadn't anticipated the level in which the industry was changing. His own studio, Pyramid, was like a turboprop commuter plane at Ithaca Regional Airport. Fantasy was like a Boeing 767 on a busy runway at San Francisco International.

I now saw Alex P in a more realistic light: he was not the all-knowing wise one, but rather, the small town amateur who'd gotten lucky with a couple of projects. Not helping was the fact that he was attempting to get me on his side for creative disputes with the other guys that I'd felt neutral about (such as snare reverb). He also attempted to bond with me over my jazz interests, saying that, though he'd never told anyone before, it had always been his secret dream to record jazz[53]. Suddenly, it felt like he was

---

[53] Ironically, while Alex P would never do anything of note in the jazz world, his own assistant engineer, Rob "Wacko" Hunter, would become special engineer to Branford Marsalis, Jeff "Tain" Watts and other jazz greats.

latching onto me as though my star was rising and his falling. It felt really weird especially when, in a breath of desperation, he begged me to keep him in mind should I pursue jazz in the future. *"Promise me you won't forget about your 'old buddy Alex' okay?"*

*

As the sessions chugged on, the problems with Alex P escalated.

A big issue appeared when the guys decided they wanted to hear the clicky quality of Slayer's kick drums. Alex ran around in circles chasing this tone. He'd argue with the guys that he'd found the sound, they'd say no, that's not it, and he'd start all over, getting more and more agitated. Sometimes, he'd start one place and then hours later, it would be exactly where he'd first started.

He blamed them, they blamed him. Whole days were soon being lost to the endless pursuit of this elusive clicky kick sound. The end result is painful: a kick drum so clicky that, when you listen to the album, it sounds as though someone has stuck his hand inside the stereo system and with every kick drum, is thumping his finger onto the cone of the speaker.

An even bigger problem was that each time we'd gain momentum, there would be some issue with confusion over the mixing desk, the computer freezing, the outboard gear not being dialed in properly or some other technical issue. All progress would then come to a halt—we'd stop, put down our instruments and wait for a staff-engineer to come in.

Fortunately, there was one particular engineer on staff at Fantasy that everyone seemed to like, who'd end up brightening up the sessions. This young staff member would soon become a permanent fixture, our official assistant engineer. He was a warm, outgoing, tech-savvy guy, about ten years older than me, also of non-practicing, California-Jewish ethnicity.

His name was Michael Rosen.

*

With his well-groomed light brown straight hair just past his shoulders and business-casual attire, Michael Rosen could have looked in place playing in a rock band or working in the offices of a hip magazine or software company.

Having engineered in studios all over the Bay Area, with artists outside of all genres, including some of my jazz heroes on the walls, Michael had many great stories. Soon, we'd be attending local jazz gigs together. He'd introduce me to some of the top session musicians he'd worked with in the studio.

Meeting Michael would be a big plus of *The Practice* sessions. While there was still tension within the band, and especially between the band and Alex P, Michael became a really good mediator, saving the process with his enthusiasm, quick wit, humor and creative ideas. He brought much desperately needed positive energy to the table.

Alex P and Michael hit it off famously. Michael had young, West Coast energy and a firm grasp on all the emerging technology. Alex possessed East Coast old school energy and had been around the block a few times. They seemed to make a good team.

After the sessions, there would be a very close friendship between Michael and Alex P. Alex would attend Michael's upcoming wedding. They would talk of many recording collaborations in the future. But their partnership would be short-lived. Why? Because within the year, Alex P would be permanently let go as our producer.

His replacement? You guessed it: Michael Rosen.

*

Though *Practice* wouldn't be our tightest album, no one would say that the recording didn't have the best feel so far.

Some of the songs have an energy that we hadn't caught on tape yet. Being able to record with our actual guitar rigs was liberating, a far cry from the first two records, where we'd had to record with a distortion pedal through mixing channel—never again! In the future, there would be more cleaning up and overdubbing, but we'd always try to record the drums as though we were playing live, keeping the drums, then redoing most of the other parts. So while we'd never record live again, those sessions at Fantasy would be the ones that set the standard for "feel."

Anytime you record an album, you get lucky on some songs, not so lucky on others. This is especially true when you record live.

I remember during "The Ballad," one of my favorite sections, the acoustic solo section in the beginning was almost cut because there was a problem with the drums. I didn't want to lose the solo but Lou was pushing to get rid of it. Lou is the band member I've had the least problems with during all my years in the band, but at that moment I was very annoyed with him.

In the midst of the argument, we had to do a photo shoot—in one of the photos, I look furious, probably the angriest I've ever looked in a photo! Fortunately, the problem was worked out. There was a solution that satiated Lou with the drums while I was able to keep the solo. For saving the day and keeping the piece, the credit goes to our new assistant engineer and future producer, Michael Rosen.

On the other hand, Lou and I both got very lucky on the title track. His drum track was one of his best takes ever. And with the drums a real keeper, my solo happened to be my best of all the takes.

The solo in "Practice" would become something of a signature solo. It was different than any I'd played thus far—a combination of all my influences at the time, put into metal. It starts out with Holdsworth/Satriani style legato. Then goes into some Jeff Beck-style blues. Then some Van Halen-esque stuff, not the "Eruption" hammer-ons that everybody apes, but the flamenco influenced licks of "Spanish Fly" and "Somebody Get Me a Doctor." Then, there are little arpeggios reminiscent of Yngwie Malmsteen, some speed picking influenced by Al Di Meola and John McLaughlin and finally some Texas blues, a la Stevie Ray Vaughn, directly inspired by his instrumental "Scuttle Buttin'."

The solo is followed by a pattern from the scale I'd recently learned in my jazz studies, melodic minor, which I showed to Eric—it presented a nice opportunity for us to play harmonies together.

I knew in the grand scheme of the music I was now listening to, especially the geniuses like Miles, Pat Metheny, etc., that this new solo of mine was small potatoes. But I also knew that in the context of thrash/speed metal, it was unique. Interestingly, the solo in "Practice" was one of the only where I've ever used a whammy bar. I'd soon give up on whammys completely, deciding they'd become, like wah-wah pedals, flashy gimmicks, at least when overused in hard rock and metal. I decided to just imitate the whammy sound with a bend, which is how I play it today.

Practice would be our biggest selling album, nearly going gold. And for as much negativity as there'd been towards my blossoming musicianship, there would be no greater acknowledgement than the day I'd receive conflicting offers—two in the same day—to write a monthly instruction column for national guitar magazines (the first thrash metal player ever to do so). I'd eventually contribute to the Big 3 of guitar mags at the time: *Guitar World, Guitar for the Practicing Musician* and *Guitar Player.* These columns would reach a guitar-centric audience beyond the thrash scene.

And these magazines, combined with the solos from this album, particularly on "Practice," "The Ballad," and "Perilous Nation," would help bring me more attention as a guitar hero than anyone could have anticipated.

30. JAZZ INTERLUDE

Despite the fact that learning jazz would be completely at odds not only with the music I was playing, but also the people I was surrounded by, I had an increasing instinct that somehow, I was meant to head in that direction.

I'd gone to see guitarist John Scofield perform at Slim's in San Francisco. I didn't exactly understand the music, but I didn't need to. I could tell it was coming from this pure place, where sound was expressed organically and spontaneously. I also liked that everyone in his band was featured, not just the guitar. I was still listening to Van Halen and Randy Rhoads, but was getting more out of listening to my new influences.

As recommended by my occasional teachers, I started listening to Django Reinhardt, Charlie Christian and Wes Montgomery. I'd also gone to hear Joe Pass who, unbeknownst to me, would pass away a scant few years later. Some of their music was too difficult to understand, but at least now, I was starting in a place that was better suited for my level than Scofield, Chick Corea etc...

Upon realizing I'd been living with a girlfriend who'd descended into a deranged meth-addict, I'd moved back in with my parents, my tail between my legs. I figured I'd be on tour most of the time anyway. My parents were really difficult to live with. I tried to be home as little as possible.

Fortunately that glaring symbol of failure—the never used dark room in the backyard, now provided a roof over my head, enabling me to live at home without being stuck under the same roof. The little backyard shed became my laboratory, where I hooked up a fine stereo system. I would pour over the *Charlie Parker Omnibook*.

*

Around this time, I experienced several more epiphanies relating to jazz, including a couple of incidents that felt strangely coincidental and bordered on supernatural. I wasn't sure what their meaning was, if any, but they felt like signals to dive deeper into jazz as a listener, a concertgoer and, unheard of for someone who played the music I did—as a guitarist.

At the very least it became clear that my interest in jazz was no passing phase. And one other thing was certain: if God, Nature, The Universe, or whoever else was in charge didn't want me to be drawn deeper into jazz, then I sure as hell shouldn't have been placed in Fantasy Studios at the moment I was.

*

Fantasy Records, housed a few floors above Fantasy Studios, had just taken over the catalogues of several legendary jazz record labels including Prestige, Impulse, Riverside and Pablo. Thousands of legendary jazz recordings, including some of the biggest names, were being re-mastered for CD and put out on the Fantasy Label.

One day, outside one of the smaller rooms, I heard the most incredible sound—a honking and squealing interweaved with effortless cascades of notes, as if the entire range of human emotions were being expressed in one musical statement. It was very raunchy and intense, yet delicate at the same time.

I was reminded of how I'd felt when I'd first heard Van Halen's "Eruption" in Junior High. Nothing since had inspired me like that, until now. I knew I'd never be able to get that tone on guitar; this was a wind instrument, a tenor sax. Maybe, if I studied for many, many years, I might one day be able to capture the feeling of it and some of the patterns.

Suddenly I felt a new purpose: to somehow combine what I was now hearing with heavy metal. It was like the moment in *The Blues Brothers* movie, where Belushi and Akroyd go into the church. Overtaken by the gospel music led by the Reverend James Brown, they scream to each other about putting the band back together. I absolutely felt a spiritual calling, although what it was I couldn't be sure. But one thing I was sure of: whoever was in that room had to be the best saxophonist in the world.

I was afraid to meet him. In fact, I didn't want to meet him. It would be like meeting God. I refused to look through the door. Still I wondered: who was in there playing the horn like that and putting me into a state of truth and higher consciousness? I had to know.

That's when a staff engineer whom I'd been introduced to a few days earlier walked up, nodded hello and was about to walk into studio B.

"Excuse me?" I asked. I must have looked shocked. "Can you tell me who that is? That's the most amazing music I've ever heard!"

"Well, you've got really great taste in music." He looked pleasantly surprised to hear such appreciation, especially from a long-haired rocker. "That's John Coltrane."

John Coltrane?! I could've sworn that John Coltrane, one of the most influential musicians in jazz, had passed away in the late '60s. But that tone was so raw and alive—he had to be right there in the room! Just then the cadenza ended and I heard the rest of the band, drums, bass and piano play

240

the final notes of the song.[54] "He's not actually in there right now," the engineer said with a smile. "What I mean is, I guess you could say he's *there*, he's just not in there physically."

He explained to me that what I was hearing was Coltrane's *Live at Birdland* being remastered for CD. The album was on Impulse, one the labels Fantasy had just picked up. This recording was of a live gig, which features an amazing two minutes or so of unaccompanied sax.

The mastering engineer added that since I was an official client of the studios, it would be no problem for me to get promo CDs of anything in the Fantasy jazz catalogue, which had just expanded by leaps and bounds. The album I was hearing now probably wouldn't be ready for a few months, but I could order it in advance. And in the meantime, I was welcome to order as many as I like. Some of them, the more in-demand ones, might cost a buck or two, but most of them they'd throw in for no charge. Would I be interested?

"Can I order every single one?" I asked.

"Hope you have room." He laughed. "There are thousands to choose from."

The next time I saw him, he handed me a typed list of albums with a checklist, designed for jazz radio stations, magazines, conferences and other organizations eligible for the discounted promo CDs. He told me to go through it, check off the ones I wanted, and in a week or so, towards the end of our session, he'd have them all in a box for me. I ordered more than a hundred CDs, the entire batch costing me around $20 or so. These albums included many by Miles Davis, Thelonious Monk, Wes Montgomery, John Coltrane, Charlie Parker, Joe Pass, Cannonball Adderly, Bill Evans, Art Blakey, Sonny Rollins. Some of the first licks I'd transcribe were on these records, and I still listen to them more than twenty years later.

Thanks to this kind mastering engineer working at Fantasy studios, my jazz collection was under way.

*

I mentioned earlier that while I've generally been a realist and a skeptic, there have been several occurrences in my life that are downright *freaky*. These incidents haven't changed my principles or how I plan my life, but they have gotten me to question the rigidity of these principles and learn

---

[54] "I Want To Talk About You," John Coltrane, *Live at Birdland*. This exact same section of music would later be played for me in a blindfold test by a journalist from *Guitar for the Practicing Musician,* who had no idea about this story, which I've never told until now.

to be a little more open to the concepts of signs from the universe. The Coltrane incident was one such freaky incident. Here's another…

I'd been working on learning some licks all day—Wes Montgomery's version of Thelonious Monk's "Round Midnight."[55] I was still on the very first section. Every day, I'd forget the licks from the day before and have to review those licks, then try to squeeze in a few more notes. The process was so slow, it felt like my life was drifting away. I'd started a month ago and felt barely any progress. How long was I going to keep this up?

Exasperated, I decided to take a break and drive downtown. I was hungry. I walked outside, planning to head to Telegraph Avenue, near the UC Campus, and grab some ethnic food, maybe browse Tower records. I needed inspiration. Silently, I wished for some sign that I should even continue trying to learn jazz guitar.

As I got in the car, the licks I'd been working on were still running through my head. I turned the keys in the ignition; the engine started and the stereo turned on. When I heard the music, I froze—it was the exact same Wes Montgomery track I'd been working on all day.

How was this possible? Had I, without thinking about it, brought my new portable CD player and plugged it into the car stereo? After all, I was getting fried from all those hours of practicing guitar, I must have just hooked up the CD player without thinking about it and…NO! What I was hearing was coming from *the radio.*

It turned out, I'd gotten in the car at the exact moment the same song was being broadcast on KJAZZ, the Bay Area's jazz station.

Ok. Now before you dismiss this as some meaningless coincidence, like the time you may have hummed a U2 hit while it was in massive rotation, and heard it on the radio later that day, there are a few things to consider here. For one thing, I've never heard Wes' version of Round Midnight on KJAZZ or any other radio station, before or since. Even more important is this: "Round Midnight" happens to be the most recorded jazz tune of all time with literally thousands of interpretations.

Of course, I can never prove any of this actually happened, so you'll have to take my word for it. But I have a pretty good track record for honesty. And I'm not saying any of this proves there's a higher power or that one should believe in a higher power. All I'm saying is this—if one is to be

---

[55] From the album *Wes Montgomery Trio.*

an artist, then at least *entertaining the notion* of some undefined[56] mysterious forces at work not only makes it more fun, it is more conducive to the creative process.

In fact, I'm willing to bet that if you conducted a controlled study of artists who allowed themselves to be open to possibilities of mysterious forces (whatever they may be) versus those who didn't, the believers would produce better results. Maybe it's just a placebo effect, but that's my theory.

Having grown up around family and friends who are rigid skeptics, sworn to the scientific method,[57] I understand that I risk coming across as someone who's completely lost his mind. But the truth is, these experiences are based on my own observation. No, they can't be proven in a controlled environment, but I don't see how that makes them invalid or irrelevant. And I'm sorry to say—I'm not exactly seeing any rigid skeptics creating great art.

Herbie Hancock is a Buddhist. Miles Davis believed in spirits. J.S. Bach, a loyal believer, composed for God as interpreted by the Lutheran Church. Most great works of art have been created by those who believed in a higher power, at least on some level. Were they all wrong to be drawing from these beliefs? I say the answer is in their art.

Churches, temples and other tenets of organized religions don't do it for me (although their architecture sometimes does). But that doesn't mean that those who derive genuine feelings of spirituality aren't tapping into some of the same undefined entities as felt by myself and other artists who are skeptics by nature but open to certain unexplained phenomenon.

So while I'm hesitant to define myself by any label or subscribe to any formal belief system, there is one definition that seems to fall in line with my own experiences. It comes from Deism, whose practitioners included Benjaman Franklin, Thomas Paine and John Locke. While I don't subscribe to Deism or any other movement, I do appreciate this description:

"A universal creative force greater than that demonstrated by mankind, supported by personal observation of laws and designs in nature and the universe, perpetuated and validated by the innate ability of human reason coupled with the rejection of claims made by individuals and organized religions of having received special divine revelation."

*

---

[56] I draw the line at describing any mysterious entity with a face or a name or other identity. I don't believe you can possibly know what that entity is, if it exists at all.

[57] Scientific Method: the process of observing reality with one's five senses, making logical theories based on observation and then proving or disproving the theory with experiments.

Less surreptitious than these events, but equally influential, was the discovery of a local establishment that brought together two things I would forever hold sacred: the sound of American jazz and the culture of the Far East. It was about a fifteen-minute walk from our house, just past the Berkeley/Oakland border.

Yoshi's was like a dream in my backyard—the best Japanese food in the East Bay and a prestigious jazz club so tiny, it was like having legendary jazz artists in your living room. This combination of Japanese cuisine and jazz music was a symbiotic, surreal combination—two elements that couldn't have been more disparate, yet somehow went hand in hand, like a Sukiyaki hot pot filled with the sophisticated soundtrack of 20th century urban America.

There was this nice feeling you got at the Japanese restaurant, from the positive energy of the staff and the elegance of the décor to the hot face towel, its refreshment setting the tone for what was to come: a wide assortment of flavors, colors and textures unlike any other type of cuisine. The miso soup, raw or cooked fish, rice and steamed or sautéed vegetables made you feel alive and refreshed, not dull and bloated like you do after greasy burgers, fries, pizza and wings.

After the meal, you'd move into the music room where the variety of sounds reflected that of the meal—a unique combination of tones, rhythms, notes and an energy level that ran the gamut from the loud and pulsating to the delicate crystal-quiet, proving that the intensity levels of soft and loud could be equal.

Just a few feet away from me, I could watch the masters at work. Some, like guitarist Joe Pass and pianist McCoy Tyner, would conjure the mystique of the night with elegant straight ahead jazz. Others enabled you to travel to distant lands in the course of an hour or so. Al Di Meola's tango music conjured visions of Argentina and Italy while John McLaughlin's ragas captured the flavors and enlightenment of India (both guitarists could fill much larger halls with electric bands, but chose Yoshi's as the perfect setting for their intimate acoustic projects).

Pianist Gonzolo Rubicaba was like a perfect combination of these two elements—his jazz piano took you to New York City after hours, but he'd incorporate Afro-Cuban influences that brought to mind walking along the piers of Havana, breathing in the salt water air. One of my all-time favorites was the now late tenor saxophonist Michael Brecker, who seemed to cover all the bases—straight ahead bebop, world music and pure funk.

But as life-changing as these experiences were at Yoshi's, there was one other Japanese establishment that would have an equally profound influence on me, perhaps more so.

*

Early on a Sunday evening, when I'd finished my guitar overdubs for the *Practice* album, Michael Rosen, the house engineer at Fantasy assigned to our project, suggested that he, Alex P and I go out to San Francisco to celebrate. "You've got to hear this band!" he said.

The Frank Martin Band played all the West Coast jazz festivals and events, but their training ground was Sunday nights at the Kanzaki lounge—a tiny bar located in the heart of San Francisco's Japantown.

Michael had crossed paths with most of these musicians while working as an engineer for producer Narada Michael Walden across the Bay. Narada had been one of the most influential jazz-rock drummers of the 1970s. He'd replaced the once irreplaceable Billy Cobham in John McLaughlin's Mahivishnu Orchestra, as well as played drums on Jeff Beck's seminal album *Wired,* composing half the tunes on the album. In the early '80s, Narada had relocated to upscale Marin County in the San Francisco Bay Area and switched from jazz/rock drumming to pop/R&B producing, his clients including Whitney Houston, Mariah Carey and Aretha Franklin.

Narada's right hand man in the Bay Area studio scene was keyboardist Frank Martin. Frank reminded me a bit of Joe Zawinul of Weather Report. Like Zawinul, his hippie-like appearance belied the seriousness of his work ethic and keyboard wizardry.   Frank played on most of Narada's sessions, hiring the other local musicians. Most of these players would turn up on Frank's own gigs, depending on who was on the road and who was in town, where they'd leave the pop behind and delve into some of the most serious electric jazz I'd ever heard.

The line-up of the Frank Martin Band consisted of a staggering who's who of the best in the Bay many of whom held regular positions with legends of jazz and R&B. Regular players included drummers Will Kennedy (The Yellowjackets), Billy Johnson (Patty LaBell) and Hillary Jones (Robbin Ford), bassists Gary Brown (Airto Moriera) Keith Jones (Wayne Shorter) and Beny Reitveld (Miles Davis), guitarists Stef Burns (Sheila E.), Garth Webber (Miles Davis) and Vernon Black (Mariah Carey), saxophonist Norbert Satchel (Diana Ross) and percussionist/vocalist Vicky Randall (George Benson, Dr. John, Kenny Loggins). Their music covered the gamut, from straight jazz, to funk, ballads and pop: Thelonious Monk to The Crusaders, Weather Report and The Brecker Brothers.

It was fascinating not only to hear this music expertly played but to rub elbows with so many master musicians.

*

On the first night I heard them, Frank had Billy Johnson on drums, Keith Jones on bass and Vicky Randall percussion and voice. This was about two years before Branford Marsalis would call her to LA to perform on *The Tonight Show with Jay Leno*. Stef Burns was on guitar.

All of the players blew me away, especially Stef. I'd never heard any guitarist cover all the bases like Stef before—he had the jazz vocabulary of John Scofield and Mike Stern but could also make the guitar sing like Jeff Beck. At one point, they did Beck's "The Pump." Stef's sound was so direct, sensitive and captivating that it wasn't until I'd hear the real Jeff Beck almost twenty years to that day in New York City that I'd hear anyone with that feel or sound. Some moments were reminiscent of my old teacher Joe Satriani, who by this time was riding a wave of popularity. But unlike Joe, Stef's playing felt improvised, not planned in advance. Joe had great musicians, but they were basically providing a static backing track for his guitar playing. Like the Jeff Beck show I'd see years later, this music was about the *band*, not just one person. I liked Frank's keyboard solos as much as Stef's. Stef's comping underneath was just as interesting as his own solos.

Stef immediately became my favorite local guitarist and represented my new direction. I'd never study with him formally, but he gave me some great pointers, such as getting deeper into the blues before taking on jazz standards.

Interestingly, Stef and I almost seemed to want to switch places— just as I began my moving towards jazz, he was stepping into hard rock, jamming with Y&T and Alice Cooper, even appearing with Alice in a scene from the film *Wayne's World*.

*

I began going to the Kanzaki Lounge on my own whenever I was in town. I spent many a Sunday night driving home hours after midnight.

The Frank Martin Band's music made you feel like you were traveling. It took you to a different place. You could leave all your petty worries behind for a few hours. Like a movie, it brought you out of your current world and took you someplace else. The technique of the musicians was amazing, but the music wasn't there for the purpose of technique, it was all about the interaction between the musicians as well as the audience. You felt like you were a part of the performance just by being there.

And though the gigs were relatively small, in front of just a dozen or so people, unlike the big rock shows with hundreds or thousands, I was knocked out by their incredible intensity. I also knew that if there was ever a way this kind of experience could somehow be brought to rock fans, they'd appreciate it. Perhaps one day, through my own music, I'd be something of a jazz evangelist, bringing that art of improvisation to metalheads and others who might not be aware how great the experience could be.

Also on Sunday nights, whenever I didn't make it out to the Kanzaki, there was a program on TV, co-hosted by saxophonist David Sanborn and pianist Jools Holland, called *Michelob Presents: Sunday Night*. On this show, I'd watch such diverse artists as Branford Marsalis, Dizzy Gillespie, George Duke, Willie Dixon, Dianne Reeves, a then mostly unknown Harry Connick Jr. (no singing—just playing brilliant up-tempo New Orleans style piano) and others. Many of them would be thrown into jam sessions with others they'd never met—the results were usually magic. In between, there would be these old jazz clips of all the greats—Parker, Powell, 'Trane, Monk and more. Today, it is so hard to believe this show, with its cultural depth, artistry, creativity, hipness and sophistication, was ever allowed on the bastion of mediocrity that is American network TV.

Even the commercials had style. The slogan "The Night Belongs to Michelob" inspired a series of great ads that included Phil Collins singing "Tonight, Tonight, Tonight" and a particularly cool one featuring Eric Clapton's "After Midnight." It showed Clapton leaving his concert with a guitar gig bag on his back, wandering the streets of New York and slipping into an after-hours gig, sharing some laughs and a Michelob with some New York musician friends, then plugging in and jamming. I always loved that ad, even though it was a bit sobering (pun not intended) to think that Eric Clapton was in the Betty Ford Center at the time, recuperating from alcoholism.

For me, Sunday night had become *Jazz Night*.

In a few years, Yoshi's would move into a larger space in Jack London Square on Oakland's waterfront, becoming the number one spot for jazz in the Bay. It's still a great place to catch a show, but it has never had the immediateness or intimacy of the original location. The Kanzaki Lounge would close down, permanently burying one of the Bay Area's already hidden treasures. *Michelob Presents Sunday Night* would be cancelled by TV network execs attempting to try their hand at higher ratings by airing a movie of the week instead.

I felt lucky to have stumbled upon these things when I did and to have had the good sense to embrace them and absorb as much as I could at the time. This experience taught me to never take anything for granted because it may not always be there.

31. ON THE ROAD AGAIN

It was in Minneapolis, at the rock venue First Avenue,[58] where we were introduced to our new co-headliners, Savatage. Like Raven, Savatage was a band I'd listened to while in high school. It felt strange to find yet another band I'd looked up to from afar sharing a bill with us in the clubs.

Savatage had suffered a serious setback in momentum due to unfortunate business circumstances. The band's powerful debut album, *Sirens,* had been so poorly distributed that fans had been forced to resort to second and third generation homemade cassette tapes in order to listen to it. While this was great for the band's street cred, it killed the album's sales. Meanwhile, the band got tied up in litigation in an attempt to free themselves from their label and management at the time.

Since then, they'd signed with Atlantic Records, which was our own distributor, making us like step-label mates. But while their distribution problem had been solved, Savatage had unfortunately been forced to cave in to pressure from Atlantic to make a shamelessly commercial album. Its cover

---

[58] First Avenue was used as primary location for Prince's 1984 movie *Purple Rain.*

photograph showed the long haired rockers re-creating the raising of the US flag on Iwo Jima in order to, to quote the album's title: *Fight for the Rock!* The reactions from fans and critics were painful.

More recently, the band appeared to be getting back on track. *Headbanger's Ball* had been playing their video for "Hall of the Mountain King." The song recaptured their original sound—a darker, more gothic version of the Scorpions mixed with Black Sabbath. The video was a tad Spinal Tap-ish, featuring a midget in a gargoyle suit (there was a hilarious story about having to turn the midget upside down and stick a straw up his nose in order to help him snort cocaine while in costume), but the band was regaining momentum. They'd been the opener on the previous year's tour with Megadeth and Dio. Now they were about to tour behind one of their most respected albums, *Gutter Ballet.*

Savatage probably would have been best off supporting a melodic hard rock group like Queensryche, whose hit album *Operation Mindcrime* had a rock opera concept more in alignment with theirs. But like us, Savatage hadn't found any opportunities to support any bigger, well-matched bands this time around. So as long as we both had to play the clubs and we were both Atlantic bands (us indirectly), it made sense to join forces.

While Savatage co-headlining with Testament presented risks for both bands, it would turn out to be the first mutually beneficial tour we'd done. Savatage would bring in a lot of new fans who'd get turned on to us, not knowing they could like thrash. Our own fans would realize they could like Savatage, despite the tempos not being 500 miles an hour and a few songs even featuring (heaven forbid): piano. In other words, neither band was piggy-backing off the other, each bringing a fair share of the draw.

That was not the case with all our tours. On a previous tour, a music biz lesson had been learned by our manager, Elliot. Hoping to gain points with Atlantic, he'd promised to take out one of their metal bands, Wrathchild America. It was a huge mistake—the band didn't go over well, and despite having a very good drummer,[59] they did not add to the draw and were very quickly forgotten by the metal public. In exchange for his generosity, Elliot was shamelessly ignored by this same A&R woman at the label for whom he'd done the favor. At one point she screamed at him to stop calling. This was further proof of what I'd long suspected—that Elliot, although a good man and fine lawyer, was not necessarily cut out to be the manager.

*

[59] Shannon Larkin, who'd go on to become the drummer for Ugly Kid Joe and later, Godsmack.

When I first heard them at sound check, I swore Savage must have a new guitar player. Not that the guy on the albums sounded bad, but this guy sounded amazing. It turned out it was the same guy, Chris Oliva. He'd grown by leaps and bounds.

Later, one of the techs would confide that Chris was shy around me—adding that there weren't many guitarists he openly respected (apparently I was one of the few). I was flattered and told his tech it was definitely mutual. Although Chris and I wouldn't get to know each other well, we'd gradually open up, passing a guitar back and forth backstage, him teasing me about "putting him out of a job." Kind of creepy when you think about the fact that in five years, he'd be dead and I'd be his replacement in Savage.

This group had added a second guitarist who seemed more insecure than anyone I'd ever met. Unlike the rest of us, whose insecurity was reflected in a general quietude, this guy's insecurity manifested itself with a highly pompous act reminiscent of Jerry Lewis' character Bud E. Love in *The Nutty Professor.* He'd talk incessantly, boasting about banging chicks, most of whom were repulsed by him (although to his credit, his persistence would occasionally pay off) and repeating the same things he'd said minutes earlier. Talking to him, you'd think the whole show revolved around him. I wasn't sure what he was even doing there, as he seemed unqualified to share the stage with the other guys. Then someone told me he'd only been brought along as a favor to the band's producer. The band had agreed, on the condition that this new kid not be allowed on stage. Which had been the case up until that point. Now they were finally letting him play and be seen. His name was Chris Caffery.

In the distant future, Chris and I would be thrown together as guitar partners for the Trans-Siberian Orchestra, created by Paul O'Neil with Savage founder John Oliva as co-writer. Although we'd eventually learn to work with one another, initially, I'd experience a lot of the same competitive guitar resentment I'd experienced with my brother and then Eric.

One night, the Savage crew, Testament crew and a few band members were all seated having dinner in the darkness of the club at some tables set up in the back of the room. It was about thirty minutes till doors. Chris decided that right then was the perfect moment to try out and show off his brand new Jackson Guitar. Oblivious to the fact that we were all enjoying our meals amidst a precious moment of quiet, he went on stage, turned on the amps and began blaring sloppy licks at full volume, recalling Michael J. Fox's failed attempt at conjuring Van Halen in the High School dance scene from *Back to the Future.*

What followed was a verbal riot—from his own camp as well as ours (although he couldn't see who it was, since it was too dark). Everyone was chucking loud insults at him, like a food fight of verbal slop, a simultaneous stew of venom, the screaming overpowering his amps: *"Turn that shit down!" "Who the fuck?!" "We're trying to eat!" "What the fuck is this shit?!" "Go home!" "What a fucking joke!" "Put down the goddam guitar! You suck!" "Give it up, buddy!"* His masturbatory wanking petered out like a failed erection.

The various crew and band members got right back to eating, as though nothing had happened; all was dark and quiet again. But if you listened closely, through the ringing of your ears, you could just barely hear him mumble something from the stage, spoken with a dejected whimper just before unplugging and walking away, his tail between his legs: *"I was just playin' with my new toy…"*

It was further evidence that you should always gauge the room you're in, be sensitive to your surroundings, never rudely play over someone else's conversation—verbal or musical—and never impose your own playing on an unwilling audience.

*

At first, Savatage and Testament existed in two totally separate worlds. We were unsure how to communicate with one another. Both bands had their own expressions, their own mannerisms, their own inside jokes. We were from radically different regions of the US, both referred to, ironically as the Bay Area: Tampa and San Francisco, respectively. On top of that, our music and theirs fell into completely different categories.

For about the first half of the tour, things were a bit distant and awkward between the two bands. But in the course of one evening, that would all change. A full scale bonding of the bands would occur, courtesy of a huge post-show bar room brawl that pitted the camps of both bands against some overly aggressive security guards, resulting in black eyes and bruises for some of our crew guys and broken windows for the club.

*

Occasionally visiting me on this tour was my new girlfriend, Lyla, a strikingly pretty African-American girl of mixed descent. She'd reminded me a bit of Lisa Bonet from TV's *The Cosby Show,* whom I'd had a bit of an infatuation with *(who didn't?)*. I'd met her at my gym, where I'd done something that required more courage than anything I've done, including playing in front of 60,000 people: asking for her phone number.

The fact that Lyla was just a stranger at the gym had made this feel like a ridiculously huge accomplishment. You have to understand, I'd felt useless without the crutch of being at my own show where the girls would talk to me first. My buddy Ben was at the gym with me at the time, in a state of shock that I'd pulled off such a coup. We'd had very little competition between us, but he suddenly seemed very jealous.

In a sense, living in the Bay Area had felt like living in Alaska. It's not that there weren't any women around, it's just that there weren't many who were smart, feminine, funny and attractive. The ones who fit that description usually got picked off quickly and, for the most part, the girls in the metal scene just couldn't measure up (at this time). The few desirable normal girls in the Bay were very closed off, limiting their interactions to their immediate circles. A good pick-up artist may have had hope but none of my friends had that skill. If you were shy, you had it especially rough. I'd been the shyest of us all, but at last, being on stage was starting to bring me out of my shell a bit, as evidenced by my picking up on Lyla. Shyness around women was something most of my Berkeley crew would never overcome, even into their 30s. Some guys I knew would go for years without female contact, a few resorting to the services of prostitutes. The Bay Area was a sad environment to be single.

Lyla was the first girl that I'd noticed, truly *wanted* to go up and talk to, and went for. All the others (except for my short-lived high school romance with Chandra) I'd dated strictly out of desperation. But being able to approach, talk to and, to my surprise, cultivate a relationship with Lyla represented a breakthrough with women for me.

The fact that Lyla was a black girl wasn't something I dwelled on, but I couldn't help feeling proud. Dating her felt like a statement, in this sense: she was the opposite of the stereotype of the girls we were expected to date: blonde, "Barbie Doll"-types. I loved the fact that dating her felt like a big *F.U.* to what was expected.

Although Lyla and I wouldn't be meant for each other long term, lasting about a year and a half, she was a very nice person and we were great for each other during the time.

*

During the *Practice* sessions, Lyla, a makeup artist and aspiring dancer, was called in to do makeup on a music video by a local rap star from Oakland. "Is it *Too short?*" I asked excitedly, having recently met the rapper in the hallway of Fantasy Studios. She told me it was this newer guy I hadn't heard of yet. His name was MC Hammer.

During the shoot, the director decided that an additional dancer was needed for one particular scene that featured several similarly dressed girls dancing in formation against a black and white background. They asked around the set, crew girls, extras, catering girls, if anyone was a dancer. Lyla, being the only one who could do hip-hop dance, was immediately chosen.

By the time Lyla came to visit me on the Testament/Savatage tour, the video she'd danced in had just come out. The song, which sampled the Rick James classic "Super Freak," would become one of the most popular rap videos of all time.

One day, we got stopped on the street by another couple about our own age. "Excuse me," they both said. I was so used to getting stopped for autographs at this point, I took out a marker from my jacket. This guy and girl just looked at me like I was crazy. Then they looked at Lyla with big smiles and said, *"You're one of the girls from that new Hammer video, right? Can we have your autograph?"*

*

Time quickly blended into one of those movie scenes, where a bus or plane is superimposed over a map, driving from city to city, flying from country to country. We toured the US, Europe, the US again, Europe again, as well as some places we'd never played before, including Brazil, Eastern Europe and most memorably, Japan.

Playing in Japan for the first time was like visiting another universe. It felt like we were The Beatles. There were dozens of fans lined up to meet us in the airport, predominantly female. They would turn up in the hotel lobbies, at the train stations and outside every show, clamoring for photos and autographs. Many were bearing gifts—bags of rice crackers, chocolates, candies, dried fish and other Japanese snacks. Some had drawings of us, immaculately done. Mixed in were numerous cards and letters.

It was quite a feeling to have so many people acknowledging us as worthwhile human beings, explaining how much we'd meant to their lives. This really helped give all the struggle and hard work a sense of purpose.

My bounty soon including a couple of very exclusive gifts that were quite unique: one was a little pillow-like doll of myself, holding a soft red guitar, modeled after my red Ibanez and threads of black yarn (and one strategically placed white one) for hair. The other was a giant oil painting, based on a photograph of me from a magazine but enhanced in magnificent luminous colors, like the artist Maxfield Parrish.

In both cases, I was so moved I didn't know what to say. Each girl would hand the gift to me and I'd ask if she was sure. Although neither girl spoke English, each seemed to understand the tone of my voice, insisting through gestures that I take the gift. I'd hug each girl and kiss her hand, just before getting rushed into a van with the other guys, a screaming mob of fans looking on.

I couldn't believe someone would put so much time and energy into capturing my image. I wished I could show these things to all those jerks who'd tormented me in Junior High.

Interestingly, the doll and painting would serve as a bridge of diplomacy to my parents, specifically my mother—the one-time artist who'd forever turned her back on music and art. Somehow she couldn't help admiring the skill and artistry that went into making the Japanese doll and painting, which seemed to awaken something within her. It was as though the artist she'd locked away in the closet was timidly peeking out of the keyhole.

Upon my arrival home, she'd asked if she could keep the doll in the living room and put up the painting nearby, I'd obligingly say yes. It somehow felt right that she should keep them.

My cards, letters and gifts from the Japanese fans began to pile up. Many of the letters were touching. These fans seemed to really notice the emotion expressed in my guitar solos, as though they related my pain to their own lives. This was incredibly interesting to me—here was this culture that was largely based on keeping expression and emotions in private. Yet they were actually hearing what I'd been trying to express through all the double kick drums, crunchy riffing and growling vocals.

Back home, I'd begun to feel a hollowness from the local scene—it seemed to be all about everything but the music—endless blathering, getting drunk, doing drugs and not really paying attention to the art. But the Japanese were renewing my faith in metal, giving it the honor and respect of listening with the same dedication one might bestow upon jazz or classical.

*

As mentioned earlier, the fans were mostly female. I'd be lying if I didn't say that a few of them weren't really pretty. Yet sleeping with any of them was out of the question. Having a fling wasn't worth the loss of what felt like a sacred bond between them and myself. It felt so good to have them respect me as a musician and as a person, it would have felt like a violation somehow.

I'd also seen the mistakes of a some others on the tour who'd rushed into flings with suggestively dressed girls, almost immediately upon arrival. In each case, after the fling, these girls would hang around in the lobbies waiting for them, following them on the streets, giving them more gifts in desperation and finally, breaking down crying in the lobby in plain view of all the other fans. Although these girls should have known what they were getting themselves into, it was very hard to see them brokenhearted like this. It further strengthened my resolve not to sleep with fans.

*

We'd been brought to Japan by the legendary promoter Mr. Udo. Udo was a bit like a Japanese version of Marlon Brando's Godfather character, Don Corleone. He wore Italian business suits and wire rim glasses. A gentle, yet imposing man, I would later read about him in a compelling narrative by Nikki Sixx from the Mötley Crüe book *The Dirt.*

Udo had several associates who went out of their way to show us extreme honor and respect but could be downright frightening. In one instance, a car full of fans was following us. Our driver screeched on the breaks, got out and barked something to the driver of the car following us. Their car immediately made a u-turn and sped away as if the passengers' lives were in danger. No one is sure exactly what the driver said. He wouldn't tell us. The entire exchange took no more than a few seconds; it seemed only one or two words were spoken.

At the concerts, the fans showed us so much respect it was unnerving—they sat quietly during the songs and clapped politely afterwards.

As it turned out, the most legendary band still in operation, The Rolling Stones, was visiting Japan at the same time. Being clients of Mr. Udo's, we were set up with center row tickets. It was thrilling to watch one of the most important bands of all time, whose music I'd grown up listening to. Sure, the show was a little kitsch, nothing like the band I'd seen in the *Gimme Shelter* movie. But all these years later, they weren't bad. It was the Stones' first time ever in Japan—thanks to a series of drug busts of a certain Mr. Richards, the band had always been denied entry by the Japanese government, until now.

Mick Jagger was determined to make it up to the crowd with an extra-long show in which he spoke to them in fluent Japanese. This audience, after being denied a tour for so long, deserved extra special treatment, which they got. How many performers, especially ones at the highest level, come to a foreign country and eloquently speak to the crowd in their native language? I was really impressed. I became determined to learn the language of each country, at least a little bit.

Upon finally setting foot in Japan, the realization that these fans heard what I was playing and really got it inspired me like never before. Japanese food was my favorite, and I'd already had strong associations with Japanese culture and high musical appreciation, thanks to my experiences back home at Yoshi's and the Kanzaki Lounge.

In Tokyo, Osaka and Nagoya, the band had some of its best shows ever. The technology was so cutting edge that we actually had clear sound. We could hear ourselves and the audiences could hear us clearly for once. Finally, there was a sense that maybe, just maybe, our place in the grand scheme of the music business was rising even if we were just, to quote the expression, "big in Japan."

*

When we got back to the United States, it was a serious dose of reality. There were no fans waiting at SFO airport or at the BART[60] stations. Japan and Brazil had been great, but now we were back home and we didn't have much to show for it. *Practice* was getting a lot of play on college radio and MTV's *Headbangers Ball* but it wasn't the breakthrough record we'd hoped it would be. Meanwhile, a band we'd hung out with in Houston during the making of the "Practice" music video, Pantera, was all over the place, jettisoning right past us in sales.

We were still a struggling band, with three records out in stores and some touring under our belts, but struggling nonetheless. I was feeling the frustration of just doing this kind of music and nothing else. Eric was even more frustrated with the attention I was receiving. Chuck was frustrated that we weren't further along, feeling our music needed to get darker. The other two guys were just confused, caught up in the whole circus.

However, there was one shred of good news on the horizon—Judas Priest had a new album coming out, and they were interested in taking some younger, heavier bands out on tour. Megadeth had been picked to support and we'd been offered the opening slot.

Perhaps a tour with Judas Priest was just what we needed? After all, this would be our long sought after, elusive arena tour. Priest wasn't exactly current; I'd been listening to them since that moment I first heard "Breakin' The Law" while standing outside Fosters Freeze in ninth grade. But hey, they were legends and represented a chance for us to finally make a go of it in the arenas.

There was just one downside: being the support act on an arena tour doesn't pay. You have to take a huge loss, think of it as advertising and chalk it up as the cost of doing business. Of course, we were ready to do it, even if it meant spending the rest of our reserves.

Unfortunately, we didn't have the reserves to spend. After being around the world three times in support of *Practice What You Preach,* the

---

[60] BART=Bay Area Rapid Transit, the commuter rail system that connects the East and South Bay to San Francisco.

well was dry. And when we turned to the record label for help, neither Megaforce nor Atlantic would cough up any more money.

*

There was one solution to our predicament: go into the studio and bang out an album fast. This would be the only way to get our record label to kick down tour support, for an entirely new album cycle.

It was still early in the year (1990). The Priest tour wasn't until the late Fall. We could do it, but realistically there was no way this band could match the level of our previous effort in that amount of time. Still, we did our best to come up with decent material as fast as we could.

I recalled an idea for a riff that had been done by a friend back at Berkeley High—he'd taken the opening to Metallica's "Seek and Destroy," changed a few notes around and played it with a 12/8 feel, like a blues shuffle rhythm. I remembered it sounding really cool, nothing like the original source and wondered if perhaps I could do the same type of thing with that now classic Metallica riff. The key of E made this new riff different from both "Seek and Destroy," and my friend's variation on it, both of which were in A. And while the first measure had those dissonant "Seek and Destroy" notes, it was answered with one of the modes I'd been studying, followed by an intervallic pattern I'd learned out of a book, *For Guitar Players Only* (by Tommy Tedesco). But used here, it didn't sound like an exercise, but a cool lick.

Once the riff was in place, I imagined an intro on bass. I'd recently traded Greg one of his Ibanez basses for one of my Ibanez guitars. Now I was putting the bass to work, coming up with a chordal pattern that set the pace for the guitar riffs to come. I knew showing the pattern to Greg would be painstaking (it was), and he'd actually have to practice it consistently. But he would and it would give him a nice, deserved little bass solo at the beginning of the tune.

Now, the challenge would be getting Eric to agree on it. Fortunately, he had a powerful riff he'd come up with that was a bit faster than mine, but I could simply adjust it to fit his. By this time, I'd learned a psychological trick for getting him to accept my parts—claim I'd written a part simply to go with his riff. And with Eric on board, we almost had a song.

Then, as would happen often, Chuck decided he didn't like it and wouldn't sing over it. We pleaded and pleaded, finally getting him to work with it, begrudgingly. It would be the strongest song on the new album and become the title track.

*

Sometime in 1990

Walking through the front lounge of the tour bus I overhear the following conversation:

"Everything's fucked," Chuck says through a cloud of marijuana smoke pluming from his mouth. "Fuckin' label won't give us any tour support. Shit, Elliot and Jeff ain't fightin' for us. Fuckin' bullshit!"

He passes the joint to Eric, Eric takes a hit and coughs. "Fuck it. Let's just put out a heavy record. Fuck Practice. *I'm fuckin' bored playin' that shit. Let's be more heavy. Dark."*

Through the green narcotic haze, a television news anchor describes that the mayor of Washington DC has just been caught on a surveillance video smoking crack with two hookers. Meanwhile, the oil company Exxon has been indicted in court on five criminal counts, a result of the Valdez oil spill.

Chuck takes back the joint. "See? Shit's all fucked up. Fuckin' political lies, corporate decisions."

"That sounds like lyrics," says Eric who takes a hit.

Lou turns to watch the screen, not realizing that Eric is trying to pass the joint to him. Eric pushes him hard in the shoulder. "What, Eric?!" He grabs the joint and turns back to the TV before taking a hit. "It's fucked up, yeah. Everything's dark."

He passes the joint back to Chuck who says. "Yeah, we'll teach 'em a lesson. Make the album fuckin' dark."

Eric: "Yeah, dark like dark souls or something. Or black, let's make it black. Black souls—souls of black, fuck them, we'll be heavy, dark, black! Souls of Black!" He makes a giggling noise like the creature from Gremlins.

Chuck: "Yeah... Souls of Black."

32. THE BEGINNING OF THE END

The *Souls of Black* recording should have been a great situation: Fantasy Studios (one of the most respected recording studios in the country), a budget of $100,000 (enormous by today's standards), and a new producer (Michael Rosen). It was a tremendous opportunity to do an album that stood out among the herd. Unfortunately, the atmosphere was unpleasant. The pressure of having to crank out an album in so little time was affecting everyone and carrying over into the music.

Whenever anyone had an idea, there would be shrugs, tsk sounds or silence. If an idea was accepted, it was begrudgingly. Lou would sometimes agree with me, then get dirty looks from Eric, who seemed to expect Lou to side with him no matter what. Lou would then whisper to me, "*I really like your idea, Al. But you know how it is.*" (Remember, Lou had left in 1985, Eric had lobbied to bring him back a year or so later—Eric never let him forget). I kept pushing for additional melodies, arrangements and key changes, which weren't going over well. But to be fair, the guys were no more positive and supportive of each other's ideas as they were to mine. And I imagine that with my frustration, I was no picnic to deal with either.

The stress that we were all under was crippling the recording process, creative energy and morale. But this album had to happen so we could tour with Judas Priest. We would finally get a chance to play in concert arenas, like the Cow Palace, where I'd first seen Kiss. If only for that reason, we had to survive.

Desperate, I took some consolation in the fact that I wasn't the only one who felt that this band was becoming its own worst enemy. During the sessions, I'd look over at our new producer, Michael Rosen. A year ago, he'd been one of the calmest, most positive people I'd ever met in the music industry. Now he had circles under his eyes, frazzled hair, disheveled clothes and was frequently found with his head in his hands.

*

There are too many stressful memories of the *Souls* sessions to write about. But one stands out more than others. That of the song "The Legacy."

"The Legacy" had been one of the band's earliest songs, from back when it was called "Legacy," and until recently, the only ballad—an island of calm in a sea of brutality. Although it shared a title with our debut album, until now it had never been recorded or performed live, partly because an exact arrangement was never settled on (it needed at least two additional verses) and partly because of Chuck's apprehension to do slow songs. Even now, he was only agreeing to record it since, under pressure to put this album out, we were forced to mine the trenches for songs.

I once again received desperate calls from Eric, Lou, Elliot and Jeff in a rare stance of unity pleading with me to write more lyrics. I replaced the original lyrics from "The Legacy," something about a castle on a hill, to describing the tribulations of former child stars, whose stories were making big headlines in the early '90s. Although largely tabloid based, these stories fascinated me; I'd grown up looking to these young actors as people who had everything—now they were reduced to jail, rehab and bankruptcy.

The chorus of the song had been written by the guy I replaced, Eric's cousin Derek Ramirez—a walking cartoon character with a high nasally voice. Derek was so far out, he made Eric look like a poster boy for a model citizen. An overgrown kindergartener, he spouted giggly, perverted inappropriate comments, usually about male and female genitalia, at inopportune times. During this period, he'd accompany Eric to the *Souls* sessions where, among his topics of conversation, was his obsession with Nazis, *"The Nazis were cool—they were eeeeevil!! Hee hee!"* Michael Rosen and I just laughed, despite our Jewish backgrounds. Derek was a certifiable idiot, and if he knew better he'd be aware that being of Mexican descent, the real Nazis would have strung him up by his balls.

In the '90s, Derek would briefly return to Testament on bass, in an act of desperation on the part of the band. Having years of regret for leaving in the first place, he'd make up for lost time by snorting and screwing everything he could. Many years later, I'd run into him on the street. Noticing the smartphone device in my hand, unable to differentiate between Blackberry and BlueTooth technology, he would say, *"Hey, is that a blueberry?"*

Yet, despite his cartoonish demeanor, offensive humor, child-like immaturity and the fact that many of his musical ideas had been incomprehensible fits of noise, I still had to hand it to Derek. He was the one who'd originated and come up with the chorus melody for "The Legacy," which I still consider to be one of the strongest melodies and most accessible choruses of any Testament songs

*

"I'm doing a lead in 'The Legacy'!" Eric announced. As indicated earlier, his lead work at this time would have sounded fine in a group like Venom, Motörhead, even Slayer. He'd done a couple leads and they were okay. Now however, he was eying a section in "The Legacy" that seemed

simple, but was deceptively difficult: it had a subtle key change and was very exposed.

I was not about to make an unhealthy, dysfunctional hostile environment even worse by telling Eric he couldn't take that solo and taking on what was shaping up to be, to quote a certain Middle Eastern dictator who would soon rise to prominence, *the mother of all battles*. I tried to help him by explaining what notes worked and what didn't. He insisted he could play anything I could and was determined to prove it. I suggested he not try to play so many notes. But when he finally did try slowing down, the pitch and the timing were off.

Aside from Michael Rosen, who had to man the controls, Eric wanted no one else in the control room while he recorded his solo. After hours waiting around in the lounge, we were all called in to gather around and listen. I told Eric he'd done a good job, which was true, he'd worked hard on it for the last few days. *"That's good, Eric,"* Lou said to him. *"Yeah."* Greg nodded in reluctant agreement. But if I had to be totally honest—I didn't really like what I heard. It might have worked really well over a heavier riff, but frankly didn't fit this clean, exposed section.

It was Chuck who said flat out what everyone else was afraid to say—that the solo shouldn't go on the album. Michael agreed, pointed out that it was very late, they'd been working a long time, there was much more to do, and the album was on the verge of being late and over budget. Eric said he'd keep trying. Michael diplomatically suggested we all go home sleep on it; after all, everyone's tired, we can figure out what to do tomorrow. Greg, totally oblivious to the situation, smiled a toothy smile and made a suggestion, "I know! Why not just have Alex play the lead? He'll make it sound killer!" He quickly received a piercing death stare from Eric, who pointed out that it wasn't possible anyway, since my gear was already broken down. But what he didn't know was that Michael and Chuck had recorded a couple of extra solos of mine, just in case.

It was hard to sleep that night. I knew my solo would be played for everyone, and if it was chosen over Eric's, he'd be unforgiving. The whole thing really shouldn't have been an issue but sadly, it was a crisis.

When we all gathered around the mixing console the next day, we listened to his solo and everyone just looked down uncomfortably. Then the track was played with my solo; there were discreet smiles and heads nodding. Michael announced that his recommendation was that we print the song with my solo, and just wanted to make sure a majority of us agreed.

An awkward, tension filled vote was taken (I abstained) and it was decided. Eric huffed out of the room and wouldn't speak to any of us for several days.

As I look back, there's no doubt in my mind that the Eric of today, with years of experience doing solos in his own black metal band, Dragonlord, would have no problem nailing that part. He's become a far more capable player—no longer struggling to emulate me or other high profile advanced soloists, instead focusing on ideas that work within the straightforward style and musical personality he has developed over time.

I longed for a situation where things like this didn't happen, where I could just do what I do, have it be appreciated and not have anyone feel like their toes are being stepped on. There'd been plenty of drama surrounding this album, mostly involving other band members—I was usually able to stay out of it—but the guitar situation was unavoidable. On the one hand, I understood where Eric was coming from and felt bad. But from my vantage point, it felt like I'd done something wrong simply for becoming the best I could be.

*

As the *Souls of Black* sessions came to a close, I wiped the sweat off my brow, uttering a silent "Thank you" to God, the Universe, Mother Nature or whoever else was in charge—grateful that the whole ordeal was over. I dreamed of one day working in a mutually respectful environment with similar standards of musicianship and a generally positive atmosphere.

I wasn't sure how to feel about the album. There were some good moments, particularly the title track, but overall, it felt as though we'd taken a step backwards. I knew the sales would follow.

I realized that we'd really had something with *Practice*, an album whose title track Wikipedia now describes as a "hit with substantial MTV airplay" and lyrics that were more about "politics and society than occult themes." This should have been a very good thing—music that was heavy enough for the thrashers, but more mature and lyrically relevant. *Practice* had also brought in a whole legion of guitar-oriented fans that had been previously avoiding thrash. This had helped the band's reputation, album sales and ticket sales. Yet the band seemed ignorant of this.

In the near future, there would be a sense of bewilderment as other bands—Pantera, Sepultara, Machine Head and others—would catch on with larger audiences and surpass us in sales. It would be blamed on external factors—management, press, etc. But the truth was that we failed to recognize the stronger qualities in the music of others, as well as our own. Many of our best riffs were brushed aside, thrown away or relegated to mere bit parts or transitions in favor of riffs that seemed louder and faster, but in reality weren't as interesting to listeners.

I had imagined us being the first thrash band to have production and songwriting that competed with the big league pop and rock acts. What I didn't know was that for more than a year, Metallica, having already achieved greatness, had been holed away working on an album that would not only enable them to catch up to the Van Halens, Scorpions and Iron Maidens of the world, but align them with the Madonnas, Springsteens and U2s. Though I would never have suggested being as mainstream as Metallica's *Black Album* (which would sell in the tens of millions), I felt that with *Practice*, we'd found a healthy balance between thrash credibility and just the slightest hint of accessibility and in the process, something we'd hit on for the first time—originality.

Somewhere along the way, the others became convinced that the only answer was to go backwards—less mature and less musically interesting. Not helping were the occasional underground mags that would eclipse the truth in the minds of Chuck and Eric. For every cheap "fanzine" that dissed *The Practice* album, there had been dozens of positive reviews in widely read, highly respected, internationally distributed magazines and newspapers. These were the sources everyone should have been paying attention to.

I did agree with the guys on a couple of things, however: the label had screwed us by cutting off our tour support. And our managers had stood by helpless.

*

It started to dawn on me that as much as I liked Elliot and Jeff, knew they meant well and were unquestionably good people, I couldn't help but feel they were out of their league. Legally they'd had their hands tied behind their backs—the label was under no obligation to continue supporting *Practice*, that much is true. But as time went on, I became convinced that changing this situation would have been possible. It wouldn't have been easy necessarily and not every manager could have done it. It would have required diplomatic skill, maneuvering and creativity.

It comes down to the difference between a good entertainment attorney and a good manager. A good manager must have the personal skills to avoid situations like this. Personal skills are not written down in clauses, paragraphs, line items and amendments.

Our attorneys, through no fault of their own, lacked the creativity and initiative necessary to navigate the murky waters of the music business in a manner that was conducive to artist management on the level we needed (and as a band we weren't exactly helping with certain decisions). Their next clients, a young punk band called Green Day, would reach this exact same conclusion, deciding not to renew their contract as things really took off. Regardless, it would have been more than justified to try diplomacy, negotiation, begging, fighting, some combination of the above, or anything to prevent us being forced back into the studio at that time.

Not only weren't we ready to go into the studio, we'd barely started our then current album cycle. Most bands seemed to get a year or two to tour a record in the hopes that it might break (reach the next level of sales). Had we toured behind *Practice* for the Judas Priest arena crowds, there's no telling where it could have gone. *Practice* had only come out in August 1989, it was now Spring 1990, barely half a year, and we were forced to crank out a whole new record? It went against all logic.

So as frustrated as I was with my band mates, a part of me could understand why they weren't happy.

*

Alas, there were a couple of bright sides.

For one thing, the title track of the album, which I'd commenced with that little bass riff on a four-track, would be one of the band's strongest songs. And I had some other things to feel proud of. For one thing, I'd started to find myself in terms of guitar tone. Even more than twenty years later, I'd still be asked, *"How did you get that tone on* Souls of Black?"

It was something I hadn't seen a lot of other people do—using a separate pre-amp unit with an amp head (as opposed to a power amp). This was risky, as you risked overpowering the tubes. I had read stories of Van Halen using a variac (voltage regulator), which would fry his amp tubes in the process, but create the best tone imaginable. In this sense, Eddie was like the great Les Paul—an inventor as well as a great musician, truly a rare breed. Unlike Eddie and Les, I'd never been technically or mechanically minded. To borrow an old cliché: I couldn't solder my way out of a paper bag. I was a complete jackass when it came to the inner workings of amps, guitars, pick-ups, circuit boards and wires. But I did have one thing on my side: I was creative.

It dawned on me that using a blend of a distortion unit and an amp might give me some of the same smooth, thick overdrive without frying the amp. It was just a matter of finding the right balance between the overdrive of both components.

I'd also incorporated a bit of advice from our soundman at the time, David Pigg. David, a memorable character who'd come aboard around the same time as Mark Workman, had the distinction of being the loudest front-of-house engineer many had ever heard. He mixed us so loud in fact, that every show prompted numerous complaints from audience members (including Metallica's own James Hetfield, who had to walk out). PA systems were blown up and lawsuits were threatened against the band. It's amazing we hung onto him as long as we did. But David did impart some valuable advice in regards to my tone: keep the midrange no more than halfway up and emphasize the presence. Somehow, it seemed to work, and I still use that as a guideline when dialing in amps to this day.

Since that time, music equipment manufacturers have designed amp heads with a lot more gain, rendering set-ups like the one I used for *Souls* unnecessary. No doubt the success of Metallica, and other multi-platinum acts with metal tone has had a lot to do with this. But even back in 1990, most of the high gain amps seemed to produce a sound better suited for '70s' bands like Foreigner. But thanks to experience and experimentation, I was able to achieve a lead guitar sound on *Souls* that I could call my own and which would seem to resonate with listeners.

Souls was also the album where I developed my technique for recording solos. On the previous albums, I'd tried to do as few takes as possible and as few fixes as possible. I felt guilty anytime I had to fix or edit a section. It felt like cheating. But what I hadn't realized was that everyone else was cheating too. The hottest players of the late '80s and early '90s, Satch, Vai, Eric Johnson, were clearly fixing and editing their solos in the studio. In some cases, they were composing them first, then piecing them together note for note. As technically good as these guys were, it felt like something was missing—the spontaneity and off-the-cuff quality of Jeff Beck, Hendrix, Clapton, or Page.

I'd gotten really lucky with the "Practice What You Preach" solo, but there were many other solos I'd had to live with on the album that I wished I'd fixed. I knew that I couldn't depend on always getting it right the first time.

Adding to the dilemma was the fact that the sound quality on albums had gotten so much cleaner, it was pretty unavoidable to fix and edit. Just two years earlier, only the biggest groups, Def Leppard, Madonna and Phil Collins, for example, were releasing CDs that had the DDD symbol, which meant that the entire process was digital (recording, mixing, mastering). Now the digital revolution had trickled down to the rest of the industry. We were living in a digital world.

Though I'm not a believer in astrology, like my sign Libra, denoted by a scale, I have coincidentally always had an increased awareness of the concept of *balance*. For tone, I needed a balance of processed and raw sound. For solos, I needed a balance of live feel and polish.

I would start by playing the solos spontaneously, off the cuff.

Occasionally I would get lucky and end up with one I liked right off the bat, with maybe just a few fixes and punch-ins.[61] But more often than not, I would have to develop the idea, never playing it exactly the same way twice, keeping that sense of edge and unpredictability. And occasionally I'd use a technique that years later, would come in very handy as I learned to improvise over jazz changes—compose the solo, then add variations, never playing it the same way twice.

For *Souls of Black* and everything that followed, most of the solos were done this way, a combination of spontaneity but polished enough to compete with everyone else out there. If I had to edit or fix a solo too much, I'd abandon it, even if I really liked the licks. I needed these solos to maintain the quality of being first takes, even if they weren't, otherwise, I couldn't live with them.

*

All in all, recording *Souls of Black* had helped me get in touch with my sound and documentation of my own solos, making it a valuable experience. These personal advances were the glowing headlights shining through the thick fog of challenges surrounding the album.

And when all was said and done, we had done what we'd set out to do: we would have a new album (albeit a flawed one), just in time for the Judas Priest tour.

---

[61]Punching in and out = overdubbing in the middle of a section, replacing any existing content.

Living Colour's
Vernon Reid
"What I question are guitarists who use technique to make themselves invincible—an 'I'm gonna blow you away with my chops' attitude. The real battles are within yourself, not in impressing others." Guitar World, November 1988.

Sonic Youth's
Thurston Moore
"We like to have things be amusing and at the same time kind of terrifying." —Option, 1986

Testament's
Alex Skolnick
"I consider what we do to be an art form. Whether it will have lasting significance, I don't know. It's challenging, new and different, which always scares people."—Guitar World, October 1989.

Winger's
Reb Beach
"We were opening for Bad Company. It was a great show, except four songs into the set we had to stop because the kids broke down the barricades and jumped on stage. All the chicks ran to Kip... and all the dudes ran to me."—Guitar World, June 1989.

33. YOU'VE GOT ANOTHER THING COMIN'

Meanwhile, another offer had come in for a tour of Europe—this one involved Megadeth, who, slated to be the middle act on the Judas Priest tour, had made sure it ended just in time for them to fly to Canada and join Priest. Their co-headliner in Europe was Slayer. They had room for two support acts—the middle slot went to us and the opening slot to a Venice, California, band that was considered more punk than metal: Suicidal Tendencies. This line up—Slayer, Megadeth, Testament, Suicidal Tendencies—would hit the road the following September, in a tour billed as the "Clash of the Titans."

I don't recall a tour before or since with less comradery between the bands—fraternizing and visits to different dressing rooms were infrequent. One journalist who'd interviewed everyone described the experience as a *"Clash of the Egos."* It wasn't that the bands specifically disliked each other, it's just that they were mostly composed of uncommunicative people.

The all band tour photo, always an awkward and uncomfortable experience, was even more tense with this tough crowd—no one dared crack a joke to break the ice, except our own Chuck Billy, who, having already had several bong hits that day, called out to the visiting photojournalists and gave them an interesting sound bite: *"Welcome to the Clash of the Penises."*

I never saw much of Suicidal Tendencies, who kept to themselves, an exception being the guitarist, Rocky George, the sole African-American on this tour (which was like a white guy performing on a gansta-rap tour). Despite being a lifelong resident of Los Angeles, Rocky wore an ever-present Pittsburgh Pirates cap, which caused him to remind me of one of the "Baseball Furies," those bat wielding hoodlums from the apocalyptic gang movie *The Warriors.*

That's how Rocky looked the day he approached me while I was practicing outside the venue by the trucks, sitting on a road case, an unplugged guitar in my hands and a stack of music books by my side. At first it felt like I was about to be shaken down for my lunch money.

Instead, Rocky was interested to know what I was practicing and which music books I was using. He said he'd been trying to expand as a guitarist but was in a bit of a rut. I showed him a few chords and patterns on the guitar. Then, he wrote down some of the book titles, *Chord Chemistry* by Ted Green, *Thesaurus of Scales and Melodic Patterns* by Nicolas Slonimsky and *The Advancing Guitarist* by Mick Goodrick (who'd been one of Pat Metheny's teachers).

Soon, Rocky and I were meeting regularly between our sound checks to jam and exchange ideas. Our hanging out would get a few funny looks, as though we were violating some unwritten code with our interacting, working on music and having a good time. Rocky turned out to have a self-deprecating sense of humor and genuine interest expanding his musical vocabulary. And to think I'd always thought of this band as a bunch of thugs from Venice.

It turned out Rocky wasn't the only dedicated musician in Suicidal Tendencies—their bassist, Robert Trujillo, was excellent. He would be announced as the new bassist in Metallica about a dozen years later.

*

Meanwhile, we hardly ever saw much of Megadeth, especially their distinguished leader. I imagined Dave was like Batman—hanging upside down in his hotel room until he got a call that it was time for the show, then rushing over to get the job done. The rest of his band followed close behind, lurking in the shadows. They never seemed to have time for more than a quick hello, but they were polite, especially Dave Ellefson and Marty Friedman, whom I'd get to know better in the '00s after this was all over. I accepted Mustaine as a peculiar character, difficult at times but who got things done—you had to respect him as a songwriter and artist even if he rubbed some the wrong way.

The only person in Megadeth I flat out didn't like was drummer Nick Menza. You'd think starting out as their drum tech, he'd maintain the humility of such humble origins like Anthrax drum tech John Tempesta, who'd never lost his coolness, despite moving on to distinguished gigs— becoming the drummer for White Zombie, Rob Zombie and The Cult. I don't remember one interaction with Nick Menza, other than a music store signing that all of us Ibanez guitars/Tama drums endorsees attended—he signed his name so big, you'd think he was Elvis and we were his backup band.

*

Other memories from the Clash tour:

Getting picked up by a cab driver in Edinburgh, Scotland, and for the first time, being unable to understand a word from someone who was speaking English. Chuck, after very many drinks in a hotel bar in Spain, smashing a mirror in a hotel elevator and Tom Araya from Slayer (who'd worked in a hospital), overseeing the stitching job of a half mad doctor.

Then there was the time I was in a hotel bar in Scandinavia and jammed with a jazz piano player in the lobby. I recognized some of the songs he was playing—"Autumn Leaves," "All The Things You Are," and "How High The Moon." During the break I went up and told him I loved jazz and was working on some of these same songs he was playing. He asked me to grab my guitar and a cable so I could plug directly into the speaker system and play with him. To describe my jazz guitar playing at that time as formative would be too kind, but I knew some melodies and basic jazz licks, so I went for it.

It was going well enough until Jeff and Tom from Slayer, along with Rocky, came in from a bar down the street, snickering, pushing and stumbling over each other. They came over and stood around me, howling crude lyrics to the music and detuning my guitar pegs. At first it was kind of funny, but it got old quick. I didn't take it personally—I knew they were in "drunk idiot" mode and laughed it off as best I could. But right then I decided that perhaps it was a good idea to pack up the guitar, thank the piano player whose expression of discomfort was now veering on borderline terror, apologize for the forwardness of my inebriated friends and call it a night.

*

We had exactly three days in between the last day of the European Clash of the Titans tour and the first day of the North American Judas Priest/Megadeth/Testament tour. There was barely enough time for us and Megadeth to catch our respective flights from London, get checked into hotels in Montreal, have a day off to try and catch up on sleep, followed by a day of set up/pre-production before moving into our rolling homes for the next two and a half months. I had to hand it to our crew for getting us transitioned from one tour to the other in such a short time.

By now, we had more or less our classic road crew. The hardcore guys—the ones who would have long, if occasionally troubled, careers on the road—included Mark Workman (Sergeant Slaughter) on lights and tour management, Rick Diesing on Monitors (both of whom would come back to work for the band in the '00s), Lorenzo Banda, systems tech (who would later do sound and monitors for Dio, among others) and David Pigg—the FOH engineer mentioned earlier. The rest were what is known as backline crew—the ones who deal with the guitars, bass and drums. For some reason, the group of guys we had here would all end up leaving the road soon after.

I was finding that crew members were a different breed. Where we'd get breaks from touring, some of these guys seemed to never leave the road. Many had interesting stories. One of my favorite techs, let's call him Quint, was educated and mild mannered. He'd had an unusual path to touring life: he'd been a student in a seminary, destined for piousness as a full-fledged Catholic priest. Then one day, he'd met a girl who would show him the pleasures of male/female relations, particularly oral pleasures, thus ending all ambitions for a life in the priesthood.

Then there was a certain crew-member who shall remain nameless. He'd have romances worthy of the Sade song "Smooth Operator" and one day get busted by his long-term girlfriend who would have his beloved wiener dog—the self-professed symbolic avatar of his own manhood—

neutered in retaliation[62]. In Brazil, he'd hit on a woman in line at the airport and join the Mile High Club under a blanket in plain view of all of us. Years later, he'd experience a true life *Midnight Express* story: while touring with another band he'd be caught with a massive amount of prescription drugs in a Middle Eastern airport, thrown into a prison for two years before being pardoned, narrowly escaping a life sentence.

*

Watching Judas Priest that first night in Montreal, I felt like I was witnessing a sleek well-oiled machine as represented by Rob Halford's chrome Harley Davidson that he'd ride out on the stage each night for "Hell Bent for Leather." It was surreal—as though one moment, I was back at the Foster Freeze on University Avenue across from West Campus in Berkeley, listening to a worn out cassette tape of *British Steel* blaring through someone's ghetto blaster, surrounded by a half dozen of fellow ninth graders. Somehow I'd channeled that moment into a career—here I was in an exclusive area just below the side of the stage hearing this music played every night by the musicians themselves.

Halford's voice was one of the best I'd ever heard, period. KK Downing and Glen Tipton on guitars had a razor precision, polished yet still biting. The rhythm section, Ian Hill and new drummer Scott Travis held it down like their lives depended on it.

In the world of rock 'n' roll, receiving an education like this was the coveted result of hard work, talent, luck and timing, unlike the rest of the world, where education was dependent on such factors as grade point averages, SAT scores and ability to pay tuition. Now we had our tenured professors wearing chrome-studded denim vests, leather pants, shiny guitars and riding motorcycles. Certain that Priest's commitment to professionalism—from their use of strong choruses, interaction and audience participation—would rub off on my own band, I felt a brief glimmer of hope.

*

I'd be lying if I didn't say that doing the Judas Priest/Megadeth/Testament tour in 1990 was a reality check.

As great as it was to be touring with the mighty Priest, the fact was this: we were third on the bill, which meant going on early, when most people were still filing in. Many who were there were fans of Priest and/or Megadeth, who didn't get what we were doing and stood with their arms crossed. Eric, by insisting on doing as many 300 mph songs as possible and

---

[62] Thankfully, the dog was neutered under anesthesia by a veterinarian. The symbolic castration was particularly harsh to the crew guy's psyche.

barking at Lou to speed up on every song, was not helping win them over, ignorant to the fact that in a concert arena, an onslaught of speed for a whole set doesn't translate well out front. Our whole set was only thirty minutes long; afterwards there was nowhere to go and not much to do except watch Megadeth and Priest which, truth be told, didn't hold the same magic after a whole month than it did that first day.

After every third or fourth show, Priest would take a day off. It seems we almost never had a day off. During one stretch, we played every night for three weeks straight. We'd fill in by doing a club show on our own or with Megadeth, who always seemed to do much better with the crowds (I understood why—Dave employed several of the same techniques as Priest as far as pacing, timing, key changes, etc.).

It was hard work. Here we were doing the long sought-after arena tour, yet I couldn't help but feel something was amiss: the whole rock star dream—driving nice cars, owning homes, and attaining financial security.

After five years, we could barely afford cheap used cars. I was lucky to pay rent on a small apartment in Oakland and with recording budgets, tour support and merchandise advances to recoup, the prospect of us gaining any kind of financial foothold was grim. And it's not like we were just starting out, with our whole life as a band ahead of us. We were on our fourth album! I'd once dreamed we'd do what Metallica had done—multiplying our audience with each new album. But it wasn't happening.

Still, I tried not to concentrate on this and just enjoy the fact that at least we were farther along than we'd been. We were also far ahead of the local bands that just a few years ago, we'd been sharing the same club bills with. I was just a few years out of high school and whatever the situation, this was an education few were able to have.

We crisscrossed through Canada—Montreal, Quebec City, Toronto, Winnipeg, Regina, Saskatoon, Calgary, Edmonton, Vancouver. For the most part, the arenas would be full by the time Priest came on—yet that all changed when we got to the US, where we cruised down the West Coast, across the Southwest, through Texas and the South, up the East Coast and Midwest. Some of the shows went really well, and almost felt like real arena shows. But at other shows, the arena was only half-full, even for Priest!

It was a painful realization. It would be one thing if we were touring with Judas Priest in '82, hot on the trail of their album *Screaming for Vengeance*, sold-out arenas from coast to coast and a genuine smash hit on the radio: "You've Got Another Thing Comin'."

But things were different now. As much as I loved Priest and they were sounding as great as ever, one thing was painfully obvious: in terms of popularity in the US market, the band was now past its prime.

*

The Priest tour has its share of memories that stand out....

We've long heard rumors of Rob Halford being gay and any doubts we have are quickly dispelled with one glance of the company he keeps. At some shows, he has an all-male entourage that look like the Village People, some of them wear tight leather, furry animal patterns—leopard skin, zebra stripes, etc. At other shows, he has this little blonde muscleman with him, wearing the tightest shorts I've ever seen and ballerina slippers and assumed to be his boyfriend.

A few years later, Rob will finally publicly "come out" as gay. By doing so, he will reveal to the world that Judas Priest's whole leather and studs look has come from his visits to gay fetish shops in London, the rest of the band (not gay) adopting this new look in the early '80s.

There is a terrific irony here: metal fans are not exactly known for their tolerance, yet here is one of metal's biggest heroes revealing that there had been gayness right under their noses. Metal will be forced to reconsider its homophobia, especially when Rob rejoins Priest in about ten years.

Somewhere in Canada, Dave Mustaine sends his TM (tour manager) over to demand that we stop using the smoke machine, arguing that Testament, being openers, should have minimal lights and production. Not wanting to provoke the situation, we play a "smoke free" show. Afterwards, Mark Workman, our TM, goes to the Judas Priest production office, apologizes for the intrusion and explains what happened. The TM from Judas Priest, normally a dry British fellow, expresses wide-eyed interest, assuring Mark not to worry and thanks him for the information. The next day, Priest's TM visits Megadeth's dressing room, tells Dave and his TM that if there is ever a problem or concern in the future, to please go directly to him, not the opening band or their crew; in the meantime, Testament will be using the smoke machine and if Megadeth doesn't like it, they are more than welcome to leave the tour. After our set that night, Judas Priest's guitarist, Glen Tipton, whom none of us have met yet and are still star-struck by, will walk by our dressing room en route to the stage, poke his head in the door, give the thumbs-up sign and ask: *"Did ya get yer smoke, boys?"*

In the Bay Area, we play at the Oakland Coliseum, where I've seen many shows and have often dreamed of playing. A shoe flies on stage hitting my guitar as I'm playing the intro to "Trial By Fire," causing me to flub my delicate arpeggio. I refuse to let it get to me, so I just ignore it and play on. Also at the Oakland show, my father, in a story he'll tell often in the future, reports going to the men's room and being overwhelmed with the amount of beer-drinking, black-clad, drunk, barely coherent metalheads in there, several of whom are face down in the toilets vomiting. One of them turns around, notices my dad with his bald-head, grey sideburns and glasses, then says *"Man...you must be the world's oldest headbanger!"*

In LA, there is a party backstage and among those attending are Kerry King of Slayer, Kirk Hammett of Metallica, the new sensation and new soon-to-be-forgotten Bullet Boys and the biggest celebrities I've seen at one of our shows thus far, including Mötley Crüe drummer Tommy Lee and his wife, actress Heather Locklear.

In Texas, our common sense-challenged drum tech, Ben Linton, notices a bathtub in one of the Judas Priest dressing rooms. He decides to take a bath, ignorant of the fact that he is taking a bath in Priest's production office. The steam carries over, causing fax papers to wilt. As the Judas Priest TM returns to his office, he finds his paperwork nearly ruined and his fax machine in danger of death by moisture, then finds our tour manager Mark and tears him apart like a drill sergeant. All Mark can do is apologize profusely.

When Mark sees Ben, the shouts can be heard across the arena.

Ben Linton, whose very name inspired parody, had almost gotten us thrown off the tour on the very first day. After our set, the other backline guys had our gear off the stage instantly, clearing the way for the mighty Priest, whose throne of gear dauntingly stood behind us. All that remained was our little drum riser and Ben struggling with a hammer, pulling out nails. Priest's stage manager, Bobby Schneider, rushed over to Ben and looked at his watch, screaming, "What the fuck is going on here? Get that riser off the stage!" Ben looked up hopelessly and told him it was stuck. "What the fuck! How the hell can it be stuck?" Ben answered that it was nailed to the floor. Bobby turned into one of those other cartoon characters that gets so mad you can fry an egg on his head, screaming like Rob Halford mid-verse: *"You nailed your fucking drum riser to my fucking stage?! Are you a fucking idiot?!"* The rest of our crew and a few of the Priest crew guys came to the rescue, grabbing hammers to pry the rest of the nails out of the stage.

We were lucky the Priest crew was so forgiving that night, simply laying down the law that this cannot happen again and billing us for a new section of marley (flooring used for dance, theater and stage). The show almost went on late; if it had, we would have been dropped from the tour for sure. Fortunately, a few weeks had gone by before Linton's idiotic bathtub incident.

The fact that people like Ben Linton continue to work for the band underscores the lack of standards this band has, carrying over into all of our affairs, assuring us a place as a second-or third-rate band. As the tour goes on, Mark Workman decides to make Ben's life miserable with the *Hire The Handicapped* routine (see chapter 26): *"Hire the handicapped! Ben fucking Linton! That's right, Testament takes pity on the specially challenged and less fortunate—hire the handicapped!"*

There are many other comedy routines at Linton's expense.

Finally, the constant taunts get to be too much. At a one-off club gig between Priest shows, Ben can't take it anymore. Like a petulant child, he throws down the drum-sticks and screams: *"Dammit, I don't have to take this shit anymore! I deserve respect! Back home, I was the drummer for two great bands: Doctor Mastermind and Evil Genius!"*

He will be quoted for many tours to come.

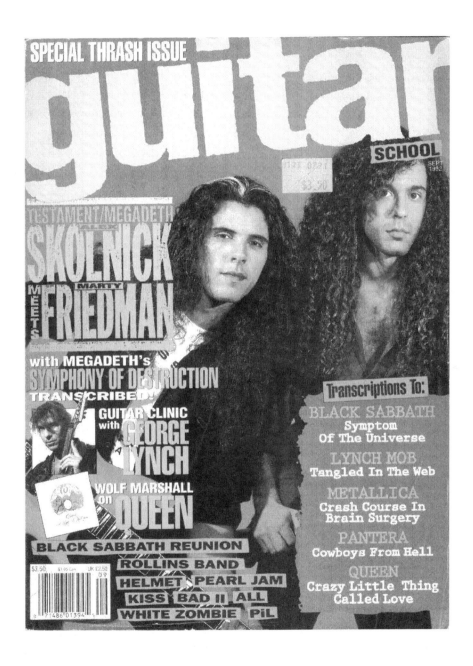

SPECIAL THRASH ISSUE

guitar

SCHOOL

SEPT. 1992

$3.50

TESTAMENT/MEGADETH

SKOLNICK
MEETS MARTY
FRIEDMAN

with MEGADETH's
SYMPHONY OF DESTRUCTION
TRANSCRIBED!

GUITAR CLINIC
with
GEORGE LYNCH

WOLF MARSHALL
on
QUEEN

BLACK SABBATH REUNION
ROLLINS BAND
HELMET PEARL JAM
KISS BAD II ALL
WHITE ZOMBIE PiL

$3.50 $1.95 Can   UK £2.50
09

0 71486 01394 1

Transcriptions To:

BLACK SABBATH
Symptom
Of The Universe

LYNCH MOB
Tangled In The Web

METALLICA
Crash Course In
Brain Surgery

PANTERA
Cowboys From Hell

QUEEN
Crazy Little Thing
Called Love

34. BREAK ON THROUGH (TO THE OTHER SIDE)

As I returned home from the Judas Priest/Megadeth/Testament tour, I prepared to smile and give a glowing report to my parents, letting them know how perfect everything was going. What else could I do? Just for kicks, I imagined how it would sound if were to be completely 100% honest:

"Yeah, Mom and Dad, it's like this: I thought when I finally played arenas, the answers would all be clear. I'd be happy with the situation, making good money and playing music that was an extension of who I was. I thought it would be the answer to everything, but it's not how I imagined it at all. It's kind of like when I lost my virginity to that girl—I lied that she'd just come over that morning, but I'd snuck her in overnight, the skinny young blonde. But she and I barely knew each other—it was awkward. But just because my first time with a girl wasn't all I thought it would be didn't mean I didn't want to try again, to experience it with someone I relate to on a deeper level. And the exact same thing is true of music. Now you won't understand this at all, but I can't imagine not playing guitar for a living!

"And as much as these guys have shown very slow personal and musical development, it hasn't changed the fact that the experience of being in the band has helped me make the first steps towards healing after growing up in an unsupportive and damaging environment. Still, I'm not sure how much more of my new family's dysfunction I can take. They don't listen to me—acting like I'm still 16 even though I'm the most responsible one in the group. But that doesn't mean I'm giving up hope in music as a whole and not going to try again and again. I just want to play music with people who have similar high standards and musical appreciation.

"Of course, there's no way you will ever understand any of this, you'd just lecture me and tell me to 'go to school,' and try to steer me into being more like you. Well guess what—that's never going to happen! Truth be told, as awful as some of the drama that I'm dealing with is, it's a hell of a lot better than I felt growing up."

*

"Everything's going great!" I say with a smile as we walk into Yoshi's. This is going to be our holiday dinner. It's not Christmas, not Chanukkah. We don't know what to call it. My brother is away somewhere, now frequently living in ashrams and other communal living situations.

As we're being led to our table, we pass by the nightclub connected to the restaurant, where a band is sound checking. Suddenly I'm star struck—that's Billy Cobham, one time drummer for John McLaughlin's Mahavishnu Orchestra and leader of his own great jazz/fusion project in the '70s, Spectrum. He must be playing here tonight with his band—it appears to be a trio. I had no idea.

For a brief moment, the excitement is soured by yelling. It's the keyboard player of the band throwing a fit. *"What the hell is this?! Didn't you guys get the tech rider? I expect more from a professional establishment like this...You bring me what I asked for or I'm not gonna play!"*

This guy is acting like a textbook case of the musician as complete jerk. It's a little embarrassing. As the hostess leads us to our table, I'm not sure what to say about what we've just witnessed.

During dinner, I tell my parents how wonderful it's going with Testament, especially on the Judas Priest tour. I only concentrate on the good aspects—playing arenas and opening for one of my favorite bands.

On the way out, the show is in full swing and we happen to catch Billy's open drum solo, which ignites my father's interest. Surprisingly, he seems drawn in. Just then I remember—he'd wanted to be a jazz drummer once.

The experience of catching a Billy Cobham gig, irate keyboard player and all, underscores something I'm feeling: as much as I still love and respect metal music, my tastes are growing. I need another outlet for my guitar playing.

And little do I know, one is waiting for me, just around the corner. It has a random, bizarre connection to this gig at Yoshi's.

*

A week or so later, I receive word of an amazing opportunity—the bassist Stu Hamm has expressed interest in having me audition to play guitar for him in his upcoming Summer tour.

Stu is associated with the two biggest names in guitar right now. One is Steve Vai, who after stints with Frank Zappa, David Lee Roth and Whitesnake, is now one of the most publicized solo artists in the world. The other is my old teacher, Joe Satriani, who by now has songs in regular rotation on FM Radio and sold-out gigs for thousands across the US and the world.

I'd gone to see Joe at the Fillmore a couple of years ago—Stu practically stole the show that night with his bass solo, incorporating an amazing two-handed tapping version of Vince Guraldi's "Linus & Lucy" (known as the "Peanuts" theme) which morphed into a mind-bending interpretation of that banjo piece from *Bonnie & Clyde* (actual title: "Foggy Mountain Breakdown."). *That guy* is considering trying me out to play guitar for him?! Wow.

The timing is symbolic. After touring pretty much non-stop for over a year, Testament is planning to take the Summer off, so I'll be free.

Stu's manager leaves a message inviting me to come hear another client of his, a guy who is also being considered to play keyboards on the Stu Hamm tour. His name is T Lavitz, and he is best known for playing in the Dixie Dregs.

When I call Bill to let him know I'll be attending, he puts me down for the T Lavitz guest list, then lets me know that there's some uncertainty about T doing Stu's tour. Apparently T has been showing a bit of an attitude problem and frequently throws temper tantrums at his gigs.

I laugh and tell him that coincidentally, barely a week or two before, I'd witnessed this angry keyboard player causing a scene at a gig in Oakland. He pauses for a second and says "By any chance, was this guy you're talking about playing keys for Billy Cobham's band?"

"Uh huh."

"At Yoshi's in Oakland?"

"Uh huh."

"That's him."

*

A few weeks later, I'm at the Great American Music Hall in San Francisco, having a conversation with T Lavitz. I tell him that I saw a bit of his Billy Cobham gig but don't mention catching his temper tantrum.

T talks to me as if we've known each other a long time, confiding in me, venting about the monitors in this goddamn place, the promotion sucked, they changed his set time on him, etc..... He also claims that Stu's manager isn't really managing him, at least officially. It's a trial basis and the way things are going, he's done.

I'm surprised he seems so bitter. I'd somehow figured advanced instrumentalists like this, especially keyboard players, would be all quiet, introspective types. Wrong.

I decide that T Lavitz is not a bad guy. In fact, I quite like him. It's just that, he shoots from the hip, is brutally honest and easy to catch at the wrong moment, as was the case as I happened to walk by him at Yoshi's.

I enjoy T's music very much that night and end up grateful to him for telling me about a guitarist he recently crossed paths with in Atlanta, whom he describes as the best he's ever heard. I know I probably won't remember the name of this guitarist. But I won't soon forget the name of his group: *Aquarium Rescue Unit.*

The next day, I'm combing the racks at Amoeba Music on Telegraph Ave., a veritable goldmine of new and used CDs, in search of The Aquarium Rescue Unit. That Telegraph Ave. smell of incense and pizza wafts in from the street. While in the record store, I hear an amazing guitar duo, Strunz & Farah. They remind me of the duo of Al Di Meola and Paco De Lucia. Playing along to them will add a strong Latin, Flamenco influenced element to my acoustic playing. In about twenty years, my listening to them will come in handy as I'll be asked to perform with another acoustic guitar duo: Rodrigo Y Gabriela. I'll guest on Rodrigo y Gabriela's album, *11:11*. The sole other guests on the album? Strunz & Farah.

Aquarium Rescue Unit and their guitarist (whose name, fittingly enough is Jimmy Herring), as well Strunz & Farah, seriously influence my direction as a player, combining the power of rock with the vocabulary of jazz and the finesse of world music. I become even more inspired and determined to prove to the world that I can hold my own amongst serious musicians.

As much as I still like thrash-metal as a genre, I no longer wish to be trapped within the limitations of the bubble. I become determined to go for it at all costs, learning Stu Hamm's music including guest solos by some of the world's most respected guitarists: instrumental rock phenomenon Eric Johnson and the mad scientist of prog/fusion (and Eddie Van Halen's biggest influence), Alan Holdsworth.

I will make this happen.

*

I head to LA to audition for Stu Hamm.

At the Power Station rehearsal space, Ray, the drummer whom I'd heard play with T Lavitz, auditions with me. He won't get the gig. But Jeff Saltzman, our manager, has accompanied me—he wisely tells me to pay very close attention to the drums while I play. Good advice.

We play Stu's tunes "Lone Star" with the solo by Eric Johnson and "Radio Free Albameuth" with the solo by Alan Holdsworth. Stu tells me he's impressed I learned those solos but encourages me to come up with my own. I tell him I'm happy to do so, but wanted to be prepared in case he wanted it like the record.

The drum gig will go to Ron Riddle who, coincidentally, is from a tiny town not too far from Ithaca, NY. He's part of the Ithaca music scene there and his biggest gig so far has been Blue Oyster Cult, the legendary hard rock band who hails from Upstate New York.

The keyboard position will go to the guy auditioning with me,

Jimmy Yager, a NY session player. T Lavitz and Stu have already decided not to work together, which is probably a good thing.

Stu pulls me aside and says, *"Alright Shmendrick—you want to make this happen?"*

"Uh, It's Skolnick," I say. *"And yes, let's make it happen."* We shake hands.

"You don't mind if I call you Shmendrick do ya?"

Forever after, Stu Hamm's nickname for me will be Shmendrick.[63]

*

I now have a new band, albeit a temporary one, but one of first-rate musicians. Upon arriving back home, the congratulations start pouring in.

First, I receive a call from my editor at *Guitar for the Practicing Musician,* John Stix. *"You know who recommended you, right?"* I say, "No, who?" before correctly presuming he means it was him. I thank him and assure him they were going to tell me.

Then, in an almost mirror image of the day I got calls from the two East Coast guitar magazines about writing an instruction column, I hear from Brad Tolinski, the editor of *Guitar World,* also calling to congratulate me. "You know who recommended you right?" I almost blow it and say, "John Stix" (his biggest competitor, who by now has stolen me from *Guitar World*[64]). Instead I say, "Yes, I heard, it was you! Thanks so much."

I'm learning.

Apparently, Stu's management and label had gone to all the guitar mags for recommendations. I was thankful to both and all for recommending me. Apparently Joe Satriani had put in a good word as well.

My friends, Niall, Alex, Ben, etc. are all congratulatory and happy to see me spread my wings, saying it's about time. In short, I can't remember a time in my life where I've felt so much support, acknowledgement, gratification and purpose.

It was only three years ago, during the making of that second album, *The New Order,* when I made a commitment to myself to buckle down and start listening to those instincts inside which pulled me to open my mind, expand my horizons and realize that I had more potential. I began taking music seriously, taking myself seriously, not getting dragged down by

---

[63] Schmendrick is a name Stu remembers from a movie, unaware of its Yiddish origins.

[64] I've switched because *Guitar World* temporarily had their budget cut and had to cancel all the instruction columns. We were all let go, then called back a few days later and told that it was straightened out; we were hired again. But by that time, I'd already been hired by GFTPM.

limitations.

Just a few years ago, I was only a thrash guitarist. To some, that's all I will ever be, and I'm violating a cardinal role for considering otherwise. But now I'm a guitarist who does instruction columns and can hold his own with serious musicians like Stu and his band. For the first time that I can remember, I feel happy. Best of all, everybody is happy for me.

Well, almost everybody....

*

When the guys in my metal band hear about my plans, there are no congratulations, no expressions of pride. In fact, they don't know how to react—it's as if someone just shot each one of them with a stun gun.

At first there is a painful awkward silence, then the reaction is split between wary support and dismissal. "That's cool, Al" is the forced reaction from Lou.

"Damn, Stu Hamm? Dude's hella bad," says Greg.

"What d'ya wanna do that kinda trip for?" says Eric.

I try to explain in his words. "It's a different kind of trip."

Chuck just shrugs.

I feel as if I am breaking some pact or code of ethics in some unwritten book in which we've all signed our name in blood.

*

After three weeks at home, most of which have been spent learning Stu's music and drinking Peet's coffee, I'm back in LA at the Power Station for rehearsals.

In what seems to be a running theme in my life, my good feelings in the wake of musical triumph have been dampened somewhat by events involving a girl. Cindy has cancelled plans to move to California and date me in the wake of my break-up with Lyla (which was largely due to the fact that I was in love with Cindy). Cindy's decided that she's been unfair to her boyfriend of three years, never giving him a chance, because she was so consumed with me. A day or two before I flew back to LA, she called in tears letting me know she was going back to him, causing me to be heartbroken during the entire rehearsals. I throw myself into the music. Once again, the guitar is there for me even if a girl is not.

I'm reminded of the Berkeley party during the summer before ninth grade. There was finally a pretty girl that liked me. She showed up to the party with her friend and was looking for me, hoping to get together. But the place was wall to wall with people and I'd been jamming in the garage outside—my most successful public jam yet. When I went back into the packed house, still high from playing and receiving high fives and compliments from the jam, her friend came up and told me that they'd been looking for me. But while I'd been downstairs jamming, this aggressive guy from school had interfered, wandered off with her and they'd disappeared. I'd soon find out, this guy had swooped in, filled her up with drinks and taken advantage of her, just like my brother had done (same girl). I supposed she allowed these incidents to happen and was partially to blame, but that didn't make it any less traumatic.

It is not the last time I will experience something like this.

The hurt inflicted upon me by these types of incidents—having a girl I really like snatched away from me in an instant by an aggressive older guy with purely carnal interests—is severe. It will haunt me well into adulthood, lead to trouble in relations with women and take many years to begin recovering from the damage.

But there's no time to be depressed right now. My world, musically and otherwise, is expanding.

*

Rehearsal with the Stu Hamm band is a very different situation from Testament and not just in terms of music. For one thing, these guys are conversationalists. As each one of us arrives, there are hellos and playful teasing, not the blank stares or silly talk I'm used to. Stu is clearly the leader but the other guys talk as well, and everyone is allowed to have their say. Although we're in LA, everyone in this room is originally from back East. I like the East Coast energy. Everyone is supportive and encouraging of one another, like when suggesting that parts be different. It's a great feeling to be complimented as opposed to being sneered at. They respect my determination to catch up with them, get up to speed on reading charts, knowing the musical terminology, etc…

I begin to catch on to their systematic communicating, where the music is discussed in an orderly fashion with terms like transition, sequence and modulation. Sections are referred to as intros, A Sections, B and C sections, bridges, verses, choruses, etc. It's completely the opposite of what I'm used to.

The Testament rehearsals now seem like a distant galaxy away, the dialogue like an alien language:

"No, Lou! Don't go 'doot dju dju dju doot,' go 'dju dju doot dju dju!"

"That's what I fuckin' did, Eric—dju dju doot dju dju!"

"Nuh uh Lou! You went 'doot dju dju dju.'"

"Did not! I went dju doot dju dju!"

"It's not dju doot dju dju! It's dju dju dju doot dju."

"That's not what you fuckin' said before!"

"Fuck you, you're trippin'!"

"No, you're fuckin' trippin'."

"Nuh uh!"

"Uh huh!"

*

Rehearsing across from the Stu Hamm band is Toto, a legendary band of LA's top studio musicians whose hits such as "Roseanna," "Africa," and "Hold the Line" are staples of FM radio. I saw them once at a Day on the Green show at Oakland Stadium, supporting Journey and was very impressed with the guitarist Steve Lukather. I hope to get to meet him.

Someone from the Toto camp keeps popping into our room and making obnoxious jokes with Stu. He has wild, jet black frizzy hair and a loud mouth and appears to have been drinking. I try to avoid him.

On the second or third day, this same crazy guy points to me and says, *"That guy, right there! He's too good! Hey, buddy—who said you're allowed to be that good?"* I'm caught off guard and just laugh shyly thinking, *Oh no. He's going to torture me now.* I do a double take and I recognize his face. *Holy shit, that's Steve Lukather!*

He looks nothing like the clean cut, LA studio-guy image that I'm used to seeing. What happened to him? I'll later find out he's morphed into sort of a rock 'n' roll Wildman and taken much of his money from in a messy divorce.

Steve is full of one-liners and quick jokes. I'll remember these two:

Q. What's the least heard phrase in the English language?

A. *That's the banjo player's Ferrari.*

Q. How many lesbians does it take to change a light bulb?

A. *One to change it, one to write a folk song about it.*

Over the next few days, Steve, better known as "Luke," will take me under his wing somewhat, inviting me over to watch the Toto rehearsals, introduce me to everyone, show me his guitars and elaborate set up (a Bradshaw rig).

Toto's rehearsals are marked by a fierce professionalism. There is a guest vocalist, Phil Perry, a soul singer who sounds like no one I've ever heard. There are three pretty black back-up singers, one of whom I can't seem to take my eyes off of. Luke's playing is phenomenal, as are the rest of the players, particularly the drummer Jeff Porcaro, one of the best I've ever seen.

Unbeknownst to anyone at that moment, Jeff Porcaro will tragically pass away within a few years under mysterious circumstances—it's said to be a gardening accident but it's suspected to be some form of substance abuse— so these rehearsals I'm witnessing are even more priceless than I realize.

Between the Stu Hamm band's rehearsals and getting to hang with Luke and drop in on Toto pretty much every day, I feel as if I am privy to an exclusive educational experience beyond the Ivy Leagues.

*

I have two more extracurricular activities that will have a profound impact on me.

One is taking a private lesson with LA based guitarist Scott Henderson. He played on an album I have by Joe Zawinul, founder of Weather Report. Scott's currently managed by Bill, Stu's manager.

Bill takes me to watch Scott's amazing band, Tribal Tech, rehearsing in their drummer's suburban garage which has been converted into a nicely organized rehearsal room. Scott, a super down-to-earth guy with a sense of humor, opens up the mysteries of chromaticism, which involves those jazzy notes I like so much. My one lesson with Scott enables me to formulate my own plan of self-study, giving me so much mileage I don't feel the need to study with anyone else for years.

My other great extracurricular moment happens when *Guitar World Magazine* calls to ask if I might be interested in conducting a one-on-one interview with jazz guitarist Tuck Andress. "Like you have to ask," I tell editor Joe Bosso, who inquires on behalf of GW.

Tuck, best known as one half of the husband and wife team—the amazing jazz guitar/vocal duo Tuck & Patti—has just released an incredible solo album, *Reckless Precision* and happens to be in LA doing press this week. It is a bit of a bold move to put us both together—you couldn't put two guitarists from more opposite acts—Tuck & Patti's audience is primarily made up of well-to-do baby boomer couples drawn to T&P's songs of love, healing and enlightenment; Testament's audience consists largely of belligerent twenty-somethings eager to say "fuck you" to the system with every headbang, mosh and stage dive.

Despite these differences, the interview is a smashing success—it garners a lot of positive attention for the magazine, allows me to get more "multi-dimensionality" cred and gets fans of mine to check out Tuck, who sounds like two or three people at once with his combination bass lines, percussive grooves and chords all on the guitar.

One of my favorite guitarists, Tuck is also one of the nicest people I've met. He is not condescending or prejudging about my being a metal player, despite being someone that wouldn't know Metallica from Meatloaf. He holds no prejudice against the music, and confesses to wishing he knew more about it.

I ask Tuck about some of his techniques, especially where he makes the guitar sound like a harp. He not only shows me how to do it, but gives credit to where he first heard it—from a jazz guitarist named Lenny Breau.[65] Like T Lavitz turning me on to Jimmy Herring, Tuck has just turned me on to a major influence. (It will be about five or six years before I finally develop my straight ahead jazz playing, and am able to incorporate their techniques.)

Not sure what his reaction would be, I confess to having some old lessons of Tuck's that were Xeroxed for me by a former student of his. Tuck doesn't mind one bit. He's just happy to see his knowledge spread into the world and encouraged me to share the lessons with others.

Meeting Tuck Andress and Scott Henderson are experiences I'll never forget. Both are master musicians and examples of the type of person one should aspire to be.

The opposite is true of the guy I'll bump into soon at the rehearsal place. On the one hand, he's a master musician among master musicians. But on the other, he is tormented by his own demons.. This is all the more disappointing because he's my biggest hero and one of the most influential guitarists of all time.

*

During a break in our rehearsals, I walk down the hall to grab a coffee from the machine in the lobby, when I notice two knuckleheads laughing obnoxiously, wrestling each other and trying to push the other down, oblivious to any attention their juvenile antics may bring. I'm just about to turn away to avoid them when I notice one of them is Luke, on break from Toto's rehearsal.

The guy that Luke is wrestling, he looks oddly familiar, like I've seen his face somewhere but can't place it. Who is that? I know him. Wait a second…his shoes—Converse sneakers that are striped like Eddie Van Halen's guitar. That's funny, I've never seen Converse like that before, they must be a custom pair. Who would wear shoes like that anyway unless it was….

Suddenly, I'm shaking. Eddie Van Halen is a god to me. There are not many other people that could ever cause this reaction, maybe Jimi Hendrix, and he's not even alive… What is he doing here?!

Of course…Eddie Van Halen and Steve Lukather…I'd read all about them. On Michael Jackson's *Thriller* they'd both played on "Beat It," Luke had played the rhythm, Eddie played the now-famous solo. They hang out all the time, play golf together, and have reputations of being out of

---

[65] Lenny Breau was one of the most influential jazz guitarists of all time, yet never a household name and tragically died broke and destitute in the '80s.

control drinkers.

One of Toto's techs walks by—he and Eddie start talking and walk back towards Toto's room. As soon as they're gone, Luke high fives me like any other time. Noticing the weird look on my face, he asks if everything's alright. I confess to being totally freaked out by seeing his friend Eddie. He offers to introduce me. We enter the room and here he is, Eddie Van Halen, in the flesh.

When you meet someone like this, it is hard to imagine that they actually exist. You think of all the pictures, the magazines, the album covers, the sounds that have been a soundtrack to your life that this person is responsible for. It is very surreal. You want the moment to be like you've met this kindred spirit, but how can it be? This is someone that gets hounded for autographs and photos all the time.

Eddie's new guitar is being passed around from Luke, to the Toto techs, to a couple other band members, then to me. Eddie is spouting some nonsense to the small crowd, everyone laughing as if on cue. Then everyone pays attention, as Luke tells a joke, but Eddie looks away, spacing out. I use this opportunity to hand Eddie his guitar and talk to him for a moment without everyone else listening in. I tell him it's great, that the neck reminds me a bit of the feel of a classic Charvel, which I feel is the ultimate compliment—after all, the original guitars he played had Charvel necks. Eddie takes the guitar back in a huff and reprimands me, claiming the neck is *his* design, not Charvel's. He's slurring his words. I'm not sure he even knows what he's saying.

Then one of the techs taps him on the shoulder, grabbing his attention, thus ending my encounter with one of the most influential, legendary guitarists of all time. As I sulk back to our rehearsal room across the hall, I'm in shock at having somehow offended my ultimate hero. I take some consolation in fact that his behavior is alcohol induced—it's only one in the afternoon and he's not too coherent. Besides, it's just one moment for him, one he'll never remember. Unfortunately, it's a moment that will stick with me forever. My crossing paths with Eddie Van Halen causes me to become more conscious of how I interact with my own fans.

Over the years, I'll try not to blame myself, a process made easier with each new story I hear about him: In about a year or so, Eddie will receive some embarrassing press in the magazine *Vanity Fair,* something about showing up drunk at a show by this hot new band, Nirvana. He'll beg them to let him join them on stage; an awkward encounter that yields no jam (of all people to not know the unwritten rule mentioned in Ch. 19, about never inviting yourself to jam on another's gig). And in about twenty years, his current singer, Sammy Hagar, will release a book that portrays Eddie as a more troubled addictive, difficult individual than anyone could have imagined.

But right now, my Eddie Van Halen encounter affects me on several levels. It reaffirms that despite certain people thinking I'm special and despite me being here in LA to be part of Stu Hamm's band, there are still situations where I feel really, really small, like a nobody.

*

By week's end, the rehearsals are over and I'm feeling years older and wiser. I've had a glimpse into some musical worlds outside of the bubble in which I've existed. It has been eye opening, invaluable and for the most part, positive.

All our gear is packed and being loaded out the door. By this time tomorrow, I'll be making my very first appearance in front of a non-metal crowd.

35. OUTSIDE THE WALL

On a sunny spring day, I watched the smoggy skyline of LA disappear in the rear view mirror, soon to be followed by the California State line. Earlier, as we'd pulled out of the rehearsal building in Hollywood, I felt like I was being shipped off to duty. Rehearsing with people at this high level of musical proficiency had been challenging, but fun and rewarding.

For the first time in several years, I was no longer on a tour bus with a refrigerator, ice cooler and my own bunk. And in a strange ironic twist, I was back in a blue van.

This was a quandary that would be a running theme throughout my career—on a comfort and business level, I was taking a step down. Stu was pretty much broke and financing this out of his pocket from his Satriani tour earnings (which really weren't as much as I'd have imagined). This meant endless drives in the van, cheap motels and mediocre pay for the gigs. But I didn't care. The fact that my heart was in it negated all "practical" connotations to the contrary. And there was no question I was doing the right thing. By accepting this opportunity, grueling conditions and all, and not just sitting around the Bay Area doing nothing, I was opening the door for new possibilities.

Being handpicked by a respected musician like Stu—the bassist associated with Satriani and Vai—was not only a win for me, it felt like an honor on behalf of any thrash musician or for that matter, anyone who has ever been marginalized and underestimated. It's not that I was trying to place myself above the metal world; I only wanted to show that it was okay for one to follow his or her own heart while ignoring the increasing sneers, insults and negative energy that came with it. The seeds were being sown for that which would define part of my purpose as a musician: to inspire others to spread their wings, face their fears, expand their horizons and not let anyone else bully them, literally, figuratively and musically.

As the blue van and our accompanying Ryder truck barreled down the Arizona highway, it became more and more clear that while so many life changes had happened in those few years since finishing high school, I was now on the road toward a whole new set of experiences. And leading the way was this quirky character I was about to get to know a whole lot better, Stu Hamm.

*

With his wire rim glasses, curly hair, slightly hefty build and ever-present baseball jersey, Stu was a not exactly an image-conscious musician. Passionate about sports, he would seek out golf courses and batting cages on tour. He seemed happiest sitting at the bar downing beers while analyzing whatever game was on TV with strangers.

I was very grateful to Stu for turning me on to several books he'd read at my age and had been influenced by, including *Siddhartha* by Hermann Hesse.[66] Stu's next books for me were *Neuromancer* by William S. Gibson and *The Sirens of Titan* by Kurt Vonnegut. Stu had been a sci-fi geek

---

[66] In the 2010s, I'd meet a brilliant, gifted and beautiful young woman, a Canadian architect named Maddy who had just moved from Cambridge, MA, to New York—she'd inspire me to read Hesse's *Steppenwolf* and *Narcissus & Goldmund,* both of which would have profound parallels to my own life.

who'd seen every Star Trek episode as a kid, so these books represented his primary focus. But it was the latter author, Vonnegut, who moved me beyond his storytelling—his books had a deeper message and had transitioned from just being a science fiction writer. Vonnegut further strengthened my quest to not be just a guitarist and planted the seeds for me to one day try my hand at being a writer myself.

Stu would also turn me on to his favorite albums. These included *Night Passage* and *8:30* by Weather Report and the Yes albums *Close to the Edge* and *Relayer,* which featured keyboardist Patrick Moraz—a friend of Stu's who would come to some of our shows. Stu also turned me on to albums by Bill Bruford with Allan Holdsworth on guitar, early recordings of John Mclaughlin, such as *Extrapolation* and *Lifetime,* with former Miles Davis drummer Tony Williams and several albums by an early '70s group I'd never heard of, called Brand X. Brand X had consisted of incredibly dynamic musicians, especially their long-haired, scraggily, bearded drummer named Phillip Collins—he would later join Genesis, become their vocalist and embark on a successful solo career shortening his name to Phil. Then there was King Crimson, whom I'd heard of but never listened to before, specifically the early '80s' period with Adrian Belew on guitar.

There was even an album by Joni Mitchell whom I'd never considered listening to before. I'd always thought of her as a folk singer, associating her with the whole Woodstock, hippie movement. But as it turned out, Joni was a very high level musician. Some of my favorite jazz musicians—Pat Metheny, Michael Brecker and Jaco Pastorious—had been eager to tour with her. Her tour with these guys was documented on her album *Shadows & Light.* I'd had no idea how great her music was, and this album was a perfect gateway into her catalog. Stu had an equal passion for classical music, particularly the instrumental sections of Wagner's *Ring Cycle* and his favorite, Beethoven's *Moonlight Sonata.*

The new blue van tour was peppered with discussions of the music and literature mentioned above, as well as independent film, art and current events. I couldn't remember ever feeling so inspired on the Testament bus with all the childlike interactions, debauchery and the TV constantly blaring, whether anyone was paying attention or not, with a constant barrage of mind-numbing entertainment (the equivalent of today's *Keeping Up with the Kardashians, Real Housewives* and *Twilight*).

*

Having never met Stu before, I'd somehow gotten this impression of him as someone quiet, soft-spoken and pensive. This probably came from reading his reflective album liner notes and the fact that his glasses caused him to look studious. He was clearly very intelligent. But this impression of him as demure couldn't have been farther from the truth. On tour, Stu was quick to react to things and had strong views on everything.

I wasn't used to musicians having opinions on current events, especially ones that were well-formulated and articulated. For example, when it came to the recently launched Operation Desert Storm, the reactions of the Testament guys had amounted to something along the lines of *"Saddam's fuckin' trippin'."* Stu's assessment was more like this: *"This whole so-called 'war' is all about oil and selfish interests. It's a pathetic waste of lives and trillions of dollars. When are the taxpayers of this country gonna wake up to the hypocrisy imposed upon them by our own government?"* Stu had an equally liberal attitude on the Pro-Life Movement, one that manifested into a funny question he'd pose to audiences from the stage: *"Why is it that people who are against abortion are FOR the death penalty?"*

I also quickly realized that Stu was tired of being questioned about Steve Vai. At this time, Vai was *everywhere*—covers of all the guitar mags as well as full-page and double page ads, life-size posters at Guitar Center. Ever since he'd become so wildly popular, with the guitar community fawning over him like he was an instrumental Elvis, I'd begun to think something might be wrong with me—I was never influenced by Vai's playing style. His playing, especially on recordings, felt "too" perfect, lacking the natural quality and rawness of someone like Jeff Beck or Van Halen. Unlike those guys, Vai seemed to have very little authentic "blues" feel, which was especially ironic because he'd appeared in a dramatic film about blues guitar, *Crossroads*.

Lately, Vai had been presenting himself as this sort of Dalai Lama of guitar. In interviews, he'd shift the focus to his belief in higher powers, pyramids, aliens, metaphysics and God. What was going on there? Was he really religious or something? Stu looked annoyed at me for having asked, *"Yeah, he's about as religious as my left sneaker."* The image of depth, piousness and altruism soon came across as largely fabricated. Stu, along with others I'd meet, would later reveal to me that Vai was a ruthless dictator in the studio, recording in a meticulous manner that was so controlled and edited that any live quality was pretty much removed. I'd suspected as much.

Still, I respected Vai's musical knowledge—after all, he had gone to Berklee and played with Frank Zappa. He was a master at transcriptions and theory. I'd seen him up close with David Lee Roth on that Monsters of Rock gig a few years earlier and his technique was impressive—technically flawless. But something about listening to him never quite sat right with me.

And his playing wouldn't have the long-term influence you'd expect from someone getting that kind of exposure.

I was learning something interesting about the entertainment industry and the tiny piece of real estate occupied by guitarists. There'd been very few authentic giants—guys like Hendrix and Van Halen—geniuses whose music had, through the right set of circumstances, struck a major chord (pun not intended) with popular culture. Then, there were the quiet masters, those who might not be household names who were undeniable *musicians' musicians* whose playing was so good, it was enjoyable to listeners beyond the guitar scene—Tuck Andress, Scott Henderson, Jimmy Herring and Jorge Strunz came to mind. But among household names, there were some (not to be named here) who, while worthy of respect, happened to be in bands whose popularity was so great that they were propped up like puppets—the public mistakenly placing their individual talent above that of the true masters in readers' polls—which encouraged wider exposure from a media who secretly knew better but had sales figures and marketing to consider. And then there was Vai, someone with legitimate guitar skills, but whose chutzpah and self-marketing abilities enabled him to exaggerate to the point of creating the illusion of being "otherworldly". He struck me as a musical version of the man behind the curtain in *The Wizard of Oz*.

*

Stu's not-so-secret desire to be a stand-up comedian was apparent—he exuded the tortured soul of a comic. One of those individuals who expressed his own truth through jest, he would speak, whether on stage or off, with a delivery fitting for an appearance at LA's Comedy Store venue.

He was especially self-deprecating about his musical career. For example, he would talk about his days at Berklee College of Music, working at a local deli to make ends meet. *"Guys would come in, order a sandwich, then say, 'Wait a second. You play bass, right? I've seen you! You're a really great bass player!' I'd thank 'em and they'd say, 'Uh...Buddy?' I'd say, 'Yeah?' 'Is there any way I could get a little extra swiss cheese on that sandwich?"*

He would also joke about his recording contract, telling audiences that he'd just signed a new record deal with Columbia Records, quickly followed by a disclaimer: *"It's a really great record deal! All I have to do is buy ten records for a penny, then they send me a record every month, which I can either buy at the regular price or send back at no additional charge."*

*

The Stu tour would be far from perfect: we'd be crammed and uncomfortable, sleeping in the van late into the night while one of us drove;

there'd be tension between Stu and the drummer Ron, who wanted some kind of guarantee he'd be playing on Stu's next album; there'd be a dark day, which Stu kept referring to as Black Friday, when it became conclusive that his manager had completely mis-budgeted the tour, causing Stu to pull each of us aside with a heart to heart talk about "economic reality" and the need for pay cuts. I'd be okay with it—but the other guys would be in really foul moods, begrudgingly accepting, since the only other option was to cancel the rest of the tour and go home early.

But these situations were the exception, not the rule. Most of the time, it was four guys playing music and having a great time. I saw that it was actually possible for a group to tour together, get through some tough challenges, maintain an aura of respect for one another and keep generally positive attitudes.

Overall, being in our little van with these highly respected musicians was a lot more pleasant than the Testament bus which by that time had become a cesspool of uncontrolled juvenile behavior and negative energy. However, after so many late nights driving the van into the wee hours, our backs and necks began to hurt. Those tour bus bunks had been a lot more comfortable on overnight drives.

*

As indicated above, Stu's career was not being helped by his manager, Bill Detco. Bill had a smile that seemed to say *"I could sell a used car to a used car salesman."* He was not unlikeable—he was in fact quite personable, and he'd always been very nice to me. But I was beginning to see him as cocky and unqualified.

People I knew at various instrument companies confided to me that while they really liked Stu, they wouldn't endorse him simply because of his manager. They claimed Bill was hustling them, as though he were Michael Jordan's agent negotiating with Nike.

Adding to the problem was his handling of lodging. No one was asking to be put up in the Ritz Carlton, but Bill had us booked into every boondock, ghetto, flophouse, outhouse and hostel—all in the name of saving a buck. I could understand the need to conserve the tour budget by not overspending on hotels, but Bill did so in total ignorance and disregard for the band. On the rare occasion he'd found us a decent hotel, he usually had us booked on the wrong day or in the wrong town. It became almost routine to arrive at a hotel exhausted after a show or long drive, only to have to turn around, hit the highway again and search for a new one (these were the days before iPhones, Google Maps, or Mapquest).

Each time this happened, we would utter his name in disdain: *Bill*

Detco! It was one of those names that just lent itself to being spoken in derision, kind of like that problematic drum tech on the Testament tour—a name that was similar phonetically: *Ben Linton.* And there would be one day that we'd utter his name more times than any other, a day none of us would ever forget. It would be the worst hotel booking on record—one in which Bill Detco, in one phone call, would manage to outdo everyone, even himself.

*

It began on the day Stu and I were driving separately with two girls who were at the show the night before (Dayton, Ohio, if I'm not mistaken). We'd had drinks with them at the bar afterwards. At that point in the tour, it was highly refreshing for Stu and I to talk to new people outside our entourage, and a little feminine energy didn't hurt. We just pretty much hit it off with these girls. There was no weird guy/girl stuff going on, just a great dynamic between us—totally platonic.

The girls had liked our show so much that they'd been thinking about driving to the next gig in Cleveland. So when we offered to put them on the guest list, they offered to take us in their car. *Why not?* we figured.

The girls came by our hotel early in the morning, picked us up and took us to a really great breakfast spot. Then the four of us had a leisurely four-hour drive to Cleveland, arriving at our hotel in time for lunch. That's when the unthinkable happened...

***Ohio Turnpike, 1991**. This is fun. Stu and I have been getting a break from the crowded van driving with these two girls. For the whole drive, we've been telling them funny stories about what's happened on tour so far. Soon, we are all laughing uncontrollably, the delirium from several hours of driving setting in as the Cleveland skyline approaches.*

When we get to the hotel, it is as though we are checking into a monastery. There is no music overhead, no chatter, only the hum of air conditioners. The walls are green and spotless, with bland pictures of flowers on the walls. The woman behind the counter speaks softly and sympathetically, like a funeral director. We all still have the giggles but do our best to check in like adults, restraining our laughter until we get into the connecting restaurant, where we hope things are a bit more alive. It is difficult not to laugh.

The restaurant is even gloomier, with two tables of people barely touching what looks like hospital cafeteria food. They are not saying a word. No one even looks over as we sit down—it is as if we are ghosts, our incessant chatter and giggles nonexistent. A waitress comes over with a blank expression—she just hands us the menus and walks off.

It feels as though we are in a David Lynch movie. When I mention this to the group, we all burst out laughing. Then we feel guilty, as though we are causing a disturbance.

As we look at the menus, two more people are escorted in. One is in a walker—he looks shriveled—like a concentration camp victim who's undergone chemotherapy. A few minutes later, a woman is wheeled in who looks even worse—she is also shriveled up and near death but with multiple IV units attached to her wheelchair and tubes sticking out of her throat.

At this point, we stop laughing.

I excuse myself, walk past the cash register and back out to the front desk. I say to the woman who checked us in, "Can I ask you something?" She nods. "I was just wondering…is this some sort of special hotel or something? What can you tell me about it?" In a sad whisper, she explains to me that the Cleveland Clinic Medical Center is attached to the hotel, (the name of which "The Clinic Hotel," should have tipped us off). I thank her, walk back into the restaurant and sit back down.

At first, I don't say anything as Stu and the girls look to me for information. I just shake my head and glare back at them.

"Well?" says Stu.

"Congratulations, Stu!" I finally say. "Your manager, Bill Detco, has booked us into a hotel for families of the terminally ill."

*

In Hollandale, Florida, I found myself back at the Button South, where barely a year earlier, there'd been a riot at a Testament show.

Overly aggressive security guards had been rough with the fans from the get-go; two songs in, a security guy tackled a stage diver and while doing so, knocked over one of my guitars. As Chuck stopped the song, we noticed several other fights happening between security and fans. As we walked offstage, a storm of flying chairs and fists inundated the seating area. For the next ten minutes, we peeked out from the tiny dressing room, hunkering down while our crew dismantled the gear. Things were only getting worse; pandemonium as more fights were breaking out. By now the police were arriving, sirens were wailing—a scene right out of a TV police drama. Soon, we escaped out the back door, jumped onto our tour bus and were rushed out of town, a police escort following close behind.

Since I was a member of Testament, I was a bit nervous they might not let me in for the Stu Hamm gig. But I was welcomed as though nothing had happened. I talked to several guitar-heads who'd attended the ill-fated gig and were thrilled to get a chance to hear me play with minimal chance of riots. It would turn out to be a nice, normal gig, erasing all associations with my previous visit.

Yet what I'll remember most about Hollandale was not the show itself, but the special guests of Stu's who joined us backstage—the Pastorius family. They were the kin of one of Stu's heroes and a favorite musician of many, myself included: the late great bassist Jaco Pastorius.

*

Jaco had died tragically four years earlier, his later years marred by mental illness and substance abuse. He'd been a native of this area.

There was Jaco's brother, a gifted visual artist who drove Stu and me to his house to view his work in progress—a life-size, haunting sculpture of Jaco. There was Jaco's teenage daughter, to whom he'd dedicated one of the most beautiful and influential solo bass pieces of all time, "A Portrait of Tracy." There was one of his sons and several other relatives.

While Jaco's solo efforts for CBS Records, not to mention an outbreak of bootlegs, were earning hundreds of thousands if not millions for various record companies, Jaco's family was barely getting by. In an effort to win back the rights to some of Jaco's music, they'd been hampered with substantial legal fees and forced to live frugally at best. One of their biggest court battles was with a European record distributor, who'd been releasing live bootlegs of Jaco's last tours in Europe.

I myself had purchased several of these recordings from record stores. How could I have resisted rare live recordings of Jaco and Birelli Lagrene, the phenomenal gypsy player on electric guitar? But when Jaco's brother told me the true story behind these CDs, how they were unauthorized, released without permission and only financially beneficial to the slimeball who'd illegally put them out—I felt terrible. I would not be buying any album in this series again.

We couldn't help noticing our guests were all eyeing the deli tray, veggie platter, chips and other backstage refreshments with longing eyes. Stu encouraged them to eat but they said they didn't want to impose. When Stu insisted that they eat, we all concurred, telling them to please take whatever they like, we were having dinner anyway and they could have it all. They coyly thanked us before diving into the deli tray like a flock of ravenous pigeons.

The Pastorious family was a heartbreaking casualty of the music industry and a reminder of how cruel it could be to those it left behind.

*

There were many other adventures on the Stu Hamm tour:

In New York City, Will Lee, the great bassist from David

Letterman's late night talk show, came to our show and hung out; it was energizing to be in the presence of a musician whose mastery and diversity had inspired me on late night TV for years. Also in New York, we picked up a new crew guy and I was the one who drove the van around Port Authority Bus Terminal. At first I was made into minced meat by the yellow cabs, city buses and other New York drivers, who honked, screeched, cursed and cut me off unrelentingly. It became an instant confidence builder—I decided right then and there that they were going to be no match for me. Suddenly, I was keeping up, not letting them cut me off, cutting them off when necessary and armed with my hand on the horn. I felt exhilarated—I was holding my own with the tough guys.

From there, we headed upstate to Rochester, NY, where we did an in-store appearance at the largest, craziest music store I'd ever seen, House of Guitars. They had every type of guitar imaginable, new and used, in piles, untuned and unstrung. It was run by these two brothers Bruce and Armen, very nice guys and oddball characters. One spoke very quietly and the other hardly said a word. Both had frizzy hair that stood straight up. They appeared as mascots on the store's psychedelic t-shirts and posters looking like they would have been right at home in Berkeley hanging out with the likes of Abby Hoffman or Wavy Gravy.

In Texas, I came down with pneumonia and I could barely stand up. I didn't move for the whole show—it was the sickest I've ever been playing, but at least my fingers could move. I saw a doctor who set me up with antibiotics—fortunately, we had a couple of off-days afterwards. In Oklahoma, we played the Samurai Sake House (yes, in Oklahoma). In Arkansas, we played Juanita's, a great venue with incredible Mexican food. It was said to be a favorite spot of their Governor, Bill Clinton, whose name I'd never heard before but would soon be hearing a lot more of.

Eventually, we crossed the California state line, only this time heading back West with thousands of miles, thousands of notes and dozens of gigs under our belts. Indeed by the time we played San Diego and LA, we were really sounding tight—like we'd been together for years.

In LA, one of my teenage guitar heroes, the German guitar player Michael Schenker (from UFO, Scorpions and MSG), came to the show but I had no idea he was even there. He was checking out our drummer, Ron Riddle, and considering him for a future tour. Ron told me about it later, then apologized for not letting me know, having no idea I was such a huge Schenker fan. A few years later, I'd meet Michael at a group photo shoot for *Guitar for the Practicing Musician* magazine and tell him how I was disappointed I didn't get to meet him that day. He'd say to me, *"I remember zat show. You ver dat guitar player? You ver good!"* I'd be on cloud nine. In San Jose, the great Steve Morse from the Dixie Dregs was in town and came to the show, sat in and jammed with us. The on-stage jam was great, but not half as exciting as the jam backstage, where Steve and I played together for about twenty minutes. It was surreal trading licks with one of my true guitar heroes.

But it would be our show at The Stone in San Francisco that stood out—a night I'd never forget.

*

By the time we hit San Francisco, the band sounded tighter than ever. I felt great about my playing. Most memorably, Joe Satriani—not just my old teacher but Stu's boss—sat in with us.

I couldn't believe I was on stage with Stu and Joe. I kept flashing back to a few years earlier, seeing them at the Fillmore on Joe's Surfing with the Alien Tour. Then I'd flash back to 1984 and my guitar lessons with Joe in that tiny room in the back of the guitar store in Berkeley.

By most accounts, I held my own that night, not necessarily matching Joe's pyrotechnics, but contributing parts that were musical, professional and worthy of my being up there with the "big guys."

Meanwhile, the gig felt like that classic TV documentary show *This Is Your Life.* Everyone was there—people I'd known in the Bay Area music scene, people I'd gone to high school with, many whom I hadn't seen in years. Who would think this was that same shy, awkward, invisible kid from Berkeley? I was incredibly moved to feel such love from so many friends and strangers alike—many who seemed to be living vicariously through me. While this wasn't the Grammy awards, it was, for me, just as symbolic.

I was no longer confined to the thrash bubble.

Even my parents were surprised. As hyper-intellectual academics, they knew the music world about as much as that of monster trucks or professional wrestling. But they understood one thing: something really special was happening in this room, all these listeners showing an outpouring of respect and admiration. Even better, this was music that they could actually handle, unlike that of Testament.

Speaking of which.....there they were—over in the corner table, wearing blank expressions and sipping Jack & Cokes, the guys from my metal band and their girlfriends. The moment I saw them, like the drinks in their glasses, was bittersweet. On one hand, I was really appreciative that they'd made the effort to come and see the show (I suspected our managers told them it was the right thing to do). Yet at the same time, it was strange and awkward, how could it not be? They didn't know how to react. Certainly a guy from a thrash band wasn't supposed to do what I was doing—playing with virtuoso musicians, building a presence outside of the band and creating a reputation in the world beyond this exclusive genre.

Yet, for as much grief as they'd caused me, I felt bad for the guys. They seemed really unhappy with each other. This didn't make sense to me. One day they might open up to some of the ideas I had: greater discipline and diligence, taking responsibility for your actions and being as honest and up front with others as possible. But that could take many years.

I couldn't blame them for not being 100% behind my endeavors. After all, Eric had started this band under the guise of an "evil metal band" (even wearing priest vestments at their first gigs). The lead guitar template had been Venom/Slayer/Angel Witch, not Van Halen, Rhoads and Satriani. But now, here they were watching their lead guitarist on stage with Stu Hamm, not to mention a guest appearance by Joe Satriani himself, in front of a packed house of diverse listeners who were openly showing their appreciation towards my playing.

It must have been weird for them.

*

After the San Francisco show, I lay in bed staring at the funky décor in a hip Geary Street hotel, a little drunk but too excited to sleep. There was less than a week to go on tour.

I kept thinking about the evening. I couldn't remember ever having such feelings of accomplishment. All my life, it had been others who scored the home runs, touchdowns and points, while I'd been the last to be picked for any team. I'd had no honor roll mentions, no perfect grade point averages, no highest test scores or any other scholastic achievement to speak of.

Looking at the challenges of my upbringing and specifically my lack of a support system, it made sense that I'd sucked at everything. Thank goodness for the guitar and the fact that I'd gotten an early head start on it, showed some talent and stuck with it. I felt grateful to all my teachers, specifically Gary Lapow, Joe Satriani and more recently, Tuck Andress and Scott Henderson, as well as the advice of those whose interviews I'd read in magazines—John McLaughlin, John Scofield, Jim Hall, etc. These were people I'd never even met who had been the supportive, encouraging voices I so desperately needed.

I finally tasted the sweet fruit of knowing that I was unique—maybe not a Jimi Hendrix or an Eddie Van Halen (in truth, there would never be a guitarist with those levels of influence again) but perhaps one day, someone along the lines of guitarists like Tuck Andress, Jimmy Herring or Scott

Henderson—not acknowledged by the establishment (*Rolling Stone, Spin,* The Grammys, MTV, etc.) or even guitar magazine readers' polls or front covers. I simply hoped to be a real, bona fide musician's musician, one whose playing stands out independent of any record sales, gimmicks or other hype. Becoming this type of guitar player—frequently underrated, often overlooked but deservedly respected—would be just fine. My own rigid, self-imposed regimen of music studies, self-improvement and enlightenment was finally beginning to pay off.

Soon, the exhaustion, not to mention the beers and whiskey shots began to creep in. Before allowing the looming mask of sleep to take over my body, I granted myself one final rumination:

As a youth, certain "friends" had shown resistance to my guitar, complaining when I brought it to camp and showing sour faces whenever I took it out to play. Yet tonight, I was surrounded by friends all there to cheer me on, let others know that I was now one of the best and tell anyone who thought otherwise just where they could stuff it. My parents' unyielding discouragement was a hurdle so high that at one point, I'd considered running away—yet earlier tonight, there they were watching me spread my wings on that stage, hanging on every note I played and offering a glimmer, just a glimmer of something I'd never seen in their eyes before: pride. Meanwhile, the very source in which I'd sought my solace from all that resistance and discouragement had been this metal band which I'd joined five years earlier. Now they're the ones from whom I feel most of the resistance and discouragement...

It was true. All I wanted to do was play guitar and play well, for artistic reasons (not ego-driven ones). Why all the resistance from others?

This thought caused me to utter something which, in a rare instance, seemed to express my Jewish ethnicity: in a tone like comedian Jackie Mason or a classic Borscht Belt comic, I shrugged my shoulders and, just before falling asleep, said aloud: *"What the hell does a guy like me have to do to play guitar in peace?"*

*

After a few more Northern California shows, we wrapped up in Ventura County, just north of LA. Stu, the band and our crew guys all had our final beers together and said goodbye. After this awesome but grueling van tour, I was glad to be going home for a bit. At the same time, I wished to keep going, playing this music and reaching new heights of musicianship. Adding to the bittersweet feeling was this: a short follow-up tour had been booked for Stu in the early fall and I had to regretfully decline.

I'd felt bad about this—Stu really wanted me there, told me as much and asked if he could offer me more money from his own pocket, which wasn't very deep. I explained that it wasn't money at all—only a sense of responsibility. It was responsibility that had enabled me to develop my playing to a level where I could play with someone at his level. But now that responsibility was drawing me back to the fold, where a new album had to be written and recorded for 1992 (for the first time, we'd gone a whole year without a new album). It pained me to have to let my sense of responsibility win out over what my heart wanted to do (and it wouldn't be the last time I'd be in a predicament like this). But I'd already taken the whole summer for myself to follow my heart.

Now, pressure was being mounted back home. There were the band members complaining that I was out here on the road when I should have been back there working with them in rehearsals. There were our managers Elliot and Jeff who, while graciously supportive of my tour with Stu, felt it was time to get back to my main job.

Finally, it was the acceptance of reality—by now Testament had indeed turned into a job, one I had quite a few issues with and that I might not have forever. But for now I had to get back to work, as much as it pained me to let Stu down.

*

As the plane lifted up from the tarmac of the runway at Burbank Airport, I looked outside the window and said a silent goodbye to Southern California. My finger touched the button to lower the seatback. I started thinking about the tour and all I'd experienced this summer of '91.

First, the crowds—they couldn't have been more different from the audiences I was used to. They'd been mainly open minded, music loving folks—more for the art than the social scene. There were many different age groups, education levels and occupations. There were even a fair amount of African-Americans, drawn to Stu's funk bass technique, which placed him in line as heir to the throne of Larry Graham and Stanley Clarke. I liked the diversity of these listeners, none of whom judged me for being a "thrasher," or "metal dude." Many were surprised to hear I came from a genre not known for producing musicians that could fit into a sophisticated musical situation like this. They treated me like I belonged and helped me realize I could play for anyone—not just crowds dominated by angry white guys from the suburbs who started fights, snorted meth and drank till they puked.

I thought about my guitar playing: I'd felt the most noticeable improvement in years, yet there was so much further to go. I was pulling off Stu's jazz influenced rock just fine, but I wasn't close to where I wanted to be with the music I felt the strongest connection to at the time—the real deal:

Miles Davis and his disciples (Herbie Hancock, Chick Corea, John Scofield, etc.) and my favorite traditional jazz guitarists (Wes Montgomery, Jim Hall, Pat Martino, etc.). Touring with Stu, jamming with Morse and Satriani, I was sure I'd have felt a sense of having arrived. Instead, I felt I had only just packed for my journey.

Finally, I thought about the shows. The fact was this—our instrumental songs had all gone over amazingly. Our solos had prompted applause that reminded me of hearing music at Yoshi's and Kanzaki Lounge. But the vocal songs, especially the pop-oriented ones, just hadn't gone over well. They might have been okay had one of us been a "real singer." But it wasn't working with Stu as a vocalist or a front man (a lesson I'd learn when I tried it a few years later). Admittedly, the rest of the band and I were making things much worse with our back-up vocals that were horribly off key. Night after night people would tell me it was a great show, *but*...then they'd bring up the vocals. It certainly hadn't been my place or anyone else's in the band to break this to Stu. And while the shows may have been flawed in that respect, overall, they were getting a tremendous response. With a few tweaks, Stu should be able to parlay this into a successful solo career, maybe even selling out the Fillmore and Irving Plaza (in San Francisco and New York respectively), or at least Slim's and The Bottom Line. [67]

The tour had been fraught with challenges. Financially, it had been dangling by a thread, almost getting cancelled midway through due to money running out (hmm, why did *that* sound familiar?). Stu's brilliant musical skills, literacy and comedic wit hadn't translated into intelligent business decisions—he'd chosen a manager who wasn't up to the standards a musician of his caliber deserved. He'd drink too much on tour, on a level that would challenge anyone in the Testament entourage. His record label rep and others had encouraged all of us to "keep an eye on Stu," who'd been gaining weight recently and appeared to be older than his early thirties. Certain other guys in the band had been all too happy to down shots and occasionally share other, less legal substances with him during late night hours at the lonely motels across America and have debates about whose pitcher was looking better this year, the Red Sox or the Yankees.

---

[67] It wasn't to be. Stu would wisely part ways with his manager, but eventually be dropped by his label, Relativity (on his birthday, which he would painfully joke about). In fairness to the label, Stu's case of writer's block would cause a five-year gap before his next record. By that time, all the momentum from our tour and the album we'd been supporting (*The Urge*) was gone. In the meantime, I'd accept an opportunity to record with another great bassist, Michael Manring, which would irk Stu.

This had caused me to become a bit disillusioned—here were guys I saw as "serious" musicians. I was sure they'd be spending more of their time and energy focused on creativity and long-term goals. But at least they saved the partying for after the shows. More importantly, everyone was nice to each other and had a good time. Most pleasant for me was that the conversational intellect of these guys (intoxicated or not), when compared with the environment of the Testament bus, was like comparing the dialogue of NPR's *All Things Considered* to that of *Beavis and Butthead*.

So when all was said and done, touring with Stu had been an invaluable experience. I'd always be grateful. Sure, in some ways, it had been far from perfect, but if given the choice, I'd have done it all over again. The Stu Hamm tour opened my eyes to the world beyond thrash metal, raised my musical skills tenfold, taught me some valuable life lessons, including the following realization:

The grass may indeed be greener on the other side, but the lawn is not always well cared for.

36. UNWANTED ADVANCES

Back in the Bay Area, I had barely a week to rest up before heading down to start getting the new album together. The process would become similar to getting a root canal.

On day one, I showed up on time to find Eric's new rig had been set up by his tech, while all my stuff remained buried under various road cases in a storage room, untouched since our last tour. When Eric finally arrived, two hours late, I couldn't help but ask: if someone had been paid to come down and set up gear, why wasn't mine set up too? "He's my tech. He came to set up my stuff." I tried to explain, unsuccessfully that his tech worked for the band, not just for him, and should have had my stuff set up too. "Have your own tech set it up." I reminded him that I didn't have a tech, and his tech was the band's only local tech. He said that since I had gone out on another tour—it was now my responsibility, not the band's.

Recognizing this as a passive-aggressive way of expressing bitterness with me for going on the Stu Hamm tour, I let it go and began the daunting task of excavating my gear from the storage area. Now, before you think I'm a sissy who can't set up his own gear, keep in mind that setting up a "rig" for this type of band, with its heavy cargo of amp heads, speaker cabinets and labyrinth of black cables buried under various gargantuan road cases which weren't even clearly marked, was no joke—there was so much lifting, sorting, organizing, it was like working at a construction site. I finally got my stuff all set up only to find out that we were still unable to jam. Why? Eric couldn't figure out how to use his own rig which was brand new. He just stood there glaring at it as if it were a strange science project, trying a switch here, turning a knob there. Practice would have to wait until the next day.

It turned out that while I'd been away, Eric had ordered a Bradshaw rig, similar to the one Toto's guitarist had been using in LA. I could understand someone like Steve Lukather using one—after all, he was one of the top session guitarists in LA and played for Toto, which required quick changes between many different sounds. But Eric only had a few sounds—he didn't require a custom switching system that cost thousands of dollars. These types of impulse purchases, at the band's expense, had gotten to be routine—every time he saw or heard about some new piece of gear, he decided he had to have it, made an argument for it till no one could bear to listen to him anymore, then received it, all expenses paid. He'd use it briefly, never more than a few months, before selling or giving it away and moving on to the next one, chipping away at the band bank account in the process.

Not wishing to be a burden on the band, I chose to pay for whatever equipment I didn't receive through endorsements out of my own pocket. It seemed more ethical. Besides, I didn't wish to contribute to the fiscal cliff eroding the band.

And there was no greater evidence of this financial erosion than the acceptance of two recent cash advances.

*

While I'd been away, the band had procured a brand-new merchandise deal that made each member of Testament twenty thousand dollars richer. That was the good news.

The bad news: our business managers had been strongly advising the band against this deal—it essentially held each one of us accountable for the entire amount of the advance. It was a terrible deal and ill advised.

A typical merchandise deal at that time was a bit like a record deal—you'd get a lump sum of money up front, which you'd have to recoup (pay back) over time through your sales. But in this case, in order to recoup their advance money should our t-shirts sell less than expected, we were allowing the merch company, Brockum, full rights to come after each of us individually. Making matters worse, it didn't matter that there were five of us splitting the money and it didn't matter that our managers had taken their commission —each one of us would be held liable for the entire amount: over $100,000. It was insane!

In the past, we'd used our merchandise advances wisely, placed in the castle vaults of our protective knights in San Francisco: Siegel, Feldstein and Duffin. The firm divvied it up into modest salaries for each of us. This time, however, the guys were acting upon a newly realized mind frame: *the business managers work for the band, not the other way around. They have to do what we tell them.* The band wanted all the money in one lump sum and they wanted it right now.

Our point person at SF&D, Fred Duffin, urged them to hold out for a better deal. It started with a phone call to each one of us warning us of the potential consequences of signing. He then issued formal notices that he and his firm would not be accountable for any aftermath of the deal, urging the band to reconsider signing something potentially detrimental, an unmitigated mistake.

How could I have agreed to such a horrible deal? Good question.

Being on the Stu Hamm tour I'd been distracted and out of the loop. I got a message to call Fred from the road, which I did—he told me the possible repercussions all of which, I agreed, sounded awful. He said something I was hearing often from our elders trying to work on behalf of the band—*Alex, you're the only responsible one. You seem to be the only voice of reason, the one with his head squarely on his shoulders. Perhaps YOU could talk some sense into these guys?*

I just wasn't in a place to be the sole voice of dissent. Who was I to try to reason with them? The Stu tour, although not exactly perfect, had been my cozy shelter from the torrid rain of Testament drama. I was not about to spoil it by getting sucked back into that black hole. I was away branching out into new forms of music, while they were sitting around doing whatever it was they did: watching TV, smoking weed, playing Nintendo games.

So when I received a contract via Fed Ex and was told that everyone had agreed to this and were all waiting on me, I signed.

The other guys immediately put down payments on new vehicles (a Harley Fat Boy for Chuck, a black Dodge pickup truck for Eric), bought entertainment systems, Excalibur swords and other frivolous purchases. I opened a retirement account and a separate brokerage account where most was invested in mutual funds. I would add to this account whenever I could and another one that I'd eventually put towards my own recording projects.

Like Murphy's Law, our t-shirt sales would fall flat during the next couple of tours—any profit the band earned had to be designated towards repayment of the advance, with interest being tagged on at all times. "The Brockum Debt," as it was known, would cast a dismal shadow over Testament—a haunting reminder of the band's collective irresponsibility and inability to recognize the reality of their decisions, foreshadowing a continued plunge to the lower rungs of the music industry.

Sometimes merch debts are forgiven, other times they are collected. While it was more likely the debt would be forgiven or overlooked, there was always a chance of the alternative. Though it fortunately never came to pass, I would spend much of the '90s in fear that this merchandise company's attorneys might come after me at any time like repo-men, eyeing any savings and possessions I had.

*

Another development that had taken place while I'd been gone: the band's management contract had come up for renewal. The guys had briefly begun investigating possibilities for new managers, but unable to resist a $2500 carrot dangling in front of all our noses in the form of a "signing bonus," had decided to renew the contract with Cahn-Man.

I voiced concern that this was not a good idea and was overridden. I was in the awkward position of liking them personally—Elliot Cahn, who'd been a colleague of my father's at UC Berkeley, was still a close friend of my family—but I didn't feel they were right to manage the band. Had I been able to express how I was feeling clearly, I might have said the following: *Elliot and Jeff are good guys, but they just aren't cut out to manage a metal band, especially one like this. Let's face it, we're no piece of cake. Don't sign a renewal just because of money and convenience. Let's keep looking.*

Not helping us was the fact that within the group, we had no business-smart visionary steering the band (like a Lars Ulrich of Metallica or a Dave Mustaine of Megadeth) and needed to make up for that lack with extra-savvy management. Complicating things further was the fact that our band was plagued by stunted personal development, collective low self-esteem issues and an inability to communicate with one another. This band needed more than a manager—it needed a surrogate parent, uncle, guidance counselor and therapist.

Elliot and Jeff had helped guide the band to the best of their abilities but they were never really about metal music anyway—it was more like they tolerated it. And in fairness, it had been the band that had approached them, begging Elliot to manage when he was still just our attorney, not the other way around. This new young band they were managing, Green Day, seemed to be much more in line with their own tastes.[68] Now here was a chance for both parties, Cahn-Man and Testament, to move forward with dignity.

Had that decision been made, a whole lot of trouble could have been saved, along with countless legal fees, bad blood and accusations of Breach of Contract.

*

Just before signing the management renewal contract, and cashing their checks for the advance, Chuck and Eric had briefly looked around to see what, if any, options there were for new management. There were few prospects.

One company spoken to was Q Prime, the firm that managed Metallica.[69] A representative there, who worked under partners Cliff Burnstein and Peter Mensch, told them point blank what was going on. Finally, someone whose advice they would actually listen to.

The conversation with Q Prime caused them to realize that we'd had a great thing going with *Practice What You Preach*. It was an album heavy enough for the original fans but that also managed to reach out to an audience beyond the metal underground. There was no better evidence than the fact that *Practice* continued to be our biggest seller. Had we followed it

---

[68] After Green Day severed ties, Elliot would continue to practice law and Jeff would move on to producing—one his first groups being The Killers.

[69] Q Prime still manages Metallica as of this writing, among others, including Muse, Mars Volta, and the Red Hot Chili Peppers.

up with an album that would've built upon what we'd established, rather than taking a step backwards, both in terms of music and sales, then we'd have had a shot at that next level—headlining large theaters across the country, larger festivals and higher financial returns. But now, it was too late.

A high profile management firm like Q Prime just wasn't interested in a band that had made some permanently damaging miscalculations, losing its potential to be a platinum act. Perhaps this could be turned around with the next album and if so, they could have another conversation with Q Prime in the future. Until then, best of luck.

It took the biggest, most successful hard rock management company in the world to get these guys to listen to what I'd been trying to convey all along—that we never should have tried to go "backwards" musically. They'd dug their own hole.

As a last ditch effort, they now wanted to do an album that was more like *Practice What You Preach,* but even *more* melodic and accessible. Now they were asking me to contribute a bigger role on this record, as I had on *Practice,* to recapture that success. While it was good to finally be validated for being right, it was hard not to view their pleas as somewhat sad.

Reluctantly I agreed, but the truth was this: their flagrant disrespect of everyone, of myself as well as each other, was driving me away. Although I'd initiated the title track and a couple other key moments on *Souls,* their stubbornness had led to a lackluster album. It was not being helped by an inability to recognize their own great musical ideas and an all-out butchering of the few good ideas they begrudgingly accepted from me. I'd mostly kept quiet; I'd lost the energy to argue.

Furthermore, I'd had enough of living on a bus with no place to escape the constant pot smoke, debauchery in the halls, and all the annoying hangers-on. The behavior on our fourth album cycle was no different than on our first. They hadn't learned to get it out of their system, focus and start behaving more responsibly and making better decisions. The bigger bands understood something they didn't—how to conduct yourself with dignity, when to say no (especially to friends and hangers-on there to take advantage) and most importantly: *work before play.*

It had all gotten to be too much. I just didn't care anymore.

But out of a sense of responsibility, I agreed to do what they were asking: have more of a role writing this next album, which they hoped would be more "accessible." Knowing privately that this would probably be my last album with these guys, I told myself I'd hang in there. Who knows, maybe they'd pull their shit together and start acting like men, not little boys. And as long as they were somewhat open to my musical ideas, I'd write as many parts for this album as I could.

But little did I know that I was setting myself up to take the fall for what would become the most criticized album of the band's career.

37. SWAN SONG

There is a huge public misinterpretation about our album *The Ritual*.

A perfect album? No. It doesn't have any high speed "thrash" songs, something I concede was probably a mistake. Unfortunately, this fact has overridden the reality that *The Ritual* has some of our best playing and most interesting musical ideas in the band's history. The songs "Electric Crown" and "Return to Serenity" are among the strongest the band has written and never failed to get a huge response live. If we were to go back and swap just a couple of songs with some old school "thrashers" as people had come to expect from Testament, the album would stand as one of the strongest. Instead, it continues to be ripped apart and tarnished unfairly.

How I became the perfect scapegoat to pin the blame upon, I'm not exactly sure, but the twisted notion that I'm somehow responsible for the album's shortcomings continues to prevail. These flames of ignorance are fanned by self-appointed critics—many of them anonymous, hiding behind on-line handles—who equate the stronger melodies, clearer production and musically interesting ideas with an attempt to be more "commercial." While it's true that high-speed thrash rhythms were not at the top of my priority list just then, it's not as though I insisted on them not being on the album. According to legend, I confronted the giant Indian warrior-like Chuck Billy and band founder Eric Peterson and demanded, "No thrash songs!!"

The notion that I, at that time still displaying the confidence of an abused animal, was somehow able to take the reins, control these guys and make demands is ridiculous. The truth is, I was on my way out and didn't really care either way. And as long as they were suddenly open to trying songs that weren't done at breakneck tempos, which I'd be able to do more memorable lead guitar parts over, then I wasn't going to argue with that.

Nonetheless, while *The Ritual* is generally listed as being the band's "weakest" album, I cannot count the number of times I've heard comments by those who, upon hearing it, find themselves scratching their heads, wondering why that is and insisting it's a great album.

Comparisons to Metallica's multi-platinum *Black Album* would be inevitable and not helped by the fact that we'd chosen to record in the very same studio, One on One in North Hollywood, where the *Black Album* was recorded. My own thoughts about Metallica's monumental, controversial album were as follows: someone finally recorded a heavy band and made it sound good, with production that stood up against the Bon Jovis and Mötley Crues of the world. I thought this was a good thing, although I can understand some of the fans not relating to the material as much; even I was a bit taken aback by the "mainstream" quality compared to *Master of Puppets* and *And Justice for All.*

At the same time, I always knew that the first band of this type to be recorded well and have structured songs would have a massive hit album. I had wanted us to do it first—certainly not as polished and mainstream as the *Black Album*, more like the best of *Practice* and *The New Order* but less noisy, clearer with more definition (the type of sound that modern metal bands like Machine Head and Gojira would do in the '00s). I wasn't even listening to the *Black Album* that much anyway. I'd been listening to more and more straight ahead jazz, as well as the music Stu had turned me onto—Weather Report, Yes, King Crimson, etc. But the definition and clarity of the big albums was something I thought we needed more of.

So I suppose there is some truth in the sense that the *Black Album* may have opened the door for us to explore more melodic, definitive ideas and get away with it. But anyone who says *The Ritual* was "Alex pushing the *Black Album* on everyone else in the band" has no idea what they're talking about.

*

We decided not to hire Michael Rosen to produce again. *Souls of Black* had felt unsatisfactory, much like *The New Order* had. There had been glaring oversights, which, truth be told, the band should have noticed, but to have a producer not notice them was inexcusable.

"The Legacy" was the song with the most obvious flaw: Louie's cymbal hits were completely left out. How nobody noticed this before mixing is anyone's guess; it only became obvious when we filmed the music video and, watching it back, realized Louie was hitting his cymbals with no sound!

We chose to work with British producer Tony Platt instead. He was my favorite of all the producers; he seemed to be the most professional and was the first who wasn't trapped producing B-list albums (Michael had diverse credits as an assistant engineer, but not as a producer). I wished we'd have started working with him earlier. I'm convinced that, had he been around on the earlier albums, they would have been captured better.

I really liked working with Tony who, in a bizarre coincidence, would many years later end up recording a group my own jazz guitar trio would inevitably (and a bit annoyingly) get compared to because of their use of rock covers, the jazz piano trio, The Bad Plus. There wouldn't be much to tell about the actual recording of the album—perhaps because of Tony's presence during pre-production, his diligent insistence that issues be worked out in advance and his unwillingness to let the guys run him around in circles. Things would go comparatively smoothly for once.

I enjoyed recording my lead guitar sections, which were more along the lines of *Practice*. And, since we were in LA, we rarely had our whole band down at the same time, which made the atmosphere more peaceful. But while there was little band drama compared to previous albums, there were incipient changes happening in the world outside.

*

Just past the door of the studio control room was the lounge—a plush room with sofas, a large coffee table, an ever-present bowl of fruit and a big screen television that was usually tuned to MTV, but occasionally had news flashes. Four police officers were on trial for the beating of Rodney King. Nearby LA was simmering towards a boiling point. Fortunately, the recording would be finished a month before the infamous LA Riots. And somehow, the tensions of the daily news seemed to parallel an impending storm brewing within the music industry.

The biggest star in the world, Michael Jackson, was on his way out—his controversial lyrics, crotch grabbing and other odd behavior not going over well with fans and critics. And the King of Pop's imminent downfall was only a mere symbol of an even bigger change, one that would greatly affect the world of heavy metal. It had started earlier in the year with these strange, quirky, promo spots on MTV, many featuring young, hip-looking people whispering to each other, "The music revolution will be televised."

It was only now, in the studio lounge, that it started to dawn on me just what had been going on with those segments: the "trend mongers," as famously described by Frank Zappa[70] had been working overtime in some Viacom/MTV boardroom, plotting an overhaul of popular music. MTV (which would one day replace music entirely with reality shows like *Teen Mom, My Super Sweet 16* and *Jersey Shore*) was out to prove once and for all that they now ruled. They were tragically right—the rest of the industry had no choice but to bend over backwards. Any label that didn't send MTV the type of artists they were looking for would be ignored. Any radio station that wasn't on board could watch its ratings plummet. The quirky early-'80s anthem by The Buggles couldn't have proved to be more true: "Video Killed the Radio Star."

For hard rockers, if you were lucky enough to be a Metallica or Pantera, established enough to be a formidable opponent, yet viewed as anti-establishment, you were going to be okay, as long as you played by the rules. If you were a platinum-selling group that was a prime target of the revolution, such as Warrant or The Bullet Boys, you were doomed—your career was already over. And if you were a band like us, which was heavy but hadn't broken through enough to escape the stigma of being considered "80's," "dated" and "old school," you were in potential trouble.

So at that very moment, as Michael Jackson's number-one chart position was being snatched by Nirvana, a band that would come to symbolize the so-called "music revolution," we began seeing new groups with loud, heavy guitars on MTV with angry, aggressive riffs and vocals.

At first, this seemed like a great thing—perhaps a door was opening for us? It felt like the "music revolution" could be beneficial to all the heavy bands. Victory was in the air.

Or was it?

*

The first sign that our hopes may have been off was that there was something noticeably different about all of these new groups.

For one thing, none of them wore leather, bullet belts, chains, skulls, studs or any other hint of heavy metal fashion. Some had long hair, but it

---

[70] Frank Zappa, *The Adventures of Greggery Peccary* (Studio Tan)

wasn't styled like ours—it was scraggily and unkempt like the skateboarders, stoners and surfers I'd known in Berkeley. Then there was the sound—unlike the tone of '80s' hard rock drums, the drums on these tracks didn't sound processed at all, as if they'd been recorded in 1974. The songwriting style had more in common with '70s' classic rock and folk than metal. There were "power chord" riffs (with just two or three low strings) but they also weren't afraid to use full sounding chords on all six strings, which was very rare in metal. There were even happy major chord progressions. I had to admit, this was a refreshing break from the sound of hard rock that had gotten so typical.

I had just one glaring problem with this "new" sound: the guitar solos. For the most part, the solos were very raw and basic, owing more to Neil Young or The Stooges than to Eddie Van Halen or The Scorpions. [71] I didn't mind at first—I never felt a virtuosic solo should be a condition for liking a song; some of these songs were really good. However, it wouldn't be long before it started to get on my nerves. It wasn't the original wave of bands—Nirvana, Soundgarden, Pearl Jam—I understood how the raw basic solos were part of the package. But when all the imitators would start coming along—Bush, The Offspring (whose riff for their mega-hit "Come Out and Play" was nearly identical to my riff for "Burnt Offerings") and others, I wouldn't be able to listen anymore.

Gone were the days of Blackmore, Rhoads and vintage Van Halen; guitar artistry no longer mattered. I'd soon turn off the rock stations, stop watching MTV for good and focus all my energy on Wes and Scofield. Jazz was *all* about the solos!

As we watched these early-'90s' videos, I don't think any of us realized what was going on—the entire landscape was being bulldozed. The music revolution would play a part in us being unable to break through that next level, despite releasing an album that just might have put us there had we delivered it a year or two earlier. It would cause our album sales to drop significantly, as well as our t-shirt sales, further placing us in danger of one day possibly facing legal persecution as a result of that ill-advised merchandise advance.

The guitar had been the very foundation of rock 'n' roll up to this point. Now, for the first time ever, its virtuosity was about to take a back seat in the very music it had helped create. Modern Rock stations would pop up

---

[71] There were a few exceptions such as Jerry Cantrell of Alice in Chains, Dave Navarro of Jane's Addiction, and a year or so later, Peter Klett of Candlebox, all of whom had good feel, warm tone and moments which reminded me of Dave Gilmour from Pink Floyd.

everywhere, playing music that sounded like old punk and new wave. Multi-platinum artists would appear who called themselves alternative.

The '90s would prove to be a strange time for music.

*

As *The Ritual* recording wound down, we each flew home one by one, depending on who was needed and who wasn't. Once we were all back in the Bay Area, we did a photo shoot for the album. This took place in a parking lot off San Pablo in Berkeley, a stone's throw from my very first gig at Ruthie's Inn, which had now closed.

The pictures eerily captured a see-through appearance on one side of the photo, something not unheard of with the right combination of light, movement and shutter speed, but odd in the sense that it was unintentional and limited to just one side of the frame.

In the image chosen, I am the only one who appears ghost-like.

38. CH-CH-CH-CHANGES

By now, a few relationships had developed that changed the dynamic of the band somewhat.

Chuck was still with his girlfriend and future wife, Tiffany. She wasn't a bad person, and many years later, I'd grow to really like her a lot. But at the time, I avoided her, for a couple of reasons. For one thing, she'd become the self-appointed ring leader of the band girlfriends (and ex-girlfriends). As a group, their behavior reminded me of *Goodfellas*, which had just come out—that scene where Lorraine Bracco's character meets all those mafia wives, gossiping and doing their nails. Furthermore, she needed to know everyone else's business—where they were going, what they were doing, who they were dating, etc. But the biggest reason was her continued indifference to her friend's stalking and harassing of me which, by then, had escalated to the point where I should have filed for a legal restraining order, had I been wiser (see chapter 22).

By now, I was living with Cindy, the bartender we'd all met in Ithaca many years earlier (and whom our then-manager had unsuccessfully attempted to win over by placing his hotel room key in her hand). She'd finally left her boyfriend, flown across the country and moved into my small apartment in Oakland. Ultimately, we'd only last a couple of years and our in-person relationship lacked the promise of our long distance relationship. But she'd give me someone to talk to while going through all this, which was invaluable. I also knew Cindy would never get dragged into the band girlfriend network.

Meanwhile, Eric's previous relationship had ended, paving the way for a new girlfriend: the ex-wife of Metallica lead guitarist Kirk Hammett. Rebecca had been living off a hefty divorce settlement (said to be in the multiple six figures) and certainly seemed to have a thing for guitar players—she was rumored to have flirted with and/or dated other guitarists including her ex-husband's arch nemesis, Dave Mustaine (the very guy Kirk had been brought in to replace in Metallica). Soon, at a European festival, Dave would say to me in a raspy whisper: "Is that *Rebecca*?!" I'd answer him and he'd respond with a wink: "Uh...she's really workin' the area, if ya know what I mean." I just didn't have the heart to relay this to Eric; he'd find out in a few years after their divorce. But there'd be a consolation to their short-lived marriage: a beautiful daughter.

Louie, meanwhile, had struck up a relationship with someone new: her name was Sherry and she was from Long Island, NY, where Louie's family was originally from. Being from the East Coast and working for a major record label, Sherry seemed more worldly than the girls he'd dated previously. She immediately scored points with me by avoiding the band girlfriend network. It wouldn't have raised any eyebrows had it been one of my girlfriends. But the fact that this was Louie's girl would cause the entire entourage to eye her suspiciously.

*

As Sherry and Louie began spending more time together, Louie began, for the first time in all these years, to stop following Eric like Sancho Panza to his Don Quixote. This was a major development. It was one thing if I avoided their clique and kept my girlfriends away from theirs—with me it was expected at this point. But Louie? He was part of the inner circle, the holy trinity.

Sherry was helping Louie realize he needed to stand up for himself and establish independence from these guys. She opened his eyes to how unfocused the band was and how unhealthy his relationship with them was. I knew this would cause a chip in the glass and place a wedge between what was considered the core of the band. I wasn't sure what the outcome would be. I had my own issues to deal with and was just trying to survive long enough to get through another album and tour cycle.

Complicating matters was the fact that Sherry, based in LA, worked as an assistant A&R rep for the label we'd just been transferred to: Atlantic Records.

*

A little background: when the distribution deal between Megaforce and Atlantic Records had come up for renewal, both parties had agreed that the partnership had been more or less a failure. For their part, Atlantic hadn't felt that being the umbrella for Megaforce had been worthwhile—no hit albums had been provided during the five-year affiliation. Meanwhile, Megaforce hadn't obtained the growth it had hoped for being associated with a major label and felt Atlantic's support, or lack thereof, was to blame.

So as part of the mutually agreed upon severance deal, Atlantic Records had retained the right to choose two acts from the Megaforce catalog to keep as their own. It had been uncertain whether Atlantic would even choose to invoke this clause (most Megaforce artists would probably never be picked by Atlantic on their own). But somewhere in a boardroom high above Rockefeller Plaza in New York City, a decision was made: Atlantic would add Testament to its roster.

This could have been a great thing. Had we been brought over by a powerful person at the label, such as then-president Danny Goldberg, or department head Jason Flom,[72] who could take us under their wing and make sure we had all the promotion and tour support we needed, things would have been different. Unfortunately, we'd been brought over as the result of a contractual clause. While it was validating to finally be on a legendary major label, it was a difficult period to sign with this particular company whose strategy at the time was to sign several new acts a year, get behind only the one or two that showed the strongest initial sales, and drop the rest.

So with no one there to nurture our album or act as the point person we needed, being on Atlantic Records essentially meant we were now part of a big tax write off.

*

A conference call was set up with Johnny Z for a bittersweet goodbye.

God knows we'd been ripped off by Johnny—especially during the *New Order* tour-support fiasco (see chapter 24). But somehow, he had always been more like our corrupt uncle who just couldn't help himself. In this sense, there'd been something very Jersey/Italian/Mafia about the whole Megaforce experience (one which fortunately didn't involve violence and murder). Now, we were potentially moving up the ladder, but Johnny was still family, and now we had to let him go. He had been the one willing to get behind this band when no other reputable label would, opening the doors of the music business at the national and international level.

Who could forget that?

All past grievances were put aside as we called Johnny to thank him for everything and wish him luck. During the call, he let us know that Atlantic had not only taken us, they'd snatched up Kings X, Megaforce's other biggest selling band. Losing both of us essentially crippled Megaforce, meaning Johnny's only viable option was sale of the label. It was the first step towards retirement from the music business.

It was all over for Johnny. I'd never heard him so down and out. All he could talk about was how he and Marsha were devastated. Then he began sobbing uncontrollably. In his gruff Jersey voice, he told us, in between sniffles: "We're cryin' da blues over here, ya know?"

---

[72] In further evidence of how small the music world is, Jason Flom would be in charge of projects such as Savatage, the Trans-Siberian Orchestra and was close friends with the manager of Ishtar, an Israeli world music singer I'd play guitar for in the early '00s.

Torn between his thrash past and jazz-fusion aspirations, Testament's Alex Skolnick attempts to make both ends meet on *The Ritual*.

BY BRAD TOLINSKI

PHOTOGRAPH BY BOBBY NEEL ADAMS

DOUBLE VISION

39. THE FINAL COUNTDOWN

With our new album in stores and the video for "Electric Crown" in occasional rotation on MTV's *Headbangers Ball*, we set out to tour behind *The Ritual*. First, we hit the US with the mighty Iron Maiden, who was experimenting with the idea of having heavy bands supporting them. We were in the support slot with the Southern hardcore band Corrosion of Conformity opening.

Like Suicidal Tendencies, I'd had the impression of COC as out of control punk rockers but found that wasn't true at all. In fact, the guitarist,

Pepper Keenan, carried around a Dobro guitar—he turned out to be a very good southern, slide blues guitar player, and we had some great jams.

Then, at one of the shows, some young concertgoers were tailgating in the parking lot not far from our bus, passing around an acoustic guitar. It looked like they were having a lot more fun than I was. Everyone else on the bus had turned into stoned zombies. So I walked out and approached the fans—they recognized me immediately and were pretty much in shock as I spent the next hour with them passing the guitar around and having a great time. It was so nice to just play music.

It suddenly dawned on me that as a band, we'd completely forgotten how to have good clean fun.

*

The Maiden tour was overall a lot like the Judas Priest tour of 1990—a dream tour supporting our idols—but much more glamorous on paper than in reality. Here was another great British metal band from a few generations before ours—metal royalty in our eyes. Onstage, they sounded as good as ever, but offstage, it appeared they were going through a difficult period. They were aloof, not just from us but from each other. And, just like Judas Priest, they would part ways with their lead singer soon afterwards.

There were a few good moments, such as playing The Cow Palace in San Francisco, the very same venue where I'd seen Kiss as a ten year old (the concert Chuck, Greg and I had attended before knowing each other a mere thirteen years earlier). But at the same time, there was a sense that we weren't crossing over to Iron Maiden's audience, while our own audience just wasn't bringing in the numbers to make up for it. And touring with Iron Maiden in 1992 wasn't the same as touring with Iron Maiden in 1984.

With Judas Priest, I'd wished we'd been touring with them on their *Screaming for Vengeance* tour. With Iron Maiden, I harkened back to the days of their monumental album *Number of the Beast.* When I'd seen Metallica supporting Ozzy Osbourne, every arena was sold out; Metallica's set was tailor-made to satisfy its core fans and reach out to Ozzy's as well. But now things weren't the same. We were supporting these bands when it was too late. Making matters worse—we just weren't going over that well. Still, I was getting written up as a guitarist worthy of special attention, which felt odd.

I was realizing that as nice as a good instrumentalist is, it is not that important in the big picture to a band's success. No matter how hard I worked at my own playing, it was being crippled by our overall decision-making and lack of leadership. And the better I got at guitar, the more depressed I was getting about the limitations of the band.

*

We headed to Europe where we opened for Black Sabbath. After several years of lackluster albums and misguided moves[73] they appeared to be on the right track. They'd just come out with their strongest album in years, *Dehumanizer*, which was helped by a recent reunion with their former vocalist, the great Ronnie James Dio (who'd famously replaced Ozzy).

Since Sabbath had been around since the time I was born, it was one of the most diverse audiences we'd played for. I believe it was our monitor guy, Rick Diesing, who described the crowd as a "father and son picnic."

While it had been a thrill to support Maiden and now Sabbath, the negativity brewing within the band—and not just towards me—was overshadowing the bright moments. I couldn't help feeling like I was trapped. I thought about the future: If I stayed, then for the rest of the '90s, I would probably remain on the exact same level of playing, but wouldn't improve. With *The Ritual*, I'd taken my playing as far as I could. But now they were back on the kick they'd been on just before *Souls of Black,* wishing to get darker and starting to buy into this whole anti-solo mentality that was infecting all hard rock, including metal.

If I left, I had no idea what I was going to do. I certainly didn't want to join a similar band. Yet all the momentum I'd built had been in the world of metal, not improvised music. Then again, more than anything, I wanted to rise to higher levels of musicianship—to be able to play like the diverse, improvising musicians I liked to listen to—jazz, world music, funk as well as rock. Yet I was so far from that in terms of ability. Perhaps I could try to do instrumental rock à la Satriani, but somehow that genre just wasn't calling me either. I realized that as much as I'd been influenced by Satch as a student, that style of music—with a live band essentially functioning as a backing track—wasn't what I felt in my heart and soul.

So what *did* I feel in my heart and soul? I honestly had no idea. I was full of conflicts. It would take years of false starts, failed bands and life changes to finally get to the point where I could compose and improvise comfortably what was in my heart. Of course, I didn't know any of this yet. But as I reflected more deeply, I began to realize one thing for sure: I would have to get out of this band, sooner rather than later.

The other members were becoming more and more rude to others, as well as to each other, burning one bridge after the next, partying too much and spending money beyond their means. I'm certain they didn't realize the

---

[73] Most bizarrely, there'd been a Sabbath album produced by rapper Ice-T. I like Black Sabbath. I like Ice T. Just not together.

damage they were causing, but they were going down a hole that I didn't wish to go down with them. I believed there was more to music and to life. I became increasingly inspired by the great artists I was discovering on my own—musicians, writers, painters, thinkers—who provided a light in the darkness.

The band was building up a skyscraper of problems, one that would not be easily demolished. In addition to the t-shirt debt, which was equivalent to a bad mortgage, they were fighting with management about problems too numerous to solve, some of which were legitimate gripes, but the majority of which had been self-inflicted wounds.

One day, the band finally fired our managers, not realizing they'd signed a contract that more or less protected Elliot and Jeff's interest and not our own. Now, on top of everything else, there was a major legal battle ahead.

What did they expect? Things could have easily been worked out had the band just walked away from the renewal contract. Instead they'd chosen to sign it and accept the signing advance. And trying to separate in the middle of a contract with your managers, especially when they happen to be practicing attorneys, is a really bad idea.

The rest of the Europe tour was consumed with how to break from the contract with Elliot and Jeff while keeping the signing advances that had already been spent.

*

While in Poland, I'd found a beautiful hand carved wooden chess set that I paid for with Polish Zlotys, which amounted to about twenty US dollars (I still have it). Greg, Chuck, a couple of crew guys and I actually knew how to play, so we would have games. In fact, there was a festival with Slayer where Tom Araya walked past our dressing room and peered in—his face wore an expression of complete bafflement at not seeing the usual scene of liquor shots being downed, joints being smoked and death metal in the background. Instead, there was complete silence as I played a chess game with my guitar tech Dave, the others silently watching as if it were a tournament between Gary Kasparov and Bobby Fischer.

The chess games represented a rare moment of respect and civility in the midst of all the insanity—the one avenue of escape that involved being in the moment and thinking for yourself, not surrendering to the scene, or the TV. It was refreshing.

Soon, this new activity became polluted when, in a strange, hashish-influenced manner, the guys began using chess terms to describe their battle with our now ex-managers. Every time they thought of some way out of the contract, one of them would yell out, *"Check!"* before describing some juvenile scheme for getting out of the contract. But what they hadn't realized was this: they had already checkmated themselves.

*

With a few weeks left to go on tour, the bands funds dwindled in the wake of legal fees, tour expenses and other debts. A decision was made to cut the pay of the crew, something I completely disagreed with. I'd been against renewing the management contract from day one, but since the others had decided to sign, we'd have to live with the consequences, which by now included a legal battle. Money was tight, yes. But cutting the pay of the crew?

The entire crew, which included a couple of long-term friends of the band and my new tech Dave Kohls whom I'd brought over from the Stu tour (and apologized profusely for bringing into the mess that this organization—or lack thereof—had dwindled to) went on strike. They refused to lift another finger until they were promised the wages they'd signed on for. The show would have to be cancelled. I sided with the crew, which didn't exactly help relations between myself and the rest of the band.

After several tense hours, a compromise was reached—the crew would continue to work for less pay until the band got the next tour support check from the record label. Then the crew would promptly be paid the lost wages. Of course, this wouldn't happen—by the time that check would come in, the band would be even further in the hole and need the money for unforeseen expenses. Several years later, Dave K. would tell me he still hadn't been paid.

I could no longer in good conscience be in a band that conducted business this way, especially towards the crew—these fiercely loyal people who were working so hard to make every show happen. Not that I needed another reason to get out, but the reasons continued to pile up like casualties of war.

Soon we'd be headed back to the US for a club tour. Here was when everything would unravel completely.

*

We were back in the clubs.

A mere six months earlier, we'd been supporting Iron Maiden with one last shot at getting carried over into the big leagues. Now, our ticket sales weren't strong enough to put us in the larger theaters, even the ones we'd comfortably headlined a couple years earlier. The big leagues were no longer in the cards for us.

Instead of blaming everyone else for the failures, the band should have been looking inward. Sometimes it's hard to admit your own flaws. But there's no excuse for not being conscious about how you're treating others and wasting valuable, precious time of your own life constantly getting high and losing focus.

In retrospect, it was amazing we'd come as far as we did. It dawned on me that the previous summer, I'd been on a club tour with pro-musicians who were able to act civil towards each other and create a functional working environment. Now I was in an environment that felt unprofessional. It's not that I expected these guys to be the type of dedicated musician I was; only that they'd show progress in terms of work ethic and personal interactions.

Adding to the growing list of challenges was this: I wasn't even being heard at the shows. Fans would come up to me telling me that the very thing that got them to buy tickets to the show was my playing. They'd show up only to find they couldn't even hear me—I was buried in the mix. I'd hear live tapes of the shows and I was simply was not there, as though I did not exist. As further proof, at one show, my cable came unplugged and no one seemed to notice.

A fan said this to me one night: *"Dude, these guys have so much potential but it's obvious they don't have their shit together. You're worthy of a multi-platinum act. What are you doing here?"* I began hearing similar assessments from other fans, journalists and music business people but would ignore them. I didn't want to think that way. I wanted to believe in my band as the best band out there and that things were going to finally just fall into place. But it was getting more and more difficult to believe this.

I'd tried my hardest. I'd hung in there as long as I possibly could. I suddenly realized I couldn't take it anymore. I knew right then that I wasn't going to make it till the end of the touring cycle. It was no longer just about musical styles, it was about personal values.

I just hoped to make it through the end of this tour.

*

I'm not sure what it was that finally flicked the switch for me. I suppose it was an honest assessment of where things were heading: the personal and musical incompatibility, the negative attitudes toward everyone including the crew (and even each other), not to mention the continuing fiascos such as the management and merchandise situations, all of which had been easily avoidable. But there was more than that: there'd been one member's competition towards me, peppered by an unwillingness to accept that my dedication as a guitarist had contributed to the very success the band had achieved. There'd also been the diminishing sizes of the audiences, whom I couldn't blame for expecting more from us.

On top of all that, there was the fact that solos were disappearing from metal. In the future, Pantera and even Metallica would release albums with few or no solos. There would be no place for me anymore—take away my precious half minute or so of soloing and I'd have nothing.

Then, there was disappointment with the metal scene at the club level in the US at this time. I was tired of watching fights, people throwing up and acting like candidates auditioning for the *Jerry Springer Show*. Not helping was the ironic prospect of me, a Jew, being protected from stage divers by the occasional hired skinhead bouncers with giant Swastikas tattooed on their backs.

Never overly sensitive about being Jewish, I was appalled not so much by the skinheads, but by the fact that no one else around me seemed to have any consciousness of the implications of this type of imagery.

In fact, there was one experience with a wannabe Nazi—a stage diver in a Swastika t-shirt, somewhere in the South. He landed on my foot pedals, which I used as an excuse to kick him with all my might, hard enough to do some damage, in the name of all Jews.

Afterwards, he confronted me—my tech Dave was there to back me up in case things got ugly. He said he didn't mean to land on my pedals and I said then in that case I didn't mean to kick him and he said, "Cool," and left. I should have explained to him how I really felt, how his shirt was wrong, how he needed to reconsider the idea of wearing such a thing, but I didn't know how to properly express what I was feeling.

While the situation had been defused in real life, that was not the case in my head. What the fuck was I doing playing gigs where I had to come into contact with those who wore Nazi imagery? Was this a sign of where the metal scene was headed? This incident appeared to be yet another sign that I should walk away in the name of dignity.

I had no problem with the concept of "lower class," but it was another thing to be low class. What had happened to this scene that once showed so much potential? It was supposed to be about thinking for yourself, but it was becoming just the opposite.

Out of a sense of obligation, I made a list of reasons to stay and reasons to go. The reasons to go were overwhelming. Did I need any more reasons to leave? Why hadn't I left already? I was just in my early twenties—my whole life was ahead of me.

It wasn't too late to develop into an all-around versatile musician like the ones I'd mentioned earlier (Herring, Henderson, Andress, Strunz &

Farah etc…). I wanted to play for people who were there to listen, not just mosh, talk, fight and puke. I hoped to play with musicians who had a similar work ethic and maybe some who could teach me a thing or two. Most importantly, I just wanted to create music in a functional, supportive environment. Perhaps I'd return to this world in the future, but only if the musicians and others in the scene learned to show a little class and respect.

It was time to announce I was leaving.

*

A part of me wanted to just run away, but that wasn't my style. I would be a gentleman, help them find a replacement, not leave them hanging. By leaving in this way, I was setting an example—being honest and upfront—that I hoped might catch on. Showing respect and doing the right thing had become core values. So while I knew it would be awkward, I was going to finish out all the shows booked so far, which went until the end of the summer.

It would have been so hypocritical to run away. I'd run away before—from my upbringing, from my education, from my past. It was time to start over, find out who I was outside of the black stretch jeans, high top sneakers and black t-shirt. The shy, introverted boy who'd joined this band at sixteen was growing up.

*

"Mark, I have to talk to you about something," I said on the following day off. Mark, our tour manager, was the only straightforward one in our whole organization. I knew I could go to him first. Though it might pain him to see me step down, I also knew he'd understand, respect my decision and offer assistance. He didn't disappoint.

"Al, you know there is no bigger motherfucking fan of this band than me. And you know as well as I do that you're an integral part of this band. A part of me hates to see ya step down. Who knows what the fuck they'll do without ya. But ya know something, Al? You're right. This whole tour has descended into an unmitigated clusterfuck."

I told him the tour was only the tip of the iceberg; he had no idea what it was like in rehearsals, in the studio and other situations. "I don't know what goes on between y'all. That's none of my motherfucking business. But I know one thing, Al: the way they're tryin' to do things, they're gonna run this motherfucker into the ground. There's still hope for you, Al. You're young. Get out while you can. Do your jazz or whatever the fuck it is you want. Like I said, this is my favorite fucking band in the world. But the way they're carryin' on now? You're above all this goddamn horseshit, Al."

By now, Mark had built up a reputation as one of the best lighting designers in heavy music, juggling tours that included Danzig, Megadeth and his other favorite band, Slayer. And as it turned out, Mark had his own, albeit less dramatic, announcement he'd been planning to make to the band: he was going to have to miss a few shows on the next tour with his shift covered by another guy he'd lined up. He'd committed to some shows with Slayer—they were important festival shows and Slayer was proving to be an increasing source of employment for Mark. He'd been planning to hold a meeting with us in one of the hotel rooms on the following day off, about five days later, in North Carolina.

The plan was that he would say what he needed to say, and then turn the floor over to me, let them know that I had something I needed to say as well. I thanked him for helping me out, then walked back to my room. I breathed deep and tried to calm my nerves.

Things were set in motion. There was no turning back now.

40. SEPARATE WAYS

In North Carolina, the sky was filled with clouds of gray, the rain pouring intermittently between claps of thunder. It was like the opening of the very first Black Sabbath album—a 1970 recording that marks the exact moment heavy metal began. But now the rain was real, each drop seeming to announce that metal, as it had stood in my own life for seven years, was coming to an end.

The cover of that album *Black Sabbath* depicts a witch-like woman in front of a centuries-old building, bringing to mind the Salem Witch Trials of 1692. Here it was 1992, exactly three hundred years later, and I felt like I was on trial for my own brand of witchery: individualism. Lying on the unmade bed and looking out the wet window, I imagined the haunting bells from "Black Sabbath" morphing into other bells that opened metal tracks: "Hallowed Be Thy Name" by Iron Maiden, "Hell's Bells" by AC/DC and the groundbreaking tune by Metallica, its title borrowed from the great Ernest Hemingway novel: "For Whom the Bell Tolls."

As I opened the door and crossed the motel parking lot, a light mist clung to my face as the sound of all these bells rang simultaneously in my head. I was being summoned to the chambers to plead my case.

I knocked on Mark's room, he invited me in and I sat down on the bed. One by one, the others knocked, were let in and sat down either elsewhere on the bed or on chairs. Nobody said much. The ensuing silence was only broken by the occasional ticking of a bedside clock—it replaced the ringing of the imaginary bells.

I mentally went over everything I was about to say as if rehearsing the lines to a Shakespearean drama. As I did so, my pulse raced and my stomach tightened—I wouldn't have been able to eat anything if I tried. This was without a doubt the hardest thing I'd ever had to do in my twenty-three years. When the last of us arrived, everyone was now seated on the bed or on the chairs.

The trial was about to begin.

*

Each moment in the room dragged on for an eternity. But now, the seconds were plummeting forward, as if someone had pushed the button for light speed in the hotel room, like Han Solo in the Millennium Falcon space ship from *Star Wars*.

In all of what must have been two minutes, Mark had made his presentation—he had to miss some shows, these were the dates, here's all the info on the guy covering for him, he's sorry about it, but it's going to be fine, he knows his sub is going to work out great, he's here to answer any questions. Everyone just shrugged. *"Ok. Now, before y'all go, Al has something he needs to say..."*

Just like that, it was here: my moment. A few words spoken, the consequences of which were going to affect everyone in this room and many others as well.

All my life, I'd hated being invisible. I'd hated feeling unimportant. Now I was finally important—what I did and said mattered to a lot of people. What I was about to say would impact a lot of lives. But I didn't enjoy this part of it.

I pleaded my case.

"After this tour, you guys will need to find a new guitar player."

*

I'd done it. I felt reborn. So much that I was able to make light of it.

"Well," I said. "That wasn't too hard, I guess."

That brought a snicker or two.

Other than that, everyone was pretty much in too much shock to react. When they finally did, they were calm. How else could they be? I'd made a difficult decision and made the even more difficult move of being upfront and honest about it. There was no use fighting, arguing. All I'd said was that I wasn't going to be doing this much longer, I wanted to play different kinds of music, I would do the rest of the tour and help them find someone if they liked. I didn't go into any details on the personal aggravations that, truth be told, would have driven me out either way.

"I knew, Al," Chuck said. "It's cool. Gotta do your thing, I guess."

"I'm kinda trippin'," said Eric. "I mean, I don't know what we're gonna do. But I understand, I guess." There was silence. I looked at Lou, and he looked away, not saying a word.

Then Greg spoke: "Dude, you're hella bad. Playing with dudes like Stu and them. You don't need to be slummin' it with us."

"It's not like that," I insisted. "You guys are the best—at being this band. No one else could do these songs like you guys. The problem is I have other things I need to do, and I wouldn't be able to do that if I stuck around. I know the situation sucks. But it just has to be. If there was any way around it, it'd be different. But I've thought a lot about it."

I was about to launch into a speech about how their daily behavior contributed to this decision, helped bring about the downfall of the band and had instilled permanent damage—but I chose not to. It wouldn't help matters. I chose to keep things positive.

For the first time since I could remember, we were interacting in a civil manner, honestly and with respect. No, this hadn't been easy. But we were actually communicating, better than we had since I can remember. It was all on the table. Nothing left to lose.

*

For the rest of the tour dates, things were surprisingly cordial.

I'd been prepared for the worst—a bitter divorce from four ex-spouses, with all of us forced to live under the same roof until one of us moved out. But it wasn't like that at all—it was more like we were experiencing a natural disaster—one that forced us to put old grievances aside, lend a hand to one another and just get through this tour alive. Negative attitudes hadn't helped before and certainly weren't going to help now. Somehow, everyone seemed to grasp this.

True, we weren't exactly spending much time together. I was a loner for the most part. But that's pretty much how things had been anyway. And now, with the big shake up, the attitudes and hostility had been replaced by bewilderment. One of us had actually stepped up and done the unthinkable: removed his part of the collective umbilical cord to which we were all bound. The fact that it was me, the kid, who'd stepped in at sixteen barely able to utter a word, unable to look anyone in the eye nor overcome his nervous smile, really threw everyone for a loop.

I'd confronted them head-on, letting them know how I felt and done it in a way that was respectful. In itself, that was a statement against all the sneakiness and passive aggressiveness that had ruled our camp. I'd always been looked at as the weak one, now I was doing something that required more inner strength and bravery than anyone would have guessed I was capable of.

For my part, I suppose I felt some sense of guilt—this was going to inconvenience them. But hadn't I been inconvenienced as well?

Surprisingly, the only one who seemed angry with me was Louie. He didn't have much to say and was suddenly difficult to communicate with. Yet he'd been the one who'd always secretly agreed with me most of the time, the one whose behavior was the least out of line and the one with whom I'd had the least issues with out of anyone in the band. When everyone else was begrudgingly okay with me, why the hell was he suddenly copping an attitude toward me?

"I'm really sorry about that, Al," he would later say. "It was because as soon as you made your announcement, I knew that I was gonna have to leave too."

*

It was late at night after a show at The Boathouse in Virginia. The bus was minutes from leaving, everyone else was on board and I had to make a quick phone call in the club. I made sure to let him know:

"Mark, I have to run in and make one phone call. I'll be right back."

"No problem, Al, try to come back in five minutes, alright? Thanks, buddy."

Mark had been the one person throughout the whole history of the band that I'd never seen drop the ball. For the most part, that remains true—with this one exception.

I came back outside and heard an engine from down the road leading away from the club. I turned my head and saw our bus about thirty feet ahead and gaining speed. I started running as fast as I could, the pace of thoughts in my head matching the speed of my feet.

How could this be happening? I told him I was going in, I'd be back in five minutes. He must have forgotten. Was this a practical joke? Was this revenge for me leaving the band? Maybe they had to go somewhere quick and would come right back? No way, they've forgotten I'm not on the bus. Fuck. They're going faster and faster!

I started yelling and waving my arms *"Hey! Hey! Heyyyyyyyyyy!"* but it was futile. I continued to run but couldn't gain any headway—the bus was now going at a full pace. The faster I went, the more the bus's speed multiplied, its size getting smaller and smaller until finally there was nothing but two fading taillights far ahead, followed by a cloud of dust in the starry, Virginia night.

Soon, the taillights disappeared as the distant sound of the engine gave way to silence, save for the splashing of the dark water just off the pier of the aptly named Boathouse nightclub. It was as if my vessel had just sped away and I was left floating in a life vest. What was I going to do? Maybe they'd realize I wasn't there and turn the bus around. But who knew how long that would take? And what if they didn't?

At least I had my wallet with me. Adding to my fortunes, the club wasn't locked yet. I'd just run in there to use the pay phone. Someone had to still be there.

I trotted back down the dirt road toward the venue. The door was still open. The club was completely dark save for a dim light in what looked like an office. "Hello," I called out. "Anyone here?" A head peered out. It was a guy I'd met earlier, Todd, the manager of the club, who'd seemed like a nice guy. Thank goodness. "Heya! I thought I heard the bus take off! Whatchoo still doin' here, son?"

As soon as I'd explained, he was ready to help in any way possible. First, we did a little bit of assessing; he would stay and wait with me if he could but, being a newly single parent, he had to be back home to relieve his babysitter; I couldn't stay inside since he had to lock up and close the club; if I waited outside I'd risk being stranded if they didn't come back and the club was pretty isolated, nowhere to go, especially at that late hour; I somehow needed to get to Philadelphia in time for the next show; there was a Greyhound station he could take me to, but who knew when the buses left the next day and whether I'd arrive in time.

Finally, we had the answer: there was a small regional airport. He could drop me off there and I could just wait until the first plane to Philly left in the morning—that sounded like my best bet. I'd recently gotten a week's per diem, so I had cash as well as a credit card.

In the meantime, Todd left a message on the voicemail of the venue's phone:

"Thank you for calling the Boathouse. If this is anyone from Testament, Alex is here, and I'm taking him to the airport. He's planning to fly to Philly first thing in the morning and meet y'all."

He then left an exact address of the airport, should they come looking for me. Then we jumped in his pickup truck and he drove me to the airport.

With just a few gates and a handful of benches inside, the airport was one of the smallest I'd ever seen. There were no flights until 6 am. All the lights were on, blinding like hospital lights. It wouldn't be comfortable, but at least I'd have a roof over my head. I graciously thanked Todd and sent him on his way. Then I went to the only open establishment in the airport— the gift store, which was thankfully open 24 hours. Basically all I would need to do is brush my teeth and set up camp on one of the benches.

The nice elderly lady working there sympathized with my predicament, and gave me a discount on a XXL nightshirt clearly meant for a female—it was pink with a grumpy-looking cartoon bunny rabbit in slippers and pajamas, holding a cup of coffee. In giant letters it said, **I DON'T DO MORNINGS**, followed by, in smaller letters *Virginia*—this would be my blanket. I also purchased a travel toothbrush, travel toothpaste, and a pair of cheap sunglasses to shield my eyes from the blinding lights.

With nothing but the clothes on my back, my wallet and my instant overnight kit, I went to the men's room to wash up and brush my teeth. Then

I settled into one of the benches. It was hard, but I had no choice—this was home for the next few hours. Worst of all were those lights; they reminded me of classrooms and hospitals. I put on the sunglasses—they didn't help much, but it didn't matter. I covered myself with the pink **I DON'T DO MORNINGS** nightshirt and fell in and out of a light sleep, as if I were on a plane.

Perversely, it felt kind of good to be off the bus and in my own space, even under these circumstances. I looked forward to my flight and was vaguely excited by the break in the routine and sense of adventure. Soon, exhausted from the show and then the whole ordeal, real sleep set in, my body not knowing the difference between this stainless steel airport bench or a queen size bed at the Hilton.

Sometime around 4 am, I dreamed I was on a tiny rowboat to the next gig. I'd departed from the Boathouse in Virginia and was now heading towards Philadelphia by sea (the fact that this routing is impossible didn't register in the dream). Suddenly, I hit a strong wave that caused the boat to rock back and forth. Then, it happened again—the boat rocked back and forth. Then again and again.........a large set of arms was on my shoulders rocking me and the boat back and forth.

Then I heard a voice: *"Hey... bud... wake up..."* I didn't know if I was asleep or awake. *"We're here for ya, man, let's get up,"* the voice said again. Just then, the vision of my boat on the water in my dream split in half like a giant poster being ripped in two—the bright lights of the airport seeped in from behind. When my eyes opened fully, there was a giant ZZ Top beard staring straight at me. Behind it was a friendly, familiar smile—Jim, our bus driver. I'd been rescued.

"We was halfway to Philly when they realized they ain't seen ya back there. Then they checked yer back and...yep! He's missin'. Sorry about that, bud! We got the message at the club—smart move there. Let's getya back to yer bunk. I'm sure you'll sleep better in there!"

When I got back on the bus, everyone had gone to sleep except for Mark. Sgt. Slaughter gave me a huge hug and an apology. He felt terrible and couldn't believe it—somehow, my telling him I was going in had completely slipped his mind.

I wasn't mad. Something had to be going on with him. I knew he was the type who'd take a bullet for us, especially me. I forgave him.

*

It seemed like the stress of Mark's dealings with the band were getting to him, causing him to drink a lot. I chalked up my being left at the club as evidence of this. Over the next week, he would apologize at least once a day. I laughed it off with a joke, saying it had been an adventure, which was true. I couldn't be mad—he'd always been so on top of things.

The guys, meanwhile, had been having many serious arguments with Mark. Most of the time, I agreed with Mark that they were being unreasonable, although there were a few times when I felt he should reconsider his own actions. But I stayed out of these things, since I had enough on my mind as it was.

With just two weeks left in the tour, the guys awkwardly told Mark that they were replacing him. As usual, Mark didn't hold back his feelings. *"Y'all can go fuck yourselves...except for you, Al!"*

*

By now, the band had plenty to fret over besides my imminent departure. The falling out with Mark, the battle with Elliot and Jeff, the faltering merch sales, the looming merch debt, their own personal debts, etc...Meanwhile, the band had instantly settled on a new guitarist without so much as an audition, something Louie fiercely disagreed with.

The handling of the guitar situation was only the tip of the iceberg for Louie. Realizing he'd have to speak up more and become the sole voice of reason now that I was on my way out, there were more and more disagreements between him and the other guys. Soon they were dismissive of him, mocking him and casting him out as if he were suddenly the oddball at school with no one to eat lunch with at recess.

But Louie had a new ally, Sherry. She was someone to take his side and let him know that he wasn't wrong to be feeling the way he was. The other guys showed an increasingly negative attitude towards her. Adding to the tension was the fact that she was someone he cared deeply about.

Indeed there was now so much fallout and drama within the band that my leaving had become the least of their concerns.

*

September arrived, and I was home, a free man.

I couldn't believe all I'd been through. I was uncertain what to do, but I'd made a very difficult and necessary step. There were possibilities, but I wasn't even going to think about my next move yet. I just wanted to catch my breath. It was a strange feeling.

For the first time in years, I took it easy for a couple of weeks. At the end of the month, I had a quiet birthday with a few close friends. It felt good to reconnect with people outside of the confines of buses and graffiti-covered dressing rooms.

Meanwhile, the other guys spent September working with my replacement, Glen Alvelais, from the band Forbidden. They wasted no time booking more shows for October, including Hawaii and Mexico.[74] Before going home, the band and I had agreed to have a ceremonial last show once they passed through San Francisco on the next leg of the tour. Despite still feeling years of baggage, I was happy that the guys and I could at least put on a display of unity for the fans.

I woke up that morning ready to head to the Warfield Theater. The first phone call of the day was from Troy, the tech I'd seen working for Danny Gill back at the Keystone Berkeley, who'd later become my tech before moving over to Anthrax—he was back in the fold.

Figuring Troy was calling to brief me on load-in time or sound check, I wasn't surprised to hear his voice. But right away, I could tell something unusual was happening.

"What's going on?"

"I guess you haven't heard."

"Haven't heard what?"

"Wait 'til you hear this."

"Hear what?

"Louie disappeared last night!"

"Get out! What do you mean disappeared?"

"I mean disappeared! They took off! Left town!"

"You're kidding, right?"

"I couldn't make this up if I tried."

"What about the show?!"

"Well, that's also why I'm calling. They don't want to cancel. They're trying to round up different drummers in the Bay Area. They might even call guys out of the crowd. It's kind of stupid, they really ought to just cancel. But whatever. Anyway, just wanted to let you know in case you hadn't heard. The show is still happening, but it's going to be a little different." Then he gave me the details for the sound check and show.

My final show that night was total chaos. Different Bay Area drummers, from different bands, Vio-lence, Death Angel and others, jumped up and played. A couple of fans came up out of the audience. Even the drum tech gave it a go. There were several false starts and incomplete songs. It was like we were auditioning drummers in front of 1,500 people.

It wasn't exactly the last show I had envisioned, but it was one we'd never forget.

*

---

[74] At the Mexico show, two young guitarists named Rodrigo Sanchez and Gabriela Quintara would attend and be disappointed I wasn't there. They'd tell me this years later, when they were a well-known musical act, Rodrigo Y Gabriela.

Two weeks later, Lou called to tell me the whole story. I immediately asked how and where he was.

He and Sherry had been traveling around a bit till things cooled off, keeping a low profile. He said I wouldn't believe how awful things had gotten after I left—during the October dates, there'd been increasing hostility towards him and Sherry. The other guys wouldn't even look at him.

Things had come to head at the LA show when Sherry was not allowed to ride the bus. It wasn't clear if this was directed specifically at her or to save face with their own girlfriends, who'd been begrudgingly complying with the "no wives/girlfriends" rule on the bus, maybe a combination of both. Whatever the situation, it was made clear to Lou and Sherry that if they were traveling together to San Francisco, it would be on their own. The rest was pretty much as Troy had described it—they'd thrown all their luggage into a cab, gone to pick up a rental car facility, picked up a car and driven off into the sunset, never to return.

Lou apologized for everything—being mad at me on tour, ditching the band and ruining my last show. He said he knew I was right all along and didn't know how to deal with it. Walking out on the tour was the only way he knew how to escape.

How could I be mad at Louie? If anything he had validated my own cause. While I didn't condone bailing mid-tour, I was still proud of him for doing what he felt he had to do. I had my way of leaving; he had his. We were both standing up against what we felt was wrong, by any means necessary. Clearly I wasn't the only one who'd had it. For me, it was better to peel off the band-aid slowly and gently. For him it was better to just rip it off and run.

We agreed to meet up soon, catch up and hang out on our own terms. We'd become better friends outside of the band than we ever were while in it.

Part VI

LOAD OUT 11:00 PM

"Caged in that little round skull, imprisoned in that beating and most secret heart, his life must always walk down lonely passages."

-Thomas Wolfe

41. THROUGH THE PAST, DARKLY

It was all over.

I was back in Berkeley. I spent many days walking around, thinking. Each morning, after a neighborhood stroll, I'd walk into Peet's coffee. There, I'd listen to a relaxing Haydn or Mozart symphony playing on the speakers overhead as the smell of fresh-roasted coffee beans began to invigorate my senses.

As the cup of thick black liquid would engulf my mouth, a mental flood of biblical proportions would enter my brain. I felt like a soldier from the days of the Roman Empire, who'd returned from years of duty to find that the land he'd left behind had changed.

Bands that had been on the verge of greatness had been reduced to rubble, while others who'd been toiling in obscurity were now superstars. Lääz Rockit, who less than ten years ago, had headlined over Metallica and Slayer in each of those bands' first visits to the Bay Area, continued to churn out lackluster albums and play dives around the US. Metallica had become the biggest metal band of all time, and Slayer had exceeded all expectations with sold-out tours and huge numbers in merchandising. Meanwhile Diamond, who'd had tremendous commercial potential and had been rising through the ranks towards becoming the Bay Area's answer to Van Halen, was now a mere footnote, forgotten by all but those of us who'd been there. The Freaky Executives, our version of Morris Day & The Time, had broken up and morphed into a great new group, the Latin-tinged Los Angelitos, who were on their way to repeating their whole cycle over with packed clubs, terrific high-energy shows and a major label interest—only to once again fall apart in the studio amidst meltdowns and mutiny against the charismatic but intense Peo.

I supposed it was some consolation that compared to those Bay Area bands I'd gone to see and looked up to, we'd done alright.

*

So what was I going to do?

I didn't have a clear career path or vision. In fact, since joining this band seven years earlier, I'd never had time to adequately reflect on all I'd been through, who I was and who I wanted to become.

Having travelled the world, I'd noticed that certain cities helped instill character in their residents. In the US, New York, Boston, Philadelphia and Austin all came to mind, as did international cities such as London, Dublin, Paris and Madrid. Of course, there were many others, but these were the ones with personality and cultural traits that had struck me. Then I thought about the character of Berkeley. I couldn't relate to it.

I had no local role models. My non-musician friends in Berkeley provided no inspiration—some were in college, like Cal Berkeley and Hayward State, and it seemed they were only attending because they didn't know where else to go.

One example was Ben, who'd stowed away in the truck on that first tour. Now he was moving on to a job as an accountant and later a CFO for a Bay Area-based software firm. He'd certainly come a long way—as someone who once wore a hood every day at Berkeley High (giving him the nickname The Hood); he was now the big success story among us and had the highest income. Yet, he'd admit over the years to never feeling a hint of passion about his career and simply not knowing what else to do with himself. Our other friend, Andrew "Fish" Fischer, was now working at a respected architecture firm but didn't seem very passionate either.

Despite my friends' career misgivings and my own career crossroads, Ben, Fish and I were the shining examples—others we'd grown up and hung out with in Berkeley were experiencing rehab, single parenthood, jail and borderline homelessness. What was it about growing up in Berkeley that had instilled such a lack of direction in so many of our lives?

Most local musicians I knew were still struggling. Others were quitting music altogether.

I was too strong to give up music, I knew that much. But it might take a year or more to sort things out and find the path that was right for me.

(It would turn out to take nearly a decade). I only knew that I needed to take some time to get my head together.

I suppose I shouldn't have felt like I'd come back from the front lines empty-handed—after all, I'd earned a respectable reputation as a guitarist. But I was still massively unfulfilled. People took me for this metal-dude they'd seen in pictures, yet the pictures and for that matter, the music, didn't reflect the complexities of how I felt inside, the life experiences, the conflicting messages and the diverse interests.

I was easily underestimated. There was so much more to me than my image—it felt as though no one knew who I really was. But come to think of it, I wasn't sure that I knew who I was either.

*

Financially, I was experiencing a huge wake-up call: I seemed to have more savings than most local musicians I knew and was thankful that I'd had earned enough money to get by for the next year or so. Still, I had to budget sensibly and wasn't close to being able to purchase a home, especially in the skyrocketing Berkeley/San Francisco real estate market. In fact, the only musicians I knew who'd purchased houses were the members of Metallica.

Come to think of it, there'd always been a massive disconnect between Metallica's success and that of the rest of the Bay Area metal scene. In a way it mirrored the situation with my father and the rest of my nuclear family—one towering giant of success in whose shadow the rest of us resided with no chance of ever being in the same league. Not that Metallica didn't deserve all the success they had—after all, Metallica had started with nothing, worked hard and paved the way for many of us in metal. But while they'd been able to amass wealth beyond anyone's wildest dreams, it seemed everyone else in the scene created in Metallica's wake could barely survive off music alone. This disheartenment wasn't directed towards them, but towards the music business as a whole.

Where was that Ferrari I'd dreamed of since I was twelve? I was sure I'd come out of all this with at least a Porsche. Instead, my brief attempt at owning a ride worthy of a rock star had been comically disastrous. I'd settled for a used 8-cylinder Pontiac Firebird, which was like a poor man's Corvette. My bank account had hemorrhaged from the gas costs, monthly insurance and massive repair bills. Then, it turned out that this particular make of car was on a list of the most stolen cars in the United States! I'd found this out the hard way—walking outside my apartment one morning to find my car missing. In retrospect, the thieves had done me a huge favor.

I used the insurance money to buy a blue/gray Toyota Corolla that was great on gas, never broke down and lasted right up until my move to New York in 1998, when I sold it for nearly what I paid for it. I knew it was the right move, driving something more practical, reliable and financially sensible over a car that looked "cool."

Still, it had been a very humbling experience switching from a Pontiac Firebird to a Toyota Corolla. It was a bit like exchanging a shot of Jagermeister for a glass of milk. My rock star fantasies were fading.

*

I ordered a refill of my Peet's coffee, sat back down and looked out the window. It was almost one o'clock, and people were on lunch break. Everyone appeared to be coming and going from work or school. They all seemed to have a place in this world and a knowledge of where they were headed. Where was I headed? What was my place in the world?

Other questions continued to permeate the ocean of thoughts in my head, such as this:

What had gone wrong? I couldn't help but wonder why my own band, despite rising above the locals, had failed to scale the mountainous terrain of the music industry in such a manner as the bands that have since become known as the "Big 4," Megadeth, Slayer, Anthrax and of course Metallica (sometimes referred to as "Big 1"). Granted, they'd all had years of a head start on us. But what about the groups that had come from behind and overtaken us, such as Pantera, Sepultura and Machine Head? Hadn't all of these groups been at one time just as unlikely to succeed as we were?

I took one last sip of coffee and enjoyed the blazing harpsichord cadenza from Bach's Brandenburg Concerto Suite; it reminded me of Van Halen's "Eruption." Then one more thought dawned on me:

It was always the core team of every successful band steering the ship. The secondary members were part of the overall sound, contributed valuable ideas, and voiced opinions, but ultimately it was one or two members who were in the role of being key decision makers. With Metallica it was Hetfield/Ulrich. Aerosmith had Steven Tyler and Joe Perry. The Rolling Stones, Jagger/Richards, The Beatles, Lennon/McCartney and so on, so forth. Sometimes there was one person steering the ship, despite the sound being a group effort—an example of this might be Sting and The Police, or, within the thrash genre, Dave Mustaine of Megadeth.

Successful bands have a power structure—it is clear who the primary members are, and they are ultimately in charge. Unfortunately, that was never clear with us.

*

Walking back to my apartment, I thought about everything I'd been through for the last seven years.

On the surface, I'd been living the dream. I'd thought it would have been the answer to all my problems growing up in Berkeley. But as it turned out, I'd gone from one dysfunctional family to another. Still, while it was not the dream I had hoped for, it was far from a loss; the whole journey had been invaluable.

I'd started as a sad-faced nobody, an invisible mute unable to stand up for himself, repeatedly taken advantage of by phony friends, male and female. I'd become someone who saw the world outside of Berkeley, traveled to many countries and had experiences on musical, social and other levels. I was no longer afraid of confrontation or speaking my mind. I had been forced to learn how to talk to people—record executives, producers, lawyers, journalists, fans, etc. You couldn't be in the music business and remain in a shell. Though it had taken years, music forced me to develop my communication skills and overcome my shyness. It also gave me access to girls and helped provide a crash course in relationships with them.

I recognized a strange irony emerging: by playing heavy metal, I had become enmeshed into a world that was the subject of my father's sociological studies at UC Berkeley: hobnobbing and rubbing elbows with drop-outs, substance abusers, strippers, drug dealers and in some cases, hardened criminals.

*

The band would continue, but ticket and album sales would plummet, never matching the level we'd once had, essentially regressing to one notch above a local club level. Greg would leave a year or so later, leaving only Eric and Chuck, as the band entered a period of constantly revolving drummers, bassists and lead guitarists. There would be interviews where they'd play the victim, describing themselves as "fighters."

Reading that, I couldn't help but think of this band, or what was left of it, as an attack dog running around in circles chasing its own tail. Some people fight and fight, never realizing that their only true enemy is themselves.

At the gym where I worked out, a new song by a much older artist who'd been through a lot more than I had, Elton John, was playing, and it resonated with me: *"I'm Still Standing."*

I could relate.

42. DON'T YOU FORGET ABOUT ME

As you can see, being where and what I am today didn't quite fall into place easily. I am finally the person I always wanted to be, but it certainly didn't happen overnight.

During the '90s, I'd drop off the national radar and keep a lower profile for some time, focusing more on self-discovery. I needed time away to find myself and figure out who I really was. There was a lot of living to do outside of the bubble I'd been in. In terms of visibility, this period would feel like the proverbial "lost years." However, it would be purely a time of personal growth, void of the destructive behavior that sometimes affects those going through sudden life changes. I always knew I'd be back in the spotlight. It was just a matter of when. And how.

There'd be many more stories, too many to narrate here. These would include starting several bands of my own, performing in the band Savatage (see chapter 17) a couple of high profile auditions, including a gig with Ozzy Osbourne (see chapter 10), a great deal of teaching guitar workshops and private lessons and finally, attending college.

Fast forward to 1998: I applied for a transfer to New School University in New York and got accepted. I packed up, left Berkeley for good and worked towards my music degree in New York. Being there amidst all the music, art, culture and intellect, and the city's general pace of life, everything felt right somehow. In 2001, I graduated and made ends meet by teaching at a music school, performing musical theater, doing odd gigs and recording sessions, and soon, touring with the Trans-Siberian Orchestra (a hit holiday concert with platinum albums—it had been built off the band Savatage). We headlined arenas across the US and featured special guest artists including Roger Daltrey (to whom I gave an impromptu guitar lesson) and Steven Tyler. I had plenty of sideman and studio work, from local jazz artists to musical theater (*Jekyll & Hyde*), Jewish folk music (Debbie Friedman), world pop music (Ishtar) and scoring for TV spots.

In 2002, I released my first jazz guitar album and, to my surprise as much as anyone else's, it got covered by Downbeat, Jazziz, The Village Voice and other jazz-based publications. The trio's second album was even featured by NPR as part of a special series named *Take 5: A Weekly Jazz Sampler*. The Alex Skolnick Trio was my primary project, with shows all over the world and several well-received albums, which I produced myself. Our most recent album *Veritas*, released in 2011, reached the Top Ten of iTunes jazz charts at no. 7, positioned between Miles Davis and Esperanza Spalding.

Then in 2005, I started playing with Testament again. At first, it was like a bunch of former athletes kicking the ball around for some reunion shows. But in just a couple of years, it morphed into a triumphant comeback with a critically acclaimed album and shows with Judas Priest, Heaven & Hell, Slayer, Megadeth and other metal survivors.

We were back.

*

The guys had grown a lot since the old days.

Chuck, having miraculously survived a serious bout with cancer, had become a responsible person deeply rooted in his Native American heritage. Eric had married a great girl, Rachel, become a dad and was raising beautiful, smart and, to the surprise of us all, very well-behaved kids. Lou lasted the first year or so before deciding he wasn't in for the long haul, preferring to run his successful antique business with his girlfriend Christy (he and Sherry had divorced after a few years). He and Eric became best friends again. Lou was at every East Coast Testament show, occasionally jumping on the bus for days at a time, his role morphing into that of official advisor. Bassist Greg returned with a life of baggage—dysfunctional relationships, various legal woes and an unhealthy lifestyle—but somehow always managing to hold down the bottom end of the bass.

My return wasn't the only unforeseen return to the fold. Things were patched up with Mark, who returned as TM/LD[75]—there were other occasional fallings-out, always to be patched up again. Even Elliot came back as a legal representative—his relationship with the band, without the pressures of trying to manage the group, a healthy one.

With each returning figure from the past, I'd utter that quote from *The Godfather*, which has been repeated on *The Sopranos, Seinfeld* and elsewhere: *"Just when I thought I was out...they PULL me back in!"*

*

Meanwhile, a whole new generation of fans had discovered the band and was showing a level of devotion and support that we couldn't have foreseen, rejecting the corporate grunge that hard music had become.

Metal had come a long way, and so had its fans. Metal's audience had diversified considerably: a modern metalhead could be found behind a desk in a real estate brokerage or law firm, in an orchestra pit (as opposed to a mosh pit) and many previously unlikely places. I'd meet a diverse array of

---

[75] Tour Manager/Lighting Director

fans, including Ph.D students in Ivy League universities and other educated types, engineers, doctors, architects, as well as celebrity chefs, star athletes and comedians who were loyal metalheads. Of course there were the usual drunk and crazy types, but many fans had grown into the very figures that were once prime targets of their wrath—there were responsible parents, teachers and even police officers who were metal and proud.

Metal would even be cited as a movement of change in oppressive countries. One example would be a band whose debut EP I'd have the pleasure of producing: Accrassicauda, from Iraq, the subject of a critically acclaimed documentary *Heavy Metal in Baghdad*. Another is an upcoming documentary I'm currently involved with—about a heavy metal band in Cuba.

Heavy metal was no longer limited to disenfranchised, working class youth in American suburbs.

*

As this book was being finished, my second post-reunion album with the band, *Dark Roots Of Earth* was recorded. It entered the Billboard Charts at #12 overall, reached #1 on the Billboard Rock and Hard Rock charts, made NPR's Top Ten Metal Albums (NPR? Metal? How times have changed) and became Metal Album of the Year on iTunes in the US. The music video for our song "Native Blood" went on to win the award for best music video at the annual Native American Film Festival in 2012.

Eric and Chuck, despite being the sole official partners of the band, often confide that the other one is driving them crazy (they're a bit like an old married couple). But things are a heck of a lot better than they were before.

No, it hasn't been easy at all times. We've had so many drummers in the past few years, it's a bit like *Spinal Tap*.[76] I've had to have a few honest, heart to heart talks with the guys and at one point, came close to leaving again. But there's never been the sense that it would be at the expense of our friendship.

There's no question we've all come a long way since that very first gig in Berkeley, at the now folkloric Ruthie's Inn. We've all accepted that no matter what happens, we're family, albeit an unusual one—a weird, bizarre mishmash of characters thrown together like that film from my high school years, *The Breakfast Club*.

*

---

[76] The subject of the mockumentery film *This Is Spinal Tap* is a hapless rock band which, among its many problems, is constantly losing drummers, often to a mysterious explosion of green light.

As for my biological family, there is another movie that parallels my struggle, one that was mentioned much earlier in the book: *Star Wars*. A young, directionless fellow finds a higher purpose by going up against a world of darkness that threatens to engulf his soul. He achieves victory through the difficult task of mastering the same skills his father has mastered, that are disguised as something else.

Like Luke Skywalker, I fought against my own father and discovered a shocking truth: that he's not a bad guy after all. He was never wicked or ill-intentioned, just misguided and in the dark about certain things, as much the product of his own difficult experiences as a youth as I was. It became my mission to right some of the wrongs that took place under our roof and apply these lessons to the world at large through my art, whether musical notes or words on a page.

Today, my father brags about my career to his friends, nudges them to read my reviews, gives my jazz CDs or concert tickets as gifts and, if they can't attend a show, rubs it in their face by telling them they don't know what they're missing. My mother is always by his side, as a regular and welcome presence at my performances, whether at jazz nightspots, theaters or concert arenas. They're both favorites among friends of mine, who love talking to them. As my father basks in the glow of the applause and love I receive from audiences, he brings to mind the shimmering, holographic image of Anakin Skywalker at the end of the original *Star Wars* trilogy, his Darth Vader helmet permanently removed.

My brother is no longer doing drugs, practices yoga and seems to be finally finding peace in lands far, far away: Israel, South Korea, Mexico and Vietnam, with a career teaching English.

These days, both parents reside permanently in New York, where they belong.

I suppose in our own unique ways, we have all escaped from Berkeley.

Part VII

BUS CALL 12:00 AM
(Overnight Travel to Next Show)

"The fact remains that getting people right is not what living is all about anyway. It's getting them wrong that is living, getting them wrong and wrong and wrong and then, on careful reconsideration, getting them wrong again. That's how we know we're alive: we're wrong. Maybe the best thing would be to forget about being right or wrong about people and just go along for the ride..."

-Philip Roth

Gibson Les Paul BFG | Wygraj efekt EHX | Kings of Leon
z mostkiem tremolo | Germanium 4 Big Muff | wybrali D'Addario

TOP GUITAR

Nr 5
2011
MAJ
Cena: 13,70 zł (w tym 8% VAT)

www.topguitar.pl

MINITESTY:
Lag T200ACE
Cort X-6 WS
Line 6 M5 Stompbox Modeler
Brace Audio DWG-1000x
TC Electronic Flashback Delay & Looper
DV Mark Over Marker

TOPTESTY:
ZT Amplifiers Club
Vocalist Live 5
Fender American Special Jazz Bass
Epiphone Joe Bonamassa Goldtop Les Paul
Cort Mirage M520
Danelectro '56 Single Cutaway Aqua
DBZ Barchetta Eminent FR Trans Red
VOX Mini3
Comba T.Burton MG
Roland Cube-80XL
Roland R-05

METALOWY JAZZMAN

Alex Skolnick

Zabrzmij jak
JOE BONAMASSA

TopRelacja
Musikmesse 2011

TopSpecial
Dlaczego gitara nie stroi?

BASS

Targi Muzyczne
Musikmesse Frankfurt 2011

FENDER
Jazz B...

DWA SUPER DODATKI!
studyjny i basowy

DOKTOR G: BEZPIECZNY GITAROWY SPIN

43. PRIEST FEAST AND PEACE

Journal Entry 2/11/2009 1:46 pm Belfast, Northern Ireland
Day 2 of Priest Feast tour with Judas Priest/Megadeth/Testament

I can't believe I'm in Northern Ireland. Although I miss my friends, my neighborhood and my apartment in New York, I am thrilled to be out in the world, experiencing life outside our tiny little comfort zone of the USA. Sure, the US may be large geographically, but historically, we are like a tiny little child, especially compared to lands like Ireland. This is especially true when one thinks about how rare it is for the majority of the population to leave the US and view the world from outside our borders. We're not encouraged to do so.

I feel very fortunate to be in a position that involves frequent travel (much as I may whine about flight delays sometimes). Either you're lucky and have an occupation that involves travel, like mine, or you have to be very motivated and financially secure enough to do so. I only wish I had more time in these places I visit, instead of the typical duration of one day. But one day is what I have so I'm going to make the most of it.

While most of the others on the bus are asleep, I get out early, check out the surroundings and soak it all in. It's about 10 am and my body thinks it's 5 am, the time back in New York. The snowcapped mountains in the distance add to the windy chill in the air and the first thing I notice is that we're parked next to the water.

I walk along the dock and a sign informs me that the area we're in is known as "Titanic Quarter." It turns out that this is an abandoned shipyard, formerly known as Queen's Island, given its new name in the mid-'90s as part of a peace initiative and slated for future development.

Of course, Titanic Quarter is named after the most famous ship built there, one that would inspire an overrated Hollywood film almost a hundred years later. The exact spot where the *Titanic* was built is not too far off in the distance. I'm glad to be experiencing this while it still has the desolate feeling of an abandoned shipyard. In a few years, this place will be a Mecca of gift shops, luxury condos and restaurants, similar to Sydney Harbour in Australia or Pier 39 in San Francisco. I admit to having enjoyed these areas which have somehow avoided much of the cheap tourist feel that has destroyed places like Fisherman's Wharf in SF or Times Square in Manhattan. (Most of my friends and I avoid these areas like the flu.) Still, I often wonder what they'd be like with a bit less tourism and more authenticity of the original sites. Maybe they'll pull it off here and capture some of that classic Irish shipyard feel in Titanic Quarter.

A short distance away, two giant cranes, nicknamed Samson and Goliath, silently watch over a city that, until recent years, has been anything but silent. These cranes were put up in the '60s by Harlan and Wolf, the same company that built the *Titanic* and give the Belfast skyline its character. As I walk along the road past Samson and Goliath, I let it take me wherever it goes. Soon, I cross an overpass into a neighborhood with a lot of character. It looks very working class and tough but has a sense of integrity. Spray-painted messages and murals are everywhere. Images of fists, crests and cryptic messages abound, but unlike graffiti in places like the inner cities of the US, these messages seem very organized, thought-out and well-placed. There are reminders of the violence that plagued the region for several decades, commonly referred to as The Troubles.

One of the murals is a museum-quality work, with the image of a man in a suit and tie, an image of a lion, mountains, a sword and the name *Narnia* in deep red lettering. I'm convinced this is code for some fallen hero from the neighborhood who died in battle. Later, I'll feel silly when, after doing some research, I realize that the image in the mural is a portrait of C.S. Lewis, the author of The Chronicles of Narnia, (which I admittedly haven't read—another book to add to my list) and this is where he's from, although he spent most of his life in England.

Eventually, I find a small downtown area with a few shops. I find a bank, the Ulster Bank, and see a line for the ATM and decide to get cash. I'm given twenty pounds of Northern Irish currency. I find out that this is good only in Northern Ireland, though they will also accept English pounds as well (outside Northern Ireland, you have to get these notes exchanged). I settle down at a cafe and order two poached eggs, toast, grilled mushroom and stewed tomato, which I commonly think of as an English Breakfast. But I don't dare call it that here. I know better. My mind harkens back to the first time I was here.....

August 1987. Belfast, Northern Ireland (Anthrax Among the Living Tour)

We're a few shows into the tour with Anthrax. Last year at this time, I was approaching my senior year of high school. This year, I'm on tour playing this music known as thrash/speed metal. My parents were sure I'd be in college now. I'm glad not to be home.

Tonight's show is at a place that functions as a gymnasium during the day, and it's packed with people. Most of the other guys in my band decided to pass on taking a shower, because the shower area is communal, not private. In fact, there is a crowd of a dozen or more naked Irishmen in there joking, whistling, talking. Everyone is carrying on like they're at a common lunch table, just as comfortable naked as they are clothed. I really want a shower and decide to join the crowd, thinking to myself, "When in Northern Ireland..." My shower is fine and no one makes me feel odd, even though my hair is halfway down my back and they all look normal by comparison. Everyone is comfortable, and it's no big deal. Suddenly it seems weirder that so many guys I know from the US, not just the ones I'm on tour with, have hang-ups about nudity.

After the shower, I find out we still can't sound check because there was a bomb threat at the venue. The entire place has been evacuated. It's going to take a couple hours at least for an investigation. In the meantime, one of the promoters has offered to take us to try the best pint of Guinness we've ever had. It's all the way across town, and we'll have to be driven with an armed escort.

"I'm not going," says Louie.

"Me neither," says Greg.

"Yeah, fuck that," says Eric.

Chuck says, "I'll go. You wanna go, Al?"

"Sure," I answer. What the hell. I'm up for a little adventure and haven't seen any of Belfast beyond this gymnasium. I'm curious. Somehow I get the feeling that the guy driving us knows what he's doing and feel safe. Hopefully I'm right.

A few minutes later, we're heading across town in a camouflage jeep. It's Chuck, myself and our driver (whose name I don't remember). The first thing I notice are the old buildings, many of which look condemned. Cars are overturned left and right. Indecipherable graffiti is spray painted on the cars and the buildings. I'm hanging on to the dashboard to keep from bouncing. Although it's quiet at the moment, there is no question about our surroundings. We are in a war zone.

Before he was our singer, I used to hear about Chuck Billy, and how he was part of a sort of suburban gang known as the Dublin Death Patrol (that's Dublin, CA, on the outskirts of the San Francisco Bay Area, not Dublin, Ireland). The DDP used to go to parties and local gigs, get into fights and strike fear into the hearts of us mortals, who would hear the stories as they circulated across the Bay Area. But now, as Chuck and I are being driven through the trenches of war torn Northern Ireland, we're both out of our league and he's as helpless as I am. Our driver is the tough guy now, and he's small potatoes compared to the guys we're about to meet.

"Win ya goh inside," our driver says. "Doon't talk to 'em unless they talk to ya first. And if ya do talk to 'em, whateveh ya do don't say yer English. And fer fuck's sake, don't ever say yer Protestent."

"How come?" asks Chuck.

"Cause they'll kill ya."

"We're both from the US. He's Native American. I'm Jewish," I say.

"You'll be just fine then, won't ya?"

I'm not sure whether to be comforted or not. How can hatred run so deep among people from the same land? At the same time, there are so many places where I can be hated just for having Jewish heritage, and it's not even an issue here. Weird.

We pull over and there surrounded by rubble, is a tiny shack, with barely enough room for six people. There are two barstools inside and one tap on the other side. Behind the bar are two men who resemble off-duty soldiers, with their strong builds, tattoos and their short haircuts. Both maintain cold expressions and eyes which have seen the unthinkable. Each one gives us a cautious, tentative nod, looking each of us straight in the eye, never looking away. We nod back. The driver throws some money on the counter and one of the bar guys proceeds to pour a black liquid into a pint glass, pausing half way, then pouring the rest. He does the same with the second pint glass.

We sit on the stools, do a timid toast and proceed to take sips of our beverages. With its light texture, extreme freshness and creaminess, the beer is as far from the Guinness I've tasted in the US as we are from our country geographically. As promised, it is the finest cup of Guinness we've ever had.

"Ello there! Would ya like anything else?" It's a friendly female voice. My waitress. I'm back in 2009. Irish breakfast is finished. I pay the check and walk back towards the venue. Soon I will be back in my routine, and it will be like many other shows.

I have so much humility and respect for this land and the situation it has had to overcome. I don't attempt to understand what the people here have gone through and offer no opinions. It is not my place. All I know is that it feels peaceful now, and that says a lot given the glimpse of scenery I witnessed back in 1987.

Back then, I would never attempt a walk through a neighborhood here alone, or for that matter with anyone else. While the paintings of fists and crests are reminders of what has taken place, there is a sense of progress, of moving forward, of letting go. Indeed, it feels that if peace is possible here, it can be possible anywhere.

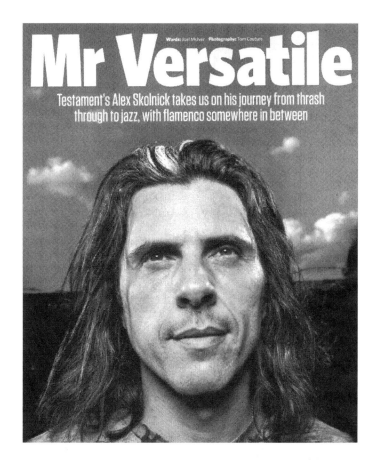

Words: Joel McIver Photography: Tom Couture

Mr Versatile

Testament's Alex Skolnick takes us on his journey from thrash
through to jazz, with flamenco somewhere in between

44. ON BEING METAL

**(Updated version of a post that originally appeared on MTV
Headbangers Blog, Oct. 2008)**

W ho is metal? Who is not? Who decides who is and isn't?
Recently I found myself pondering the answers to these
questions.
It started after a story I'd posted on my blog, "SkolNotes," was picked up by
other websites and generated a lot of comments. The story was about
meeting the Iraqi metal band *Acrassicauda*, and the film that made me aware
of them: *Heavy Metal in Baghdad,* which sheds light on the US invasion of
Iraq and the subsequent aftermath.

Now, I try not to get trapped in the quicksand of comments online.
Like television, the internet can suck you in and waste your valuable time
and mental energy, especially when it comes to comments. But here was an

important story, one which had political, musical and most of all, human overtones. Not your typical metal website news. So in this case, I was very curious to see what people were saying online and couldn't have been more surprised by what I saw.

The reaction was 100% positive. I was touched that the fans were taking such an interest. One comment, which was echoed by others, stood out in particular: *"This is what metal's all about."*

The statement struck a bit of a chord, pun not intended. Why? Because I haven't always been "Mr. Popularity" on the internet, especially in metal forums. Admittedly my own "metalness" has been called into question several times.

*

Most would probably agree that part of being "metal" is putting it out there: honest, shameless self-expression, regardless of what the reaction is. This is part of what defines the music and the attitude. Metal fans, myself included, wouldn't have it any other way. And the endless parade of comments on metal websites is a reflection of this.

On the positive side, there are many intelligent, thought-driven internet users who have something to say, whether you agree with them or not, and do so with class and respect. On the other hand, there are others who consistently insert brainless, insulting, profanity-laced drivel into an otherwise interesting dialogue, although (knock on wood) I didn't see any of those related to this story.

This *Jerry Springer Show* mentality of some internet users is a big reason why I try not to get too caught up in web comments. But, like a driver passing the scene of an accident, sometimes you just have to look.

And in doing so, I've noticed many comments by very loyal fans that appreciate everything I do. They go out on a limb to support and defend me and for that I'm grateful.

I also have some detractors. I have no animosity towards them. Many of them are young and will grow out of it. I've already heard from some of these "haters" who, as they matured, started to realize that maybe I'm not such a bad guy after all. But there are others who are determined to hunt down my online reputation like Captain Ahab's pursuit of the great white whale in Herman Melville's classic novel *Moby Dick*.

*

So what did I do to become such a target of wrath for these guys in the first place?

I did the unthinkable. First I left my metal band. Then I started playing...*(gasp)*...jazz.

As mentioned in the previous chapters, I needed to fill some gaps in my life: a university education and jazz guitar. Two things seen by some as "not metal."

I realized I'd offended the "metal police" with this move. On the other hand, it could be argued that what I did, by shocking people and going against the grain was...very metal.

It was simply that there was a world beyond it and I needed to see it and prove to myself that I could exist in it. I moved from the SF Bay Area to New York where I immersed myself in jazz, literature, and other art and culture. I earned a music degree from my school (New School University), and launched an improvisational music project, Alex Skolnick trio. I also began working as a guitarist for hire playing and recording rock, world music, pop and jazz. This is something I'd always wanted to be able to do but had felt limited by only being a metal player.

Eventually, I felt the time was right to return to metal while continuing my other pursuits. This began with some guest appearances with Testament in the early 2000s. It was at this time that I became aware of all the metal website forums out there, and the onslaught of fired-up fans verbally duking it out online from their bedrooms every day.

As my name seeped back into the metal world, I found myself a "controversial" musician, one that some love and others love to hate. Suddenly, I felt like a Gene Simmons or Lars Ulrich, on a much smaller level commercially. You know, those musicians who mirror "bad guy" characters from professional wrestling.

The comments were funny: I was a "traitor." I had polluted Testament's music with key changes, harmony and melody (Is that a bad thing?). Most bizarre was the suggestion that I had "sold out" to play jazz. How do you *sell out* to the least commercially successful genre of music?

These types of comments have shown up less and less frequently, especially since I've started playing regularly with Testament again and we've released two well-received albums in recent years, *The Formation of Damnation* and *Dark Roots of Earth*. But this wouldn't have happened if I hadn't been able to step away and find out who I really was.

*

Some folks naturally fit the metal ideal. For example, my friends Kerry King, Zakk Wylde and the late, great Dimebag Darrell all come to mind. These guys are all straightforward, in-your-face personality types whose image is enhanced by the fact that they're excellent metal guitarists. I'm no psychologist (disclaimer: my mother is), but I'm willing to bet that even if they weren't famous metal guitar players, Kerry, Zakk and Dime would still satisfy the perceptions of what is "metal" based on their personalities alone. It's just who they are.

Me, on the other hand? I'm kind of a nerd. I admit it. I only have one tattoo. I read a lot of books. I'm somewhat of a "wine connoisseur." I occasionally enjoy a good cigar. I prefer fine dining to fast food, and read up on noteworthy chefs and restaurants. I also like symphonies, art museums, architectural exhibits and other culture outside the metal world. In short, there are elements of my interests and lifestyle that could cause one to say, "NOT metal!"

But when you see me onstage, clad in black, blasting a screaming guitar through a wall of amps, a sweaty mosh pit circling the floor to songs like "Into the Pit" and "Over the Wall" (both of which I helped write), then I'm willing to bet that you'll say, "THAT'S metal!"

Of course, I couldn't do it without the other guys in Testament who, despite our differences in appearance, speech and lifestyle, are like my brothers.

In some ways, I relate to the kid in the movie *Hustle and Flow* played by the actor DJ Qualls. In this film, Qualls plays a young, brainy, white musician who, despite having a very different social background and personality, develops a strong connection to the hip hop world. Even though he's the opposite of the stereotype, he's able to hang out with the "hardcore" guys, bring in new ideas and add something to the music.

I'd like to think I'm not as geeky as Qualls' character in the film. But I do feel some similarities in the sense that my role is to bring in a different perspective to the group's creative process. For this reason, I no longer feel the need to go out of my way to try to "be metal." But that wasn't always the case.

When I was in my teens I had this "rocker dude" persona that just wasn't me. I used the word *dude* a lot. I also interjected more profanity in my speech than necessary. I have no moral objection to saying *fuck* and still do on occasion. In fact, it's really funny when I do, because it gets people's attention. By not using it all the time, I feel the word becomes more powerful. But the way I spoke when I was younger was an attempt to try to fit in.

Over the years, I've seen countless people mimicking the type of images they think they should have. They become caricatures that fail to develop their own personalities. I've seen this with many rock and metal guys, but they're not the only ones.

For example, while studying jazz at New School University, I'd occasionally come across these clean-cut white guys, who, seeking acceptance as jazz musicians, felt they have to talk "black." They were nice enough, but I just couldn't take them seriously. I can hear them now:

"Skol, man! What up, dogg! You chillin' yo?"

Give me a fucking break.

There's nothing wrong with speaking this way when it's from a real place. But if not, it's really pathetic.

The late great jazz pianist Bill Evans is a good example of why that type of behavior is unnecessary. Bill was a skinny white guy who wore thick glasses and looked and sounded like he could be a math or science teacher. That didn't stop him from impressing the greatest African-American musicians of the day, including most notably, Miles Davis. This was in the fifties, when racial tension was at an all-time high and Miles, not exactly known for his eagerness to work with white musicians, hired Bill for his band. He took much criticism for this decision, but stood by it. Miles' albums with Bill Evans, including the quintessential *Kind of Blue* (a personal favorite of many, myself included) have become timeless and his decision to hire Bill Evans is no longer questioned.

Think about this: if Bill had tried to dress and talk more "hip" or "black," he would have been laughed out of the room by Miles and his fellow musicians. Instead, Bill was real and honest with himself and didn't try to change his personality. He just focused on being the best musician he could be. This helped him land the gig with Miles and go on to become one of the most influential jazz pianists of the twentieth century.

Another musician who fits this description is one of my favorite metal guitarists, the late and legendary Randy Rhoads. Randy's playing on Ozzy Osbourne's first two solo albums took metal playing to a new level. Who knows what new ground he would have forged if it weren't for his tragic death in a plane crash at age twenty-six?

By most accounts, Randy Rhoads was a shy, intellectually curious guy with a quiet demeanor. Sure there were a few moments of rock star-like partying, but he was young, thrown into a whirlwind situation and finding himself. Randy had dreamed of furthering his education, both musically and otherwise. He was also someone who fit into metal on his own terms and never tried to change his personality to fit an image. Although he may have one day stepped away to explore other types of music, no one can ever accuse Randy Rhoads of not being *metal*.

In conclusion, who is metal and who is not is totally subjective. As long as people are honest with themselves and others at any given time while allowing room to change, then they can be metal on their own terms. Sometimes it takes a long time to discover who you really are, and you go through phases on the way. It's good when you get to a place where you feel you can be real, both to yourself and to others.

Being *you* is what's most important, regardless of how well you fit into any clique, be it metal, jazz or otherwise.

PHOTO DESCRIPTIONS

PHOTO CREDITS

REFERENCE FOR QUOTATIONS

Part I: Jarrett, Keith. Interview 1978: *Jazz-Rock Fusion: The People, The Music* Eds. Julie Coryell, Laura Friedman (Hal Leonard Corporation 2000)

Part II: Murakami, Haruki *What I Talk About When I Talk About Running* (Vintage International 2009)

Part III: Hornby, Nick *High Fidelity* (Riverhead Trade 1996)

Part IV: Jong, Erica *Seducing The Demon: Writing For My Life* (Penguin Group, USA 2006)

Chapter 17: Composer: Seal   Album: *Seal* (©1990 Warner Bros. Records)

Part V: Composers: Young, Young & Scott   Album: *High Voltage* (©Jay Albert & Sons, Atlantic Records 1976)

Part V: Schopenhauer, Arthur. *The Wisdom of Life,* written in 1851 (*Aphorismen zur Lebensweisheit* translated by T. Bailey Saunders, Dover Ed. Originally published: London: S. Sonnenschein & Co. 1890)

Part VI: Wolfe, Thomas   *Look Homeward Angel* (Scribners & Sons 1929, renewed 1995)

Part VII: Roth, Phillip *American Pastoral* (First Vintage International 1997)

ABOUT THE AUTHOR

Alex Skolnick is one of the most diverse guitarists of his generation. Best known for the metal band Testament (which he joined at sixteen), he has gone on to make a mark in jazz (Alex Skolnick trio), world music (Rodrigo Y Gabriela) and more. A devoted writer, he has blogged for Guitar Player Magazine, MTV and penned a popular blog, SkolNotes. A Berkeley, California native, he relocated to New York City in 1998, enrolling in The New School University and graduating with a BFA in jazz performance. He currently resides in Brooklyn, New York.

www.geektoguitarhero.com

www.alexskolnick.com

20494140R00227

Printed in Great Britain
by Amazon